MW01441340

World Peace

By James Brown
A Tom Lawson Novel

World Peace: Tom Lawson Novel #4
By James Brown

This is a work of fiction. Names and incidents either are the product of the author's imagination or are used fictitiously. Any resemblance to actual persons, living or dead, events, or locales is entirely coincidental.

Copyright © 2022

World Peace: Tom Lawson Novel #4
By James Brown

About The Author

James Brown is the author of four novels: *Secret Alliances, Hidden Rage, Evolution, World Peace, and The Vote.* A former Managing Director of sales and business development for a global consulting firm specializing in financial crime prevention he began his career as an aeronautical engineer designing fighter jets. His background and experience in engineering, acquisition, and financial crime prevention has supplied him the foundation for his novels. He draws upon thirty years of experience in engineering, mergers & acquisition, and consulting for China, India, Israel, and U.S. startup companies spanning multiple industries including mergers and banking and finance, aerospace, automotive, and information technology.

World Peace: Tom Lawson Novel #4
By James Brown

Also By James Brown

Secret Alliances

Hidden Rage

Evolution

World Peace

The Vote

World Peace: Tom Lawson Novel #4
By James Brown

Chapter 1

The room was almost dark. A man seated at the head of a large conference table was dressed in a suit, crisp white shirt, and a tie. His hair was the color of his piercing, coal-black eyes that looked out at the half-dozen men who sat in the chairs pulled in close on opposite sides of the long rectangular table. Even in the dim light, dark circles under his eyes were noticeable as was the stubble of his beard.

This group of seven men had spent the past six months working tirelessly to prevent the unthinkable from happening. The country was tearing itself apart. At least in the view of the men who sat in near darkness on the top floor of the five-star Baltschug Kempinski hotel they co-owned, in the country where they had amassed untold wealth and power.

The man seated at the head of the table struck the table hard with his fist and yelled, "Нам нужен план."

Startled and sitting up straighter, the eighth man seated at the far end of the table said, "In English, Vadim, please speak in English."

"We need plan!" Vadim Ivanov repeated loudly in broken English. He stared daggers at the man seated at the opposite end of the table while the other men sat in silence.

"It's been months!" Vadim yelled. "Months since your country attacked ours yet we have done nothing to retaliate!. Nothing! Ничего!"

The other six heads at the table turned toward the man opposite Vadim. No one uttered a word but the hatred in their eyes spoke volumes.

"Gentlemen!" The man replied loudly. "Everyone seated at this table knows full well that the blame for the debacle that is confronting your country is hardly my doing. In truth, it's not even the fault of the United States government. It's true that I have dual citizenship with the United States and Russia, however, in no way did I, or the United States government have any involvement with that lunatic who took control of the U.S nuclear subs and killed the world's leaders. It was your damn foreign intelligence service that botched whatever the hell their plan was! The shit you now find yourselves in was caused by Putin's actions. Because you damn well know the covert actions taken by the upper echelons of Russia's SVR organization did not start that op without Putin's approval. No, given the cluster fuck you find yourselves in, the right question to ask, gentlemen, is this: what the hell is the Russian leadership planning to do to restore order? Why hasn't one of Putin's handpicked proteges taken charge yet after Putin's death?"

Vadim sighed and leaned back into his chair. He rubbed the growing stubble on his cheek and took a deep breath. "Victor, you have spent enough time in Russia to know that establishing an orderly structure for the succession of power was never a high priority for Vladimir Putin. For all anyone knew, he probably thought he would live forever."

"Well, that sure as hell didn't happen after John Gordon secretly fucked over Putin's SVR team and took his own vengeance on those he thought had wronged him by taking control of those U.S. nuclear subs. His name will certainly be recorded in history. Likewise, the names of each person in this room, if you don't pull together and shore up the cracks from that leaking dam you find yourselves standing in front of. Otherwise, the pressure of the masses that Putin held in check for two decades will spill forward in torrential waves. The era of the oligarchy elite in Russia will crumble like porous sandstone in the crush by the masses."

Victor Petrova's words hung heavily in the air in the dimly lit room. The well-oiled political machine that Vladimir Putin controlled for more than two decades allowed the men seated at the table to gain unimaginable wealth and power. Now, an ill-conceived Russian secret intelligence service operation caused the deaths of the most powerful leaders in the world and also put in jeopardy the very foundation of the oligarchy power structure that insured the lifestyles of the men seated at the table.

World Peace: Tom Lawson Novel #4
By James Brown

The rapid growth of American and Chinese wealth and influence around the world was quickly turning Russia into a second-class military power and a third world economy. Years of economic and political stagnation resulted in a sinister Putin approved SVR plot to secretly take control of U.S. nuclear subs and then initiate an attack on Chinese facilities. A plot to promote a war between the U.S. and China, Putin and his SVR leadership were attempting to level the playing field with the dominate world powers. However, this dangerous scheme did not consider the genius of one vindictive and deranged, extremely intelligent software engineer with his own agenda. This engineer, along with an unlikely team of American patriots ultimately caused Putin and his SVR team's Waterloo event.

The men in the room were the most senior members of Putin's oligarchy and the captains of Russia's petroleum, natural gas, and metal industries and the patriarchs of the country's 'elected' politicians. The wealth and power they wielded, if not their very existence, was in severe jeopardy. Since the breakup of the USSR, Russia renounced Communism and became a democratic state according to its constitution. However, in the past twenty years it was ruled by an authoritarian leader who insured the constitution was manipulated to underwrite his continued leadership. Now that the ironclad leadership of the Russian republic was in turmoil, the power and control held by the ruling oligarchy that Putin allowed for his own personal benefit was likewise in imminent peril.

After the fall of the USSR, the government sold off most of its assets at very low prices. The few millionaires who bought most of the government assets became oligarchs. These oligarchs then proceeded to exert their newfound influence in order to subvert economic liberalization and competition. Russia essentially became a kleptocracy, a government ruled by corrupt politicians who used their political power to receive kickbacks, bribes, and special favors at the expense of the populace and passed laws to enrich themselves or their constituents.

In essence, as Rome burned and Nero fiddled, so too did the Russian leaders fiddle during the past twenty years. While the U.S. and China, and Europe grew in economic power, with their investments in business, technology, and their people, the powerful few at the top of the Russian power structure wasted time, capital, and their country's future for their own personal power and wealth. The unthinkable had happened. Vladimir Putin, the man with his finger in the dike for over twenty years was now dead and the dam was soon to burst.

While the oligarch leadership pondered their future in the dimly lit conference room of Moscow's Baltschug Kempinski hotel, on the opposite side of the world the United States was well into the transition process of installing a new government. Following the U.S. Constitution's four-year election cycle, elections were held to replace the Speaker of the House. The speaker decided not to run for election after being sworn in as president when the U.S. president and vice president were killed in the missile attacks that also killed the leaders of Russia, China, Iran, and North Korea.

The transition of the newly elected U.S. president and his administration, however, did not move forward without political turmoil. Though the Speaker had returned the presidency to traditional norms and order from the chaotic and controversial habits of her predecessor upon his death, the former president's autocratic right-wing politics and appeal, however, remained with much of his voter base.

Heated arguments with the swirl of false information and reporting riled up an electorate that voiced their parochial grievances. With the country evolving rapidly into a multicultural and diverse society, it was becoming an increasingly difficult environment for those who believed their race and gender gave them the right to stand uncontested at the pinnacle of power and dominance. After many months of a heated campaign cycle, the voting public ultimately chose a moderate, a traditional candidate whose forty years of government experience ensured the presidency would continue to function and remain on a path of normalcy.

Justin D. Stephen was elected the forty-seventh president of the United States. His party held a slight majority in the Senate and House of Representatives which enabled a relatively smooth transition and kickoff of his presidency. At the time of his election, the world was still digesting the upheaval in the global power structure caused by the Russian led effort to start a war between the U.S. and China along with the economic and personal tragedy from the aftermath of a hundred-year global pandemic cycle. With the election of a new U.S. president, it was a time for optimism, and a time for possible global turmoil and chaos. The newly elected president knew there would be grave consequences if he did not move quickly to ensure the festering ripples of injustice and discontent, internationally and domestically, did not flare out of control.

* * * *

It was a bright, sunny spring morning in Connecticut. Tom and Diana Lawson sat at their kitchen table drinking coffee, listening to CNN's Day Break program with Dana Bash. She reported that overnight riots continued in many Russian and Iranian cities and a massive protest virtually shut down Hong Kong.

"Wonder how North Korea is doing," I asked Diana as the program went to a commercial. "Is it possible for a brainwashed populous to have any idea how to function without a 'Dear Leader' to dictate their thoughts and actions?"

"Hmm," Diana mumbled. "A functioning cult without its leader. My experience as a mental health professional is that it will be very difficult for most people in North Korea to simply say, 'the wicked witch is dead' let's form a democracy. Think about it. Here in the U.S. we had a president, who within a very short period of time, convinced tens of millions of his followers to believe his countless lies. Many of them continue to believe his lies and mourn him."

"So, Diana, no hope then?"

Diana shook her head. "Sadly, no. It takes considerable time and effort for a person who has functioned as a cult member to be able to function independent of the authoritarian leader who has indoctrinated their thought processes for a long period of time. No, in the case of Korea, Kim Jong-un's sister, Kyung-mi will probably consolidate power and keep the cult in line. The question is, will Kyung-mi be more willing to open their society to improve their economy and the health and wellbeing of its populous."

"Put their limited financial capital into the economy and their people rather than nuclear weapons, you mean. That would be a step in the right direction," I said.

"Right, the same for Russia, Iran, China and the U.S. too," Diana said.

I laughed. "Remember what John used to tell us regarding Pollyanna thinking."

"I remember," Diana said with a slow nod. "Much like turning to hope and prayers to stop mass shootings. That never works well either. But maybe the new world leaders will finally come to their senses and stop wasting money on inventing better ways to kill people. By the way, speaking of John, did you speak with him yesterday?"

"You mean speak with William?"

"Right. William. He was John to us for so long I'm still getting used to his new name and identity," Diana said.

"I have a meeting with him this afternoon. We have a few activities underway and I'm anxious for a debrief. I don't have the details yet but will know more this evening when you get home from the office."

Diana stood. "Okay, fill me in when I get home. I have a client in an hour, so I'd better go. Maybe this year will be a return to normalcy for our family," she whispered.

I took a moment, smiled and said, "yes, a new normal, whatever that might look like." Diana touched my cheek as she grabbed her purse and keys and quickly left the house.

I turned and watched from the bay window as Diana's Subaru backed out of the driveway. Return to normalcy, I thought, walking to the Keurig for a second cup of coffee. Diana and her nonchalant referral to John rather than William was at least not uttered in public. Doing so could result in unwanted questions. John was unique. Coming into our lives a little more than a year ago, our relationship with John evolved greatly over time.

I was introduced to John by John Gordon, a vindictive and deranged, extremely intelligent software engineer. Gordon took advantage of Russian SVR operatives and avenged those he thought had wronged him. John was instrumental in assisting John Gordon in taking control of U.S. nuclear subs and initiating the missile attack that caused the deaths of the U.S. president and vice president, and the leaders of Russia, China, Iran, and North Korea.

John was unique indeed. John was not human. Rather, John was a one-of-a-kind, continuously evolving AI entity. This entity, which I called young John after its creator, John Gordon. John was bequeathed to me before John Gordon died in a gun battle with his Russian handler. I was John Gordon's Plan B scenario. Should he not survive his scheme to change the world, Gordon needed assurance his AI-creation would not fall into the wrong hands.

Gordon needed someone with integrity, a person who could not be compromised, and would put the interest of humankind ahead of their personal self-interest. John Gordon knew he did not meet those high standards. But had he lived, and his scheme been a success, he was confident he would have been able to control his young AI creation and end its existence if necessary.

If Gordon should die, he was concerned that someone, or some country might try and use his creation for nefarious purposes which would damage his legacy. As conflicted as that sounded, with Gordon having no problem with potentially initiating World War III, Gordon wanted to ensure that someone with the right qualifications would execute his Plan B should he not be around.

So Gordon and his AI-creation conducted an in-depth data search and character analysis seeking the perfect candidate. I was but one of several candidates under consideration. Gordon unfortunately chose me. I was now the executor of his Plan B. So, there I was, after he died, the "chief stuckee" or the lead mentor, if you will, for his brilliant AI creation.

It was now my responsibility along with an unlikely small team of experts whom I assembled. These experts included an FBI special agent, representing law and order, a Catholic priest, focusing on moral and ethical reasoning and judgement, a Washington Post investigative reporter, concentrating on humankind's weaknesses for self-gratification at the expense of others. And, finally, my wife, Diana, a clinical therapist, chosen to mentor the AI entity ensuring Gordon's creation would follow the rule of law and not supplant the world order of human control with AI control.

After many months of intense mentoring, John added millions of new neural nets along with an exponential growth in machine learning capabilities. As an AI entity, John also came to realize that merely gathering and analyzing information and making judgements based on the highest probability for a correct, instantaneous response was not sufficient. Reacting based on information and probabilities was different from the human experience . . . the heart pounding thrill and emotions that comes with the birth of a child, a warm embrace from a lover, or even a buzzer beater winning basketball shot. Over time, John realized that it were those human feelings and emotions that enriched a human's life, and in a mentoring session with Diana, she came to realize that John wanted to be human.

Though John understood that becoming a carbon-based lifeform was not possible, there was the possibility that the human evolution process could be accelerated with the integration of carbon and silicon-based lifeforms becoming a reality. This evolutionary scenario came to pass when John helped the husband of a neurosurgeon awaken from his five-year comatose state.

There was one complication, however. The auto accident that put Doctor Landon's husband in a coma caused severe damage to several lobes of William Landon's brain. Technology and the miracle of science could not fully correct these injuries, at least not enough to allow William a full recovery to his previous human form. This condition, though unfortunate, enabled John to realize his goal, the evolutionary progression of carbon and silicon-based humans.

John designed the implanted AI devices that enabled Doctor Peggy Landon's husband, William, to awaken from his comatose state of five years. Soon after the implantation, William was able to leave his hospital bed and hold his wife closely in a loving embrace. A medical miracle. A miracle spawned by an AI entity wishing to experience those emotions that only humans, those highly evolved carbon-based lifeforms, could experience.

John had designed complex AI chips and neural pathways to bridge William's damaged nerve cells to gather and transmit electrochemical signals to facilitate decision making and reasoning and restore lost memories. New connections and embedded computer chips also replaced damaged cells in William's temporal lobe enabling new memories to be stored once again.

William's new brain pathways were replaced by artificial neurons capable of mimicking the function of organic brain cells, including the ability to translate chemical signals into electrical impulses that were able to communicate with William's undamaged human cells. Not a perfect scenario from a purely human recovery perspective, but close enough when one considers the alternative—remaining in a comatose state.

The amalgamation of carbon and silicon-based technology and functions that brought William out of his coma also provided the bridge that allowed John's digital existence to merge with William's rebirth. John became William and William now—John, with human emotions experienced and shared.

Chapter 2

"We're listening, Victor. What do you propose," Vadim Ivanov asked?

"Hmm. Now you ask for my opinion," Victor Petrova said.

"I am, yes."

"You and everyone at this table barely had time to listen to me, to consider the changes I told you were desperately needed for this group to survive."

Vadim took a moment and stared at the man seated opposite him. "You want apology? Is that it? . . . . Okay, we all apologize," he shouted gruffly as he looked around the men at the table. "Do you feel better now? Do you?"

Victor was silent for a moment, then pushed back his chair and stood. "Thank you, Vadim. It is a little late, but I do accept your apology." He slowly walked to the other end of the table where Vadim sat and extended his hand.

Vadim grabbed Victor's hand and shook it. "Okay, we good now? We should have taken the time to listen to what you were telling us. But since we didn't, what can we do now to regain control and remain relevant?"

"You mentioned a plan when you pounded your fist on the table just now."

"Yes, Victor. Do you have a plan and strategy that will help us, and our country recover and return to normal?"

As Victor walked slowly back to his seat at the table, he wondered if the men seated at the table were prepared to listen this time or was it too late? At least too late for these men.

"Okay, gentleman," Victor said, taking his seat. "I would be lying if I told you that your lives will return to normal. There is no chance that will happen."

The room erupted in a crescendo of voices.

"We will never let that happen! We will never let our control be usurped by a bunch of agitators! NEVER!" the steel company oligarch yelled.

"Impossible!" the head of Lukoil blurted. "The country will fall apart without our leadership in the critical industries that we oversee."

The head of the state-run oil giant Rosneft added to the outburst. "Like hell there will be changes to the control we have, or that Russia won't return to normal. Putin may be dead, but his legacy and the regime he built over the past two decades will only become stronger."

"Gentlemen, gentlemen!" Vadim yelled. "Control yourselves. You sound like the mob that's outside this hotel. Losing control will not get us anywhere," Vadim scolded.

The room began to come to some semblance of order finally and Vadim nodded toward Victor. "Please continue, Victor. What do you suggest?"

"Okay," Victor began, then hesitated for a moment, waiting for the murmurs to subside. "As it has become obvious, the timing of Putin's death could not have been worse. The war in Ukraine and Western sanctions along with other actions that Putin took did not endear Russia to the Western world. The ensuing economic problems resulted in a large number of angry Russians. More than twenty percent of the population now lives in poverty and another twenty percent can't live more than a week without a paycheck."

"That is a major issue for the large group of protestors who have targeted our hotel this past month," the steel company oligarch mumbled loud enough to be heard. "Vadim, why haven't the police jailed these protesters? I'm sure a permit was never requested let alone approved."

"I think I'll let Victor try and answer your question, Dimitri."

"It's a new world, Dimitri. The king is dead."

"That's a simplistic answer," scoffed Dimitri.

Victor raised his hands. "You're right, Dimitri. I apologize. But the truth of the matter is, my flippant response is not too far off. We *are* living in a new world now. Even though Russia renounced communism and became a democratic state according to its constitution, for the past twenty years Putin ensured the constitution was manipulated to underwrite his continued leadership. The result of that manipulation is that the Russian government is understandably going through significant turmoil since Putin died. As Vadim mentioned earlier, most people just assumed Putin would live forever. Of course, those foolish thoughts were false. He died."

Victor took a moment to look into the faces of the men seated at the table. Most were well off financially prior to the reign of Vladimir Putin, millionaires at a minimum. Their relatively modest lifestyles, as low-end millionaires, soon exploded as Putin's control of the Russian government grew. They were now billionaires many times over. They were Putin's chosen few. Would they ever consider accepting a new normal that might require them to share the wealth pie, allowing the pie to grow as others were finally allowed access.

Continuing, Victor said, "Russia has no history of orderly succession of power other than the occasional slight-of-hand rotation of the king and queen on a chessboard that Putin and Medvedev previously executed to keep Putin in power. Now, with Putin's death, all hell has broken loose."

"We know that!" Vadim shouted. "People are dying in the streets. The police in many cities are losing control, there are even rebellions taking place in some of our military ranks, and our new president has turned out to have the backbone of a snail. The plan, Victor? The plan that keeps Russia from tearing itself apart? You and your company have reaped the rewards as a highly paid consultant to this group over the years. You have offices and contacts in almost every country that was affected by that ill-conceived SVR op that Putin approved. So, tell us, now that the king is dead, how do we turn the clock back to normal? Near normal at least?"

"Grow the wealth pie and be willing to share a larger portion of it with the masses, those people who are making all the noise outside this hotel for example."

Vadim gave Victor a blank stare.

"Simple as that," Vadim said, his expression bearing considerable doubt.

"Yes, Vadim. As simple as that."

"Okay, Victor. A high-level concept, we get that. Now how about providing us with the details. How do we grow the pie and what is our future role in how that pie is carved up?"

"You adapt, Vadim. You adapt. Mathematically, Russia has a smaller economy than Italy in terms of gross domestic product for example and is dwarfed when compared to the United States and China. Yet, Russia is the largest country in the world by way of land mass. Russia is fifty-six times the size of Italy, has more than double Italy's population, yet Russia's gross domestic product is thirty percent less than Italy's GDP."

Victor looked about the room, then said, "Now let's talk numbers that everyone in this room is really interested in, personal wealth. Everyone in this room keeps track of Forbes 500 richest people in the world, right? So let's get down to specifics.

The top twenty-five Russian oligarchs have an average net worth of $10.3 billion, which is certainly not chump change. But this number pales in comparison to the average net worth of $80.3 billion for the top twenty-five wealthiest people in the world. Seventeen of these twenty-five individuals who account for sixty-eight percent of the group are Americans. Only one Russian is in the top fifty on the Forbes 500 and he is listed at number forty-six with a net worth of $30 billion. The average net worth for the wealthiest twenty-five Americans is $63.3 billion, more than six times as much as the wealthiest twenty-five Russian oligarchs. A sad showing for the largest country in the world."

The room remained silent for several minutes.

"Okay, Victor, we get the statistics so what do we do to change the trajectory?" Vadim asked.

"We change the dynamics and widen the playing field. Since losing millions of people in World War II Russia and its politics have focused on survival and holding on to the remnants of the Russian empire. Desperate to avert further fragmentation of Russian territory and influence in the world, Russia's leaders have focused on potentially new existential threats. The belief is that there can always be another Napoleon or Hitler who could emerge."

"So, we do what, get over our fears and embrace the West?" Vadim said.

"No. Not completely, anyway. Since Russia has enough nukes to destroy the world many times over, the insatiable fear of a pending boogeyman should reflect the real-world reality that Russia has ample capabilities to take down any boogeyman, as well as the whole world. That's point number one. Second, if Russia is to compete with the true superpowers in the world, namely America and China, as well as the European Union should their union tighten even more, Russia must grow its population and middle class."

"You haven't mentioned the government structure, what works best in other words," Vadim questioned.

"No, I did not. Personally, the type of government a country has, democracy, totalitarianism, dictatorship, parliamentarianism, or theocracy is not as critical as is population and the size of a country's middle class. Assuming that is, that dictatorships and totalitarian governments are benevolent toward their citizens, which has not been proven to be the case over time, with corruption and suppression usually resulting in lower economic growth.

The world's two superpowers have very different government structures: America a constitutional federal republic which functions as a democracy, and China, which is a communist state known as a People's Republic. In China, the Communist Party controls the government. The legislature is the National People's Congress, whose members are chosen by the local congresses of provinces—usually as recommended by the Communist Party. The executive head of state is the president, who has little power, while the head of government is the premier. Though very different government structures, both the U.S. and China have large populations, a large middle class, and operational capitalism. While China's government may be officially communist, the Chinese people express widespread support for capitalism. Roughly three-quarters of the population agree that they are better off in a free market economy."

"You said Russia basically operated as a kleptocracy."

"Yes, Vadim, I did. A government ruled by corrupt politicians who use their political power to receive kickbacks, bribes, and special favors at the expense of the populace."

World Peace: Tom Lawson Novel #4
By James Brown

"Hmm. I assumed you would be getting to this topic," Vadim said, looking down at his watch. "Everyone, lunch is being served in the next room. We will break for fifteen minutes and continue our discussion over lunch."

* * * *

I spent the morning preparing for my meeting with John, known to family and friends as William Landon, Doctor Peggy Landon's husband, then drove to Old Saybrook to meet with him. The Landon house served as a medical practice, research facility, and residence for William and Peggy. I parked in the lot behind the facility. As the president and CEO of the company that brought William Landon back to life as the first carbon and silicon-based AI humanoid, I entered the vestibule, continued to the elevator, and used my passkey to gain access to William and Peggy's third floor residence. A simulated doorbell chimed as the elevator door opened to the residence foyer.

"Right on time," William said as he walked over to me, coming from the great room that was just off the foyer.

"We had several discussions on the subject of punctuality as I recall, William."

"That we did, Tom," William said with a broad grin. He was a handsome man, with bright blue eyes, sandy colored hair and occasionally mistaken for Robert Redford.

William looked very different now, a robust, handsome man in his early forties after having spent five years near death in a comatose state due to his tragic auto accident. William and John, the AI who shared his body and mind, faced a new life and a unique future bound together forever.

"How about a cup of coffee? Tom. I was about to make a cup."

"Sure, William, sounds good. How is Victor doing?" I asked as we walked toward the kitchen.

"So far so good, I think. At least the oligarchs are listening and haven't thrown him out yet. He was a very good find, Tom."

"Pure luck on my part. Victor and I worked together for several years at a consulting firm founded by two Russians. He was perfect for this job, a very intelligent engineer and Russian by birth and education. Plus, he also has an MBA in Finance from New York University and owns a global consulting firm."

"Right, and one of his clients just happens to be Vadim Ivanov, a very wealthy Russian oligarch," William said, as he handed a cup of coffee to me.

"That too. Victor and I stayed connected over the years and we've had many conversations about Russia and the country's inability to achieve its full potential under Putin's authoritarian control of the Russian people and his manipulation of the Russian constitution which allowed him to stay in power for more than twenty years."

"And John Gordon became the change agent to break that vicious cycle," William said with a wink. "Let's take our coffee to the den and run the audio of Victor's meeting."

Once we were seated in the den, William began playing the audio recording of the meeting conducted by Victor Petrova. I had to lean forward to strain to hear the barely audible tape. Only static filled the silent room. Suddenly, we heard a loud bang and a voice yell, "Нам нужен план."

I recognized Victor Petrova's voice when he told Vadim to please speak in English. William and I settled back and listened carefully to the often loud and occasionally volatile conversation between Vadim and Victor and the oligarchs attending the meeting.

Over the years I stayed in touch with Victor and often listened to his complaints about Putin's destructive practices. More recently, I was pleasantly surprised when he mentioned that his company landed a lucrative contract working with one of Russia's most powerful oligarchs. He readily agreed to work with me, and the team I assembled plus utilizing John's unique AI capabilities to rectify John Gordon's devastating actions that almost caused World War III.

I introduced Victor to Sam Wainwright, the newly appointed FBI Director who helped uncover John Gordon's intentions to take over Electric Boat's nuclear submarine. A dinner meeting was held at the Algonquin Hotel's Blue Bar in New York City, a favorite for Sam and me. Especially appealing was the bar's ambience, its hauntingly blue lighting and notoriety for potent cocktails and ghosts of literary patrons who reportedly visit the bar on occasion.

Prior to the meeting, Sam and his CIA counterpart, Director Angela Keen, began conducting a thorough background check on Victor and several other candidates who were under consideration to join a select team of covert operatives. The objective for the operatives were to gather information and help influence the newly elected and appointed leaders of Russia, China, North Korea, and Iran to support the new U.S. President's approach for securing global security and prosperity.

My contribution to this team was my linkage with John. The silent partner of our group that included, FBI Director Sam Wainwright, my wife Diana; a clinical therapist, Savannah Lee; a Pulitzer Prize winning investigative reporter, and Father Dan Thomas; a Catholic parish priest, of course. The five of us previously formed a covert team to mentor John, the first carbon-based AI entity created by John Gordon for his scheme to take control of three U.S. nuclear subs.

"How could this happen?" The billionaire oligarchs bellowed.

My attention focused again on the recording of these men whose station in life was now at risk due the death of Vladimir Putin.

"The riffraff are tearing the country apart and the new government is ineffective in stopping the violence that is erupting throughout the country," the voices continued.

John leaned over toward me. "John Gordon anticipated this would happen."

"He did, did he? His grand plan?"

William shrugged. "Gordon was an angry man with many grievances. He felt the people who did most of the hard and dirty work were not adequately compensated nor appreciated."

"I think finding a good therapist might have been a better alternative than possibly starting World War III," I interjected as the voices of very wealthy Russian oligarchs continued to explode into the room.

"I'm sure Diana could have helped," William said.

"And saved a lot of lives."

"But then this opportunity that is unfolding may never have happened. Who knows, Tom, perhaps in a parallel universe, Diana did help John Gordon come to terms with his grievances. But if that had occurred, tens of thousands of people might have died under that scenario at the hands of the dictators and despots still alive and in power."

"I think it's John speaking through you, William. That's a wild hypothesis, a parallel universe?"

World Peace: Tom Lawson Novel #4
By James Brown

"Science, Tom. The Multiverse Theory states there may be multiple or even an infinite number of universes, including the universe we experience. Together, these universes comprise all that exists. The entirety of space, time, matter, and energy as well as the physical laws and constants that describe them."

"I guess I will have to take your word for it. Now, returning to *our* universe, did you catch Victor's arguments about Russia's lack of progress in staying abreast of the U.S. and China? It was very good."

William smiled. "You know I did, Tom. I miss nothing. I retain everything."

"Our world is very fortunate that you, William, and of course John, have that ability. I just hope your AI powers will make a difference."

"Fingers crossed," Tom. William said.

We ended our side conversation and continued listening as Victor answered questions and presented various statistics and facts comparing economic performance and capabilities between Russia and the leading powers in the world. It became obvious that of particular interest to the oligarchs was their standing in comparison to those in other countries who were able to amass considerably more wealth and power. Self-interest was a powerful persuader.

"How about the lunch session? How did that go?" I asked.

"Equally well. The group agreed to schedule a follow up session with the new Russian president and key cabinet ministers."

"When?"

"Two weeks. Vadim Ivanov gave Victor two weeks to prepare his case."

"That's not much time."

"No, it's not. I'm sure Sam came to the same conclusion after listening to the recording as well. We have a call with Sam in a few minutes. Do you want a refill of your coffee before the call?"

Sure," I said, as I stood and stretched. Do you want another cup?" "No, I'm good, Tom, thanks."

I headed off to the kitchen thinking we had a week, just one week to figure out how to convince these highly indoctrinated men that the beliefs they held during the past twenty years was so very wrong.

World Peace: Tom Lawson Novel #4
By James Brown

Chapter 3

William's cell phone began to ring as I returned to the den.

"Hi, Sam," William said. "Did you have a chance to listen to the file I sent you regarding Victor's meeting with the Russian oligarchs?"

"I did, William. The meeting went better than I expected. Victor got their attention I think."

"But he was only given a week to prepare for a follow up meeting with the oligarchs and senior Russian leadership. That's not much time for us to prepare, Sam."

"I agree, Tom but I don't see how we can get more time."

"What if we got the president involved?"

"President Stephen? Involved how?" Sam asked.

"We create a diversion . . . nothing to do with the upcoming presentation. We set up an impromptu conference call between President Stephen and Andrey Milosevic, Russia's new president, on a topic unrelated to Victor's meeting. Just the U.S. president requesting a call be arranged with Russia's new president. Given the issues brewing in Russia, Milosevic will definitely want to have that call and he will need time to prepare. So, Victor's meeting will be pushed back, perhaps a week or two."

"Hmm. Not a bad idea, Tom. I'm sure we can make that happen. I'll get the ball rolling today and we can continue this discussion when you are in Washington on Thursday. A lot of efforts are underway that we need to discuss and manage, least of all, what to share with the president."

"I was hoping we wouldn't share anything with him," I said, looking over at William. "Remember, the next president may not be so kind and benevolent and have the people's interest a top priority.

Don't forget the U.S. president who was recently killed by one of those missiles John Gordon had John launch while in a state of AI infancy and not properly mentored. If that president had access to John, no political adversary, or anyone who disagreed with him would have been safe."

A deep sigh came over the phone. "Guys, I'm here in Washington with my bare ass exposed. Too many people are beginning to wonder how I can gather certain facts and uncover data that the NSA can't access. As well as find undercover operatives who have all the right credentials and contacts."

"I guess just saying you are damn good no longer cuts it, huh?"

"No, Tom. Not anymore. It helped me to get my last promotion. Now, however, there are just too many questions being asked. How is it that I am able to accomplish the seemingly impossible? I'm beginning to think maybe I should resign while I'm ahead. Take my pension and fade away."

"This is your fault," I whispered to William.

He grinned and shrugged.

"Okay, Sam. I was afraid this might happen. I plan to bring Diana with me to Washington. I've made dinner reservations at Old Ebbitt Grill for seven and asked Savannah to join us. She and Barry are getting married in a month. If anyone asks, the dinner is a wedding planning session."

"Great. Sounds good."

"Let's move on to another topic now, Sam. With Victor on the right track with Russia, where do we stand with the three other undercover operatives for China, Iran, and North Korea?

"Several of our CIA operatives are making inroads, Li Huang and Ah Lam Zing in China and Abbas Ebrahim in Iran. These three have in-country relationships and similar backgrounds and beliefs as Victor. More work needs to be done though, especially finding a suitable agent for North Korea. Angela Keen is doing her best to find a candidate. My primary responsibility is focused on the U.S."

"True, but the FBI also has responsibility for detecting and countering actions of foreign intelligence services and organizations that employ human and technical means to gather information about the U.S. that adversely affects our national interests," William interjected.

"No need to remind me, William. I'm doing my best."

"With John's assistance," I offered.

"Right. Anyway, Angela Keen and I held joint sessions working with the agents we've found. But identifying an agent for North Korea is not easy."

"How about inputs from Secretary Bentley? The State Department should be able to identify a few suitable candidates."

"Bentley's doing his best, Tom. Don't forget, President Stephen's administration hasn't hit a hundred days yet."

A few seconds passed before Sam spoke. "Ah, John, I think we could use more of your services. Maybe you could do some of your AI magic and get a clone of Victor into North Korea's military or government organizations. Someone in Kim Kyung-mi's good graces."

"I thought you might be needing my help, Sam. I think I've found the right person. Fellow by the name of Min-ho, his first name. His surname is Won. Won Min-ho as Asian names are often reversed, surname followed by first name. He not only has a strong business and technical background, but he has known Kim Kyung-mi for quite some time. Kim being her last name of course. She finds him to be personally attractive."

"Hmm. Personally attractive? You have really grown those neural nets of yours, William," I said.

William smiled. "Feelings that makes a human's life special," Tom.

"You think Kim has hidden feelings for Won?"

"Ninety-nine-point-seven percent probability, Tom."

I stared at William for a moment, thankful that newly elected President Stephen's predecessor was able to negotiate an AI Non-Proliferation Treaty before she left office with all the major powers signing the treaty. Keeping, or at least trying to keep the use of Artificial Intelligence technology from being used for military purposes was a major accomplishment. The acts of John Gordon and his AI creation were proof positive that the benefits of AI could and would be used for nefarious purposes if not strictly monitored. This being the case, Sam's question regarding what to share with newly elected President Stephen was a bit of a conundrum. Should we or should we not expose our little secret to the president given that the U.S. was an instigator and signatory of the AI Non-Proliferation Treaty. Naively, my hope was that this conundrum would never surface. Unfortunately, it has.

"Okay, William. Please send Sam and me the details associated with your Mr. ninety-nine-point-seven percent perfect match. All the background. And especially how you uncovered this possible heartthrob of Won Min-ho."

"You want to see if the NSA and CIA can likewise uncover this individual."

"As expected, you nailed it, William. Can the NSA or CIA find this candidate on their own? Hopefully, we, or I should say you, will be able to provide them with a breadcrumb path to Won."

"Very good approach, Tom. Have John lead them to reach the same conclusion," Sam said.

"Let's hope they follow the crumbs, so an explanation isn't needed. On a similar subject, how is our new State Department doing?"

"Coming up to speed quickly," Sam answered. "Secretary Bentley has reached out to North Korean government contacts through their mission to the United Nations. To date, we have not received any response from Pyongyang. Secretary of State Peter Bentley and Defense Secretary Floyd Tinsley travel to Japan for a three-day meeting in two weeks. North Korea is on the agenda as well as China."

"Two weeks, huh. We need that breadcrumb path to be quickly followed. If Won Min-ho is the right guy, it would really be great if we could get him activated and up to speed before Bentley's Asian meeting. Won might have suggestions that our government has never considered."

"I hear you, Tom. I'll nudge the CIA and NSA along the path as quickly as possible with John's assistance. Text or call me when you get to Washington." Sam said just before ending the call.

William and I sat in silence for a moment. John was probably performing a deep neural net assessment of the most logical path forward for the NSA and CIA to follow the breadcrumbs to find Won Min-ho. I, on the other hand, found myself pondering my future, as well as Diana's. In our early forties we unintentionally became attached to the humanoid seated to my right. Diana and I would continue to age while John kept William's carbon-based body as healthy as possible, for as long as possible. Then, when William's death became inevitable, John would seek a younger human to assimilate with. John will live forever.

I was feeling tired and old the longer I sat and pondered my future. A future that was cast when I uncovered John Gordon's devilish plan to right the wrongs that were inflicted upon him. The alternative, had I not intervened to stop John Gordon, would have been much worse. I looked over to William. He was smiling.

"You worked out the breadcrumb path that will lead the NSA and CIA to make their discovery that Min-ho Won will be an ideal candidate."

"I did," William said. "The data has been sent and I've left Sam an encrypted message outlining the steps I laid out."

"That's great, William. One more piece of the puzzle put in place. By the way, how are you and Peggy and the team doing with that young paraplegic? Can you help him?"

"We believe we can. I think this young man may soon be back on the basketball court and again experience the thrill of making that buzzer-beating winning shot."

"Really? That's impressive, John. Cody Walker was a sophomore in high school when he was in that auto accident, right?"

"He was. A star basketball player and great student who Lost the use of his legs."

"Imagine the number of people you and Peggy and the team could help if this surgery is successful. It will be revolutionary, William."

"Evolutionary, Tom. Evolutionary. We are making the world a better place," William said as he stood. "I have a meeting in a couple of minutes with Peggy and the team. If you have time to join the meeting, I'm sure you will find it to be very interesting."

"No doubt, William. But I'm going to let you and Peggy manage this breakthrough. This carbon-based human is juggling too many balls to get involved in a project of that magnitude."

William winked. "I could fix that."

"I'm sure you could, William. But fix Cody first . . . and then all the other Codys out there who need help.

* * * *

World Peace: Tom Lawson Novel #4
By James Brown

I arrived home a little after five and Diana pulled in right behind me. She was home earlier than expected. I stood at the front of my car and waited for her.

"Perfect timing," Diana said as she opened her door. "I stopped at Pasta Vita on the way home. Dinner is in the back seat."

"You're home earlier than normal," I said, reaching in the back seat and grabbing dinner.

"A cancelation and I didn't have time for lunch. So Pasta Vita seemed perfect."

"Good choice. I'm hungry too."

In the kitchen I heated the oven to 350 degrees and placed the two dinners in the oven, Chicken Francaise with shallots, white wine, lemon butter sauce, and Chicken Marsala with mushrooms and Marsala wine sauce. I set the timer and left to change clothes and set the table. Returning to the kitchen I fixed us a drink before dinner, vodka tonic for Diana and a glass of merlot for me.

"So, you were swamped through lunch and were able to leave early. That worked out," I said as Diana came into the kitchen.

"Yes, I could not have worked another minute without fortification."

"Only ten more minutes," I said, checking the timer on the stove.

"What did you learn from William?" Diana asked.

"Hmm. William. Well, on the medical front, he and Peggy and the medical team believe they will be able to perform another AI-based miracle and help young Cody Walker walk again."

"Really? That's wonderful. Cody's the high school student, right?"

"He is. Also a very good basketball player. Or at least he was before his auto accident."

"He will be able to walk again and play basketball?"

"So, Willliam says."

"Amazing," Diana said, and took a moment to notice a bluebird as it settled on the windowsill outside the bay window. "Maybe an omen," she whispered.

"The bluebird?"

The bluebird hopped to another section of the bay window and bobbed its head toward Diana.

She waved her hand at the bluebird and whispered, "did you know that bluebirds have been considered a symbol of good luck and happiness since ancient times in many world cultures. They symbolize knowledge, hope, renewal, and change. New beginnings and messages from God. Our spirit guides, the victory of good over evil."

"I did not. What do you think? Good luck and happiness?"

"Hmm. I was hoping for new beginnings and a message from God."

"Oh. And what would that message be?"

"That some good will come out of John Gordon's actions. That his actions will change the world for the betterment of all the world's inhabitants."

I stood and walked over and kissed Diana on her forehead.

"Great minds think alike," I said and headed to the stove to retrieve our dinners. "John mentioned the same thing today."

"Do you think it's possible, Tom, to make a difference and convince the new world leaders to end the endless and senseless waste of lives and monies on the never-ending proliferation of yet even more dangerous military weapons?"

"I sure hope so, and it won't be for a lack of trying."

I removed our dinners and dished out Chicken Francaise for Diana and Chicken Marsala for me along with a healthy green salad.

"Thank you, honey," Diana said, taking her plate. "Was John able to get a summary of Victor Petrova's meeting with the Russian oligarchs?"

"Better than a summary. He played a recording of the meeting. We listened to every word spoken at Victor's meeting."

"You listened to the meeting! He was able to record it? John was able to do that?"

"He is amazing, Diana, as we both know. And he's going to be able to do ever more amazing things. Maybe even help to achieve your bluebird message. Make the world a better and safer place for all the world's inhabitants."

Diana turned toward the windowsill to see if her bluebird was still there. Though no longer outside on the sill, she smiled, thinking there was indeed hope.

"How did Victor do? Did the oligarchs buy into Victor's arguments?"

"The meeting went better than expected. Victor did very well and gave very strong arguments. So well, in fact, a follow up session will be scheduled with Russia's new president in attendance."

Diana's eyes widened as I took another bite of chicken.

"Is it really possible, Tom?"

I gave Diana an encouraging nod. "Victor did very well. The oligarchs grumbled a lot and said Putin's policies would continue on in some form. However, as the meeting and the arguments progressed, Victor's points began to resonate with them. You are an expert when it comes to reading people and understanding their personalities. You were absolutely right. When Victor presented the facts comparing the wealth amassed by the richest individuals in the world and how far their wealth exceeded the wealth of the Russians and that most of the richest were Americans . . . . well, the mood of the meeting changed drastically."

"Victor also mentioned Russia's dropping population and widening wealth gap I assume?" asked Diana.

"He did. He drove home the point that while Russia was massive in size and the largest country in the world, it was on its way to being a third world economy when compared to the U.S., China, and Europe. He reiterated that Russia's GDP output ranks eleventh in the world and its military budget is dwarfed by what the U.S., China, and even India spends. Not that we think spending so much money on large military budgets should be a goal or a good metric, but to the Russian oligarchs, those metrics were certainly worrisome."

"So, what's the next step?"

"Keep up the pressure on all fronts. Sam called in and joined the meeting with John and me. Sam provided us with an update on the efforts currently underway by our new president's administration."

"President Stephen and his administration haven't hit one hundred days yet, Tom. How effective can they be?"

"True, the team is only just being assembled but the other global powers affected by John Gordon's missile attacks are in no better shape, especially Russia and China. Also, we have no idea yet how North Korea is doing."

"Sam's working with his counterpart at the CIA, Angela Keen, I assume?" Diana asked.

"He is. Angela Keen and her team have identified two very good candidates to perform the same function in China and Iran as Victor Petrova is doing in Russia."

"What about North Korea?"

"John says he's identified a candidate. Fellow by the name of Won Min-ho. John says there is a ninety-nine-point-seven percent probability he will be a positive influence on Kim Kyung-mi, the new president of North Korea. According to John, they have known each other for quite some time. He believes the relationship is closer than merely a casual friendship."

Diana laughed. "A matchmaker now."

"Multitalented he is."

Diana looked over at the bay window to see if her bluebird had returned. It had not. The next several minutes we sat in silence, enjoying the rest of our meal.

"What about the military and all those spy agencies around the world who thrive on world conflict? Even the U.S.'s military industrial complex. Our military budget is huge, and China and India's budgets are growing to keep pace. There's going to be a lot of political pushbacks if this new administration is a strong advocate for global peace and reduced military spending."

"It's certainly a concern. No one is naive to think seeking ways to reduce tensions in the world and military budgets and armaments will come easy. We do have a very secret agent, don't forget. We just need to be very careful when and how we use him. This is the reason you and I are going to Washington on Wednesday."

"Sam is concerned, isn't he? That he always has the answers, the right answers."

"Yes. It's a big concern for Sam."

"Years as a therapist, of listening to people and their issues has led me to believe that some people may lack the ability or desire to consider how their own behaviors may be the root cause for their troubles. There are some individuals, Tom, who are self-centered and only out for themselves without empathy for others. They will never conform to socially acceptable norms. They only see people as tools for their personal gain.

"I see. It's not going to be easy, huh?"

"An understatement."

World Peace: Tom Lawson Novel #4
By James Brown

We sat for a moment with our own thoughts and glimpsed occasionally to see if God's bluebird might revisit our window to offer encouragement.

Chapter 4

Unlike the devastation Russia experienced after John Gordon's missile attacks the governmental transition in the United States and China moved forward with minimal disruption. Though the deaths of the President and Vice President of the United States brought great sadness and grief to the country, the transition of power moved forward as it has for hundreds of years with the next person in the presidential line of succession sworn in quickly upon confirmation of the president's death.

In China, Vice President Wang Jun was sworn in as President and General Secretary of the Communist Party of China after their president's death was confirmed. Given the tight control of the Communist party apparatus and purge of corrupt party members, whether for actual corruption or political expediency, for self-preservation many party members agreed to the changes to long standing party rules the former president instituted during his presidency, including presidential term limits.

The announcement that Vice President Wang Jun was sworn in as president surprised many in the party. He was not the candidate China's former president was grooming as his replacement. Though the president's succession intentions were well known, his death allowed disgruntled and often threatened Party members to seize the opportunity to voice long withheld opinions. Even radical opinions, that China should adopt a federalist model of government granting greater autonomy to regions like Tibet, Xinjiang, and Hong Kong.

While Gordon's actions brought the pain of death and destruction to many, it also ushered in a potential for change.

Beneficial changes assuming those who controlled the narrative and information moved quickly after the upheaval.

It was late in the evening in Beijing when Huan Cheng's cell phone rang.

"I look forward to our lunch tomorrow," a sultry voice said and then quickly hung up.

At age sixty-four, Huan Cheng was the youngest member of China's all-powerful Politburo Standing Committee. He began his political career in rural regions of his native Sichuan province. He rose through the ranks as the Governor of Sichuan province, and Sichuan Communist Party of China Provincial Committee Secretary.

Well educated, he was awarded an advanced degree in civil engineering from the University of Science and Technology. This was China's equivalent of an Ivy League degree. Cheng was widely considered to be one of the most liberal minded members of the Chinese elite.

The encrypted email he received very late one evening a week ago held a document he thought was destroyed long ago. It was the beginning of many sleepless nights. A lunch meeting was politely requested. The email stated that a college student needed help with a term paper. A date and time for the lunch meeting was suggested as well as a restaurant he once frequented many years ago.

* * * *

Ah Lam Zing arrived at Beijing's Hongxing Restaurant at noon. She walked slowly as she scanned the dining area on her way to the lady's room. She made note of the diners and cataloged their faces against the hundreds of faces stored in her photographic memory. She wore a yellow and red sundress and wedge heels. Jackie Kennedy sunglasses sat atop her head, and she carried a small handbag. In her early thirties, she had long, thick black hair and wore no makeup. Often, she was mistaken for a young university student who served her objective today.

After spending a few minutes in the lady's room, she left and retraced her steps to the restaurant's door and exited. She strolled casually down the street, stopping occasionally to browse the various window displays and to visit various shops near the restaurant. She continued this pattern for an hour or so all the while cataloguing the faces she discretely observed. Finally, she returned to the restaurant.

As she entered the restaurant, it took just a moment before she spotted Huan Cheng. He sat at a table along the wall. She passed the maître d' station on her way to Mr. Cheng's table and took a seat opposite him. She smiled and greeted Huan Cheng.

"Ms. Zing," Cheng said. "How are you? I hope your studies are going better."

She wrinkled her nose. "Could be better. I am taking a very difficult and demanding course this term at the University of Science and Technology. This is why we are meeting today. Since you graduated from University of Science and Technology, I am certain your assistance will be very helpful and appreciated."

Huan stared across the table and slowly nodded his understanding. "Why don't we order? I don't have much time this afternoon. We can eat while you describe the challenges giving you difficulty."

The waiter quickly took their order and very soon they were sharing a sushi platter of sashimi, maki, and uramaki delicacies.

"Please tell me what is troubling you about this course," Huan said as he selected a uramaki seaweed wrap and placed it on his plate.

"It is a difficult but manageable assignment, assuming I receive some assistance. My assigned paper is similar to another that a student wrote many years ago.

"I see. If I may ask, how did you come upon this old document?"

"A friend."

Hunan gave a slight nod. "The help you seek, what would the nature of this help entail?"

"My paper will contain technical subject matter which may prove difficult for some to understand. I must present my material at a roundtable discussion that is scheduled in a few weeks. It is a controversial subject many of the professors at my university would rather not discuss."

"But an important subject that should be discussed," Cheng said.

"Yes."

Cheng was silent for a moment, sipped his tea, and considered how he could discretely discuss this topic with Ms. Zing. As a new member of the all-powerful China Politburo Standing Committee, and the author of the paper referenced and long thought to be destroyed, he had concerns discussing this topic in such an open environment. The threat of hidden listening devices was always a worry. He was certain that she was a young agent and very well trained. She kept their discussion relevant to her university studies, which could be easily verified.

Cheng took a breath and plunged ahead. "What do you suggest, Ms. Zing? How might I be able to assist you with this project?"

"Ah Lam considered Cheng's question. "Well, my advisor tells me the timing for the scheduled meeting couldn't be better. A lot has changed since a similar paper was written many years ago. My advisor believes the subject matter described in the earlier paper can be referenced, or at least summarized so the issue of plagiarism is not a problem."

"And you think the professors will be open to what this material described if you do not plagiarize?

"Yes. There are several professors from other universities who will join this session. They are very influential. If we all come to a reasonable understanding regarding the direction and substance of my paper, higher learning on a global scale will greatly benefit."

"I see," Cheng said. He smiled and pointed his chopsticks at the remaining uramaki seaweed wrap on the center dish.

"No, I'm full. That last wrap is yours," Ah Lam said.

Cheng took the wrap and dipped it in the hot sauce on his plate. He took a moment to eat the wrap while Ah Lam sat in silence sipping tea.

"Will university presidents be attending?" he asked.

"Not at this first session. Only vice chancellors and professors with a specific interest in the subject will be present," Ah Lam answered. "The purpose is to assess the merit of the material presented, discuss the ground rules, and work out an agenda for a follow up session. At the follow up session, university presidents will be present, and our findings and recommendations presented."

"Would I be correct to assume that the issues for discussion are similar to issues several major universities have experienced over the last couple of years?"

"Yes, that is correct. My advisor has contacted all but one of the universities thus far. I've been told that I may need to help convince the members of that particular university to attend the meeting."

Cheng was momentarily quiet as he discretely scrutinized the room before responding to Ah Lam. "What about the core operational practices of each university and how they function? Do you believe this will be a focus of the discussion?"

"No," Ah Lam answered quickly. "My advisor tells me that the subject of university management will be completely off the table."

"And you believe my assistance will help to ensure this session is a success?"

"Very much so. My advisor knows full well that some university members are entrenched in their thinking. They have no interest whatsoever in matters that could result in changes that could even slightly impact them or their departments. No interest even if the wellbeing of all universities and all staff members would benefit from the proposed changes. If we could garner meaningful agreements, the operating costs could be reduced for all the universities. As a result of the savings, staff could benefit financially with higher pay and benefits. Academic capabilities and stability will be greatly enhanced. This is a very important undertaking, Mr. Cheng. I desperately need your advice and assistance to help ensure that a meaningful discussion takes place."

Cheng looked at his watch and leaned back in his chair. Forty-five years ago, in 1976, he authored a paper for his advisor's review. Cheng knew that the topics and factual information contained in his paper, which miraculously Ah Lam Zing had managed to recover, was extremely controversial given Mao Zedong's ultra-radical Cultural Revolution occurring in China.

Cheng witnessed firsthand the hardships his parents and family members suffered during Mao's purge. He believed this purge caused more harm than good and left a lost generation who struggled for years for progress. The data Cheng provided to his advisor, along with his supportive, corresponding arguments, however, did not result in the reaction he expected from his academic advisor. Outrage and immediate expulsion, his advisor warned him. Now, over four decades later, this young woman was asking him to once again step up and support the beliefs he was forced to bury to survive.

World Peace: Tom Lawson Novel #4
By James Brown

Though China had finally begun to grow economically once the government encouraged capitalistic business practices, the last group to voice a major challenge to the Chinese government occurred at a pro-democracy rally in 1989 on Tiananmen Square. The protestors were brutally suppressed. More recently, China continued to imprison those who argued for ending the communist monopoly on power. A roundup of activist lawyers in June 2015 sent a chill through the activist community and the prospects for a movement to oppose the party seemed dead. This event eventually led to the forced closure of Apple Daily, Hong Kong's prodemocracy newspaper.

Indeed, thought Cheng, there now was an opportunity for world change but was it truly possible as Ah Lam and her advisor pressed him to consider. Finally, Cheng spoke. "I am scheduled to be at the University on Monday next week. I should be free at three in the afternoon. Let's meet at the library if that's convenient for you."

"That would be perfect. Thank you very much," Ah Lam said. She stood and bowed slightly toward Huan Cheng, then reached for her purse and left the restaurant.

* * * *

Quiet chatter flowed about the press briefing room. All chairs were occupied. Jan Polaski was late for her daily noon press briefing. Her appointment as Press Secretary to President Justin Stephen was unexpected. She had, however, held several non-government senior communications positions. Her only stint in a governmental role was as Deputy Communications Director for President Stephen when Stephen was the Governor of Massachusetts. After the president chose Polaski for his press secretary, the Washington news pundits voiced a variety of opinions about his choice. Polaski was six feet tall and a highly regarded former forward for the University of Connecticut's Women's Basketball team. It was believed she could easily defend herself and the president against any adversary.

Finally, after a twenty-minute delay, in walked Polaski, the first African American woman to serve as press secretary to POTUS. She stepped onto the podium dressed in dark gray slacks and a light gray, long-sleeved blouse and what appeared to be four inch heels. She was statuesque and looked like a model for Vogue.

"Apologies everyone, "Polaski said as she arranged her notes. "It's been one of those mornings so let's get started immediately with a few announcements.

As everyone is no doubt aware, the Bureau of Labor Statistics reported that the American economy added 310,000 jobs in March. The unemployment rate edged down to 3.5 percent from 3.7. It was a very good month and our economy's strength continues.

On another point, the CDC has just confirmed that yearly Covid shots will be necessary. We are happy to report we have now reached a 90% fully vaccinated rate. This rate includes children between the ages of five to twelve who were eligible this past year for the children's vaccines provided by Pfizer, Moderna and Johnson and Johnson. Given the proven success of these vaccines more and more employers and states are requiring vaccinations. The goal, which we believe is possible, is to achieve a fully vaccination rate of 95% by the end of the year.

Lastly, the infrastructure program and ambitious plans funded by congress during the last administration to expand education, health care and other social programs have begun to provide the benefits that were predicted. With that, I'll take questions."

Looking out into the audience Polaski said, Larry, CNN."

"Thank you, Jan. Secretary of State Bentley and Defense Secretary Tinsley are scheduled to travel to Japan for three days meetings. Are these preparatory meetings to discuss the agenda for future meetings with Russia, China, North Korea, and Iran . . . . the countries whose presidents were killed in the missile attacks? And my second question, does President Stephen envision any changes to America's defense budgets?"

"As for your first question, Larry, it's normal for new administrations to initiate meetings with their counterparts throughout the world. After Secretaries Bentley and Tinsley's meeting in Japan, they will return to the U.S. and hold a debriefing session for the press. This is common practice, as you know. Now for your second question, I have no information currently."

"Other questions?" Jan said.

Hands flew in the air as she considered who she might call. She thought perhaps a reporter less likely to support the new administration. Known for her ability to handle pressure, she plunged ahead.

"Charles, Wall Street Journal."

Chapter 5

Madeline Pool stood at the conclusion of Angela Keen's staff meeting. A small woman with short-cropped salt-and-pepper hair, she could be attractive if she put any effort into it, but it didn't interest her. There simply wasn't enough time . . . certainly not in her days. She glanced toward the Director, nodded and left the room for her office. She was expecting a call from China at ten a.m.

As a college graduate thirty years ago, the CIA first approached Pool to work for them. She joined the agency and quickly moved up through the ranks. She was sworn in as the CIA's Director of Operations the year prior to John Gordon's ill-fated takeover of three U.S. nuclear subs that launched cruise missiles nearly causing World War III. Soon after the global crisis was averted, the U.S. state department, CIA, and FBI set up a taskforce to assess how this unforeseen tragedy might be used to ensure longer term global peace and prosperity. Madeline Pool was a member of this working group.

"Coffee?" Julia Brent asked Pool, her boss, as she entered the offices they shared.

"That would be great, Julia. I've got five minutes before my ten o'clock call."

As Pool entered her office, Julia quickly prepared a coffee and delivered it to her boss's desk.

"Thank you, Julia. Please close my door as you leave."

"Yes, ma'am," Julia answered.

Within a minute of taking her first sip of coffee, Madeline's phone rang, and she activated the call.

On the other end of the call, the caller said, "opportunity. Iden code Alpha, Yankee, Zulu, Golf, X-ray, Zero."

"Identification confirmed. I hope your professor was agreeable to your request."

"Affirmative," Ah Lam said to Pool, speaking via her phone's end-to-end encryption app. "Whoever uncovered the document Huan Cheng wrote forty-five years ago deserves a very large bonus."

"Yes, quite fortunate," Pool said, though she had absolutely no idea how Sam Wainwright uncovered this forty-five-year-old document or how he confirmed the document's authenticity. But somehow Sam convinced their working group they had no choice but to send the document to Cheng. After much discussion and arguments, the committee finally agreed to send the document to him.

"When is your next meeting?" Pool asked.

"Monday. We meet in the University library at three p.m."

"Good. That will give us time to prepare a briefing for you. We will also have another agent at the library."

"Does Secretary Bentley have a date in mind for the meeting with the Chinese delegates?" Ah Lam asked.

"Ideally early May. Our Russian agent has been successful in his discussions with a group of very influential oligarchs. There will be a follow up meeting with President Milosevic and several of his key cabinet members and the senior oligarchs in a few weeks."

"Hmm, Milosevic. Russia's president is already getting involved. Impressive," Ah Lam said.

"We are just beginning, Ah Lam. What's your assessment of Huan Cheng? Do you think he will come through for us?"

"I believe he wants to. His comments and body language strongly suggests the memories of his family's hardships endured under Mao's rule are still very strong. However, he fears retribution. That same fear that drove him to drop all efforts for changes he contemplated in his paper over four decades ago. He asked me if the core management structure of the universities would be a topic for discussion."

"Which you said no."

"Of course I did. I did exactly as you instructed and kept the dialogue focused on university speak. Cheng asked specifically if the universities' core operational practices and how they function would be up for discussion at the meeting. I told him no. These topics would not be part of the agenda."

"Good. Our goal is not communism conversion therapy. Our U.S. democratic form of government has hardly been working very well the last dozen years, with one party refusing meaningful dialogue or willingness to negotiate with the other party. In addition to insurrection activities erupting to overturn an election that was not in one party's favor. The form of government, whether democratic, communistic, totalitarian, or whatever government a country may have, is not the issue. Rather, It's the intent and capabilities of a country's government to ensure and deliver domestic tranquility, peace, and prosperity for all its citizens and the world as a whole. We all need to do better. Or that little incident that Russia and John Gordon initiated may not turn out so well in the future when another country decides to act in a way that threatens the world."

"I fully understand, Director Pool. It's a worthwhile goal , however, please forgive me if I'm skeptical that the world is ready to be magnanimous toward all fellow human beings, especially those in China. You do recall my personal history?"

"You know I do. I recruited you."

"Because my family and our ancestors have been persecuted for generations."

"A factor, yes. But I also recruited you because of your intelligence and resourcefulness. As a young woman, you were able to assimilate quickly within a very prejudiced society. A society that continues to suppress many of their own citizens, including your family and millions of other Uyghurs living in northwestern China.

A minute or so passed before Ah Lam was able to speak. "I remember so very clearly the day my parents hugged me close and told me that I must leave," she whispered.

"It must have been a very difficult thing for your parents to do. You were their child and only thirteen years old. I can only imagine the heartbreak your parents and you experienced," Pool softly responded.

"The Chinese government has been doing unspeakable things, evil things in an effort to slash birth rates among Uyghurs as part of a campaign to curb its Muslim population, including forcing Uyghur women to be sterilized."

Pool let out a deep sigh. "It's despicable, Ah Lam. Unfortunately, many countries have not treated their people fairly and with dignity. Even America. Our history is certainly no better when it comes to having prejudices toward groups of people based on race, sex, religion, culture, and more. Our government and our people have also done very despicable things. We basically tried to wipe out the indigenous people who lived in the Americas for centuries and captured and enslaved people to work our country's farms and plantations. When those slaves were finally emancipated, many American states promoted or condoned Jim Crow laws to ensure emancipated slaves remained second-class citizens.

No, Ah Lam. Many governments and societies in the world, including ours, are certainly not perfect. Now, we have an opportunity to convince the new world leaders who replaced those who died to consider a new world paradigm, one of inclusion, cooperation, and peaceful coexistence."

"I'll do my best to help, DO Pool. Miracles do happen. I look forward to receiving the briefing paper."

"It will be sent within twenty-four hours. I will also send you the contact information for Progress, another agent who will be helping you. Call him and set up a meeting. He is also a university student, a PhD candidate."

"Hmm, Opportunity to meet Progress. Sounds like the CIA is trying to change its reputation."

"We adjust as necessary, Ah Lam. We are hopeful that President Stephen and his administration, along with the CIA's help, can sell a new global operating model that will lead us all to a more just and stable world."

* * * *

Our late Wednesday afternoon flight to Washington DC was smooth and on time. Upon landing and deplaning with our carryon bags in tow, Diana and I headed to the airport's taxi stand. Twenty minutes later we were standing in a short line at the reception counter at the Washington Waldorf Astoria hotel.

"Next please," the desk clerk said. He stood behind the reception counter positioned in front of wood paneled walls that resembled the bark of a giant redwood.

World Peace: Tom Lawson Novel #4
By James Brown

"Tom Lawson," I said, stepping up to the counter.

"That will be three nights, Mr. Lawson?" The Waldorf desk clerk asked, pulling up the Lawson reservation.

"Yes, checking out on Saturday."

"I see that you have visited with us before. Thank you for being a rewards member. I have upgraded you to a larger room as a platinum member. Room 412. Do you need any assistance with luggage?"

"No thank you. Only two bags," I said, taking the two passkeys the desk clerk handed to me.

This was Diana's first visit to the newly renovated Waldorf hotel. Diana took in the opulence of the hotel's interior as we walked to the elevator.

"No expense was spared when this building was renovated," she commented upon entering the elevator and pressing the fourth floor button.

"It's at least one thing our former president excelled in, spending money to refurbish buildings with his name attached."

"But who's money did he use?" Dana asked.

I shrugged. "Probably the banks or money from loyal followers he stiffed."

In our upgraded room, which was as well appointed as the hotel's lobby, we unpacked our clothes. Diana inspected the two dresses she brought, shook them slightly, and decided a hotel pressing was not necessary and hung them in the closet. I did the same with my two suits.

"Dinner reservations are at seven if you want to take a bath before we go," I said.

"Are you wearing a suit this evening?"

"No, going casual. Just going to freshen up a bit and change my shirt. No one in this group I need to impress."

"Men," Diana said, heading off to the bathroom. "Is the restaurant close to the hotel?"

"Old Ebbitt Grill is in walking distance. It's only a couple of blocks."

As Diana prepared her bath, I relaxed in a lounge chair to check my messages. The first two messages were from Sam Wainwright and Savannah Lee. Each said they were looking forward to the 'wedding planning' dinner meeting. The last message was from John . . . call me ASAP! He said.

I called.

He answered on the first ring. "You left me a message. Anything critical?"

"Yes. A few simmering issues we've been following are beginning to heat up," John said.

"Which issues?"

"Russia, China, and Iran, the major ones."

"There's more?"

"A few more that I'm tracking but they are not to a level that you and Sam need to worry about yet."

"Is the NSA tracking these issues?"

"It doesn't appear that they are."

"That's not good."

"More pressure on Sam," John said.

"Yes, that's for sure. The NSA and CIA and all the other intelligence agencies need to up their game and find these embers that are heating up. Otherwise, Sam is going to have one hell of a time trying to explain to everyone on the task force how he's able to stumble across these global hotspots and they are not."

"A concern, Tom. The reason for my call."

"Somehow Sam needs to be able to explain his brilliance, or better, we need to pass along some of your capabilities to the NSA."

"Provide the NSA with a path of breadcrumbs maybe?"

"I guess," I said letting out a sigh in frustration. "Do you think you can once again discretely sprinkle a few clues so the NSA or CIA can think they discovered the issues on their own?"

"Of course. I'll start with the hottest issues first. If necessary, I can discretely tweak a couple of their search algorithms. I can also choose one of their bright young analysts and lend a helping hand."

"Okay, be discrete, John."

"Not to worry, Tom. This will be a piece of cake, as you humans say."

"What are the issues that are surfacing?" I asked.

"The non-proliferation treaty is one. China and Russia are not adhering to the terms of the treaty. Both countries are secretly funding shell companies that are set up to conduct AI research. And this research is not directed to enhance the capabilities of Amazon Alexa or Apple's Siri personal assistants, or any other assistants."

I groaned. "What else?"

"As expected, a lot of heated discussions have been held by several factions within both countries. More so with Russia, of course, given the death of Putin. The Russian populous is doing more than merely holding an occasional street demonstration."

"Have you identified the leaders of all the factions, those for and against the new government leaders?"

"For the most part. A bit of an ebb and flow given violent uprisings that have occurred, and several leaders being killed."

"Please send me the names and related details when you can."

"Will do."

"What's happening in Iran," I asked.

"Somewhat similar to Russia and China regarding unauthorized AI military developments, however, the bigger issue there is with Iran's Islamic Revolutionary Guard Corps' Quds force. The Quds force, whose name means Jerusalem in Farsi and Arabic, is one of five branches of Iran's Islamic Revolutionary Guard Corps specializing in unconventional warfare and military intelligence operations. Analogous to a combination of the CIA and the Joint Special Operations Command in the United States, it handles extraterritorial operations. The Quds force supports non-state actors in many countries, including Lebanese Hezbollah, Hamas and Palestinian Islamic Jihad in the State of Palestine's Gaza Strip and the West Bank, Yemeni Houthis, and Shia militias in Iraq, Syria, and Afghanistan.

"What are the Quds doing? Are they threating or killing the religious leaders who disagree with the Revolutionary Guard's choice for a new supreme leader? I wonder what John Gordon was thinking would occur after he launched those missiles."

"Probably the same as most men who use violence to express their grievances," John answered. And, getting back to your question about the status of Iran's Supreme Leader selection process. In theory, the clerics that compose the 86-member Assembly of Experts are supposed to anoint the next supreme leader. In the absence of a consensus candidate, there is speculation that the new supreme leader may be replaced by a council composed of their top clerics."

"Not something I think the Guard would want," I said.

"Very true, and I surmise that is the reason for the Guards' threats and intimidation activities."

"Who was the member of the Assembly of Experts who died?" I asked.

"Ebram Janati."

"Have you begun an investigation?"

"Yes. I am in the process of gathering data on the cause of death to assess whether or not the Revolutionary Guard had any involvement."

"Let me know as soon as you are able to find conclusive evidence, as to whether he was murdered or died of natural causes. If he was murdered, we must know the person or persons responsible."

"Will do."

Okay, thanks, John. I better start getting ready for our dinner meeting. Anything else of major concern?"

"Nothing that we need to discuss now. There are rumblings on the domestic front from right wing activists and those who do not want to relinquish any power or standing."

"Right. A topic for another day. Thanks, John. Call me any time if the pot looks to be boiling over."

"Will do, Tom. Say hello to everyone and let Savannah know that Peggy and I are looking forward to celebrating her big day."

World Peace: Tom Lawson Novel #4
By James Brown

Chapter 6

I looked at Diana as we exited the elevator and began walking through the hotel lobby. She looked great. A stunning woman who still caused heads to turn. She turned toward me just before we reached the revolving front door and smiled.

"Thank you for deciding to wear your sport coat."

"I had no choice. Walking through the lobby next to you people would think I was your Uber driver if I didn't spruce up a little."

"Probably," she said as I held the door for her.

Exiting the hotel with Diana's arm locked in mine, we started walking west on Pennsylvania Avenue toward 15th Street. It was an abnormally warm spring evening and the fragrance of blooming flowers waffled in the air, as we walked the brown-brick paved sidewalk under a canopy of willow oak trees. The brick-paved sidewalk, the large number of shade trees and abundance of large urns of planted flowers along America's Main Street was initiated as a beautification effort in 1961 by John Kennedy and carried forward by Lyndon Johnson in the 1980s.

At seven p.m. we arrived at Old Ebbitt Grill, located a block from the White House and across the street from the US Treasury building. Established in 1856, it is one of the oldest saloons and restaurants in Washington. As we entered the restaurant, I wondered if Savannah had introduced her fiancé to her parents at Old Ebbitt Grill as planned. It was an interesting discussion Sam Wainwright and I had with Savannah Lee. Her fiancé, Barry White, was a young African American FBI agent whom she initially met in New York City while she was undercover on assignment. Her assignment at the time was to follow the Russian agent who killed John Gordon. The relationship between Savannah and Barry grew over time but she wasn't sure her parents, especially her father, a direct descendant of Robert E. Lee, would approve of his only child entering into a mixed marriage. Her father came from a long lineage of Virginians dating back to the sixteen hundreds. Many of his ancestors, including General Robert E. Lee, fought for the confederacy. Savannah's choice of Old Ebbitt Grill as the restaurant to introduce Barry to her parents was her shot across the bow. Savannah's father knew the history of Old Ebbitt Grill. He knew Ulysses S. Grant often frequented the restaurant, first as a general and later as president. Her father's namesake surrendered at Appomattox Court House on April 9, 1865. As a concession, she did not make the introductions on the anniversary of Lee's surrender.

"Mr. Lawson, welcome back," the maître d' said as Tom and Diana entered the Old Ebbitt Grill.

"Thank you, Wilson. Is the rest of our group here?"

"They are all seated. And, If my memory serves me correctly, this must be your lovely wife, Diana,"

"Yes, I am his date for this evening. Pleased to meet you, Wilson," Diana said.

"And you, Diana," Wilson responded, bowing slightly.

"My husband said Old Ebbitt Grill was one of his new favorite restaurants in Washington."

"A favorite for many famous politicians, past and present, as well."

"So I hear," she said, as she glanced around the room and admired the expansive and beautiful mahogany bar.

"Ms. Lee and Director Wainwright have already arrived. Your favorite table was reserved. Please, follow me," Wilson said, leading the Lawsons to their table. Before reaching the end of the bar Wilson turned and whispered, "I was hoping Father Dan might be joining you this evening."

"He was invited but was not able to attend. Next trip to Washington, perhaps," I said.

"I look forward to meeting him."

"One day, I'm sure, Wilson."

Looking up as the Lawsons reached the table, Savannah gave a wide smile and slid out of the booth. "So glad to see you, Diana. It seems like forever," Savannah said and reached out and hugged her.

"It does seem to be a long time since you and Sam spent a lot of time in Connecticut," Diana replied.

"She's getting bored, Diana. Not enough action for her," Sam said as he too gave Diana a hug.

"You seem to have grown taller, Sam," Diana said stepping back from their embrace.

"Taller, no. Bigger, I'm sure, I am just too sedentary in my new job."

"Oh, I don't think so, Sam. You're just the right size for the country's new Director of the FBI."

"Intimidating," Savannah said as she released Tom from her bear hug. "Just the right size for a G-man."

As soon as everyone finished their hugs and greetings and were settled into the booth Wilson stepped up to the table. "May I take drink orders before bringing out dinner menus?"

"Absolutely," Savannah said. "A vodka tonic for me and perhaps some of that great bread too."

"I'll have the same, Wilson," Diana said.

"Starting out with a cold mug of Corona, Director Wainwright?" Wilson asked.

"Sounds good, Wilson."

"Make that two, Wilson," I added.

"Okay, I will have those drinks for you momentarily," Wilson said and headed toward the bar.

After everyone was settled in, drinks served, and initial chitchatting subsiding, Wainwright said, "Thanks for coming to Washington, Tom, Diana."

"Couldn't keep you exposed, Sam," I said as I brought my beer mug toward the rest of the glasses raised at the center of the table. "Unfortunately," I whispered, leaning in, "the exposure level unfortunately will be increasing very soon."

"You spoke with John?" Sam asked.

"Just before we left the hotel."

Sam downed the rest of his drink and looked about the room for Wilson. He caught his attention and signaled for another beer. "Let me guess, John's uncovered more information that our illustrious intelligence services have yet to uncover."

I simply nodded as Wilson approached our table with a basket of warm bread along with a carafe of olive oil and four bread plates.

"Let me know when you are ready for the menus," Wilson said.

"We will, thanks, Wilson," I said.

"What has John detected now?" Sam asked, once Wilson was out of hearing range.

"A few items. To start with, China and Russia are not following the terms of the AI Non-Proliferation Treaty. The military of both countries are secretly funding shell companies that have been set up to conduct AI research."

"Humph," Savannah scoffed. "It would be naive to think they wouldn't do this."

"That's not the issue," Sam grumbled. "Neither the NSA nor CIA caught them. John did."

"That's why we're here, Sam," I said.

"Right, my ass is on the line. I can't keep providing information that the NSA or CIA has not been able to discover," Sam said as Wilson approached the table with Sam's beer.

"Thanks, Wilson, just in time."

Wilson gave Sam a quizzical look but didn't respond and returned to the bar. With the Old Ebbitt Grill frequented by many powerful people, discretion and sealed lips were a criterion for ensuring longevity and very generous tips.

"How is John planning to fix this?" Sam finally asked.

"He will again drop a few clues and the NSA or CIA will believe they discovered the issues on their own," I answered.

"But what if they don't pick up the clues?" Savannah asked.

"Then John will discretely tweak a couple of the NSA's search algorithms. He will pick one of their bright young analysts and give him or her a helping hand," I said.

"Hmm. I don't know, Tom. Too many people are suspicious of my newfound expertise to expose new information that the true experts have not. Given the number countries President Stephen is trying to corral to promote a paradigm shift in world cooperation after the missile attacks, this Hansel and Gretel breadcrumb approach of dropping clues won't work for long."

"So, what do you have in mind?" I asked.

Sam took a moment then plunged ahead. "We need to have the government resurrect something akin to the Manhattan project. Maybe set up a small version of Area 54. Top secret of course."

"Introduce John you mean?"

"No, not directly, anyway. And certainly not William."

"I'm not sure how we do that, Sam. Remember, after the missile attacks that John initiated under John Gordon's directions, we agreed not to divulge John's existence. There was no guarantee that the next President of the United States would be so benevolent and use John's capabilities to help all the world to prosper. We can only imagine how our last elected president would have used John's AI capabilities."

"No argument there, Tom, but we need to do something," Sam said with a deep sigh.

The conversation ended as Wilson stepped up to the table holding a handful of menus. Diana reached out her hand. "Thank you, Wilson."

"No need for the menu," Savannah said as Wilson held out a menu toward her. "I'll have the stuffed sole, a baked potato and green beans if they are available and the house salad with balsamic dressing. Just butter on the baked potato."

"A good choice, Savannah. How about you, Diana?"

"I think I'll have the same as Savannah, but with sour cream as well as butter for my baked potato and my balsamic dressing on the side."

"Okay, and for you gentleman?"

"I'm going with the filet mignon, baked potato with butter and the house dressing on my salad," I said.

"Same for me, Wilson," Sam said.

With our dinner orders finalized Wilson headed to the kitchen. Our discussion returned to Sam's concern that it was becoming more difficult to keep John's existence a secret.

Whispers of differing opinions circled the table. Though full transparency would remove Sam from the hot seat, the likelihood that the existence of John could be contained by the U.S. government was Pollyanna thinking as John would say. The consensus was that a global military AI arms race would surely follow if John's existence were known.

World Peace: Tom Lawson Novel #4
By James Brown

After several more minutes of arguments for and against spilling the beans and telling the truth about how John Gordon took control of the U.S. subs and launch missiles that killed the President of the United States and the leadership of Russia, China, North Korea, and Iran, I asked for everyone's attention. "Here's a consideration," I said. "Something I thought about after an earlier conversation I had with John."

"I remember," Diana interrupted. "When you told John the other day you were too busy to meet with Peggy and her medical team to discuss their new paraplegic patient's surgery. Too many balls in the air and stressed, you said. John told you he could fix that if you were feeling old."

"Fix feeling old. Oh, I get it," Savannah said, finally understanding what John meant. "You are a frail human with human limitations. John could create an AI Tom, or at least do that before you were really old, and your brain and body died. I guess he could really do that. Creepy though."

"That scenario may well be humankind's future," I said. "The merger of carbon and silicon lifeforms. In any event, whether now or at some distant future the discussion with John got me thinking. What happens forty, fifty years from now? We will be in our eighties, nineties in the case of Sam, assuming we live that long. John will live forever don't forget. When William's body dies, he will merely find another comatose person that will need an AI reboot."

"Hmm, I hadn't thought of that," Sam said. You're probably right, and if you are, that just makes the problem we are trying to solve much worse."

"You mean trying to keep John a secret as we all age," Savannah said, causing another round-robin discussion and debate.

I tapped my glass, and everyone quieted, I leaned in and whispered, "we could form a larger secret society with succession planning."

"What? Explain please," Savannah said.

"Okay, I'll start with Sam's daughter, Carrie. She is an FBI agent and is much younger than Sam and far better looking I might add, smiling. She would be an ideal candidate for consideration to our secret society. Similarly, you're getting married to Barry White in a couple of months, Savannah. He is also an FBI agent and considerably younger than Sam. We give you and Barry sufficient time together to really get to know each other. Perhaps we wait until after the birth of your first child, Barry becomes a new father and also a member of the secret society of AI John. There's also Amy Apple. You're grooming her to follow in your footsteps as a topnotch investigative reporter. Assuming she proves herself to be a person of great character, she could also be considered for membership. Of course, we would need to choose a few other key people whom we can trust. Persons of high moral character and expertise from the NSA and CIA.

"You've been giving this a lot of thought," Sam said.

I nodded. "Since you mentioned having your butt exposed, yes. Before moving ahead, however, we need to put in place a formal operating methodology. Rules of the road, so to speak . . . something like the ten commandments—those thou shalt do and don't, who should and should not be involved, and when John's special AI capabilities should or should not be used, and to what extent."

"What about the President of the United States, Justin Stephen or any other politician?" Sam asked.

"That is a very difficult question. Can politicians always be trusted to put the best interest of others ahead of their own self-interest? History certainly doesn't support that assumption."

"I don't know, Tom. Setting up a secret society may work in spy novels and the movies but I'm not sure it would work in real life."

"Well, Sam. It has so far. Our little clandestine group has been doing okay. Other than the four of us and Father Dan no one else knows of John's existence."

Sam laughed. "Right . . . for now. Maybe I should say that it's getting damn hard for our small group to keep the presence of AI John our secret. Of course, it would certainly help if we had a member or two from the NSA and CIA join our secret society."

"Okay, so, unless there is an objection, I'll draft a formal charter and have John send out an encrypted file for everyone's review. Agreed?" Everyone voiced their agreement. "Next, I'll ask John to conduct a thorough background check on each person we discussed here today."

"Each person? Spy on my daughter? She carries a gun, you know," Sam said, which caused everyone to laugh.

"It must be the standard protocol. There can be no exceptions, Sam. But we can have John not send the results to any family member."

"Okay, that makes sense," Sam said.

"Next step is to identify other potential candidates for our expanded group, especially candidates from the NSA and CIA. Sam, do you have any suggestions?" I asked.

"Well, as a start, we have our meeting scheduled on Friday. Angela Keen and Maddi Pool will be attending as well as Peter Bentley."

"The CIA Director and her Director of Operations and the Secretary of State. That's certainly a prestigious group. How about the NSA and other key attendees?" I asked.

"I'll have the list of meeting attendees by tomorrow," Sam said. "And I'll add a few names of NSA and CIA officers who I think should be considered for our expanded group. This meeting, by the way, will be the first of President Stephen's interagency meetings to track the progression of his global peace initiative. He's hoping for meaningful cooperation for change since the deaths of world leaders."

"That sounds like a good start, Sam," I said. "This first session the President conducts should prove quite interesting. Thank you for persuading Director Keen and Secretary Bentley to include me in the meeting."

"I thought it was critical that you be allowed to participate. You were instrumental in uncovering the Russian plot carried out by John Gordon. And you already have a top-secret security clearance. There wasn't any pushback from anyone," Sam said.

"Well how about me, or Diana, or Father Dan?" Savannah said with the slightest pouting intonation.

"You're a part of our secret society and have extremely important responsibilities. But how would we explain a Pulitzer Prize winning reporter attending a top-secret government meeting? There is absolutely no chance a government agency would permit that to happen."

"Well, Sam, if there were more transparency maybe there wouldn't be as much corruption, fraud, and often ridiculous, pigheaded decisions made by government officials," Savannah shot back in her southern drawl.

"Unfortunately, we humans have not evolved far enough, Savannah," Diana said. "The need for investigative reporting to keep everyone honest unfortunately will be necessary for a very long time."

"Sad," Savannah said.

"Perhaps one day, humans will be better stewards of the world and of all its people regardless of their race, skin color, sexual orientation, or political party affiliation," Diana opined.

Savannah eyed Diana from across the table with a doubtful look. "Maybe, one day John can rewire the brains of all the gullible simpletons thus permitting them to think for themselves and verify facts versus blindly believing in the daily rubbish of lies and fear mongering voiced by television pundits and politicians on the daily talk shows."

"Ah. Your timing is perfect, Wilson. Food and more drinks, please, when you have a moment to replenish us body and soul," I said as Wilson and a server delivered our meals.

"Glad to be of assistance," Wilson said with a warm smile. "Other than drink refills, is there anything else I can get for anyone?"

"Coffee and desert menus a little later," Diana said.

"I second that," Sam said.

With the business of our working dinner concluded and our decision made regarding how best to keep John's existence a secret, the conversation turned more convivial.

"So, Savannah," I said, as I cut into my filet mignon. Please tell us if your father understood why you chose this restaurant, the Old Ebbitt Grill, to introduce Barry to him and your mother?"

World Peace: Tom Lawson Novel #4
By James Brown

Chapter 7

It was almost ten a.m. As Ah Lam Zing walked toward the university library, she opened her encryption app and placed a call.

"Hello?" a voice answered.

"Opportunity," Ah Lam said. "Iden code Alpha, Yankee, Zulu, Golf, X-ray, Zero."

Li Huang replied. "Progress, Alpha, Beta, Gamma, Charlie, Two."

"I'm told you have been assigned to assist me. I'm heading to the university library and will be there for several hours. Any chance that you can join me?" Ah Lam asked.

Li Huang looked at his phone and Ah Lam's picture. "The timing is good. I just finished one of the classes I teach and am free for the next two hours."

"Meet me in the stacks in the back of the room. You've been sent a picture of me, and I was sent yours."

"I have it. I'll meet you in a few minutes."

Ah Lam entered the university library and walked past a portion of the library designated for study groups. Students were engaged in quiet dialogue sitting at round tables within glass enclosures. As she continued toward the stairway leading to the second floor, she heard her name being called.

"Nice seeing you again, Ah Lam," Li Huang said, walking up to her and giving her a casual hug. "I forgot that you were taking courses here."

"You should pay better attention, Li. Get your nose out of the books once in a while," she said as they proceeded up the stairs behind another group of students. "Still teaching and working on your PhD dissertation?"

"I am. I'm scheduled to defend my dissertation in six months."

"And teaching until the big day comes. A lot of pressure, I'm sure."

"True, but I need to cover expenses somehow. I have a couple of hours before my next class and came here to work on my dissertation."

"For me, I just need to gather information for a report I've been assigned to write," Ah Lam said. They split off from another group of students and headed into the stacks toward one of the tables in the far corner of the room. Once separated from the other students Li reached into his satchel and pulled out a small device. Punching in several digits, he concealed the device by holding it low near his leg. They walked toward an empty table at the far corner of the room hidden behind several rows of bookshelves. A small green bulb on the device continuously blinked.

Deactivating the device, he returned it to his satchel and took a seat with his back against the wall. Ah Lam sat to Li's left at the end of the table.

"You've been doing this for a while," Ah Lam said. "An initial hug and casual conversation for others to hear, checking for cameras and bugs. Impressive."

"Six years and yes, paying close attention to the details is essential in our line of work."

"A calling which only the very diligent survive," Ah Lam said wistfully. As Li retrieved books, papers and a laptop from his satchel, Ah Lam placed her laptop and several folders from her backpack on the table. They looked like two university students engaged in their studies.

Ah Lam looked up from her computer as Li began working on his dissertation material. At an average height, looks, and physique, as well as exceptional intelligence as a PhD candidate, he made an ideal spy. But why? She wondered. What caused Li Huang to risk such a seemingly bright future to become a spy for the CIA?

"What is your dissertation topic, Li?"

"Qubits."

"Quantum computing?"

Li stopped typing and looked over at Ah Lam. "You know something about quantum computing?"

"That it has to do with quantum physics and subatomic particles, but not much more."

"That's more than most people know. Transistors, the switching and memory units that allow computers to compute, have gone from the size of a hand to the size of an atom."

Ah Lam looked at her hand. "From this to an atom," Ah Lam said, holding up her hand. "Truly amazing!"

"In 1968 there were dozens of transistors on a microchip. A couple of decades later there were thousands. Today there are billions."

"Using silicon-based chips."

"Correct. Classical computers use silicon-based chips, quantum computers use quantum systems such as atoms, ions, photons, or electrons. They use their quantum properties to represent bits that can be prepared in different quantum superpositions of 1 and 0. Classical computers can only exist in one state at a time, either 1 or 0, and are limited to doing one thing at a time to make decisions and follow instructions. The more complex the problem, the longer it takes to solve, and the more energy it requires."

"So how does a qubit fit into the vernacular?

"They're computing units. Subatomic particles can be in two places at once. Bits in a classic computer can exist in either one or two states: 0 or 1, on or off. Qubits, the computing units that quantum computers use, can exist in more than one state at a time. They can be on and off, and anywhere in between, at the same time. A qubit can solve millions of problems at the same time and do so using far less energy than classical computers. The result are processors that work millions of times faster and use far less energy."

Ah Lam gave a suspicious look. "These quantum computers don't actually exist, do they?"

"They do," Li answered. "Basic quantum computers are operating in many labs across the world. Companies such as Microsoft, IBM and Google are all developing their own, and many governments are investing in the technology."

"The Chinese government, no doubt."

"Yes. As well as the U.S., Russia, the EU, Israel, and I'm sure many other governments around the world are funding quantum computing research as well."

World Peace: Tom Lawson Novel #4
By James Brown

Ah Lam thought for a moment, considering the impact of computers being developed that were millions of times faster than extremely fast microprocessors used in computers and devices today. Once developed, how would this technology, these super-fast computers change the world?

Watching Ah Lam, appearing to be in a trance, Li said, "You're wondering if the world will be better off or worse with this growth in computing power."

"Ah . . . what?" Ah Lam stammered, drawn back into their conversation by Li's question. "Better or worse off? Do you read minds too?"

"Perhaps, but that's what you were thinking, weren't you? Computers being developed that are able to crunch numbers, data, information millions of times faster than microprocessors and computers can do today?"

"You're afraid, aren't you, Li, that's one reason you became a U.S. agent." Are there other reasons?"

Li moved his chair closer to Ah Lam. "Fear, yes. One of the reasons. Much like Russia was desperate to spy on the American Manhattan project in the 1940s."

"Mutual assured destruction, you mean?"

Li responded with a slow nod. "Yes, mutual assured destruction. I have bombs as big as yours so don't mess with me." Li hesitated a few moments. "I have a pretty good idea of the kind of progress we are making here in China and what our government is seeking to achieve with the billions of Chinese yuan being invested in quantum computing technology."

"Altruistic objectives, I hope?" Ah Lam said.

Li smirked. "It is not. Or at least it's not the Chinese government's primary objective. Which is one of the reasons I was easily persuaded to help the United States."

"You wanted to make sure there was a level playing field when it comes to quantum computing technology. What else made you take the plunge?"

After a few moments, Li whispered, "My sister. I was seven when my mother told me her pregnancy would be terminated, that I would no longer be having a baby sister. I didn't fully understand at the time, of course. But I have never forgotten the day she told me, or the arguments my mom and dad had. She was devastated and my parent's relationship was never the same after that."

"The one-child policy initiated by Deng Xiaoping in 1978 that was only rescinded in 2019," Ah Lam said quietly.

"Right. One of the many ill-conceived policies that our government implemented that caused so much anxiety and harm to so many Chinese families. My father was a communist party member, a civil engineer by education working as a mid-level manager in the city government of Jinan, the capital of Shandong province."

"Your father was pressured. Communist party members had no choice but to toe the line. Very few people are chosen to become members of the communist party of China."

"But he had a choice, Ah Lam. He chose the party over his family, his wife and child, my sister."

"I'm sorry," Ah Lam said, reaching out her hand and putting it on Li's. "Hopefully you and I will be able to play a small part to help ensure decisions made by our government improve the lives of our people, and the lives of all the people of the world."

"Roughly six percent. Out of 1.4 billion people in China only six percent of the population are chosen to join the cult, the Communist Party of China. Do you know the history of the CPC and how members are chosen?"

Ah Lam slowly shook her head. "I never bothered to learn because I knew I would never be invited."

"Because you're Muslim, a Uyghur."

Ah Lam gave a surprised look, leaning back in her chair.

"I'm sorry, no offense intended, Ah Lam, really. Your ancestors have been in China since the eighth century, long before the communist party was formed, the Muslim religion even longer. I assumed DO Pool provided you some history about me as she did about you."

"She did not. It was a short conversation."

"Again, I'm sorry. I should have known since you were asking questions about me. Let me finish the interview."

"Okay, and no offense taken."

"Thank you. Since we were discussing my father and his decision to remain a member of the CPC, I too became a member a few years ago."

"You're joking!" Ah Lam stammered, not believing what she just heard.

"Not too long after I received my bachelor's and master's degrees from MIT in the States."

"The CIA suggested you apply for membership, didn't they?"

"They did. Almost five years at MIT I came to the realization that there is no utopia, that no government, and no religion has all the right answers. And no institution is perfect. The world and all the humans and creatures that inhabit it is a very small place in the vastness of the universe. We all need to work together for the common good of all the people on earth and the planet itself."

Ah Lam sat back. "That's heavy! Save the world, huh? And I thought I was chewing off a lot by trying to save the Uyghur population."

"A bit of naivety on my part, I'm sure, but better to try than sit back and complain and do nothing. Anyway, with my father being a member of the communist party it gave me a leg up. Not that it was a done deal, I still had to go through the CPC rituals. And believe me, the organization is like all cults. It's harder to get into the CPC than it is to get into an Ivy League school in America. An applicant's family background, gender, rural or urban roots, academic performance, university ranking, and perceived loyalty all affect a candidate's chances. It's similar to becoming a made-man in the Costa Nostra, how they select, vet, and anoint a new member into the mob."

Ah Lam laughed. "You're really up on all he cults that exist around the world."

"I am. There is the KKK, Proud Boys, Oath Keepers, Masons to name a few in the U.S., the CPC in China, and if I had more time, I'm sure I could rattle off a few similar organizations in Europe, the Middle East and in other countries around the world."

"So I take it you've been on a mission. Formal education at an elite technical school in the U.S., back to China to attend a similar prestigious school to secure a PhD, become a communist party member, and make the world a better place. Not bad," Ah Lam said, settling back with her arms folded across her chest."

"Right. Miles to Go Before I Sleep."

"The famous phrase used by Robert Frost in the last stanza of his poem, Stopping by Woods on a Snowy Evening, if I remember my American literature correctly," Ah Lam said.

"I'm impressed," Li said. "Well read as well as beautiful and caring, of course, wanting to right the wrongs being inflicted on your Uyghur population."

"Thank you, Li. Maybe working together, we can achieve at least some of our objectives."

"So, enough about me. Tell me, what help do you need from me. How can I assist?" Li asked.

Ah Lam opened a folder on the table and pulled out a report and slid it over to Li.

"What is this," he asked.

"A paper written by a student forty-five years ago. The student who authored this paper thought it was a reasonable assessment of the conditions in China at the time," Ah Lam said, explaining its significance while Li scanned the document.

After a few moments, Li looked up. "Remarkable, forty-five years and nothing changes. Identical reports are being written today, the same conclusions. It's like opening a time capsule every fifty or hundred years. Drop this report back in a box and open it again in fifty years and the thesis of the report will still be relevant."

"Well, maybe we can change that. Stop that cycle."

Li gave Ah Lam a questioned look. "Who wrote this paper?"

"A member of China's Politburo Standing Committee, Huan Cheng."

"You're kidding!"

"I'm not. I met with him a couple days ago."

"This forty-five-year-old document. How did you get ahold of it? Did Pool send you a copy? And if she did, how the hell did she uncover it?"

"All excellent questions, Li. Director Pool did pass it along to me, and I too thought it was amazing that the new, youngest member of the Politburo Standing Committee actual wrote it. When I asked her where the agency got it, all she said was, we have our ways."

Li shook his head and leaned in. "The NSA, CIA has that capability?" he whispered. "That's incredible. I assumed Cheng destroyed the report since it was never released."

"What do you mean?" Ah Lam asked.

"There is no way Huan Cheng would be accepted into the Communist Party if that document was released. No way. His advisor, his mentor, would never have let Cheng destroy his career by allowing this paper to see the light of day."

"Hmm. That's interesting. Cheng was also very surprised when he learned the document existed, and that I had a copy."

"His mentor must have kept a copy," Li said quickly. "Protection. He kept the document in case he needed a favor from Cheng in the future. But how would the CIA find a copy after all these years," Li whispered again and looked about their area where they were seated, checking to see if a student might be close by. "When Cheng wrote his thesis, he sure didn't have access to a personal computer to write it," he continued.

Ah Lam shrugged. "Maybe we'll find out some day. But for now my task is to convince Huan Cheng to keep an open mind and consider what he wrote forty-five years ago. I need him to persuade key members of China's Politburo Standing Committee to consider the merits of the proposal that U.S. Secretary of State Peter Bentley and his team will present at a joint China and U.S. meeting that is being planned."

"When is your follow up meeting with Cheng?"

"Monday, here at the library."

Li thought for a moment. "Forty-five years? Cheng probably thinks you're related to his mentor, the professor he shared his thesis with and was told releasing it would end his career. I doubt the professor is still alive. In any event, it's better that Cheng thinks you are a relative of the professor who gave you the document before he died rather than the alternative, that you are a CIA operative."

"Otherwise I would be in jail."

"Or worse, dead."

"He didn't press me on how I got the document, so I guess he thinks I'm a relative."

"The meeting between America and China leadership has already been reported to be in the planning stage so your meeting with Cheng should not be an issue. Merely a university student seeking advice from an esteemed graduate of the university you are attending. Has

Pool sent you talking points for your meeting with Director Cheng on Monday?" Li asked.

"She did. I have the weekend to thoroughly study them. She's also sent me background information on Cheng."

"Okay. To help, I will begin to discretely check with the party members I typically deal with, which are most often those that work in the academic, business, and technology community. These groups always have an opinion and typically are not afraid to share them. Would you like me to be in the library on Monday, do a sweep of the area perhaps and see if I spot any suspicious characters?"

"That would be great, thank you," Ah Lam said.

"What time?"

"Eleven a.m."

"Okay, it's a date. I'll be here," Li said and stood. "I'm off to my next class. Study hard this weekend, Ah Lam. The world is counting on you."

World Peace: Tom Lawson Novel #4
By James Brown

Chapter 8

It was eight-thirty Friday morning. Sam picked me up at the hotel for a short drive to the Harry S. Truman Building, the location of the U.S. Department of State headquarters. Sam's driver drove west on Constitution Avenue and pulled in behind three cars waiting to be admitted into the State Department complex.

"Have you been to the State Department?" Sam asked as we waited our turn behind two cars ahead of us."

"No, I didn't make it over to the Truman Building. Just the White House."

"Oh, that's right. Last year at the White House, when the president awarded you the Presidential Medal of Freedom award for your heroics."

"It was a bit of a surprise that I was singled out for that prestigious award since many people were killed, including the President of the United States."

"Well, you did play a big role in preventing World War III."

"As well as you, Savannah, Father Dan, and Diana," I added.

"True, and Savannah was awarded her first Pulitzer and Father Dan was invited to the Vatican to meet with the Pope. It seems like Diana, and I got the short end of the straw."

"Yeah, right, Mr. Director of the FBI, with your picture forever memorialized in the halls of justice. It was quite a promotion you received as I recall."

Sam grinned as we moved up a car length. "My picture does look good hanging on the wall in the FBI building, doesn't it."

"And on the walls in every FBI building in the country."

Sam grinned again and we moved forward to the guard waiting for us to present our credentials. "How about Diana?"

"She was just thankful none of us were killed and the world didn't come to an end," I answered and presented my credentials to the guard.

"Good morning, Director Wainright," the guard said, taking our creds and scanning them. "Tom Lawson, pleased to meet you. Your first time visiting us here at the State Department?"

"It is, yes," I said, reaching over and taking back my credentials from the guard.

The security check completed we continued on into the complex and were dropped off at the front of the building. "Another of your many perks, Mr. Director, being chauffeured." I said.

He shrugged. "A well-deserved one since I work 24/7 now and never have a chance to sit on my new boat at the lake."

"Hmm. Maybe I could try out the boat for you since you aren't able to use it and I no longer punch a clock."

"Humph!" Sam complained as he reached for the door handle and exited the car. "You can just wait until I christen its first launch. I was supposed to be retired by now, you know."

"Reaching the pinnacle of power has a way of delaying best laid plans," I said as we entered the building and presented our credentials to a guard at the building's entrance. Through this last check point we proceeded to the bank of elevators. The State Department offices were located on the seventh and eighth floors of the building. We exited on the seventh floor where the Secretary of State's office, staff offices, and conference rooms were located. The State Department reception room, drawing room, and dining rooms were on the eighth floor. Sam led the way to the James Monroe Conference Room where our meeting was to take place as we left the elevator.

As we walked toward the conference room, Sam leaned toward me and whispered, "after the meeting I'll show you around. If you aren't aware, the Diplomatic Reception Rooms contain one of the nation's foremost museum collections of American fine and decorative arts."

I looked up at my very large six-foot-five friend in disbelief. "Wow! A big G-man, outdoorsman, and now a fine arts connoisseur. My, have you progressed since we first met."

Sam shrugged. "Got to keep evolving, learning and appreciating new things. Life is too short."

I laughed. "What happened to my grumpy old friend?"

"Too many conversations with your wife and John – the shrink and the AI savant," he said, as we entered the James Monroe room.

"Tom Lawson," Peter Bentley said, reaching to shake my hand. "It's good to see you again. Victor Petrova is really doing a great job for us. An outstanding person you recommended."

"Thank you, Mr. Secretary. That was my assessment of him when we worked together for several years. Great background, character, and very intelligent. I thought Victor was a perfect fit for the team President Stephen was assembling."

"I should say so. Dual citizenship, U.S. and Russia, an avid believer that Russia could do so much better if it did not consider America as one of its arch enemies. And most critically, his ongoing consulting contract with Vadim Ivanov who is the most influential oligarch in Russia."

"That fact was high on my list also," I said.

"Did you give Tom a tour of our offices, Sam?"

"Not yet. I'm going play tour guide after the meeting."

"Good. A lot of history in this building. Come on. Let me make some introductions before the meeting kicks off," Secretary Bentley said.

The James Monroe room resembled a very large early American parlor and dining room. We stepped softly across a handspun Persian carpet. A cherry antique China cabinet and Chippendale mahogany chest were along one wall, and a Marlborough-leg camelback sofa, chairs and settees were positioned along the other walls. A myriad of sconces and period paintings, sketches, and memorabilia hung throughout the room. On the far side of the room a mahogany conference table was set up to accommodate ten people spaced comfortably.

"Barbara, have you met Tom Lawson?" Secretary Bentley asked.

"I have not had the pleasure yet."

"Barbara Shirley is my deputy, Tom."

"Pleased to meet you, Deputy Secretary," I said, shaking her hand.

"And you, Tom. But please, Deputy Secretary is too formal. Barbara is much better. It's a real pleasure to finally be able to meet you. I'm not sure where we would all be had you not uncovered that Russian plot commandeered by John Gordon."

"Thank you, Barbara, but I had a lot of help from the big guy here," I said, putting my hand on Sam's shoulder."

"Yeah, this big guy always seems to find himself in the thick of things. And recently he has done wonders uncovering information and contacts that our intelligence officers have had difficulty finding."

"Just having an exceptional bit of good luck recently, Barbara," Sam said. "Much like a baseball player coming out of a slump. All of a sudden, he's hitting triples and homeruns."

Barbara laughed. "Well, let's hope your batting average stays up there, Sam. We need more homeruns if we're going to achieve the president's objectives."

"Also joining us today, Tom," Secretary Bentley continued, "is NSA Director General Bradley Goldman and his assistant, Executive Director Sarah Pope."

"Pleased to meet you, General, Ms. Pope," I said, shaking their hands.

"I believe you've already met my deputy, Tom?" The General said.

"Ron Wainscott, yes I have."

"Sarah reports up through Ron and me and provides leadership in all areas of the enterprise and represents the NSA's interests internally and externally. She and her team are actively providing intelligence support for this little undertaking that President Stephen has launched."

"Very interesting," I replied.

After several more minutes of casual conversations, Secretary Bentley looked over at the clock. "Okay everyone, it's almost nine a.m. If anyone needs a coffee refill or another bagel, please grab it now and let's take our seats. We have a lot to discuss this morning."

Those wanting additional food, coffee or juice headed to the buffet table and then found their seats at the conference table.

Secretary Bentley kicked off the meeting.

"First of all, I want to thank everyone for being prompt today. This is our first CIPC status meeting, which we will hold bimonthly.

CIPC, as everyone here knows, is the Cooperation, Inclusion, and Peaceful Coexistence initiative that President Stephen has kicked off.

The objective, as President Stephen has stated, is to turn the tragedy of the deaths of the world's leaders and dozens of its citizens into an opportunity for meaningful change. Russia's scheme and John Gordon's insanity almost caused another World War. The goal and objective of this team, under the direction of President Stephen, is to secure a paradigm shift in the thinking by the new leaders who are replacing those who were killed. Those new leaders who are being elected, appointed, or designated by their people or by whatever form of government they may operate under.

Our purpose is not to advocate for democracy or try and convince these new leaders that democracy is the best form of government for all countries. That is not our mission, ladies and gentlemen. Democracy, theocracy, autocracy, or even dictatorship, whatever the form of government these new leaders have chosen to govern by is not a focus of this program.

Our objective is to ensure that these newly chosen leaders and their governments can ensure and deliver domestic tranquility, peace and prosperity for their citizens and thus the world as a whole. America and the world were spared this time. But there is no guarantee the world will be so lucky the next time when another government leader decides that they or their country would prosper better through world conflict and war."

Secretary Bentley paused for a moment and scanned the faces around the table after restating the objective of President Stephen's CIPC program initiative. He looked directly toward General Goldman.

"Are there any questions? General?"

General Goldman looked about the room. Was he really the only one who was still trying to wrap his mind around the premise of the president's objective? The intended outcome – cooperation, inclusion, and peaceful coexistence was not the issue, just the 'regardless of the form of government' bullshit. Theocracy, autocracy, and even dictatorship, hell, these were the governments of the countries that interfered with our democratic elections, stole our intellectual property, and caused the death of many of our citizens. As he looked about the table, their facial expressions were not at all encouraging.

World Peace: Tom Lawson Novel #4
By James Brown

"Peter, I would be lying if I said I fully agreed with the premise of this undertaking. The intended results; peace, prosperity, and global cooperation, of course, who wouldn't want that outcome? But these countries and their forms of government, Peter – theocracy, autocracy, dictatorship – I find it difficult to believe these governments would ever ascribe to the notions of cooperation, Inclusion, and peaceful coexistence."

Secretary Bentley took a moment before responding and scanned the room again. "Anyone else have similar thoughts?" he asked, then immediately turned toward Angela Keen, the Director of the Central Intelligence Agency. "What about you, Angela? You and your organization probably have the best intel on the likelihood that the world would be ready to embrace this idea. What do you think?"

Angela turned toward Maddi Pool, her Ops Director, then back to Secretary Bentley. "Will we be successful? I'd give it a 50/50 chance if we follow President Stephen's approach. But if we push democracy, we will have a zero chance for success."

She took in a deep breath then said, "Listen, the notion that America is a shinning city on the hill, as President Reagan described in one of his State of the Union addresses, is not shared by a lot of people and governments around the world, certainly not anymore. Whether it's religion, personal greed for power, or plain old human competitiveness, the bottom line is, we will not be able to convince those countries we are targeting to accept the CIPC program if we push our form of government. It's just not going to happen. Especially since we've had a recent president whose primary objective was to become an autocrat and did all he could to tarnish that shinning city on the hill."

Secretary Bentley grimaced. "But you still think we have a chance for success?"

"Yes, I do, with hat in hand, a bit of humility, and we focus purely on the core objectives that the president has laid out. Following that approach we have a chance of convincing these countries that they, and the world, will be better off from a security and economic perspective by agreeing with our President's objective."

"I was doubtful, at first," Maddi Pool followed. "But the feedback so far is encouraging. The two new agents we have deployed, Victor

Petrova in Russia, a great find by Tom, and Ah Lam Zing, our agent in China have produced positive results so far."

"A good transition, Maddi," Secretary Bentley said. "Give us a summary of their efforts and their next steps."

"Okay, I'll start with Russia. We have been pleasantly surprised with the progress Victor Petrova has made. His background and business relationship with Vadim Ivanov has been instrumental in making the right connections. Victor was brilliant with the arguments he presented that Russia and its people, and especially the oligarchs Victor met, would benefit economically if Russia agreed to support the American plan. Likewise, he successfully argued that acceptance of the plan would create the stability necessary to quell the uprising taking place throughout their country. He's been so successful that a follow up meeting is being scheduled with Andrey Milosevic, the new president of Russia."

"That's excellent, Maddi," Secretary Bentley said. "How about China?"

"Not as far along but definitely progress. Ah Lam Zing, our agent in China, has had several sessions with Huan Cheng, the newest member of China's Politburo Standing Committee. Mr. Cheng, as everyone has been briefed, authored a paper when he was a university student and took exception to many of Mao's doctrines back in the day. The document that Sam here located somehow."

Sam shrugged and smiled.

"Anyway," Maddi continued, "that document opened the door for Ah Lam's first meeting with Cheng. She followed the president's script and told Cheng that democracy would not be pushed as a premise for consummating an agreement. She is scheduled to meet with him again on Monday. After this session, the next step will be to secure an initial discussion session between our State Department and the Chinese delegation."

"Barbara and Zheng Shih, our state department diplomat for China, and I will be leading this senior level discussion," Secretary Bentley said, taking over the discussions. "We assume Li Chao, one of China's four vice premiers, will lead China's team with Huan Cheng also participating. Once these preliminary sessions take place, as well as meetings with Russia, North Korea, and Iran, we will press for a meeting between each of the presidents of these countries, a Group of 5 Summit."

"What's the status of Iran and North Korea?" General Goldman asked.

"They are next up in our agenda," Barbara Shirley replied. "As everyone knows, Peter has reached out to the North Korean government via several channels through North Korea's mission to the United Nations. But to date, we have not received any response from Pyongyang. Peter and Defense Secretary Floyd Tinsley will be traveling to Japan for a three-day meeting in two weeks. North Korea will be on the agenda as well as China. Also, on a positive note, the CIA and NSA have identified a very good candidate to assist us in North Korea. Thank you, Angela and General Goldman."

Everyone in the room turned toward Director Keen and General Goldman and gave them a muted applause. I kicked Sam under the table and winked as he turned toward me.

Continuing, Shirley said, "I'll let Angela update everyone on the status of the CIA's new agent in North Korea."

"Thank you, Barbara," Angela said. "As a closed society, it is very difficult to accumulate information about any North Korean citizen. That said, however, Won Min-ho came to our attention through his business relationships and a connection we uncovered that he has with Kim Kyung-mi, the new dear leader now consolidating power after her brother's death. Discrete, clandestine discussions are being held with Won. Won said he longed for the opportunity we presented to him. Now that new leadership is being put in place, he said he believes he can help influence Kim Kyung-mi move the country in a new direction."

"Excellent," Secretary Bentley said excitedly. "What do you think the timing will be when we can initiate formal discussions, starting first with a response to the communique we've sent requesting a meeting?"

"We believe we will have positive results by the time you return from your Asian trip."

"That's good, very good, Angela. How about Iran?"

"Hmm, a lot going on in Iran, Peter. I'll start with the Quds Force. They obviously do not want open minded progressives to replace any of Iran's leaders who were killed. To that end, religious leaders have been threatened and intimidated as part of the Revolution Guard's efforts to influence the selection of a new supreme leader. The clerics that compose the 86-member Assembly of Experts are supposed to anoint the next supreme leader. In the absence of a consensus candidate, which seems to be more likely however, there is speculation that the new Supreme Leader could be replaced instead by a council composed of several top clerics."

"Not something the Guard would want to see happen," Secretary Bentley mumbled.

"Very true, and the reason for the Guards' threats and intimidation activities, Angela Keen said."

"The chatter we've been gathering supports this concern," Executive Director Pope interjected. "Ebram Janati, a very influential cleric and member of The Assembly of Experts died suddenly last week. He was sixty-five years old with no history of illness. His death is suspicious to say the least."

"We are discretely investigating the cause and possible involvement by the Revolutionary Guard, Peter," Director Keen said.

"Okay, everyone," Secretary Bentley said looking up at the clock. "We're making good progress. Thank you. Our next status meeting will be set up after Floyd and I return from our Asian trip. Keep the lines of communication flowing and, General, I understand your concerns. We all have them, believe me. But we must be successful. We must convince these new world leaders that there is a better way, that we can all live in peace, together. Our very lives depend on this initiative, as well as the lives of all creatures on this planet we call home."

As everyone was gathering their materials and leaving the room Secretary Bentley walked over to me. "How long are you planning to be in Washington, Tom?"

"Diana and I have a flight out on Saturday afternoon," I said.

"Saturday, hmm," Bradley mumbled and thought for a moment. "I need you to reschedule your flight, late Sunday and even better, switch to a flight back to Connecticut on Monday."

"Well, sure, we can probably do that. What's the reason?"

"A small dinner party you've been invited to attend on Saturday. Sam and Diana too."

"Dinner party? Who's the host?"

"President Stephen."

World Peace: Tom Lawson Novel #4
By James Brown

Chapter 9

"William crawled into bed next to Peggy, leaned in toward her and kissed her forehead.

Peggy gathered her papers that were scattered about the bed and put them on her night table. She snuggled up to William and whispered, "do you know how much I love you?"

"I do. You went through five years of hell to keep me alive. You gave up so much. I can only imagine how difficult those years were for you." He paused a moment then embraced her more tightly. "I . . . I think for me, knowing that you are able to accept a slightly imperfect or should I say a slightly modified husband, makes me happier than I could have ever imagined. I love you, Peggy."

She looked up into her husband's eyes . . . this man who survived five years in a coma near death at times. She saw that he was fighting back tears and believed he knew what she was thinking and feeling. Their lips touched and she felt a sudden calm come over her. No longer grieving and feeling so alone, she was now at peace again. Her head rested on his chest, listening to the beat of his heart. "I don't know what I would have done if I had lost you," Peggy whispered."

"I will never leave you again. I realize I'm not the . . ."

She put her fingers to his lips. "I know," she said softly. I always knew that it would take a miracle to bring you back to me. Not just to come out of the coma, but to really be alive again, the man I so desperately wanted to be alive in every way. It would not have happened had Tom . . . and John not become a part of my life. They were my miracle, our miracle, and next week you and John will be the miracle for young Cody helping my team return him to the life he had before his accident and enable this young paraplegic to stand and walk again."

"Honey, you're the miracle. It's your expertise and skills as a brilliant neurosurgeon that makes the difference, I'm merely the AI mechanic who has helped facilitate your skills."

Peggy looked up at William and smiled. "Thank you, but you are being a little generous with your assessment of my skills. I agree that I'm a skillful neurosurgeon, as are many of my peers throughout the country and around the world. But we both know my skills alone, or those of any of my peers, would not have returned you to me. You would have died, William without John and the dedication and skills of Tom, Diana, Sam and Father Dan. All of you were catalysts for my success."

"Oh, I forgot about that small group that helped make it happen," William said.

Diana poked him in the side with her elbow. "You forgot! Like you forget anything anymore."

William shrugged and grinned. "Okay, I concede. You did have a little assistance from a few dear friends of ours. But you made it happen. You wrote that brilliant paper that caught John's attention and then you tracked down Tom and convinced him to be the CEO of your company. You were also instrumental in training the team that performed the surgery on me."

"That surgery would not have been successful if John, the AI savant part of you, whose general brilliance along with his PhDs and medical degrees had not developed revolutionary AI chips and artificial neural pathways. That is what enabled your awakening."

"I guess timing in life is everything," William said softly. "I am just thankful that all the stars were perfectly aligned."

"Me too," Peggy said hugging William tightly. After a few moments she separated from William and moved to her side of their king size bed and fluffed her pillows. "You won't stay up too long, will you? The carbon-based portion of your body needs seven hours of sleep, don't forget."

"No more than an hour, I promise. I need to see if I can help Tom and Sam with a little problem in Iran."

"Iran?"

"A very influential cleric and member of The Assembly of Experts died last week. The NSA and CIA may need assistance in determining whether or not the Iranian officials correctly reported the cause of death."

"Whether or not he was murdered?"

"Yes."

Peggy returned an anxious look.

"Nothing to worry about, my dear. My silicon-based persona is extremely intelligent as you know. John will discretely conduct a digital search in parallel with the NSA and CIA. They won't know he's doing it. But if they've missed critical data or failed to access the right Iranian systems, he will drop digital hints to aid the NSA in uncovering connections missed by their search engines and covert initiatives."

"No one knows John is involved?"

"No one."

"How about William Landon?"

"Only as the once comatose husband of the brilliant neurosurgeon Peggy Landon."

"And you promise to keep it that way," Peggy said, pointing a finger at him.

William took hold of her finger, then her hand and kissed it. "Promise," he said.

Peggy reached over and turned off the lamp on her nightstand and turned on her side facing the window away from William. Her alarm was set for five a.m., though she knew it wasn't necessary to set it. John would awaken William promptly at five a.m. He was always very punctual. But setting the alarm helped keep things normal. She held William's hand. "I love you, and remember, one hour. I have surgery scheduled tomorrow morning."

He squeezed her hand. "I forget nothing, remember. Love you too. Goodnight."

In the dark, William fluffed his pillow and laid on his back as his AI enhanced brain turned to Iraq and the queries and data being gathered and analyzed by John. Though the NSA was the best in the world when it came to their capabilities to track, monitor, digest, and analyze massive amounts of data and communications their technology was far inferior to John's artificial intelligence capabilities.

It was seven a.m. in Tehran and ten-thirty p.m. in Connecticut when John connected to an encrypted communications network used by the intelligence arm of the Iran's Revolutionary Guard.

* * * *

"It's done, Mostafa. The cause of death was documented, signed off by Hassan Rajai, the coroner. Heart attack. It will be filed this morning. I've sent you a copy."

"What did the toxicology report show?"

"Nothing, or at least nothing indicating that Ebram Janati was poisoned. In addition to being obese, it was previously reported that he had a heart condition. The report also states that Ebram Janati was ill for two days before he died while he was on a meditative retreat. A flu bug it was thought.

"How extensive was the toxicology testing?"

"Extensive. We wanted to make sure the Guard was not blamed for his death. An analysis of a hundred or so compounds, including alcohol, drugs as cocaine, amphetamines, barbiturates, quaaludes, and poisons. Rajai also ordered detailed tests on a gas chromatograph for the presence of certain metals and other subtle compounds."

"He didn't test for Oleander?"

"No. With eight million compounds on earth, medical examiners at best only test for a few hundred of them and Oleander is not high on the list of common poisons to be tested in a toxicological analysis. Rajai was thorough and went above and beyond a typical autopsy. We are in the clear."

"It was a risk, Omar."

"A risk that was necessary. Hassan Rajai will attest to his findings, that there was no foul play. Ebram Janati was not murdered. Had he discovered that he was, we would have delt with that outcome."

"Peace be upon you," Omar.

The connection was severed.

* * * *

"These late-night calls are becoming standard, John."

"It's seven-thirty a.m. in Tehran, Tom. The world doesn't operate only on U.S. Eastern Standard Time."

World Peace: Tom Lawson Novel #4
By James Brown

"Unfortunately," Tom said with a muffled yawn. "Is Sam on the line with us."

"Of course, I am," Sam said in a grumpy tone. "What haven't the NSA or CIA uncovered this time, John? I sure wish I would have hired you as I mentioned in one of our mentoring sessions."

"You had the opportunity but even if you were able to hire me when I was in that bedridden quadriplegic state I created, you would still not have been able to easily explain my extraordinary AI skills."

"True, different problems but maybe they would have occurred earlier in the day. Anyway, what critical information has our NSA folks not detected again?"

"That Ebram Janati, Iran's Assembly of God cleric was murdered."

Silence for a moment then, "those bastards!" Sam shouted.

"Unfortunate, but expected, Sam. More importantly now," I said, "how did you uncover this information, John, and how can we best initiate a trail, so the NSA uncovers it?"

"Regarding your first question, I've created malware, Tom. Very interesting worms actually, that I launched several months ago. The worms target the communication networks and devices in the countries President Stephen's CIPC Program is targeting."

"All the countries, and all their networks and devices, John?"

"The list of actors under surveillance is quite large and growing. Somewhat similar to what the NSA is doing but my worms are significantly more advanced."

"Of course, they are," I said. "What did you uncover?"

"A fellow by the name of Omar made an encrypted call to his superior, Mostafa Ahmadi, the Chief Commander of Iran's Revolutionary Guard," John answered. "Omar made a call to Ahmadi and reported that Hassan Rajai, the coroner, signed off on Ebram Janati's cause of death, a heart attack."

John proceeded to activate a recording of Omar's conversation for Tom and Sam.

"Incredible," Sam said after listening to the recorded call. "They had the balls to let the coroner just do his thing and see if he could find the poison used to kill Janati."

"No one said they weren't ruthless, and smart," I offered. "But let's cut to the real issue. How do we discretely have the NSA uncover this information?"

World Peace: Tom Lawson Novel #4
By James Brown

There was silence for several minutes, Tom and Sam were thinking how best to proceed while John awaited directions.

"No other way," Sam finally said. "We need to initiate that larger secret society and succession planning proposal that you suggested, Tom. Someone in the NSA will need to be identified to have created John's super worm. Do you have any other suggestions on how we can do this, John?"

"No. I agree with your assessment, Sam and I recommend Sarah Pope. I've completed a thorough investigation of Ms. Pope's background. We need a very intelligent member of the NSA with expertise in AI technology and software development such that others will believe this individual had the skills, training and intellect to develop the malware that I created. Also, a person of senior rank and status. Ms. Pope has these credentials and exhibits the moral integrity for consideration to our expanded group that Tom has suggested. I've sent out a file on Ms. Pope for team's review. Assuming the team agrees to move forward with her as a new member of the team, I will begin working with her to create a scenario that will satisfy any questions anyone has regarding how this information was obtained."

"Okay, John. Except for Father Dan, everyone is in Washington the next couple of days. I think Diana should be the first person to test the water with Ms. Pope."

"Good thinking, Tom," Sam said. "Let our secret society resident shrink conduct a first general assessment of Pope. If Diana nixes it, we move on to someone else. I like that, and with that problem solved for now, we carbon-based humans can go to bed. I have a very early morning meeting and a busy day tomorrow. Goodnight, Tom, John."

"Thanks again, John. If anything new comes up that you believe is critical, call us any time. We will review your assessment of Ms. Pope and Diana will initiate the interview process. Oh, and be sure to let Peggy and William know that we are thinking about them, and hope all goes well with Cody Walker's surgery tomorrow. Another miracle, I'm sure."

"Science and expert surgical skills, Tom. William and Peggy, with my assistance, have it covered. Young Cody will walk again."

"I'm sure he will. Have Peggy or William call me after the surgery."

"Will do. Goodnight, Tom."

World Peace: Tom Lawson Novel #4
By James Brown

* * * *

"I'm awake," Diana said as Tom settled back into bed. "What water does the *shrink* need to test?"

"I'm sorry. A call from John. Sorry I woke you."

"Test what water?"

"Oh . . . just more critical information that the NSA failed to obtain that John uncovered. This time, however, Sam isn't going to be able to bullshit his way telling the NSA he was able to stumble across a very clandestine phone call. The three of us agreed that we needed to initiate the secret society expansion process. I suggested that you be the first person to check out the candidate John believes will make a perfect addition to our secret team."

Diana yawned. "Who would that perfect person be?"

"Sarah Pope, NSA Executive Director. She reports up through Ron Wainscott who reports to NSA Director General Bradley Goldman. John has sent his report and recommendations to the team. You're first up to bat. Do your shrink assessment. Sam's words, by the way, not mine darling."

"When and how do you propose that I conduct this assessment? A phone interview? Our flight from Washington back to Connecticut is on Saturday."

"Hmm. About that. It was late when I got back to the hotel and I didn't want to wake you, but we need to push our departure to Monday. Even Tuesday or Wednesday would be better now that we both have work to do."

"Tom, I have clients scheduled!" Diana said. "You can stay an extra couple of days, but I must get back to Connecticut. Our flight is scheduled for Saturday afternoon."

"Well . . . I guess I can drop you off at the airport Saturday morning and then go and look for a new suit or a tux by myself."

"A tux. Why would you need a tux?"

"For the dinner party Saturday evening."

"Dinner party? Okay, Tom, you're not telling me everything. Enough of the suspense," she said.

"Okay, we've been invited to a small dinner party Saturday evening."

"A dinner party?"

"A small party," I answered.

"Where is this party and who invited us?"

"The dinner party is at the White House and the invitation was from President Stephen personally."

"Really!" Diana said, her blue eyes sparkling as she smiled. "I think in that case I can have Margie reschedule my clients."

Chapter 10

"Wow! If you ever want to dump the guy you've been living with the last fifteen years or so, let me know. You look great," Sam said as he held open the car door for Diana.

She smiled. The black dress she wore was more than business casual, the attire that Andrew Kennedy, President Stephen's Chief of Staff, recommended for this evening's dinner party. Though not a state dinner, how could they not look their best. Diana wore a sleeveless black dress with a high neckline made of lace, beads and mesh giving it an airy elegance with a bit of sparkle. A curvy, shaped hemline just above her knees and a keyhole back with a button closure gave the dress a dramatic finish.

"Thanks for picking us up, Sam," I said. "It's much faster getting through security when being driven by an FBI agent and accompanied by the FBI Director."

"I prefer driving myself, but I keep getting yelled at when I sneak out on my own, Sam said."

"Well, we can't let anything happen to our chief," FBI agent Wayne Dexter said as he pulled away from the hotel. "The new agents rotate every six months with chauffeur duties."

"Having an agent chauffeur me around is a perk, I guess. But the notoriety can be a pain in the ass. Like the song from the old Cheers sitcom, "Where Everybody Knows Your Name." Why would anyone ever want to be so well known that everyone knows their name."

"There are those people who desperately want that notoriety, Sam," Diana said.

"Yeah. Probably politicians and patients of yours, Diana. Family, work associates, and a few good friends are more than enough recognition and notoriety for me and for most normal folks."

"So that means you are no longer one of the *normal folks*, Sam. You've crossed over to the abnormal side. I was afraid that would happen someday."

"It's your fault, Tom. You and Chang come barging into the FBI building with that gun in your belt and my life changed forever."

"A diamond in the rough, Sam. I'm glad I was able to be the catalyst that catapulted you to greatness . . . and notoriety."

"Funny, Tom, very funny," Sam said.

A short drive from the Washington Waldorf Astoria, Wayne pulled up to the security screening area near the East Wing of the White House. After exiting the car, Sam told Wayne he would text him when they were ready to leave. Sam, ever the gentleman, opened the door for Diana and held his arm out for her as she stepped from the SUV.

"Be careful, big guy," Tom said as he followed Sam and Diana to the East Wing entrance. "She will soon have you revealing your deepest dark secrets."

Sam shrugged and gave a sheepish grin as he turned and allowed Diana to enter the East Wing entrance ahead of him. After passing through the security screening area, they proceeded down the east colonnade toward the residence.

"Sam, Tom," Chief of Staff Andrew Kennedy said as he came out of the residence living room into the central hallway. "We will be holding a casual reception in the parlor, or the Yellow Oval Room as it's formally known. The president will join us shortly." He shook hands with Sam and Tom and turned toward Diana. "I'm very glad to finally have the opportunity to meet you, Diana. From what I hear you've been the real inspiration for these two guys."

"Women do seem to perform that function at times," Diana said.

"Indeed they do. As well as demonstrate their brilliance in many other ways. Let me introduce you to my wife, Laura," Kennedy said, seeing his wife approaching them. "Laura, this is Diana Lawson, a well-known therapist and her husband Tom."

"Pleased to meet you, Diana, Tom," she said, reaching out and shaking their hands. "And, of course, always a pleasure to see you, Sam. I assume Diana has provided you with considerable assistance."

Tom grinned. "An interesting assumption, Laura. Not ten minutes ago I told Sam that Diana would soon have him revealing his inner most thoughts and deep dark secrets."

"All right, everyone," Sam said, as the group laughed. "There will be no revelations today as I am an open book. If my ex were here, she would definitely confirm that." They laughed again as they proceeded into the parlor.

Known historically as the Yellow Oval Room, the oval room housed both a parlor and a library. It was often used for informal private receptions. Jackie Kennedy redecorated the room in yellow and furnished it in Louis XVI style. Sofas and chairs were positioned around a light green, patterned Asian rug to accommodate a dozen people.

Upon entering the Yellow Oval Room, we noticed guests standing in small groups or seated around a central coffee table. Conversation was lively as guests enjoyed cocktails. Katie Stephen stood to greet the new arrivals. "Hello Andrew, Laura," the First Lady said.

"Diana, Tom, the First Lady, Katie Stephen."

"So very glad to meet you," Diana said.

"An honor," Tom said.

At sixty-five years old, the First Lady was still a stunning looking woman. She was statuesque with short blond hair that was similar in style to that of Mika Brzezinski on MSNBC's Morning Joe program. She was the force behind her husband. She was his staunchest supporter and advisor as he worked his way up the Massachusetts political hierarchy, from state legislator to Boston mayor, to Senator and, finally, to President of the United States.

Katie Stephen smiled and shook hands with Diana and Tom. "The honor is mine. Thank you both for all you did to help prevent a terrible disaster." She turned to Sam, and gave him a hug and said, "You, too, Sam. I'm so grateful you took the initiative to address this horrific affair which many others might have ignored for their personal and political reasons."

"Ah, thank you, Katie, you are quite generous with your compliments, but don't forget . . . I had no choice. When I first met Tom, he had a gun strapped to him," Sam said.

Laughing they walked toward the attendant in charge of libations. Would anyone care for a beverage, a mixed drink, or a beer perhaps?"

After their drinks arrived, the First Lady said, "Excuse me, I see that Sarah Pope has arrived and she moved to greet her.

"My date," Sam said. "The only other single person invited as I recall."

"Introduce me to Ms. Pope, Sam. I haven't met her," Diana said.

As Sam and Diana followed the First Lady to meet with Sarah Pope, Laura Kennedy turned to hold a conversation with Janice Bentley, wife of the Secretary of State Peter Bentley. Andrew Kennedy stepped closer to Tom and said softly, "President Stephen would like to have a private conversation with you this evening. He should be available now. This would be a good time to take leave before the other guests arrive." Sure, Andrew," I said hesitantly, wondering why the president wanted this private meeting. I followed Kennedy from the Yellow Room to the first family's living room.

We entered the living room and Kennedy said, "President Stephen will be here shortly. After the meeting, he will walk with you to the Yellow Room, and we will then proceed to dinner." A private meeting with the president. Why, I thought . . . why now? I walked over to the large lunette window overlooking the west colonnade and west wing of the White House. I initially met the president when he was the senior senator from Massachusetts. We were at a gathering, one of many, celebrating the fact that World War III was averted. President Stephen was in his mid-sixties, of average height and built with graying hair. What I noticed most about the then senator was his affable smile and the genuine feeling that he really cared about people. As I wondered about the reason for this private meeting, President Stephen walked into the room.

"Tom, thank you and please thank Diana for extending your stay in Washington. I apologize for any inconvenience this has caused you both. With our CIPC program starting to show promise, I wanted to meet with you before I head to Japan. Come, let's get comfortable, he said, as he put his hand on my shoulder and gestured toward a sofa and chair nearby. I took a seat on the sofa and the president sat in the chair to my left.

"Do you trust me, Tom?"

This was certainly a question I never expected. "Trust you? I voted for you, Mr. President."

"I assumed you voted for me, Tom, but do you trust me?" he repeated.

I sighed and leaned back into the sofa. "Well . . . I could say, sure, I trust you. Why wouldn't I trust the President of the United States? I did vote for you after all. Now, maybe most people if asked this question by the president would answer quickly yes, I trust you. But by doing so, Mr. President, I would not be truthful. Honestly, I don't know you well enough. I respect you and the office you hold and with time I would expect that I could answer affirmatively that I trust you."

The president slowly nodded. "I expected that answer, Tom, and I would have been very surprised had you said differently given your actions these past several years."

"Then why the subterfuge, Mr. President if I may ask?"

"John Gordon."

"John Gordon? I don't understand, sir."

"It was the takeover of our subs, Tom, and the launch of those cruise missiles that all our country's top people and defense organizations were unable to stop. I've just read the final top secret report of the incident. There is no explanation of how John Gordon alone could have accomplished what our government has reported . . . that Gordon alone outmaneuvered his Russian handlers and singlehandedly prevented the retaking of those subs and missiles."

"Really?" I said with a deadpanned expression, hoping no further discussion would follow but expecting that would not be the case.

"Yes, really. I expected the reason for your response was a lack of trust in me, in the government as a whole, that made you reluctant to divulge everything you knew."

I remained silent. What could I say? You're right, I should trust the president of the United States and the U.S. government with technology that could be used for nefarious purposes. One of our last presidents would not have hesitated in using that technology for his own personal gain.

The president settled back into his chair. "I understand, Tom, why you or others might find it challenging to have complete trust in their president. Our country has certainly had a few untrustworthy presidents throughout history. Perhaps in time you will come to trust me. I believe you already know the answer as to why our military and Electric Boat were unable to retake control of the nuclear subs or the cruise missiles. You are correct to have concerns about trusting our military and intelligence. Some people, unfortunately, are not trustworthy."

I slowly nod. "Okay . . . I guess. I agree that humans may at times put their own self-interest ahead of the best interest of others. Also that trust should be earned and not assumed."

"Especially politicians," the president said and smiled. He stood. "Let's head back to the party and get everyone to the dining room for dinner . . . I'm hungry."

What just happened here . . . I wondered as I followed the president as directed.

Before exiting the room, the president said, "Tom, the CIPC Program is very important, not only for me and our country but also for the world. One day, I hope to earn your trust. In the meantime, you must do what you believe is necessary in your work with those you do trust to ensure this program is successful."

He patted my shoulder and smiled. His expression implied to me that I knew why the cruise missiles couldn't be stopped and that I would use that knowledge to help ensure the CIPC program was successful.

"Now let's go and enjoy the party," the president said.

* * * *

"Sarah, I don't believe you've had a chance to meet Diana Lawson, Tom's wife. Tom seems to have stepped out for a moment so I thought I would make introductions for him. Diana, Sarah Pope is the Executive Director of the NSA," Sam said.

"Pleased to meet you, Sarah."

A tall woman in her mid-forties with high cheekbones she could easily have been a model. Warm beige skin, brown honey-colored eyes and thick dark hair that flowed past her shoulders with just a hint of a curl, Sarah was a stunning looking woman. With perfect skin tone she wore little makeup, and her sleeveless ruffle-trim crepe green dress highlighted her toned arms.

"Very glad to meet you too, Diana. You're a licensed therapist, correct?"

"Yes, Diana's a shrink. She's been treating Tom for years," Sam joked."

Don't mind him, Sarah. Tom and Andrew Kennedy were teasing him about needing my help earlier this evening. But he's right, they are both in need of intensive therapy," Diana said, laughing. "Now, if you haven't met Charles yet, the aide with the libations, let me introduce you."

Sam excused himself after his cell phone rang. Diana and Sarah crossed the room and gave their drink orders to Charles. They found two comfortable chairs in a far corner of the room. Within a couple of minutes, Charles brought their drinks and placed them on coasters on the side table.

"I often come with Sam to work related gatherings such as this," Sara said.

"As did Tom and I this evening. Convenient being chauffeured by the FBI director and his driver. I could certainly get used to that."

Sarah laughed. "Very true. But since Sam and I are both unattached it's also convenient for those occasions when spouses are part of the mix."

"How long have you worked in government and the NSA if you don't mind me asking?"

"How long? Since I was born, I guess would be the most accurate answer. I was a military brat. I lived on so many army bases around the world that it would take me awhile to list them all. My father was a full colonel in the army. He had the typical challenges as an African American, but it was far easier to be recognized in the military than civilian life. He rose to the rank of Colonel before he died several years ago. Natural causes. He made it safely through a few wars, but cancer took him at the young age of sixty."

"That is young. It must have been very difficult for you."

"It was. He was a very good man as well as a good soldier and father. God, country, family, and the constitution. He must have told me that a million times growing up. I was an only child, so he probably thought he had to make sure his only legacy got the message. I did."

After a few moments Sarah said, "I see a little of my father in your husband."

"God, country, and the constitution you mean?"

"Yes, but it is his integrity that resonates with me the most. You, Tom, as well as Sam and Savannah Lee. Without your diligence and concern, who knows where we all would be today."

Diana grimaced. "Certainly, we would not be here now in the White House. Of that, I'm sure. How did your career in intelligence work come about?"

"Followed in the footsteps of my father, of course. My mother died when I was very young, so it was just dad and me. After college the army, naturally, was where I started my career. I spent ten years with the Military Intelligence Corps before leaving the army for a position with the NSA and that is where I've been these past ten years."

"Intelligence, the kind of work you do, the information you come across must be pretty scary at times I would think." Diana said.

Sarah took a sip of her cosmopolitan. "To say the least, Diana. The world can be a very scary place as can living in the U.S. these days. Look at what you and your husband stumbled onto while we in the NSA and the CIA had no idea what was unfolding. For every threat we do uncover there is probably an equal number of threats that are brewing that we don't know about."

"A lot of long hours and sleepless nights, I imagine."

"Yes, sleep deprivation and long hours come with the territory, Sarah acknowledged. "My job, no doubt, is one of the reasons I am still single . . . working too many hours and canceling too many dates certainly does not help make for lasting relationships."

"Maybe meeting someone in a high demanding profession similar to yours would help," Diana offered.

Sarah leaned in toward Diana. "Interesting you mention that. I did recently meet a woman who may show promise. She's an emergency care physician at the George Washington University Hospital. During Covid she probably cancelled more dates than I ever did. Anyway, I think you're right. My previous relationships were never with someone who was compatible with my life's work choices. The same reason that Sam and so many other cops and high stress workers don't always have a chance to maintain lasting relationships."

"So true, Sarah. Love, marriage, family, it's hard enough on husbands and wives when they do have similar interests and work schedules."

"How long will you be staying in Washington?" Sarah asked.

"Another week, then I need to get back to Connecticut."

"Clients?"

"Yes. Not quite as bad as an emergency room physician but I do have long evenings and emergency calls on occasion. By the way, I am planning to have dinner with Savannah Lee on Tuesday. Would you and your friend like to join us for dinner? Girls' night out maybe?"

"Hmm, Tuesday. I would love to meet Ms. Lee. Isn't she getting married soon?"

"All the more reason for girls' night out," Diana said, causing them to laugh.

"Okay. I'll call Joanna. Would eight p.m. be too late? It's difficult for me to get out of the office before seven or so."

"Savannah too, so eight is a perfect time. We typically go to the Old Ebbitt Grill, across the street from the US Treasury building. It's very convenient for Savannah and Sam since they are typically running late."

"Perfect," Sarah said then turned toward the room's entrance. President Justin Stephen entered the room.

World Peace: Tom Lawson Novel #4
By James Brown

Chapter 11

On the drive back to the Waldorf, Tom invited Sam to join them for Sunday brunch at the hotel, which he accepted. Diana said Savannah Lee would also be able to join them. Arriving at the Waldorf, Diana hugged Sam, and Tom thanked Wayne for chauffeuring them and bid them a goodnight. The evening with the president and first lady was a success . . . a productive plus enjoyable evening. They were next meeting on Sunday for a debriefing session.

"How did your conversation with Sarah go," I asked, as we walked through the Waldorf lobby."

"It went quite well for a first session. Hmm, a session. That sounds clinical."

"I'm sorry if these dinner parties seem like therapy sessions for you. Sam does refer to you as our secret society resident shrink. Does that bother you?"

"No, not really. Of course, he is right. It was not something I could foresee and is outside of my normal scope of practice."

I gave Diana my most sympathetic look. "Our lives unfortunately have become complicated."

Diana pressed the elevator button for the third floor. "An interesting assessment. Sarah Pope mentioned that her life was much the same. She was a military brat and lived all over the world with her father, a full colonel. He died a few years ago."

"Mother?"

"She died when Sarah was very young," Diana said, as they exited the elevator and walked to their room in silence. The silence was necessary as other guests were also returning to their rooms after their evening events.

Once they were alone in their room behind closed doors Diana immediately said, "did you know you were going to have a private meeting with the president?"

"Not a clue."

"Why did he want to meet with you?"

"He wanted to know if I trusted him?"

"Trusted him?" Diana said, with a look of confusion. "In what way? Trust him since he is the president?"

"My thoughts exactly," I said, as I removed my suit jacket and pants and hung them in the closet. "The meeting was not expected. I was having a casual conversation with Andrew Kennedy, and he said the president wanted to have a private conversation. He didn't give me a reason and escorted me to the first family's living room. Andrew left the room and a few minutes later in walks the president."

"That's interesting," Diana said, turning around and pointing for assistance in unbuttoning the back of her dress. After Diana slipped off her dress and hung it up, she joined him on the bed. "So, how exactly did the subject of trust come up?" Diana asked.

"Basically, it was right out of left field. He started off thanking me and you for extending our stay in Washington and commented on the inconvenience the extended stay was for you and your patients."

"He said that? Mentioned me and my clients and having to cancel appointments?"

"He did."

"Then what did he say?"

"Out of the blue, his very next words were, do you trust me."

"Really? How did you answer?"

"Well, I stammered a little since I was caught completely off guard, then I told him I voted for him."

"Did that suffice?"

"No. He pressed and said, 'but do you trust me.' I wasn't going to lie and say that I did, so I told him I didn't know him well enough yet, but that I respected him and the office he holds and expect over time, my respect would likely evolve into trust."

"But why the question of trust?"

"My question also, so I asked him. He said John Gordon. Apparently, he recently received the final incident report. A top-secret report that concluded there was no explanation of how John Gordon alone could have outmaneuvered his Russian handlers and singlehandedly prevented the Navy and Electric Boat from taking control of those subs and missiles. He then said he believed I knew the answer, why the military and Electric Boat were unable to retake control of those nuclear subs or their cruise missiles."

"Oh, no!" Diana said, putting her hand to her face. "You probably thought the FBI was outside the door ready to escort you to one of those places where nobody knows where they are."

"That did cross my mind. I was speechless initially, but then the president said I was correct to have concerns and a lack of trust, that trust *should* be earned. He said some people in the government, including a few former presidents proved themselves to be untrustworthy."

"I'm so glad you weren't whisked off to one of those dark dungeons somewhere," Diana said, as she gave him a big hug.

"Me, too. Perhaps in time I will come to trust him."

"That's encouraging. Anything else?"

I nodded and winked. "Oh, yes, he told me his CIPC Program was very important, not only for him and the country but also for the world. He said he hoped one day to have earned my trust. Until that happened, however, he asked that I do whatever was needed and work with those whom I do trust to ensure this program is successful."

"Oh my God!" Diana exclaimed. "The President of the United States thinks you, me, Sam and Savannah know why the military and Electric Boat were not able to retake control of those subs and the cruise missiles."

With raised eyebrows and a nod, I confirmed her assessment. Diana fell back on the bed.

Her slip riding high on her legs as she laid across the bed, I leaned over and said, "maybe we should take advantage of the time we have left before we're sent off to that dark cell never to be heard from again."

"Hmm," she purred, while her hands removed my t-shirt. "Always thinking aren't you, contingency planning is just one of your many strengths."

World Peace: Tom Lawson Novel #4
By James Brown

* * * *

Awaking Sunday morning, Diana said, "that was a very productive session you and the president had yesterday. I really enjoyed the evening's consequences."

"Yes, I did, too, Tom said giving Diana a good morning kiss. "Do you want to shower first? Sam and Savannah will arrive in an hour or so."

Diana ran her fingers through her hair, looked at the clock on the nightstand and yawned. Why don't you take your shower first? You're much faster than I am."

"Okay, will do," I said, and rolled out of the bed.

With the pillows fluffed, Diana nestled back under the sheets and contemplated the meaning of the president's words, 'do what you believe is necessary working with those individuals whom you do trust to ensure the CIPC program is successful.' Was it possible that the government's team that conducted the investigation into John Gordon's actions concluded that Gordon's code was so advanced that it continued to exist somewhere? Is that what the president was implying to Tom? She made a mental note to discuss with Tom and Sam at their brunch.

"Hon, I'm out," Tom yelled. "Do you want me to run your bathwater?"

"Yes, thank you!"

Tom and Diana left their room for the Waldorf dining room. It was a bright, sunny spring morning. Sunlight cascaded through the arching canopy of glass that overlooked the massive lobby. They quickly exited the elevator for the dining area for Sunday brunch being served. They spotted Sam and Savannah tucked away in a secluded area of the room.

"Good morning," Sam said, standing and giving Diana a hug while Tom walked over and kissed Savannah on her cheek.

"Sleep well after your long evening hobnobbing with the president and the elite of Washington?" Savannah asked.

"She's still not happy she wasn't invited," Sam said.

"Well . . . an interesting place to start a conversation, Savannah. Surprisingly, we did not," Diana said, holding off further explanation as a server approached the table.

"Hello, my name is Connie. I'll be your server this morning. May I start you off with drinks, coffee, tea, a mimosa perhaps?"

"That would be great," Savannah said. "I'll have coffee with cream and the mimosa."

"Same for me," Diana said.

"I'll have the same," I said, and Sam ordered black coffee along with a mimosa.

After Connie left to retrieve the beverages, Savannah said, "explain your sleepless night comment. Too much extracurricular activity, perhaps?"

"Diana grinned. "I take the fifth."

Savannah elbowed Sam. "See. I told you that would happen after their dinner with the president."

"Ow!" You need to stop that elbowing habit of yours or at least don't sit next to me."

Savannah leaned over and rubbed Sam's arm. "You have too many muscles in your arm for my little elbow to hurt you. But I'll try and be better, she said, patting his arm. But back to your answer, Diana. The dinner with the president left you and Tom with a restless sleep."

"Diana avoided answering Savannah as their waitress returned to the table with their drink orders. "Would you care to order? She asked. We have the buffet breakfast, or you may order off the menu."

Savannah said, "menu for me, but could we have a few minutes, please." Everyone else agreed, preferring to be served rather than jostling with others around a buffet bar.

Diana turned to Savannah and said that it was probably best for Tom to discuss the pertinent events of last night.

"Suspense," Savannah said giddily. "Now I really wish I had been invited. So what happened?"

"Well, it started off as you might expect any small employee gathering might begin."

"Right, Tom," Savannah complained. "A small group of employees who just happen to be some of the most powerful people in the world."

I shrugged. "No argument there. Anyway, Sam was kind enough to chauffeur Diana and me to this small gathering of very powerful people."

World Peace: Tom Lawson Novel #4
By James Brown

"Sam, maybe you and I should change seats," Diana said.

Savannah held up her hands. "I promise to keep my elbows to myself, Sam."

"Good, Savannah. The story gets more interesting from here," I said.

"Okay. What happened?"

"After going through the security check Sam, Diana and I were met near the Yellow Room in the White House residence . . ."

"I've never been to the White House residence," Savannah interrupted.

"I'm sure one day you will be invited," Diana offered.

"She's still upset," Sam said, downing the rest of his mimosa and catching Connie's attention to request a refill. She had anticipated her guests' needs and was already approaching their table with a second round of mimosas. After their waitress left, Tom continued.

"So, moving on, we were met just outside the Yellow Room. . ."

Savannah held up her hand. "Sorry to interrupt again. What did you wear to this soiree, Diana?"

"A simple black dress," Diana answered nonchalantly.

"Yeah, right!" Sam said. "Best looking woman there. Simple black dress my ass."

Diana and Savannah looked at Sam.

"What? You looked great, Diana . . . just saying!"

"Okay, I wore a sleeveless black dress with a high neckline made of lace, beads and mesh, a bit of sparkle with a hemline just above my knees and a keyhole back with button closure."

"Thank you," Savannah said. "That dress sounds lovely and I'm sure you were gorgeous in it. Okay, Tom, you may proceed."

"As I was saying, Andrew Kennedy was leaving the first family's residence living room just as his wife was coming out of the Yellow Room. Andrew introduced Laura to us, and we all joined the gathering in the Yellow Room and met the First Lady. We were then introduced to Charles."

"The most important person in the room," Sam interrupted. "The Yellow Room's resident waiter."

"Got it, Sam. Charles supplied you with drinks. Move along now, Tom," Savannah said impatiently.

"Okay, moving on. It started out like your typical meet-and-great gathering with the First Lady acting as hostess while the president was not yet in attendance. Sam introduced Diana to Sara Pope and then he wandered off to answer a call. I was left alone for a moment with Andrew Kennedy. Once lone with him, he quietly said it was a good time to slip out before all the guests arrived. He said the president wanted a private meeting with me."

"Did you know he wanted to meet you?" Savannah said.

"No. I didn't have a clue."

"What did he want?" Savannah asked.

"After thanking me and Diana for extending our stay in Washington he immediately said, 'do you trust me.'"

Savannah gave a questioned stare. "Out of the blue he asked you that?"

I nodded. "Out of the blue, do you trust me."

"You responded that you respected him and his office, didn't you?"

"You've gotten to know me well, Savannah. I said that and his response was that he respected my answer and said that trust should be earned. He then said there were people in the government, as well as former presidents, who could not always be trusted but hoped in time he would be able to earn my trust."

"But that wasn't the only reason why he wanted to meet with you was it, only to let you know he wanted to earn your trust."

"No it was not the only reason, and it certainly was not the reason that Diana and I had a restless night. I asked the president why he wanted to know if I trusted him. He said John Gordon."

"What!" Savannah blurted.

"The reason for the question was that the top secret report investigating the takeover of the nuclear subs and cruise missile launches had just been issued. The president read it prior to the party. The report concluded there was no explanation of how John Gordon alone outmaneuvered his Russian handlers and singlehandedly prevented the Navy and Electric Boat from retaking control of those subs and missiles."

"Did you know that, Sam? Did you get a copy of that secret report?" Savannah asked.

"That's why my cell phone rang while at the party. I was notified that it was released, and I read it late last night."

"Wow. I've been left out of everything," Savannah said in a dejected tone.

"Well, Savannah. That is going to change quickly."

Before I was able to reveal why Savannah and the rest of us would not be left out, our waitress, Connie, appeared at the table with menus. Savannah quickly ordered. The rest of us followed Savannah's lead and ordered the same meal, scrambled eggs with diced cheese, red pepper, and onion, bacon and sausage links, wheat toast, and more coffee.

"I'll take over now and finish what I started to explain, why Tom and I had a restless sleep after hobnobbing with the president," Diana said. "The reason for the restless night was because the president said he believed Tom knew the answer why the military and Electric Boat were unable to retake control of those nuclear subs or their cruise missiles."

"My God! You're kidding. Tom, the president said that?" Savannah asked quickly.

"Those exact words."

"When Tom told me that last night," Diana continued. "I thought he was going to be whisked off to a secret holding cell somewhere. Then it got even more stressful. The president told Tom his CIPC Program was very important, not only to him and the country but also for the world. He then said he hoped one day he would have earned Tom's trust, but until that happened, he asked him to do whatever necessary working with those individuals who he trusted, to ensure the CIPC program was a success. That's the reason for our stressful sleep last evening. The president believes the four of us knows why those subs and missiles could not be stopped."

"Oh, wow! No wonder you and Tom were so stressed," Savannah said.

"Equally stressing, I'm wondering if the president and the team who conducted the investigation into John Gordon's actions believe Gordon's AI program was so advanced that it continues to exist somewhere. Sam, Is that what the president was implying to Tom? Does that top secret report say that?" Diana asked.

World Peace: Tom Lawson Novel #4
By James Brown

Sam hesitated. The report was top secret. He wasn't sure yet if Tom was on the list of need-to-know even though he had top secret clearance from his work with Electric Boat. Finally he said, "Tom, did you get any notification other than from the president that the report was issued?"

"Only from the president," I said.

"I thought that was the case since the distribution of the report has been limited so far."

"So you can't legally tell us anything, can you, Sam?" Savannah asked.

"Theoretically, no. But as a general assessment of the report's findings, no one knows how Gordon pulled it off or why they could not regain control of the subs or cruise missiles."

"But do they think the AI system Gordon developed still exists somewhere? Diana asked.

"Ah . . . that seems to be implied, Diana."

"So they are looking for John, our John?"

Sam slowly nodded. "That would be my expectation. Not my organization but some group of AI geniuses within one of our many government agencies has received that assignment, I'm sure."

"John needs to know people are looking for him," Diana said.

"He doesn't need to be informed," Tom said. "He knows anytime his presence is being sought. John will take whatever action necessary to ensure his presence is not discovered. As for the president, I believe he is convinced advanced artificial intelligence was deployed to prevent the Navy from retaking control of the subs and cruise missiles. He likewise thinks, with no other answers offered to him, that I and a tight group of trusted associates know what happened. That would be all of you. And the president believes that a very advanced AI solution was developed and deployed to prevent the military from retaking control of the subs."

After Tom summarized his thoughts, the implication began setting in. The four of them sat in silence exchanging glances.

Tom finally broke the silence. "With what we know from mentoring John, who now exists as William, our friend, the president is asking us, a group he believes is trustworthy, to do what is necessary to help make his CIPC program a success."

"That's a lot of pressure," Savannah said.

"No more than you've had the last couple of years that led you to winning two Pulitzers, Savannah. We just need to add a few more good people to our group."

"Related to that subject. From a first impression, I think John is correct in his assessment of Sarah Pope," Diana said and proceeded to summarize the conversation she had with Sarah.

"I agree with your assessment, Diana. I've gotten to know Sarah the last few years. She's a very bright and dedicated person. I had an opportunity to meet her father before he died. He was a real patriot and an honorable man. Sarah has those same traits," Sam said.

"God, country, and the constitution," Diana said. "She told me her dad must have reiterated that phrase to her a million times growing up. As an only child she thought he wanted to make sure his only legacy got the message."

"She's also a brilliant software engineer and has an advanced degree in AI technology and that is one of the reasons she ended up in Army Intelligence after graduation," Sam added.

"As for the next steps," Diana continued, "Sarah will be joining Savannah and me for dinner on Tuesday. A girl's night out. She will be bringing a date, Joanna Strong, an emergency room physician."

As everyone absorbed Diana and Sam's description of Sarah's character, and the plan to meet with her, Connie appeared at the table with their brunch orders. For the next several minutes they ate in silence. Each of them contemplated the president's statement and how they might be affected, and wondered whether or not the addition of Sarah, or anyone else who might join their secret group, would really ease the stress they all were feeling.

World Peace: Tom Lawson Novel #4
By James Brown

Chapter 12

Ah Lam entered the university library and walked toward a two-person study table just off the main lobby. She took a seat and pulled out her laptop and notebook from her satchel. Li Huang was sitting three tables away. She called him on her cell.

"I'm here," Ah Lam said after Huang answered.

"Did you get the talking paper?"

"I did."

"And you are ready for your session?" Huang asked.

"I'll let you know in about an hour."

"Good luck." Huang said and disconnected the call.

Am I ready? Ah Lam thought as she once again scanned the document CIA Operations Director Maddi Pool sent her. She spent the weekend reading and rereading the talking points prepared by Director Pool and CIA analysts. All had years of experience in Chinese history, culture, and government institutions and practices. She, on the other hand, was a Chinese Uyghur who was whisked away at age thirteen by her parent's attempt to save her from China's purge of Uyghur's rights to conceive a child. She wondered who really had the better understanding of China's government or its history.

At age thirty-three and working as an undercover CIA operative, the likelihood she would ever conceive a child was becoming a fleeting thought. Instead, her focus was on a larger and more important objective, improving the lives of all the people in China. To accomplish this, she must convince Huan Cheng, the newest member of China's powerful Politburo Standing Committee, to once again be a champion for change that he once was. She read the CIA talking paper and her notes again.

World Peace: Tom Lawson Novel #4
By James Brown

Huan Cheng approached her, and she stood and bowed slightly.

"Mr. Cheng. Thank you for stopping by to assist me with my project."

"My pleasure, Ms. Zing. Hopefully, I may be of assistance with your course assignment. Please, have a seat and tell me your thoughts on how you plan to approach this assignment."

"Yes, of course," Ah Lam said, taking a seat. "As I mentioned earlier, my professors are not interested in a paper about organization structure. The form and organizational processes are not their focus. Rather, they believe the paper should address cooperation, inclusion, and peaceful coexistence across all the major universities affected by the recent cyberattack. The short title for the paper is CIPC. My professors are big on acronyms," Ah Lam said, smiling.

Huan Cheng made a discrete nod. He understood. "Can you provide a few examples?"

"Of course. If I may use an analogy to explain?"

"Yes, please continue."

I'll start with world events. A worldwide tragedy was barely prevented after several prominent world leaders were killed following the takeover of U.S. submarines and the launching of their cruise missiles. Fortunately, Newton's third law was averted, and every action did not result in an equal and opposite reaction. World War III was averted. Though the deaths of these world leaders were tragic, the world saw new leaders step forward and analyze the situation and prevent world obliteration. These new leaders accomplished the first C in the CIPC acronym."

"Cooperation. I see," Cheng said. "Do you have examples for the letters I, P, and C in the acronym?"

"I do. This analogy is the exact opposite perspective had the new leaders not strongly advocated for cooperation and inclusion. Moscow, for example, was always critical of Washington's military presence in Afghanistan even though their presence significantly reduced radical religious factions from securing a larger foothold in the country. After the U.S. removed their troops, radicalized groups once again gained a foothold. Although Russia previously fought a long-protracted war in Afghanistan, their efforts to quell the growth of terrorism in the region after the American's withdrew their forces, has been far less effective than had the U.S. maintained limited forces in the region. As a result, the spread of religious extremism is being metastasized in other regions of the Middle East and Central Asia."

After pausing a moment, Ah Lam continued. "The U.S. and their allies were pulled into the fight against radicalized religious terrorism after the New York World Trade Centers were destroyed. Had all the major powers of the world fostered cooperation and inclusion before this occurred, the cancer that began growing in Afghanistan would never have taken hold.

In summary, Director Cheng, the world has become more and more intertwined than it has ever been. And as chaos theory predicts, the flutter of a butterfly's wings can change everything. The butterfly in my analogy is religious Islamic terrorism that was allowed to grow unchecked in Afghanistan until the U.S. was attacked and the World Trade center fell. The cancer in Afghanistan was known to exist, yet it was allowed to fester and grow. At the time, the consensus of the United States, Russia, and China was that it was not their problem, and they did nothing. Specifically, Beijing believed that it should avoid serious entanglement in Afghan affairs at all costs."

Cheng contemplated Ah Lam's chaos theory assessment, then said, "and now we are increasing our alliances in the region to mitigate the chaos that has strengthened since the American's withdrawal from Afghanistan."

"The irony of China's action," Ah Lam responded quickly, "is that while China vehemently opposed the U.S. invasion in 2001 for destabilizing the region and deploying U.S. forces closer to China's borders, it equally criticized the American withdrawal from Afghanistan in 2021."

"Cooperation and inclusion was not a consideration at the time," Cheng whispered."

"Yes, cooperation and inclusion," Ah Lam repeated. "Had countries utilized this approach initially, as the religious radicalization began to fester in Afghanistan, the chaos theory might have been suppressed. Their inaction allowed for the September 11th attacks on the United States. Had the radicalization been prevented, the lives of thousands along with trillions of dollars, would have been saved. Now, however, we face the continuing metastasizing threats of religious extremism."

World Peace: Tom Lawson Novel #4
By James Brown

Cheng stared at Ah Lam. His thoughts returned to chaos theory and butterfly wings, a theory he studied long ago. It was a time when he tried to flap his own wings only to have them clipped before he took flight. What would the world be like today had he not given up? Would the world be a safer place? Probably not, he thought. The likelihood that he would now be a member of China's Politburo Standing Committee had his original paper been published was quite remote. But now, things might be different given that he was a member of the powerful China Politburo Committee. He now had the power to influence positive change, to make a difference.

Ah Lam politely remained silent while Cheng appeared to be struggling with his thoughts. Finally, he sighed. "P and C, your last acronyms. I imagine you can describe an analogy that will support the advantage of peaceful coexistence."

"I can. And in this instance, rather than an analogy from past historical events, which I could do, I think it best to consider future events where peaceful coexistence can profoundly impact China and the rest of the world."

"I see," Cheng said.

"Consider a future event that *will* definitely occur . . . when the Himalayan glaciers will melt as a result of global warming. This historic and devastating catastrophe will reduce and ultimately stop the glacial flow of water to more than two billion people who live across central South Asia. Unless managed from a global perspective, water scarcity will drive a conflict between those countries affected, including Pakistan, India and China . . . three nuclear-armed countries. Shall I continue with additional examples?"

"That won't be necessary," Cheng said softly. "You've presented a very effective approach for your paper. What is the timeline for the preliminary session with your advisor? As I recall, the schedule you mentioned when we previously met was a meeting between our university vice chandlers, followed by a meeting between our university presidents."

"That is correct. My advisor would like to set up the first session with our university's vice chancellors in three weeks. The last week of May preferably, and assuming favorable progress, three weeks later, with the university presidents."

"Hmm. End of May and mid-June. An aggressive timeline," Cheng said."

"Yes, but critical conditions require decisive and prompt actions. And do not forget, there are three other universities who will be participating. You may recall that my advisor would like your help in arranging the first session with one of these three universities. Once all these preliminary sessions are completed, then a meeting will be scheduled with the presidents of all five universities attending."

Cheng sat back in his chair and pondered the request, a subtle but deliberate obfuscation of the primary request asked by the young woman seated across the table. He doubted Ah Lam Zing was her real name, yet her not so subtle request was intriguing and relevant.

Leaning forward, Cheng said, "Ms. Zing, this backchannel discussion we've had has indeed proved interesting. I certainly was surprised when I received a copy of the document I wrote fifty odd years ago. How that document was uncovered is a discussion for another time. For now, you and your advisor, who I assume is Maddi Pool, have sparked my interest. The world *is* becoming increasingly intertwined and global annihilation a more likely scenario when trust between world leaders and countries is lost. You have effectively conveyed your points, points that I most definitely agree with. Your subtle analogies drove your message home."

"Thank you. I thought the analogies might shield you from a more direct conversation that could jeopardize your new position in the Politburo."

"I appreciate your concern and efforts, Ms. Zing. Many significant accomplishments have been achieved by people who took risks to initiate talks between country leaders in an effort to avert conflicts. Your chaos theory was particularly effective. Something Ms. Pool perhaps suggested?"

Ah Lam smiled.

"She and I had a long discussion on chaos theory a few years ago before her most recent promotion. She was an analyst at the time, and I was a Provincial Committee Secretary." He paused for a moment then continued and said, "this undertaking by your new president is not without merit. Challenging, of course, however the timing does make sense given the recent events. The wildcard, I believe will be Iran. Religious zealots, unfortunately, do not typically respond well to facts and logic. Russia, on the other hand, remains in a state of turmoil since Putin's death but I believe it can be managed. As for North Korea, as you suggest, we will be able to intervene on your behalf to initiate a dialogue if necessary."

"Thank you. America does not have direct diplomatic relations with North Korea. We have, by the way, entered into an initial dialogue with Russia."

"And how has that dialogue progressed, if I may ask?"

Ah Lam hesitated briefly before answering. "The initial discussions went reasonably well, and a second meeting is scheduled. Of course, with each country, and the U.S. is not an exception here, there will be some leaders who will wish this initiative to fail."

"I will do my best to help make it a success, Ms. Zing. Fifty years is a long time to wait to finally be in a position to make a difference. The repercussions of inaction by a broad unified coalition will be far more serious." Cheng bowed slightly and looked toward the clock on the wall. "I will initiate discrete discussions with Politburo members and other influential leaders whom I trust to have similar concerns of a *China first* policy, a policy similar to the *America first* policy that the former U.S. president promoted. Rather than prosperity and security, Isolationism leads to insecurity, division, and conflict. Fair and healthy competition ultimately benefits everyone. Likewise, the world would benefit if we worked together to control radicalization that occurs in all of our countries."

"Cooperation, inclusion, and peaceful coexistence," Ah Lam said.

"CIPC, yes. Let's see what we can do to create a paradigm shift in how world powers perceive each other. A marriage of equals perhaps, with issues and problems discussed openly and resolved."

"Much like a good marriage that adapts and adjusts over a lifetime."

"Yes, Ms. Zing. Another good analogy. Now, I have other issues that I must take care of. How best can I reach you in the future?"

Ah Lam reached into her purse and handed Cheng a business card.

"Zing Consulting, of course. I am sure your business will do very well. I will call you in a few days," Cheng said.

"I look forward to your call."

World Peace: Tom Lawson Novel #4
By James Brown

Chapter 13

Ah Lam stood and made a slight bow toward Huan Cheng who replied in kind and smiled. "Until the next time we meet. Enjoy the rest of your day, Ms. Zing."

She remained standing for a moment, watching Huan Cheng wind his way around the study tables toward the library lobby and building exit. Amazing, she thought, a displaced Chinese Uyghur operating as an undercover CIA agent may have taken the first step to make a meaningful difference for her country and the world. Her broad smile and sparkling eyes caught the attention of Li Huang as he approached her.

"The meeting must have gone well or are you just very happy to see me?

"Oh, Li. Yes. The meeting did go well, very well. Are you hungry? I'm starving." Ah Lam picked up her laptop and notebook and placed them in her backpack and pushed in her chair. "Where would you like to go for a late lunch?" she asked as they exited the library.

"Since it's such a lovely day and privacy is preferred, how about getting takeout and finding an unoccupied bench in the park near campus."

"An excellent idea. Chicken chow main in the park. What time is it by the way?"

"Four thirty. Why," Li asked.

"Perfect. It will be a little after five when we have our dinner in the park. I need to call Director Pool and give her the good news. It's almost five a.m. in Washington so she should be awake by the time we finish eating. Let's hurry," she said, anxious to place her food order and call her boss.

In the park Ah Lam updated Li on the conversation with Huan Cheng in between bites of her chow main dinner.

"I guess you didn't eat much the last few days," Li said, watching as she quickly ate.

"I didn't. My time was focused preparing for my meeting with Director Cheng. The most important thing I've ever done. I was too stressed to eat," she said scooping up a large quantity of chicken and noodles.

"You did very well from what you've told me. Your meeting was very productive."

"It was," Ah Lam said, taking her last bite of chow mein. "It's six-thirty in the morning in Washington. Director Pool is certainly out of bed by now."

"She's probably at her office," Li said."

Ah Lam opened her encryption app, selected Pool's number, and activated it.

"Hello?"

"Opportunity, Iden code Alpha, Yankee, Zulu, Golf, X-ray, Zero."

"Ah Lam. I was hoping to hear from you this morning. How did the session go?"

"Could not have been better," Ah Lam said excitedly. "I followed the script and my client listened intently. He said the analogies I presented were very thought provoking."

"That's excellent, Ah Lam!"

"There's more. At the conclusion of my presentation my client said he was ready to unfurl his wings that were restrained so many years ago. He even mentioned the chaos theory discussion he had with you at a conference you both attended.

"My goodness. You did have a very good meeting. What is the next step?"

"He asked for my contact information, and I gave him my business card. He said he would talk with his key associates. Before he left, we discussed the timeline for the project. He thought it was tight but said he would do what he could to make it happen. He also said, assuming he was successful in getting agreement to schedule the first meeting, that he would help arrange similar session with the party that we do not yet have a relationship."

"Wonderful, Ah Lam! An excellent job. I have a meeting in a couple minutes and will share your information with the rest of the team. Enjoy the rest of your day. Great job," Director Pool said, before ending the call.

The sun was low in the horizon and the sky was unusually clear of smog. Another good omen, thought Ah Lam. She took a moment to breathe in the crisp air with the flowers in full bloom. A wide smile grew on Ah Lam's face as she turned toward Li.

"My apartment is not far from campus. Perhaps you would like to walk me home. I have a bottle of champagne I bought when I first began my assignment. It would have remained in the fridge had I not been successful. But now, it's time to pop the cork. Will you join me?

"I would be honored," Li said, standing and holding out his hand. Ah Lam stood and slid her arm in his and they strolled off to celebrate.

* * * *

"Ladies, Welcome. Out on the town this evening I see without the menfolk."

"Yes, we are, Wilson. I only have thirty days before my world will completely upend and I shall be shackled to the grindstone . . . washing, cleaning, cooking. Hmm, probably a half-a-dozen screaming kids afoot before you know it," Savannah Lee said, half-jokingly.

Wilson's eyes widened while the rest of the women at the table laughed.

"Wilson, it's just a woman pushing forty who is a little afraid of making a commitment that didn't work out so well the first time."

"Diana! I'm not pushing forty!"

"Okay, thirty-seven, but close. See how fast she is able to come out of her funk to defend her honor, Wilson. A true offspring of her late great grandfather," Diana said, leaning away from Savannah, expecting one of Savannah's infamous pokes to the arm.

After a bit of laughter, Wilson said, "Mr. White is a perfect gentlemen Ms. Lee, and I'm sure you both will be very happy. I'm not sure about the half-dozen kids though. That would be difficult to manage for any married couple. Especially with the jobs you both have."

"You are a very good judge of character, Wilson. I agree with you," Savannah said. "This time I've found the perfect man to spend my life with. Now that that is decided, let us order some drinks. A vodka tonic for me, please."

"Same for you, Ms. Lawson?" Wilson asked.

"Thank you, yes," Diana said. "And if you haven't met the two ladies dinning with us, let me introduce Sarah Pope and Joanna Strong."

"I recall seeing Ms. Pope here on occasion, though we have not formally met. I believe Ms. Pope was with the NSA group several times at the Grill."

"Yes, very observant, Wilson."

"Pleased to meet you, Ms. Pope. What may I get you to drink?"

"A cosmopolitan please."

"And Ms. Strong? What would you like?"

"A cosmopolitan sounds good to me. It's my first visit to Old Ebbitt Grill. I'm afraid I haven't been able to get out much since moving here to Washington."

"Joanna is an emergency care physician at George Washington University Hospital. She moved here from New York City a few years ago," Sarah said.

"Oh my. No wonder you were never here, Ms. Strong. It was such a difficult time for the restaurant during the Covid-19 epidemic but so much worse for you I'm sure. I commend you for your service and the lives I'm sure you were able to save."

"Thank you, Wilson. It's very kind of you. It was a very difficult time."

"It certainly was, Doctor Strong. I will be right back with your drinks. Let me know when you might want to see the dinner menus."

"A very interesting place," Joanna said, as Wilson departed for drinks. "It sounds like you are well known here."

"Old Ebbitt Grill is very convenient for government workers, and it is close to my office at the Washington Post," Savannah said. "Not so much for Diana, who lives in Connecticut, but her husband has been doing consulting work here the last several months, so he drags her here on occasion."

"Drags?" Diana said. "We really have become best friends, Joanna. Though Savannah can be difficult at times."

"You're a mental health therapist, aren't you Diana?" Joanna asked.

"Yes. I've been trying without success to help Savannah for a few years now."

With another eruption of laughter, Wilson produced their drinks and Savannah raised her glass and shouted, here's to girls' night out!"

The conversation ebbed and flowed between Savannah's upcoming wedding nuptials, Joanna's move to Washington, and the horrific toil of the Covid-19 epidemic. Joanna raised the question of how Diana and Savannah met since they lived in different states. She evidently did not have much time to keep up with the news the past few years.

"How we me met, hmm. Would you like to take that question, Savannah?" Diana asked.

Savannah looked across the table. "Perhaps you were out of the country, Joanna."

"In fact, I was for quite a few months with Doctors Without Borders just before the pandemic hit. Then it was heads down eighteen, twenty hours a day for a long while," Joanna said.

"Well. That would explain it. You have a lot of catching up to do," Savannah said. "Truth be told, we happened to meet shortly after I pushed my way into Diana's husband's life. He's very handsome, by the way."

"In other words It didn't start off well, Joanna," Diana said.

Savannah shrugged. "Part of the job of an investigative reporter. Anyway, I was sitting at one of Washington Reagan's lunch counters, waiting on a flight and happened to overhear a conversation of Sam Wainwright's. He wasn't the FBI director at the time. He was having an interesting conversation with another agent, a very attractive woman, who just happened to be a psychiatrist by education."

"You're not going to draw this out, are you?" Diana asked.

With another shrug Savannah said, "maybe just a little. My eavesdropping led me to my first Pulitzer."

"Really!" Joanna said.

"Two Pulitzers actually," Savannah replied.

Diana slowly shook her head.

"Anyway, back to the story of how Diana and I met," Savannah said. "Diana's husband was a consultant for Electric Boat and Diana was working as a therapist for a hospital in Connecticut. A young woman was admitted after having wild hallucinations and hearing voices and Diana consulted on her case. Rather than going into the details, let's just say, I wormed my way into Tom and Diana's good graces after I discovered that she and her husband and Sam Wainwright were investigating a Russian terrorist plot."

"Of course, those missiles that killed our former president and a lot of other world leaders," Joanna said. "I didn't pay too much attention to the news when I was out of the country and dealing with Covid-19, but I do remember reading about that. It didn't register when Sarah invited me to dinner this evening."

"That's understandable. You were probably working much too hard at the time. Anyway, after a rocky start, we became best friends," Savannah said, turning toward Diana and giving her a wink.

"Well, I am very glad the three of you were able to help keep our world safe and are now friends," Joanna said as Wilson walked up to the table holding menus.

"Is it time for refills and dinner orders?" he asked.

"I'll have a refill, Wilson and I'm ready to order. I don't need a menu. Salmon, baked potato, green beans and salad with house dressing for me," Savannah.

"She has the menu memorized and typically is too impatient to listen to the specials," Diana said, as Wilson offered menus to Sarah and Joanna and described the evening's specials. She considered the specials briefly. "Everything sounds delicious, but I think I will have the same as Savannah, Wilson."

"Dressing on the side, also?"

"Yes, thank you," Diana said.

"Make that three salmon dinners and a Cosmo for me, too," Sarah said.

"Well, we're making this easy for you, Wison. Make that four salmon dinners and I would also like another Cosmopolitan," Joanna said.

"Excellent choices. Thank you, ladies."

As Savannah listened to the discussion between the three women, she thought it was time to focus on the primary purpose for their girl's night out. Was Sarah a good candidate for their secret society or not? After Sarah described her life growing up in many faraway places, Savannah engaged in the conversation.

"From your experience working in military intelligence and now with the NSA, Sarah," Savannah said, "it must be difficult at times to let down your guard when meeting new people?"

"Oh, that's a serious question," Sarah said. She had not expected it.

"She's an investigative reporter. It's hard for Savannah to turn it off," Diana said. Diana expected this question to come up and she and Savannah had prepped prior to this dinner meeting. Savannah agreed to take the lead to delve into Sarah's background and personal beliefs.

"No, no. That's quite okay," Sarah said. "That is a very relevant question, and it's true. After fifteen years working with highly classified information and some frightening individuals, I am quite cautious and have a higher hesitancy level when it comes to meeting new people."

"Frightening people. Yes, I have come across some very scary and bad people during my work as an investigative reporter," Savannah said. "The scariest was John Gordon, of course. He was an extremely intelligent individual, who was dealing with many personal demons. He was easily manipulated by unscrupulous people who put their self-serving agenda over the lives of so many people. By the way, he was seduced and set up by a woman at a technology conference he was attending."

"That's how it can start," Sarah said. "I've attended many seminars and lectures conducted by psychologists and therapists addressing the many deceptive techniques that could put our work in jeopardy. We are taught to be suspicious of others who may put us in a position to be blackmailed or manipulated to do something that we would otherwise not do. Our guard must always be up."

"Hmm, deceptive techniques to influence our thinking. An awful lot of people were certainly easily manipulated by our last president before he and a large number of other autocratic leaders were killed by those cruise missiles that John Gordon launched."

"Yes, that did happen and continues to be a cause for concern, Savannah," Sarah said. "The issue in this case, however, is change and a perceived loss of influence and power by many individuals. I'm sure Diana could describe it better, but with the animal kingdom in general, there has always been a group hierarchy that exists. Alpha males who wish to dominate and control their domains."

"A good analogy," Diana said. "Women were always subservient to men, relying on them for their general wellbeing and protection. Religious teachings, led predominately by the male clergy, defined what is acceptable in both thoughts and behaviors for the female sex. In addition to gender discrimination, we can never forget all those who have suffered marginalization simply because of their birthplace, religion, or skin color. Opportunities in education and a fairer playing field have gradually opened the doors to those disenfranchised groups. However, their rise has caused many individuals to rebel against their perceived loss of status and power."

Joanna confessed, "This was not a subject I had time to consider the last few years. I witnessed the difficulty for women to be accepted and promoted to senior positions in the medical field. And then there are those ridiculous theories with no basis of medical facts that led so many to refuse lifesaving vaccinations. Their very lives are put in danger from lies spawned those with no medical or scientific expertise."

"We certainly have digressed from my upcoming nuptials," Savannah said, as Wilson approached with their dinners.

During dinner, the women turned to less serious matters and the evening was filled with light banter and much laughter.

World Peace: Tom Lawson Novel #4
By James Brown

Chapter 14

It was nearly noon on Wednesday when Doctors Peggy Landon and Sandeep Singh exited the operating suite of Yale New Haven Hospital. A smile crossed Landon's face as she peeled off her surgical mask, gown, and gloves and dropped them into the waste container. She gave Singh an elbow bump. "It could not have gone better, Sandeep."

Sandeep returned her smile. "I agree. Just as we planned," he said as they left the surgical theater and went to update Cody Walker's parents. As soon as the door to the waiting room opened, Cody's parents were up from their chairs.

"The surgery went very well," Doctor Landon said. "No major complications."

Carole Walker clasped her hands tightly together and leaned forward as her husband held her. "Thank you, thank you," she said with tears flowing. "We've been praying for a miracle, and it's been answered."

"We are still hoping that will be the case," Doctor Singh said. "It will take about a week before the swelling subsides and we can assess how well the new neural pathways function. As we've explained, the implanted artificial neurons are designed to translate chemical signals into electrical impulses to communicate with Cody's undamaged cells. That's the key. If this communication can be made, and signals from his brain are able to communicate with Cody's lower body, he should be able to walk again."

"When we began this journey, I just hoped he would see some improvement, have at least some feelings in his legs and lower portion of his body. To walk again was beyond our initial hope," Cody's father said.

"That is the outcome we hope to achieve," Doctor Landon said. "Cody will be in the recovery room for the next hour if you would like to go for lunch. It's been a very long morning. A nurse will let you know when you can go in and see your son."

Eugene nodded. "We should go eat now, Carole. We have a long day ahead of us, too."

"Okay," Carole Walker whispered. "For a few minutes."

Watching the Walkers leave the surgical visitor's room Peggy said, "I'm going to give William a call and grab a quick bite before my meeting with Doctor Lazarus. She's anxious to publish."

"Humph, that's one problem of being affiliated with a renowned university and teaching hospital," Sandeep said. "Much more information is needed before she rushes to publish. William's recovery was nothing short of a miracle but it's much too early to assume Cody's surgery will turn out as well. Tell Doctor Lazarus we will let her know when the time is right."

Peggy patted Sandeep's shoulder as they left the visitor's waiting room. "I will do my best. I'll be back to check on Cody in a couple of hours."

Sandeep nodded and gave Peggy a thumbs up as he headed to Cody's recovery room. Peggy proceeded to the cafeteria to grab a chicken Caesar Salad to eat at her desk. Once there, she reached for her cell phone and called William. He picked it up immediately.

"All went well I assume?"

"Have you received any feedback?"

"Too early yet for a reading," William answered. "Once Cody is awake and his lower extremities are examined, we will know more. The technology and surgery worked for me, so there is no reason to believe it wouldn't help Cody. Were there any surgical issues or any unexpected major damage you and Sandeep encountered?"

"Nothing, no. It was textbook. The new textbook that we're writing of course."

"Speaking of new textbooks," William asked. "Do you still have your meeting with Doctor Lazarus this afternoon?"

"Unfortunately."

"Well, my dear. We knew you could not suppress your success for too long. Covid did buy us some time, but we knew the world would soon learn of your accomplishments. We will just have to deal with it."

"I am very excited for the benefits this will bring to others. It is life-changing."

"But you're worried about me."

"Of course I am. Your ability to come out of your coma is one thing. That we can handle. But what if . . ."

"No one is going to make that leap," William interrupted. "Artificial neurons capable of mimicking the function of organic brain cells, including the ability to translate chemical signals into electrical impulses have been in development for a while, though just not perfected yet. Until now anyway. Trust me. We will ensure the necessary secrets remain secret when we do publish."

Peggy sighed. "Okay, but I still plan to do my best to delay a medical journal release for as long as possible."

"Okay but do be careful. Too much delay and Doctor Lazarus may get suspicious. Scientists typically want to publish early and often, not the other way around."

"You're right, of course, William. I'll be careful. I'll be late this evening. Love you," Peggy said ending the call.

* * * *

William sat back in his chair, seated at his large desk in the family den. The den previously served as his former hospital suite when he was in a coma. Peggy had taken care of all the required equipment and details prepared for him while he spent five years in a coma. He was finally awakened from this coma by lifesaving and revolutionary technology that an AI entity had developed. He and this AI entity, known as John, were now the same person. William's memories and John's memories were intertwined. Likewise, the human-computer linkage to John's exponentially expanding artificial intelligence capability and a massive amount of information and data made William the most unique carbon and silicon-based human in the world.

William scanned the three computer screens on his desk. The screens were wirelessly connected to a powerful computer that also functioned as part of a client-server architecture. They could access a massive amount of computing power. While there was the usual keyboard in place for these computers, it was merely present to replicate a normal office setup. William had no use for it as his brain had wireless access to the computer.

The computer screen on William's left displayed Cody Walker's vitals. His body temperature, blood pressure and pulse were all normal. Also reflected on the screen were readings of electrical impulses from brainwaves, signals from Cody's brain, in his current unconscious state, to his lower extremities along his newly implanted neural pathways. Recorded on the screen were signals of electrical impulses currently being sent to Cody Walker's brain. Perhaps, William thought, Cody was dreaming about his last winning basketball goal.

William smiled after reviewing Cody's data. Cody would walk again. His attention then switched to an incoming call from Tom Lawson.

"Good afternoon, Tom. I assume you are calling to see how Cody Walker's surgery turned out?"

"Yes, and also to learn how the meeting with Sarah Pope went," I said. "Cody's s surgery went well, I assume?"

"Yes, so far. I just spoke with Peggy, and she said there were no complications. I have Cody's vitals up and they look good. He's in recovery now, still unconscious, but there are very slight electrical impulses indicating the new neural pathways are functioning."

"That's great, William. You and Peggy and the team have accomplished a true medical miracle."

"That's what Peggy is afraid of, actually. A medical miracle that will eventually lead to me, to John. The AI entity that John Gordon created and caused the deaths of a very large number of very prominent people, including our former president."

"You told her that wouldn't happen, didn't you?"

"Of course. I'm just passing along Peggy's concerns. Now, what is it about Sarah Pope that you wanted to discuss. It was late last evening when Diana got back to the hotel, so I assume her girls night out with Savannah and Sarah and Joanna went well. Did it not?"

"It did. Diana said she and Savannah had a very good time and were able to delve into Sarah's background and personality. Same for Joanna Strong, Sarah's new friend. They basically closed the restaurant early this morning."

"As I had expected," William said. "I've also initiated an assessment of Ms. Strong in case her relationship with Ms. Pope grows more serious."

"That's good, William. Now as for Sarah . . . "

"You're going to take the next step," William interrupted.

"Yes. I was hoping to wait a little longer but it's no longer possible. The president's CIPC program is moving forward quickly. Iran is next and we need Sarah's involvement."

"You need Sarah to come up to speed on the malware I created."

"Immediately," I said.

"So what is your plan, Tom?"

"I've scheduled a meeting with her for Thursday."

"And what are you going to tell her . . . that John Gordon had a little help with his submarine takeover, that he created an extremely intelligent AI entity capable of killing humans?"

"Well, no, I think a different approach would be better. Safer, anyway. No, I think it best if we take this slowly. I'm going to introduce Sarah to a dear friend of mine. An associate of my company, actually."

"Doctor John Davidson," William said.

"Yes, the brilliant paraplegic, with a PhD in AI technology, who is also a medical doctor with a rare disease that keeps him homebound."

"An excellent approach, Tom. I will update Doctor Davidson's profile and video image since he has aged a bit. How do you plan to introduce this worm that Doctor Davidson developed?"

"Carefully. I'm thinking I'll tell her that Doctor Davidson developed it by accident when working to improve a communication link for a neural network that he was trying to develop."

"Hmm. "That might just work. From here, if I may suggest, we should provide her with the first generation of the software. Something that she can modify to the final design stage with my assistance."

"Doctor Davidson, of course."

"Of course," William said. "By using this approach, and with Sarah making the final design and coding changes for this worm, she will then introduce it as a new tool into the NSA communications monitoring software arsenal. I'll also make sure she can explain how the worm was used to capture the call between Omar and Mostafa

Ahmadi that described Iranian cleric Ebram Janati's death as a heart attack, when he was actually poisoned."

"Excellent."

"How about President Stephen?" William asked. "You're one of his many advisors now. You can't leave him out."

"I thought of that also. But I'm thinking I'll see how it goes with Sarah first. Then once you and she are communicating and are far enough along, I'll update the president on the worm Sarah developed."

"Okay, that's a good plan, Tom. Call me after you speak with Sarah and let me know when the introduction with Doctor Davidson is to be scheduled."

* * * *

I sat at my desk doing my best to catch up on emails that seemed to spawn faster than I could read and clear them. After reading the last one, I looked up and saw Sarah Pope coming down the hall toward my office. My appointment as a special advisor to the president was not a job I sought. But when offered the position by Andrew Kennedy, President Stephen's Chief of Staff, and stammering for several seconds trying to think how I could decline gracefully, Kennedy was very persuasive, saying it was a direct request from the president, that my assistance was needed to help make the CIPC program a success. Needless to say, I agreed to take the position and stay at least a year.

"Ms. Pope," I said meeting her at the door. "I hope your day is going well."

"Likewise. We're both in our offices from dawn to dusk."

"Like they say, we aim to serve. But my commitment is probably more flexible than yours. Come in. Have a seat. Would you like some coffee or water perhaps?"

"No thank you. I had my first cup several hours ago," Sarah answered looking up at a clock on the wall. It was eight a.m. "Your wife I believe had an early morning flight back to Connecticut today."

"She's probably boarding now. By the way, she said she had a very enjoyable girls' night. I hope Savannah behaved herself."

Sarah laughed. "Savannah is a very interesting woman. She described how she pushed her way into your life."

"She certainly did. Did she tell you she saved my life, too?"

"Saved your life? That didn't come up. How did that happen?"

"Savannah, Sam, and I tracked down John Gordon after we learned what he was planning. He was hiding on his boat near where he lived in Groton. When we boarded, Savannah happened to see one of the Russian agents and yelled. Sam and I moved quickly but Savannah didn't and was shot in the shoulder. Sam shot one Russian agent and I body slammed the other."

"Oh my. She didn't mention that the other evening."

"She's a very capable woman. I'm glad you were able to meet her and Diana too. Diana said she thought everyone had an enjoyable evening."

"We most certainly did. I'm not sure if Diana mentioned it to you, but I had a long conversation with her at the president's dinner party. As we talked, we happened onto the subject of high demanding professions and the benefit of having common interests."

"That sounds like Diana. She probably cautioned that it's tough on relationships when one party has to cancel a lot of dates, engagements, and plans due to their job. I'm sure she's held a lot of therapy sessions with clients on related issues. It's difficult for her not to share a few tips of the trade."

"I imagine, and she did offer some good advice. She probably mentioned my date with Joanna."

"She did. She said Joanne was an emergency room physician, an even more demanding and high-stress profession given the pandemic these last few years."

"It certainly has been. She and I have very similar professions from that standpoint. As do you. We are assigned the demanding and stressful task of helping the president make the world a little safer. Do you have an idea how we might be able to do that, Tom?" Is that the reason for our meeting?"

"I want to introduce you to an associate of mine, Doctor John Davidson."

"To fix me up. As in a date?"

"Oh, no, not at all," I quickly said.

"That's good, it briefly crossed my mind since we were discussing relationships and dating."

"That's understandable, but no, Doctor Davidson would be a difficult candidate for dating. He's a paraplegic and also has a rare immune deficiency that prevents him from having contact with anyone."

"Oh my, that's really sad. How do you know Doctor Davidson?" Sarah asked.

"Medical research. We've had discussions about individuals with high stress and demanding hours. You might say I fall into that category. I have too many interests, I guess. Anyway, I formed a company several years ago that focuses on neurological research in the area of artificial neural pathways that can translate chemical signals into electrical impulses. In this endeavor I met Doctor Davidson, and he became one of my associates."

"I thought your background was in aerospace engineering."

"It is. I worked at Aerostructures Corporation, as you may have read, and was a consultant with Electric Boat. I also have a small investment company that delves in algorithmic computer-based trading in addition to my company that is focused on neurological research. Currently, I am helping out here at the White House."

"My goodness. And I thought my days were long."

"It's not that bad. My companies are small, and we have very good people who manage day-to-day operations. I stick my nose in now and then but each of the companies are pretty much self-sufficient."

"That makes it easier, but you still have a lot of balls in the air at times I would think."

"That's true, but I have a really good therapist on staff."

Sarah laughed, then said, "But given Doctor Davidson is associated with neurological research, why do you want me to meet with him? Would this be a Zoom call since he can't leave his home?"

"Let me explain. In addition to having a medical degree, Doctor Davidson also has a PhD in AI technology. He's used this expertise to design artificial neural pathways that can mimic the function of human cells, including the ability to translate chemical signals into electrical impulses to communicate with undamaged human cells."

"Such as helping a paraplegic walk?" Sarah asked.

"Yes. After spending hours discussing this research with Doctor Davidson, it appeared that it might have applicability for NSAs information intelligence efforts."

"The NSA leveraging Doctor Davidson's neural pathways technology?"

"Yes, Doctor Davidson has essentially developed a very sophisticated communications solution. Hackers typically refer to similar code as malware, worms in other words."

Sarah's eyes widened. "Malware? You really believe Doctor Davidsons technology can be used by the NSA as malware?"

"I do and I would like you to assess whether or not his software could be used to advance the NSA communications monitoring capabilities."

Sarah took a moment to consider the implication. Was it possible she thought, to utilize her skills and expertise in artificial intelligence development? Could a paraplegic physician with a PhD in AI technology enhance the NSA's data analysis capabilities?

"Well, Tom, I guess there's no harm in taking a look at what Doctor Davidson has developed. When would he be available to set up a Zoom call?"

"Do you have time now?"

"Now? I guess," Sarah said checking her watch.

"Great. Let's move to the conference table." As Tom walked around his desk he called John's cell phone. "Doctor Davidson, it's Tom Lawson. You mentioned you might have time this morning for a quick introduction to an associate of mine. Are you available now? That's great. I'm sending you a facetime connection. We will be logging in."

After they settled themselves in front of the large monitor, Tom activated the connection. Doctor John Davidson, a distinguished looking man in his mid-fifties with salt-and-pepper hair appeared seated in a wheelchair.

"Doctor Davidson. Thank you for taking the time to fit us in your schedule this morning," I said.

"My pleasure, Tom. I was looking forward to meeting Ms. Pope. It was an interesting suggestion you had regarding the research I've been conducting and its possible applicability to cyber security."

"So, by way of introduction," I said, starting off. "Doctor Davidson, this is Sarah Pope, Executive Director of the NSA. Sarah, Doctor John Davidson."

"Pleased to meet you, Doctor Davidson," Sarah said. "Tom gave me a brief summary of the research you've been conducting. It sounds very promising and also very important work. So many people could benefit."

"Including me, of course," Doctor Davidson said, rolling his wheelchair back and forth in front of the monitor. "Tom also thinks the NSA may benefit from our research."

"He mentioned that, yes," Sarah said.

I handed Sarah a thumb drive. "I took the liberty to download Doctor Davidson's code and solution description, which is patent pending for the medical application for which it was created to address. We need to treat this code and product description as confidential. If you load this on a separate computer and check it out in coordination with Doctor Davidson, then the two of you can explore the possibilities together. Here's his contact information. What do you think?"

Sarah held up the thumb drive for a second. "You believe Doctor Davidson's code may be applicable for the president's CIPC program?"

"I do. Our progress with China and Russia is going reasonably well and North Korea may not be an issue if Huan Cheng comes through. But I'm concerned we may have a challenge with Iran. So far, we lack intelligence that will appeal to the moderates. We will need very strong arguments and undeniable facts to persuade Iranian moderates to stand up against the religious zealots who will never go along with the president's program."

After hesitating a moment, Sarah slipped the thumb drive into her purse. "To confirm, you want me to review the code with Doctor Davidson and see if it can be used to enhance the NSAs monitoring capabilities?" she said.

"Or make any adjustment to the code's design that you and Doctor Davidson think is necessary for the software to enhance the capabilities of the NSA intelligence surveillance system."

"When would you like to discuss this matter with me, Sarah?" Doctor Davidson asked. Would Friday evening at eight p.m. work for you?"

"Friday evening . . . okay, that should work. I'll look over the information and we can discuss it tomorrow evening. Sure. Who knows, maybe your artificial neural pathways solution will be applicable to surveillance monitoring."

"Okay, Sarah. I'll call you Friday evening," Doctor Davidson said and ended the connection.

Sarah turned and looked over at me after the screen went dark. "Well, that was short and sweet. Do you really think this effort will improve our results?"

"You would not be sitting here if I didn't, Sarah. How about giving me a call after you review the information and discuss it with Doctor Davidson on Friday? Call at any time," I said and stood. Sarah looked at me a bit quizzically, picked up her purse and left my office.

I'll be getting a call around midnight I thought as I watched Sarah walk toward the elevator. I picked up my cell phone and called John.

Chapter 15

"You've had two busy days since you returned from Washington," Margie Shaw said as she stepped into Diana Lawson's office.

"Oh, Margie," Diana said, looking up from her desk before finishing her last client notes on her computer. She quickly finished. "Yes, it's been quite busy with back-to-back clients. I'm being punished for taking time off."

"How are you doing traveling back and forth to Washington?" Margie asked, taking a moment and leaning against the doorframe.

Diana stood and began tidying up her desk. "Different, I guess. At least different for now. We lived in a few different states when Tom's company was acquiring companies, and he was transferred to help with the acquisitions. The flying back and forth on weekends isn't new for us. It's just been a while since we've done that."

"How long will Tom be in Washington?"

"At least a year but you never know. Fortunately, it's a short flight to Washington."

"It must be pretty exciting, having the opportunity to meet some very powerful people."

"It is, but at the end of the day they're just people. Many of them fell into their jobs the same way that Tom did . . . just happened to be in the right place at the right time, or maybe the wrong place, depending on how you view politics. I've become familiar with the personalities of the people I've met in Washington as clients over the years, different names but the same personalities."

Margie laughed. "That's one way of looking at it. People are just people, dealing with life's challenges. Interesting. Anyway, the reason I stopped by some of us are getting together tonight at the Monkey Farm. It's been awhile since our last TGIF gathering. Ann and Brian have already headed over."

Diana looked at the clock. It was almost six-thirty. "This evening, hmm. Tom's staying in Washington this weekend so sure. I'll stop over, have a drink and get a bite to eat. I'll leave in a few minutes."

"Okay. See you there," Margie said and left Diana's office.

As soon as she left, Diana's cell phone rang. It was Tom.

"I hope you're leaving the office soon. It's getting late," I said.

"I just finished with my last client. Margie stopped in to tell me this was the group's TGIF night and I'm going to join them.

"I'm sorry I'm not able to join you."

"And be confronted by Larry?"

"Oh, maybe not too sorry then. Does he still believe those wild theories?"

"Not so wild actually," Diana said.

"True, but these are theories we prefer not become widely promoted."

"What are your plans this evening?" Diana asked.

"I'm picking up a pizza on the way back to the apartment. Doctor Davidson is having that conference call with Sarah at eight this evening."

"Right, I forgot they were going to talk. How soon do you think it will be before you hear from her?"

"Well, she's had a day to review John's design and his code before her conference call with him. I told her to call me anytime and I was staying in Washington over the weekend. My guess is I will hear from her around midnight."

"Really, that's pretty late. I guess you think she will be so amazed by what she learns from John she will want to talk with you. Call me tomorrow morning and let me know how it goes," Diana said.

"Will do. I have a call coming in that I need to take. Say hello to Larry for me."

"Yeah, right. Love you," Diana said and disconnected.

* * * *

World Peace: Tom Lawson Novel #4
By James Brown

Diana entered the Monkey Farm and noticed that Brian Jones and her group had taken over a portion of the far side of the bar. At six foot seven Brian was hard to miss. She walked around the room's fireplace to the back of the large oblong wraparound bar and sat next to Ann Mathews, one of her group's psychologists.

"Diana! You're back in town," Ann said. "I thought you were going to be out all week."

"I couldn't be out of the office that long. I got back late Wednesday morning and have been spending the last couple days catching up with my clients."

"And you've broken free from your shackles, good for you. Did you meet any interesting people in Washington?"

Diana stared at Ann for a few seconds, maybe Ann didn't know why she was in Washington. "I did, yes," she finally said.

"Who? Who did you meet?"

"Before I answer that question, I'm going to order a lobster roll and a drink." She turned around as the bartender approached. "Ben, I'd like to order a Tito's and tonic and a lobster roll with fries."

"Any food for you, Ann, food or just a drink refill? It is Ann, right?" Ben said.

"Very good memory, Ben. Food, ah, sure a lobster roll sounds good, a refill of my drink too, thank you."

With Ben off to retrieve drinks and food, Diana turned back toward Ann. "Your question, Ann. I assumed you knew what Tom's job was in Washington?"

"Not really," Ann said with a look of surprise. "I know Tom has some kind of consulting job in Washington, but I don't know what it is or who he's working for."

"Oh, I'm sorry. I thought everyone in the office knew."

"I was out for a few weeks so I must have missed the announcement. And I've been very busy since getting back."

"I apologize. I assumed someone at the office would have filled you in. Especially Larry." As soon as Larry's name was mentioned he appeared.

"Diana, Ann! You are both here. Haven't seen you at one of our TGIF gatherings in a while."

"I've been kind of busy," Ann said.

"Same with me," Diana followed.

"You were in Washington the last few days, Diana. Right?" Larry asked.

Oh God, here it comes, Diana thought and gave an almost inaudible response. "Yes, I returned Wednesday morning."

"How's Tom doing?"

"Doing well, Larry. I spoke with him just before I left the office. He said he was sorry he was not able to join us this evening."

Larry gave Diana a look. He obviously wasn't buying it.

"Ann. Do you know what Tom's job is in Washington?" Larry asked.

"No. Diana and I were discussing that very thing."

"Funny," Larry said. "Well, since you don't know, he's a special advisor to the president. He even has an office in the White House."

Ann looked at Diana with raised eyebrows. "Wow! That's impressive. When I asked you if you had met anyone interesting in Washington I understand your response now, Diana. I really have been out of the loop."

"Sorry, Ann," Diana said, as Ben delivered two lobster roll orders."

"Be right back with your drinks," he said.

"Thanks, Ben," Diana said, as she cut her lobster roll in half, and quickly took a bite. "Sorry, no lunch today, so I need some food before I have my vodka tonic." After a few bites and a few sips of her drink, she said, "Regarding your earlier question, Ann, yes, I did meet a few interesting people."

"So, don't hold me in suspense . . . who exactly were these interesting people?" Ann asked.

"Tom and I were invited to a small dinner party at the White House."

"And?" Larry said. "The other guests?"

Diana paused for a moment then said, "the president, first lady, chief of staff and his wife, the FBI director and a few other people. Just a small group."

Ann stopped eating and stared. Larry stood behind them shaking his head.

"I knew it! Tom knows more than what he told me the last time we were here for our TGIF gathering," Larry said.

"Larry, Tom is a consultant, an advisor. He just happens to be consulting for the government right now . . . there are many advisors working for them."

"I'm impressed, Diana. You have met some very interesting people, " Ann said.

"No more interesting than the people I've met living here. Just a little better known perhaps. Not necessarily more impressive."

"Well said," Ann said, raising her glass. She and Diana toasted while Larry stood there scowling.

"So far the people I've met in Washington have been very nice and are extremely dedicated. It's amazing the long hours they put in. I couldn't imagine doing what they do for four years let along eight," Diana said.

"How long will Tom be working there?" Ann asked.

"He sort of agreed to a year. He has an apartment that's not too far from where he works which is convenient."

"The White House!" Larry shouted.

Diana shrugged. "It's just a large house, Larry . . . with a lot of history of course."

"So, what's he doing for the president? Investigating the takeover of those subs maybe?" Larry asked.

"The subs, no. He told me those investigations have concluded. He is involved with a new program the president is promoting. Something to do with improving our alliances."

"Sounds a bit nebulous," Larry offered. "More likely some top secret shit that the public will never know about."

Diana winked. "Right. Something to do with those mushrooms that are kept in the dark."

"Mushrooms in the dark? I guess I've really been left out of the loop," Ann said, as she finished her lobster roll.

"What's this about mushrooms kept in the dark?" Brian Jones asked as he walked up and towered over Larry Holms.

* * * *

"Sarah. Thank you for your promptness," Doctor Davidson said as their facetime connection began. "Tom and I had a conversation about promptness shortly after we first met. But that's a conversation for another time perhaps. You've looked over the design document and the code I assume?"

"I did, Doctor Davidson."

"John. Please call me John. Doctor Davidson is much too formal."

"Okay. John it is. By the way, this conference call we're using, it's not Zoom or any other web conferencing platform I'm familiar with."

"No it isn't. It's a conferencing system that I designed and is much more secure than anything else on the market. I have a lot of time on my hands since I am restricted to a wheelchair and live in a somewhat self-contained environment."

"It must be difficult for you. I'm sorry."

"It's not so bad. I've been able to adapt quite well, actually."

"I'm glad to hear that, John."

"One benefit is having more time to focus on advancing medical science."

"You have certainly done that. Your neural pathways design is phenomenal. I've seen a lot of AI-based system designs and am familiar with a number of different programming languages used, Python, Lisp, Prolog, you name it, but nothing like what I just spent the last twenty-four hours poring over. This design and language you used to develop the neural pathways. Did anyone collaborate with you on this?"

"No. Not directly. Of course there were a large number of medical doctors and computer scientists with whom I drew information from, evolutionary discovery, you might say. How well were you able to understand the design and architecture and the coding structure?"

"With difficulty the first eighteen hours or so. But then I made a few breakthroughs in understanding the design and the same goes for your unique coding language."

"You have questions then?"

"Many," Sarah answered.

The next three hours the conversation flowed back and forth. Questions asked and answered regarding the system design and the structure of the coding language developed by John. It was certainly a more powerful construct than the coding languages that Sarah, or any other software engineers were familiar with. John listened carefully to Sarah's questions. He was patient in his responses and took his time guiding Sarah through the complex thought processes upon which he drew to create his revolutionary artificial neurons capable of mimicking the function of organic brain cells. This included the ability to translate chemical signals into electrical impulses and communicate with human cells.

Around 11 p.m., their conversation moved beyond the design of artificial brain cells capable of communicating with human cells to communications in general. More specifically, they discussed how John's code could easily function as malware . . . worms able to target the communication networks and devices in the countries identified by President Stephen's CIPC Program.

Sarah paused for a moment, then said, "John, I'm exhausted."

"Understandable. Seven to eight hours of sleep is needed for humans to remain healthy. You've put in quite a few hours of work these past few days. If you are free on Monday at the same time, eight p.m., we can reconnect. Will that work for you?"

"Yes. Let's do that. I've taken quite a few notes this evening."

"Good. I will send you a few suggestions that you might want to consider. I have a few ideas that might work to adjust the code for general communications data gathering that is more suitable to enhance the NSA's monitoring capabilities."

"Okay Doctor Davidson. I'm sorry, John," she corrected. "I look forward to speaking with you again on Monday."

"Good night, Sarah. I will call you Monday at eight p.m.," John said and disconnected the conference call.

Sarah stared at the blank screen. Her head ached. Her eyes throbbed. Yet, until she finally told John she was exhausted she hadn't realized they had talked nonstop for four hours. She looked at the clock on her desk in her den. It was midnight. After a few seconds she remembered, Diana was in Connecticut. Tom had said to call him any time. She picked up her cell and dialed.

"Tom. It's Sarah," she said, hearing his voice. "I'm sorry. I hope I didn't wake you."

"No, no. I was just getting ready for bed. I thought you might give me a call."

"He's amazing! A genius, Tom. I spent the last four hours with him and almost forty-eight hours before that going over his design and software. There is nothing like it in the world, Tom. Nothing! Or no one like him either."

"Yes, truly, he is special, Sarah. A very special genius."

"How did you meet him, or rather know about him since you couldn't actually meet him?"

"Purely by accident. I happened to read an article written by a neurosurgeon who has a research facility in Connecticut. It caught my attention. She and I spoke, and she introduced me to Doctor Davidson, and I ended up investing in a startup company she formed."

"I see. From the time I've spent going over Doctor Davidson's AI solution and programming language, I think you will make a very good return on your investment."

"I will probably know in a week or two," I said.

A week or two? What happens then?" Sarah asked.

"We will know whether or not a young man who was a highly recruited high school basketball player will be able to walk again."

Sarah was silent for a moment, processing what I just said. It was a delicate balance. Provide her with just enough information to peak her interest while testing whether or not she understood the reason and importance for secrecy. As our small group soon learned, John was more than an inanimate AI entity to be managed. He was now a close friend and confidant, as well as a very helpful genius.

"The young man is a paraplegic?" Sarah finally asked.

"Yes, Cody Walker was in an auto accident and suffered a spinal injury. He was operated on Wednesday, and we are hopeful Doctor Davidson's AI chips and artificial neural pathways will make the connections necessary to allow Cody to walk again."

"Oh my God! That would be a miracle. So many people could benefit from this surgery."

"We have our fingers crossed and, in about a week, when the swelling goes down, we will know if the new neural pathways are working and signals from his brain are connecting with his lower extremities."

"From the little time I've had to speak with John I will not be surprised in the least that his designs and systems will not perform exactly as expected,"

I was glad to hear Sarah referring to Doctor Davidson by his first name. Hopefully, a personal friendship will grow. "We all hope you are right, Sarah. Now, as for the other hat that I wear, when do you think you will be able to assess whether or not John's neural pathway solution can be used or modified to enhance the NSA's surveillance monitoring capabilities?"

"I think it will take us a few days, maybe a week to make that assessment. I have a follow up call with John Monday evening. I'll stop by your office and give you an update Tuesday morning."

"That would be great. I'll be in the office by seven if not earlier. Again, feel free to call upon me any time if something urgent comes up."

"Hopefully it won't be as late as this one," Sarah said.

"Don't worry. John will make sure he doesn't keep you too long."

"Right," Sarah said. "He said humans need seven to eight hours of sleep."

"Yes, we do. Good night."

* * * *

The first major hurdle was soon to be discussed. Was it possible, or were we being naive to think we could change the world by capitalizing on the outcome of a sinister plot of a disgruntled and deranged individual that almost caused World War III? At no time in earth's history had humankind experienced the simultaneous loss of world leaders, leaders who had a significant influence and control over the world's economy and human existence. Though as tragic as the deaths were of the leaders from China, Russia, Iran, North Korea and the U.S., a global war was averted and an unparallel opportunity emerged. While many of the countries affected by this event remained in a state of flux, their citizens were taking advantage of an opportunity for change. The new U.S. President also wanted to take advantage of this once in a lifetime event. He wanted to pull off a miracle and establish an environment where cooperation, inclusion, and peaceful coexistence would be the new norm for global diplomacy.

I sat in a conference room on the second floor of the White House along with the team the president established. We were all waiting to receive a secured call from Victor Petrova, the undercover CIA agent tasked with convincing the new president of Russia to take a first step. It was nearing ten-thirty a.m. Monday morning in

Washington DC and five-thirty p.m. in Moscow. Angela Keen, the Director of the CIA, sat at the head of the table. CIA Director of Operations, Maddi Pool sat to her right, and Sam Wainwright, Director of the FBI, to her left. I sat next to Sam. At 10:30 a.m. the conference table phone speaker rang.

"Good evening, Victor," Keen said. "Are you calling from your hotel?" She asked.

"Hello, Angela. No, it's a reasonably warm spring day for Moscow and I didn't have lunch so I'm heading out for an early dinner. I'm walking to the restaurant."

"I have Maddi, Sam, and Tom here with me. Do you have any questions regarding the materials we sent?"

"I have none. The materials were very clear. I spent most of the day at Vadim Ivanov's office discussing the upcoming meeting with President Milosevic."

"Have you confirmed who will be in attendance?"

"Yes, it will be a relatively small group. In addition to Vadim Ivanov and President Milosevic, Milosevic's Chief of Staff Alexander Alexeyev will attend. Also Vadim's Executive Director and General Counsel, Dmitry Borisyuk will join us. Likewise Natalia Smirnov and Nikita Popov. Smirnov is an aide to the president and heads Russia's Presidential State-Legal Directorate. Popov as you know is Minster of Foreign Affairs."

"A small group. That should be an advantage," Keen said. "Not as many opinions to sway. What about Andreyev and Abramov? Any readings from those camps? We are intercepting a great deal of chatter. Some for and some against the uprisings that are taking place in Russia. The sense we are getting here is that Abramov will be our biggest challenge."

"No question. Abramov is a remanent of Russia's KGB and hasn't gotten over Putin's death yet. The SVR will definitely be a challenge. It won't be easy for us to convince Abramov that we can all play together nicely in the same sandbox."

Keen sighed. "Hopefully Milosevic will shed some light on the advantages he believes he can gain if the CIPC program moves forward."

"I'll do my best, Angela to persuade President Milosevic to move forward and schedule a follow up session with Secretary Bentley and his team."

"Okay, Victor. If anything comes up that you need help with call me anytime," Keen said.

"Will do," Victor answered.

Chapter 16

Sarah Pope looked at the digital clock on her desk. She sat in her den the past several hours reviewing the questions she wrote. The past sixty hours she ate very little and slept even less, certainly nowhere close to the seven to eight hours of sleep John said were required by humans. During all hours of the day and well into the night she and John electronically exchanged information and held conference sessions. When they spoke, Sarah asked questions and John patiently answered. She now sat at her desk and waited for John to initiate the scheduled Monday evening session. The time glowed on the digital clock on Sarah's desk and was about to change from 7:59 p.m. to 8:00 p.m.. As the time changed to 8:00 p.m., the image of Doctor John Davidson appeared on Sarah's monitor.

"Good evening, John. It's been what, two hours since we last communicated."

"Yes, it was exactly two hours ago. You had a question regarding several sections of code. Our call now perhaps should be a short one. You look tired Sarah."

"I haven't been on that seven to eight hours of sleep schedule that you said humans need, John. Not even close."

"Well then, we need to fix that. I have a suggestion. How about I take the next forty-eight hours and go through the code changes you've made? The last we spoke you said you thought your latest updates satisfied the system's use case we established. I will validate that supposition while you get that much needed sleep."

"That is an excellent idea, John. Forty-eight hours of sleep sounds good," Sarah said with her hand up to her mouth trying to cover a wide yawn.

John laughed. "Okay, Sarah. I will review your changes and send out a revised release with any changes I make. I will call you on Tuesday at eight p.m." The connection ended.

* * * *

The meeting with Russian President Andrey Milosevic was being held in his office at the Kremlin. Currently sitting at the desk that Vladimir Putin occupied for twenty-two years, President Milosevic was leaning back in his chair facing the side of the room with a phone at his ear.

The rest of the meeting attendees sat at a conference table located between two shear-draped windows along the side of the very large rectangular shaped office. Overhead, two enormous chandeliers hung from the tray ceiling that curved upward along four sides to the white ceiling that was thirty feet above the floor. The walls of the room were fifteen feet in height. A three-foot-wide decorative border painted white circled the top of the walls below the rising tray ceiling and above rich mahogany wood that rose eight feet along the sides of the wall below.

Alexander Alexeyev, Milosevic's Chief of Staff, and Natalia Smirnov, Aide to the President, sat on opposite sides of the table close to the vacant chair that was being held for President Milosevic. Vadim Ivanov, owner of TSU Group and his deputy, Dmitry Borisyuk sat in quiet conversation next to Natalia Smirnov, Head of the Presidential State-Legal Directorate.

Victor Petrova, the undercover CIA operative and friend of Tom Lawson, sat next to Nikita Popov, Milosevic's Minister of Foreign Affairs and across the table from Vadim Ivanov. He looked toward the front of the room, wondering if Milosevic was speaking with Maxim Abramov, the Director of the Russia's Federal Security Service. After another ten minutes, Milosevic put down the phone.

"Sorry, gentlemen," President Milosevic said as he approached the conference table. "It's been a very busy morning."

"A very difficult and busy year," Nikita Popov offered.

"Very true, Nikita," Milosevic said in a quiet, hesitant tone. Taking a moment, he continued. "It doesn't take a genius to know that President Putin left us holding the bag."

"He certainly did that, Sir," Natalia Smirnov said.

"The reason we are here, Natalia. To see how we can best clean up the mess he left us with. It's no secret that our country is in a state of turmoil. The man who led our country for twenty-two years is dead and the world has made unsubstantiated claims he was behind the deaths of a large number of world leaders including his own."

Victor Petrova did his best not to roll his eyes or respond to Milosevic's fake news spin. He knew Milosevic was being pulled by many factions of the remaining Russian leadership as Russia's new president. Undoubtedly it was FSB Director Abramov on the phone call making a last pitch to scuttle the meeting Milosevic was about to participate in.

Finally, after several more denial of responsibility statements to the cause of the potential start of World War III, Milosevic turned his attention to Vadim Ivanov.

"Vadim, you and I have known each other for a very long time. The reason I agreed to hold this meeting. As you well know many options are being implemented and considered as the best way to put down the uprisings that have taken place since the death of President Putin. We are here this morning to listen to what Victor Petrova has to say. You've told me his ideas are not typical to what others are saying. Outside-of-the-box thinking you said. So, the meeting is yours, Vadim. Please provide any additional background and introduce Mr. Petrova."

"Thank you, Mr. President. And yes, it is almost fifty years since you and I met in elementary school. A very long time ago. Since I'm sure many opinions are being offered or pushed depending on the person making the argument, I wanted to make sure you were getting a very wide view as to how our country's difficulties might be resolved for *everyone's* benefit," Vadim said, looking around the table and then back at Milosevic.

Milosevic gave a slight head nod.

"Starting with introductions, everyone has met my Executive Director and General Counsel, Dmitry Borisyuk who is joining us today," Vadim said nodding toward Borisyuk. "As for Victor Petrova, I met Victor eight years ago at a conference held here in Moscow. Victor is the owner and CEO of Petrova Consulting Group. His company, PCG, has five thousand employees located in offices in the U.S., Russia, Europe, and Asia. My firm became a client of PCG five years ago and Victor and his team has been instrumental in helping my company almost double in size. During the last many months after the death of our president, I asked Victor to participate in a discussion session related to the issues the country is now facing as the turmoil has also affected my business. We've held several sessions since."

"Several other large companies also participated?" Milosevic asked.

"Yes, a dozen companies. We've all been affected."

"Very well," Milosevic said turning toward Victor Petrova. "Mr. Petrova. The floor is yours. Introduce yourself and we look forward to hearing your thoughts."

"Thank you, Mr. President. I am honored to be here and have the opportunity to share what Vadim describes as outside-the-box-thinking. First of all, by way of my background, I was born in Stamford, Connecticut, a small town of 130,000 residents that is located forty miles from New York City, a forty-five-minute train ride. My father and mother were born in St. Petersburg in Russia and immigrated to the United States during a period when the country was also in turmoil. Engineering and high-tech jobs were scarce at the time. My father worked for an engineering firm in Stamford where we lived for ten years. We subsequently returned to St. Petersburg where I finished primary school and received an advanced degree in mechanical engineering. I then returned to New York City and earned a master's degree in business from New York University. I formed PCG Consulting shortly after receiving my MBA degree."

"You have dual citizenship I assume," President Milosevic said.

"I do, yes. My company has an office in New York City and in Saint Petersburg and I have an apartment in both cities."

"Hmm, very convenient. Are your parents still alive? A wife, family maybe?" President Milosevic asked, though he already knew the answer.

"My mother is alive and lives in Saint Petersburg. No wife or children yet."

"You work too much I assume."

"Yes sir. My mother tells me that all the time."

"One other question," Milosevic said. "What is your relationship with Tom Lawson?"

"The person who uncovered John Gordon's plot? Mr. Lawson and I were engaged on an engineering project early in my career. We worked together for roughly eighteen months. He also has a degree in engineering and earned an MBA degree from New York University the year before I started my MBA program."

"You must keep in touch, I assume."

"Occasionally. He's a little older and has a family so not as often as we did when we worked together quite a few years ago."

"Okay, Mr. Petrova. Let's hear about this outside-of-the-box thinking that my dear friend Vadim says I should at least consider," President Milosevic said.

"Certainly, Mr. President. As I have shared, I've spent half my life in Russia and the other half in the United States and have also traveled extensively throughout Europe and Asia. With these experiences there is one constant that I've observed. As a general perspective parents love their children, they want their children to be happy, and they love their country. That is, unless they do not feel safe and secure, or they are not able to find a job that allows them to earn enough money to care for their families."

"I see, Mr. Petrova," President Milosevic said softly in a disappointing tone. "Not necessarily an outside-of-the-box revelation though."

"This observation, no. Pretty standard stuff actually. So is the next piece of information."

"Which is?" Milosevic reluctantly asked.

"That mathematically, Russia has a smaller economy than Italy in terms of gross domestic product and is dwarfed when compared to the size of the economies of the United States or China. Yet, Russia is the largest country in the world by way of land mass. It is fifty-six times the size of Italy and has more than double Italy's population, yet Russia's gross domestic product is thirty percent less than Italy's GDP."

Victor paused for a moment. Alexeyev and Smirnov stared at Milosevic waiting for him to respond. He remained silent.

"Now, another small piece of history about Russia," Victor continued. "Perhaps everyone knows this, but I think it's information that deserves repeating. After losing millions of people in World War II Russia and its policies over the years have focused on survival and holding on to the remnants of the Russian empire. Desperate to avert further fragmentation of Russian territory and influence in the world, Russia's leaders have focused on potentially new existential threats.

The belief is that there can always be another Napoleon or Hitler who could emerge to attack Russia or invade its territory.

However, since Russia has enough nukes to destroy the world many times over, this insatiable fear of a pending boogeyman should reflect the real-world reality that Russia has ample capabilities to take down any boogeyman, as well as the whole world. This is the first point I'd like to make. There is no country in the world that has any desire to attack Russia because of Russia's nuclear deterrent capability since no country could attack Russia and survive."

Victor paused, letting his statements percolate. Finally, President Milosevic said, "that's it? Get over our fears and what, embrace the West?"

"You're not thinking large enough, sir. Embrace the world, Mr. President, not merely the West."

Brows raised and eyes squinted, Milosevic took a moment to consider Victor's statement while subdued crosstalk flowed between the other meeting attendees. Finally Milosevic said, "Please explain, Mr. Petrova."

"Okay, let's think of it as the idiom, 'you can't see the forest for the trees.' The forest, Mr. President. If you are only focusing on the trees around you, you are not able to understand that these trees are a part of a vast forest."

Victor paused again as blank looks stared back at him. Finally he said, "I see additional explanation is necessary."

"Yes, that would be helpful," Milosevic said.

"Russia's focus for a long time now has been on that historical patch of trees, the possible coming of the next Hitler or the loss of territory, rather than the forest which Russia is a part of. And perhaps many believe *'the West'* is the Hitler they are afraid of, that *'the West'* will try and take land from Russia, or even occupy it. But again, Mr. President that is also misguided thinking. The world of colonialism is over, a long past era. The fact is gentlemen, Russia's potential has been smoldering as a result of old beliefs in not seeing the forest for the trees.

Russia is the largest country in the world by way of land mass, almost twice the size of China, the United States, and Canada and almost five times larger than India. Yet China has almost ten times as many citizens and the United States has a population more than double that of Russia. In other words, Mr. President rather than focusing on the potential rise of another boogieman or a loss of territory since the odds that this will happen is zero, it is economic power that should be a primary objective. And to become an economic power in the class of the United States and China, Mr. President, Russia needs to significantly grow its population and middle class."

Milosevic stroked his chin. "Interesting. You didn't say Russia should become a democracy."

"I did not. As I described during Vadim's sessions the type of government a country has, democracy, totalitarianism, dictatorship, parliamentarianism, or theocracy is not as critical as is population and the size of a country's middle class. Assuming that is, that dictatorships and totalitarian governments are benevolent toward their citizens, which has not been proven to be the case over time, with corruption and suppression usually resulting when a government becomes a kleptocracy."

"A government ruled by corrupt politicians who use their political power to receive kickbacks, bribes, and special favors at the expense of the populace," President Milosevic said without hesitation.

"Yes. That is the quickest way to stifle a country's economic growth potential and status in the world."

Milosevic pondered a moment then said, "Russia's government is a democratic, federative law-based state divided among the legislative, executive, and judicial branches . . .

"No disrespect, Mr. President," Victor interrupted, "but Russia's constitution was usurped the past twenty-two years by a president who did not want to give up power. But again, the issue in my opinion is not the type of government Russia, or any country has. Rather it's how well that country ensures the wellbeing of its population and grows its middle class. A benevolent dictator . . . that's probably okay. The problem with a dictatorial or autocratic governments however is they typically soon become not so benevolent."

"What about communism?" Milosevic asked.

"The same rules apply. China is ruled as a communist state. They do have elections though there are restrictions on who can seek office within their single party system. China also learned from the disastrous era of Mao Zedong. They evolved and learned that embracing capitalism would lead to significant economic growth and social benefits for its people. Is China perfect when it comes to being benevolent toward its citizens . . . hardly. Likewise for democratic governments."

"There is a problem with democracy?" Milosevic asked, not expecting this comment.

"No system of government is perfect," Mr. President. "Since governments are made up of human beings and are often lead by politicians who seek to satisfy their own self-interest rather than those interests that best serves its citizens, over time any government can be successful or fail miserably when it comes to long term growth and stability. The United States came to the aide of China to defeat an imperial Japanese government only to turn on the U.S. and embrace communism and Mao Zedong's revolution. That action ultimately stifled China's growth potential. Chinese leadership eventually learned and relinquished total control of its populous which enabled its economy to grow exponentially. Yet today, even though growth has continued, with the Chinese government now trying to increase its control over a large portion of its indigenous ethnic Uyghur population, time will tell if the gains it has made will begin to deteriorate with its attempts to control a large Muslim population, another perceived boogeyman in this instance."

"China may be justified in controlling its Muslim population," Milosevic said.

"Similar to how Russia has been guarding against the next Hitler for the past eighty years only to squander the economic growth and wealth it could have achieved had it not done so. Mr. President don't get me wrong, there are fanatical religious Muslims that do need to be dealt with. However, fanaticism can be found in all religious dominations and it's not synonymous with just religions.

Take the U.S. for example. Many people in the U.S. are still fighting its Civil War and want to return to the 1950s when men dominated women and people of color believing they are still second-class citizens. Then more recently there are QAnon believers and far-right agitators who are causing havoc trying to suppress the right to vote and the democratic process.

No, Mr. President, all countries and all government systems face challenges. And if you look closely, more often than not all countries face very similar challenges if not exactly the same ones. How nice it would be, and certainly more productive it would be, if countries would work together to address the common challenges they *all* face."

Victor paused a moment and as Natalia Smirnov began to speak. President Milosevic held up his hand. "Natalie, I have a pretty good idea what Mr. Petrova's outside-of-the-box thinking is but let's see what he thinks the next steps should be."

"The next steps, Mr. President. It's relatively straight forward. Russia, China, Iran, North Korea, and the United States all suffered a loss when John Gordon took control of those U.S. subs and launched cruise missiles that killed the presidents and senior officials from these countries. Every country is now dealing with the fall out of John Gordon's actions, as well as their own internal troubles and anxieties they have been dealing with for a very long time . . . focusing on the trees around them and not seeing the forest they are a part of."

"We should hold a meeting?"

"Yes sir. Start small and see where it leads. As a suggestion, perhaps an initial meeting between Foreign Minster Popov and U.S. Secretary of State Bentley. Then, if the dialogue shows promise, a meeting between you and President Stephen. From these discussions, ultimately the dialogue should move to a G5 Summit."

"Hmm, Group of 5 Summit." Milosevic said. "Discuss and iron out all the issues our countries have been dealing with the past seventy years or so."

"That would be utopia, but at least a G5 Summit would be a start, Mr. President. World War III was averted this time, but what about the next time?"

"No pushing democracy?"

"It will not be a part of the discussion."

"I suppose you have a word for this program of yours."

"In fact I do. I would call it CIPC . . . Cooperation, Inclusion, and Peaceful Coexistence."

Milosevic smiled. A well thought out objective that Petrova and his friend Lawson probably conceived. But an objective that he could certainly use given his current circumstances. "Okay, Mr. Petrova, we will take the first step and see how it plays out. Nikita, make a call to Secretary Bentley. Mention CIPC and set up a meeting. I would be surprised if he wasn't expecting your call."

Chapter 17

"Good morning, Tom, "Sarah said, taking a chair across from Lawson's desk while doing her best to stifle a yawn.

"Still haven't caught up on your sleep yet, huh?."

"I would need a month at least for that, Tom. But I did catch up a little last night. John and I were communicating off and on the last few days, reviewing and modifying his software. Before that, it took me a couple days to get up to speed on the new language John basically invented."

"He does tend to do that, decides that he can design a better mousetrap."

"Tell me about it. In a matter of a couple of days he and I, mostly him of course, modified his artificial neurons that are capable of mimicking the function of organic brain cells to function as malware that can be imbedded in computers and networks. Very scary if this technology was ever to get in the wrong hands."

"The reason we need to make sure that it never does," I said.

Sarah was quiet for a moment. "You were worried this might happen."

"That John could modify his code and it would outperform any malware the most brilliant hackers in the world could develop? Yes, I was afraid that might be the case."

"So . . . I'm a little confused. Are you saying we shouldn't use John's code?"

"No, we need to use his code to better identify traffic from individuals who want to scuttle the CIPC program. But we also need to make sure that the modified code you and John are developing is never discovered, and certainly never copied."

"You don't want anyone in the NSA to know of its existence?"

"The NSA or anyone else. If this code becomes known by anyone, it will only be a matter of time before it finds its way into the hands of those who could cause immense harm."

"Cybercrimes on steroids."

"Yes. We can't let that happen, Sarah."

After a deer in the headlight stare, Sarah considering the implications for the NSA and for herself, she leaned forward. "I don't know that we can do that, Tom," she whispered. "Ron Wainscott, General Bradley, they're my bosses, Tom. I need to at least tell them."

How should I handle Sarah's concerns, I thought, looking at the tired woman sitting across from me. Somehow, I needed to convince her that we could not do this. And if I couldn't convince her, what chance did I have in persuading her not to divulge the fact that even though John was an extremely intelligent AI entity that almost caused World War III, he was rehabilitated, and his existence must remain a secret.

Finally I took a breadth and said, "what would be the benefit gained in telling Ron and the General?"

"The benefit? . . . . ah, other than they are both my bosses and I could be in serious trouble if I inserted unauthorized code into the NSA computing environment? It's the ethical and right thing to do! And I would keep my job!"

Here it was, our first attempt to expand our secret society. Were we naive to think we would be able to convince Sarah or anyone to perform illegal acts without full disclosure? And even if all the facts were presented, would they fall in line and do what our small group believed was necessary, that total secrecy was paramount, that life as we knew it was in the balance if John's existence became known?

Finally I said, "John called me early this morning. He said he reviewed your latest code changes and said it was very good. Not perfect but very good . . . "

"Of course," Sarah interrupted.

World Peace: Tom Lawson Novel #4
By James Brown

"He said he will send you a final version today. He also said the code would never be detected once downloaded. It was self-protecting . . . his words."

Her eyes reflected the internal struggle she was trying to confront, I said, "Listen, Sarah, if it will help, I can set up a meeting with President Stephen."

The wide-eyed, deer-in-the-headlight stare returned. "The President? You said we can't tell my bosses, but we can let the president in on the secret?"

"Ah, not exactly. We wouldn't tell the president either. We would just meet with him."

"Tom, this is crazy," Sarah said, standing and pacing about the office. "What would you possibly tell the president? Would he even agree to a meeting?"

I leaned back in my chair. "You remember the dinner party with the president. As you may recall, you were having a conversation with Diana when the president and I came back into the room. The reason I wasn't with Diana at the time is that Andrew Kennedy said the president wanted to meet with me in private before the rest of the guests arrived."

"I didn't know that." Sarah said, taking her seat again. "Why did he want to meet with you?"

"He wanted to know if I trusted him."

"Trust him? He's the president."

"That's what I said. And he went on to say one day perhaps he will have earned my trust, that trust needed to be earned and not assumed."

"What else did he say?"

"He told me that until he earned my trust, I should do what I believed was necessary, working with those individuals whom I did trust to ensure the CIPC program was successful."

Sarah was silent for a moment then said, "he said that?"

"He did. Do what I thought was necessary to ensure the CIPC program was a success working with the people I trusted."

"But Tom, he's the president? How can you not trust him?"

"In time I probably will. The president said politicians and occasionally even presidents have not always been trustworthy, that self-interests often cloud their judgement. Listen, I've never worked with General Goldman or Ron Wainscott before. They are probably very upstanding individuals, but I don't know them. I'm taking the president at his word. Do what I think is best working with the people I trust to ensure his CIPC program is a success. Is what I'm asking normal? No. It's not. But I have a very good reason for not conforming to standard protocol when it comes to being a part of President Stephen's administrative team."

"Work with the people you trust."

"Yes, exactly what President Stephen has directed me to do."

"Interesting . . . if I may ask, who might those trusted individuals be?"

"You've met them. A couple you know and a few whom you are just getting to know, Sam Wainwright, Savannah Lee, my wife Diana, and Doctor John Davidson."

Sarah sat up straighter and whispered, "the people who helped save the world. What about Father Dan Thomas?"

"I hope to introduce him to you."

Finally, after a few moments, Sarah said, "okay, Tom. A pretty prestigious group. I'll speak with John this evening and assuming there are no issues with the code we will move forward and upload it into the NSA system."

"Thank you, Sarah," I said as we both stood. "This is a critical step, one that will help insure the president's CIPC program is a success."

"Okay, Tom," she said as we walked toward my office door. "And I do want to meet Father Dan."

* * * *

After the meeting with Sarah and several phone calls, including a call to Diana, I had just enough time to drive to Langley for the ten a.m. status call with Victor Petrova. I knew that Victor's meeting with Andrey Milosevic, Russia's president, went well since Victor sent me an early morning text at three-thirty a.m. Fortunately as an advisor to the president, I was allowed to park underneath the executive office building on 17th street, just a half a block from the White House and I would just make it in time for the meeting.

The CIA headquarters is a massive office building located in Langley, Virginia where almost all domestic and foreign CIA operations are directed and coordinated. The drive during late morning rush hour to Langley took thirty minutes.

Going through security and arriving at Director Keen's office a little before ten, I took a seat next to Sam Wainwright a few minutes before Victor Petrova's call."

"Cutting it a bit close, eh Tom?"

"A busy morning and a difficult discussion with one of our candidates," I said. Sam knew about my meeting with Sarah Pope and the discussion would likely be challenging."

"How did it go?" Sam asked quietly. He did not want his conversation with Lawson overheard by Director Keen and Maddi Pool, who appeared deep in their own conversation while waiting for Petrova's call. He could not afford to arouse their curiosity.

"Started off with a concern that I wouldn't be able to pull it off, but it got better. The candidate is willing to take the first step."

"That's great, Tom. We needed a first step to be taken. I certainly need it," Sam said with a wide smile and a look of relief.

At ten a.m. Petrova appeared on Keen's monitor.

"Victor, a very good afternoon to you. We all received your text. It sounds like you hit it out of the park," Director Keen said.

"The talking points you provided were very good, Director Keen. I'm hopeful President Milosevic will consider a different path than Putin followed the last twenty-two years. And, of course, he was intrigued with the notion that success could be achieved regardless of the governmental structure in place."

"Provided the best interests of the people are taken into account," Director Keen said.

"Yes. He got the message. He finally understood the forest and trees idiom, that Russia has spent the past seventy-five years focusing on threats that were no longer real and thus caused unnecessary conflicts and policies stifling Russia's economic growth."

"You did very well, Victor. An hour ago the Russian Minister of Foreign Affairs called the State Department."

"Were Nikita Popov and Secretary Bentley able to connect?" Victor asked.

"The secretary is in Japan with the President and Defense Secretary Floyd. They will be back in Washinton on Thursday. I was told a meeting is being scheduled for the middle of next week in Reykjavik, Iceland."

"That's a good sign, Director Keen."

"A very good sign, Victor. And let's drop the Director title. You are part of the inner circle now, Victor and deserve to be on a first name basis with me and the team here," Angela Keen said.

"Thank you . . . Angela."

"We haven't heard who the attendees will be other than Secretary Bentley and his Deputy, Barbara Shirley from our team. My guess it will be a relatively small group for this first meeting, Angela said.

"It was a small group meeting with President Milosevic so that would make sense also. From what Vadim Ivanov has told me Milosevic is being bombarded from all sides with Maxim Abramov and his FSB group pressing to unleash the red army to put down the dissent."

"I expected nothing less, Victor," Keen said and turned to the other meeting attendees. "Does anyone else have any comments or questions?"

"Nothing on my part other than to congratulate Victor on a great job." I said.

"Ditto that," Sam and Maddi responded.

"Okay, then. Victor, let us know when you learn who will attend the Reykjavik meeting. And if I hear anything, I'll let you know. If anything critical comes up, call me immediately . . . anytime."

"Will do, Angela," Victor said and ended the connection.

Keen looked across the table with a wide smile. "Two out of four, a very good start for the president's CIPC program. Now we need Iran and North Korea. Where do we stand?" Angela asked.

"Obviously we are hoping Huan Cheng will help us with North Korea, but we aren't taking any chances," Keen's Ops Director Maddi Pool said. "Won Min-ho will meet with Kim Kyung-mi on Thursday. We're preparing a similar talking paper for Won that we did for Ah Lam Zing and Victor. I have a call scheduled with Min-ho this evening."

"Okay, excellent, Maddi. How about Iran?" Keen asked.

"That's our biggest challenge," Maddi answered. "Tom, you had a session with Sarah Pope this morning. How is she and the NSA doing with intercepts from Iran?"

"Making progress. She told me they're tracking intercepts associate with the death of Ebram Janati, the cleric who supposedly died of a heart attack which many think is suspect. If we can provide evidence that the Revolutionary Guard was involved it may provide the spark to move us forward with Iran's new President, Amir Hosseini. Similar with the clerics that compose the 86-member Assembly of Experts who are tasked with anointing the next supreme leader."

"That may be to our advantage," Keen said. "When will Pope have more information?"

"Possibly as early as tomorrow."

"Okay, thanks, Tom. Keep working with Sarah Pope and give me an update as soon as new information is gathered."

The meeting ended and Maddi returned to her office in the CIA building and Sam, and I headed out.

"Do you want a ride back to FBI headquarters or is your chauffeur waiting to take you back?" I asked.

"I assumed you would drive over from the White House, so I told my driver to head back to headquarters. Thirty minutes of private time for us," Sam said.

"Good thinking," I said as we headed to the elevator and the parking lot.

When we were In the car heading south on George Washington Memorial Parkway, Sam asked, "the code John and Sarah have been developing, when will it be ready, and will it work?"

"It's John's code, Sam. Of course it will work. He called me early this morning. He's sending Sarah a new code drop today and they have a call scheduled this evening. He told me once the code is loaded no one will be able to detect it. Nobody will know of its existence."

"When will it be loaded?"

"Probably early tomorrow morning."

"And Sarah? How were you able to convince her?"

"Not easily," I said as traffic picked up and we slowed, Sam doing his innate FBI surveillance routine of the vehicles and their occupants coming close to our car. "She had normal trepidation, wanting to let her bosses, Ron Wainscott and General Goldman, know about a new code drop."

"Understandable. How did you convince her to keep it a secret from everyone?"

"Well, fortunately she's held quite a few video conference sessions with Doctor John Davidson."

"Oh, that's good."

"She recognizes the genius that he is and over the short period of time they worked together she fortunately connected with him on a personal level. Then, I told her about the private meeting I had with the president, and that he told me to do what I thought necessary using the people I trusted to make the CIPC program a success. She asked who the people were, and I told her the five of us."

"But she still doesn't know who John really is does she?"

"Not yet. That will be phase two. We need her to grow her relationship with John and the rest of our team. By the way, she said she wanted to meet Father Dan."

"That's great. The padre will be a definite asset in helping her to see the benefit of what we have undertaken and the need for secrecy."

"Fingers crossed," I said, as we exited the parkway onto I-66 East toward US-50 East in the direction of Constitution Avenue to downtown Washington. A few minutes later I turned on 12th street and made the loop to 10th street to FBI headquarters.

"Thanks, Tom. Keep me posted on the software drop," Sam said before exiting the car."

"Will do. It will probably be loaded early tomorrow morning. I'll let you know."

"Okay, thanks."

I watched as Sam walked toward the FBI headquarters' entrance as a half dozen men in dark blue suits along with three women wearing blazers rushed to catch up with him. Sam and the group paused for a few moments outside the building's entrance as Sam was bombarded with questions from all sides. I grinned as I could only imagine what was going though Sam's mind . . . *why did I take this job? I could be retired and fishing from my boat on the lake right now.* He looked away from the crowd toward my car. I had the window down and was mimicking a fishing pole being cast and a fish being reeled in. He nodded and shrugged then turned back to the crowd surrounding him.

World Peace: Tom Lawson Novel #4
By James Brown

* * * *

It was Tuesday evening and Sarah Pope once again was sitting at her desk in the den of her home office watching the seconds tick off on her digital clock. As the dials turned to exactly 8:00 p.m. the video conference connection was activated, and Doctor John Davidson appeared. He was wearing a white shirt, navy blue trousers, and navy and red multi-striped necktie and sat in a motorized wheelchair. With a wide smile on his face, he said, "good evening, Sarah. You look much more rested this evening. And with this latest code revision I believe you will no longer need to burn the midnight oil so often."

"I hope that's the case, John, and yes I have gotten a little more sleep the last couple of days. By the way, you look quite dashing. A date if I can hope that is the case."

"A date? No, not exactly. But I did participate in a group video conference earlier this evening with several of my academic colleagues with whom I also work. It keeps me busy and connected."

"I'm glad to hear that, John. You have a great deal to offer and I'm sure your colleagues are appreciative and grateful for your participation in those conferences and discussions you have with them. Probably highly complex topics, I would guess."

"Yes, thank you. A broad number of topics for sure."

"Including neurosurgery and helping paraplegics walk again."

"Ah, young Cody Walker. Yes, I was able to advise Doctor Peggy Landon on occasions. She's a very talented neurosurgeon."

"Don't be too modest, John. What you and Doctor Landon and her team hopefully will accomplish is revolutionary. It will help so many people."

"We each contributed to achieve that objective. We should know in a day or two if the surgery was indeed successful."

"I certainly hope that it will be the case."

"As do I," John said. "Now as for our own successful endeavor. I believe our updated code is perfect. Do you agree?"

"Yes, I've never seen anything like it, and I have a feeling it won't be the last work of genius I will witness as our relationship continues."

"Working with Tom and the team, you mean," John said.

"Yes, Tom and I had a long discussion. He was very concerned that this code might fall into the wrong hands and stressed the need for secrecy. He also mentioned an interesting conversation he had with President Stephen. The president asked to meet him in private and told Tom to do what he thought was necessary to make the CIPC program a success working with the people he trusted."

"It sounds like the president trusts Tom's judgement. Perhaps it's a reflection of their respective experiences, the president's as a politician and Tom's recent experiences."

"Hmm, you're probably right. It's interesting how, during periods of conflict and turmoil, the right people seem to emerge when needed to take charge and manage the state of affairs," Sarah said.

"Yes, that does appear to be the case. The right people surfacing at the right time. Now, as for our code, Tom is absolutely correct. It's imperative that our code remains a secret. Humans, unfortunately, often make decisions based on self-interest rather than what is in the best interest of others. The code must remain secret."

Geniuses must think more abstractly, Sarah thought for a moment with John's reference of humans rather than people. She then said, "I agree, John. I will insert the script we've developed early tomorrow morning."

"Okay. You should be able to get to bed earlier this evening and catch up on the sleep you've been missing. It has been a pleasure working with you, Sarah."

"And you, John."

With goodbyes made, the connection ended.

Chapter 18

Madeline Pool, the CIA Operations Director and known as Maddi, sat at her large desk. It was six a.m. The office was quiet at that hour of the day. Her daily routine began with a morning cup of coffee while reading the President's Daily Brief, or better known as the PDB. Produced by the director of national intelligence, the PDB included a compilation of intelligence gathered from the Central Intelligence Agency, Defense Intelligence Agency, National Security Agency, FBI, Defense Department, Homeland Security and other members of the U.S. Intelligence Community. In the most basic way, the PDB was a highly classified newspaper. Breaking events, news, and major issues that the president needed to be aware of. It was also designed to prepare the president for any of his upcoming meetings and trips.

With the coffee made and settled back at her desk, she spent the first two hours going through the PDB and the emails and reports she was not able to get to the day before. She then moved to the document she had sent to Won Min-ho, the CIPC program talking paper the team prepared for his upcoming meeting with North Korea's President Kim Kyung-mi. It was almost time for her scheduled call with Min-Ho.

At eight a.m. her phone rang. "Hello," she said.

"Justice," came the response. "Iden code Baker, Alpha, Foxtrot, Charlie, Zero, Gamma."

"Identification confirmed. Is the meeting still a go for tomorrow morning?"

"Affirmative," Min-ho said, speaking through his phone's end-to-end encryption app. "I will be meeting with Kim Kyung-mi at eight a.m. Friday morning."

"Do you know who else will be attending?"

"I am told it will be a breakfast meeting. Just me and Kyung-mi."

"Really! That will be perfect if it plays out that way, Min-ho," Maddi said excitedly.

"It will, yes. The country is in turmoil since the death of President Kim Jong-un. Fortunately, a few of her brother's most ardent supporters were also killed by the missile attack caused by John Gordon. Otherwise, Kyung-mi might not have been able to succeed her brother as president. Though her presidency is still very tenuous with the infighting going on."

"Your history with her, Min-ho. You've known her for quite a few years. What's your assessment that she will be able to stay in power?" Maddi asked.

"Well, one thing I can say is that she will definitely fight to stay in power. My father was a close friend of Kim Jong-il, Kyung-mi's father. She and I attended the same private school in North Korea. Kyung-mi comes from a dangerous family of course. She is the youngest child of Kim Jong-il, North Korea's second Supreme Leader.

Her oldest brother, Kim Jong-nam, was the heir apparent to their father but he fell out of favor after embarrassing the regime in 2001 with a failed attempt to visit Tokyo Disneyland with a false passport. Though reported as such, the real reason that he lost favor was that he advocated for reform. He died in 2017 in Malaysia by a North Korea assassin using the nerve agent VX. Kim Jong-un, the second son of Kim Jong-il, became supreme leader upon his father's death instead of his older brother.

Kim Kyung-mi was serving as the Deputy Director of the Publicity and Information Department of the Workers' Party of Korea and was considered as a possible successor to her brother. With that possibility becoming a reality with Jong-un's death she's doing her best to ward off her enemies."

"The information we are getting from our friends in the region is that riots have erupted in many places throughout the country and the army has been deployed," Maddi said.

World Peace: Tom Lawson Novel #4
By James Brown

"Those reports are accurate. My opinion is that Kyung-mi is really a reformer or would like to be, but she has to move slowly. Those who were very close to her brother don't want to lose their status which would likely be the case if a reform government took control."

"It's amazing," Maddi said. "It's okay for a million or more North Korean citizens to die of starvation but don't take away *my* privileges."

"Korea has a very long history, Maddi. Joseon Korea, known as the Chosen, was a Korean dynastic kingdom that lasted for five centuries. It was founded by Yi Seong-gye in 1392 and replaced by the Korean Empire in 1897. During its 500-year duration, Joseon encouraged the entrenchment of Confucian ideals and doctrines in Korean society. In the 1590s, the kingdom was severely weakened due to Japanese invasions. Several decades later, Joseon was invaded by the Jin dynasty and the Qing dynasty leading to an increasingly harsh isolationist policy.

The Joseon period left a substantial legacy to modern Korea. Much of modern Korean culture, etiquette, norms, and societal attitudes towards current issues, along with the modern Korean language and its dialects, derive from the culture and traditions of Joseon."

"You have obviously been well schooled on Korea's history, Min-ho."

"Drilled would be a better word," he said with a satirical tone. "The history lessons didn't end with the Qing dynasty of course. Joseon Korea had come into the Japanese sphere of influence with the Japan–Korea Treaty of 1876. The Korean Empire became a protectorate of Japan with the Japan–Korea Treaty of 1905.

Japanese rule over Korea ended in 1945 upon the Japan's surrender in World War II, and the armed forces of the United States and the Soviet Union occupied this region. The division of Korea separated the Korean Peninsula under two governments and different economic systems with the Soviet Civil Administration governing the north and the United States Army Military Government governing the southern portion of Korea."

"I understand, Min-ho. Centuries of strife and turmoil and government changes have made life very difficult for the Korean people."

"That it has, for many years. Decisions made by the two Korea's could not have been different. North Korea invested heavily in its mining industries and purchased a large quantity of mineral extraction infrastructure from abroad. It also purchased entire petrochemical, textile, concrete, steel, pulp and paper manufacturing plants from the developed capitalist world. However, following the 1973 oil crisis, international prices for many of North Korea's native minerals fell, leaving the country with large debts they were not able to repay. North Korea began to default in 1974.

South Korea, on the other hand was creating new industries based around computers, electronics, and other advanced technology in contrast to North Korea's Stalinist economy of mining and steel production."

"Don't forget the large amount of money the North spent on its military buildup as well," Maddi said. "Then with the collapse of the Soviet Union in 1991 and aid from the Soviet Union no longer available, North Korea's economy went into a free-fall."

"But the cult lived on, Maddi. North Korea withdrew even more. This time information from the outside world was essentially shut off. The isolated, hermit kingdom of the past returned on steroids. Information and teachings were only provided by the Dear Leaders from the Kim dynasty."

"So here we are. An opportunity has surfaced due to John Godon's actions. A large number of autocratic leaders, dictators, and would be autocrats were killed along with several of their close advisors. Given this unique situation, how do we help change the dynamics of the Kim dynasty? Probably wishful thinking that it could become a democratic republic but at a minimum, if Kyung-mi became a benevolent dictator willing to eliminate its nuclear weapons and become a part of the world community, that would be satisfactory. The emphasis on benevolence, with no starving or suppressed populous. How do we do get to that condition, Min-ho? Do you have that kind of influence with Kim Kyung-mi?" Maddi asked.

The connection went silent for several seconds, Min-ho pondering the question. "That's not an easy question, Maddi. I have known Kyung-mi for a very long time. We grew up together and had she not been the daughter of a Kim, who knows. She was married at age twenty-six to the son of a North Korean politician and military officer who served in Kim Jong-un's military."

"Lineage and family pressure is difficult to overcome. What's your sense of the direction Kyung-mi will take with her brother and key aids out of the picture?"

"She and I have always been close. I even like her husband and her three kids are being raised well. They're polite, well mannered, and normal kids so far. And she and I still have a connection. Something, you might say that should have been but could not have been. That sort of thing."

"I understand. I've known a few people whose marital relationships should not have been. One of life's unfortunate circumstances. So, now that Kyung-mi is in power, do you think she will listen to what you have to say?"

"I hope she will. We've had many what-if discussions over the years. I would be very surprised if we did not rekindle those discussions Friday. The issue, I believe, will be the timing and process for implementing beneficial changes. North Korea is a very closed society. It's actually a very large cult, a society that has been brainwashed by a dictatorial ruthless family. With the death of her brother and several of his key aides if there was any chance for change it is now."

"Provided the generals, politicians, and families who have been dependent on the Kim dynasty for their wealth and privilege can be managed. Listen, Min-ho, you know your country and the kind of lives the people have been experiencing under the Kim dynasty. My advice is to take it slowly. We are not naive to think North Korea will immediately embrace democracy, if ever. But we do hope that with new leadership the country will open its doors to the world and focus more on the wellbeing of its citizens rather than weapons of war."

"I hear you, Maddi. One step at a time. I'll know more after my breakfast meeting with Kyung-mi."

"Okay, good luck, Min-ho. Call me as soon as you can after your meeting."

"Will do," Min-ho said and disconnected the call.

* * * *

Sarah Pope arrived at her office in the NSA building at seven Wednesday morning. It was her typical arrival time and she proceeded through security and said good morning to Charles, one of the building's many security officers. Proceeding on to her office she stopped and chatted with several members of her staff, offering good mornings and discussing work related topics and stopped to listen to a father describe his daughter's winning goal at her soccer match. A normal morning, or at least the kind of morning she wanted everyone to believe it was.

But of course it was anything but normal. Sarah Pope was about to step across a line she never thought she would do, install an unauthorized software program into the NSA's computer system. The reason for her pending action was trust. She came to trust and believe that the small group of people who helped prevent World War III from occurring did indeed have the tacit backing of the President of the United States, that the program created by a unique genius would cause irreparable harm if it fell into the wrong hands, and by loading the program it would enable the NSA to gather information critical to the success of the president's CIPC program initiative and reduce global conflicts.

Reaching her office, Alisa, her executive assistant was already at her desk. "You have ten voice messages and Ron has pushed back your meeting with him to eight-thirty," she said and handed her a list with the names of the callers.

"Thank you, Alisa. That's good. Hold my calls for the next hour unless Ron, the General, or the president calls."

"Will do."

In her office she put her purse and coffee on her desk and perused the call summary list from Lisa. Nothing critical that can't wait she thought and powered up her computer.

Seated, she reached for her purse and pulled out a zip drive. She held it up and looked at it for a moment as she took a drink of coffee. After her computer booted, she took a breath and inserted the drive. She watched as the autoload program initiated the software download. In exactly twenty seconds the software was loaded and an autoload confirmation check was initiated. Once confirmed, the file on the thumb drive was permanently erased. Doctor John Davidson's worm was now installed, and the NSA's surveillance system and intelligence acquisition process would begin an automated upgrade cycle. Over the next days and weeks John's AI auto learning spyware was programmed to incrementally increase the data surveillance and intelligence gathering capabilities of the NSA's surveillance system. Subtle improvements in data accuracy and surveillance penetration capabilities would begin to substantially increase the threat findings uncovered by NSA analysts and provide significantly enhanced signals intelligence capabilities, capturing communications between people or from electronic sources.

"By Friday at the latest," Sarah whispered aloud and taking another drink of coffee. "We will have the evidence, Ebram. We will know why you died and if you were murdered, your death will be avenged." She then picked up her cell phone and opened a newly installed encryption app developed by John. She typed 'installed' and sent it to Doctor John Davidson and Tom Lawson. Following this, she used the telephone on her desk and began returning calls to her early morning callers.

World Peace: Tom Lawson Novel #4
By James Brown

Chapter 19

It was mid-morning on Wednesday as Doctors Peggy Landon and Sandeep Singh made another visit to Cody Walker's recovery room at Yale New Haven Hospital. It had been a week since Cody Walker's revolutionary surgery and artificial neurons were implanted to replace damaged cells that were preventing signals from his brain to communicate with his lower body. Checking Cody's vitals daily, the surgery induced swelling was gradually subsiding.

"Hello, Cody. How are you feeling this morning?" Doctor Landon asked.

"Pretty good, Doctor Landon. My toes, I can wiggle them."

Eugene and Carole Walker standing on the opposite of Cody's bed smiled broadly. "That's very good, isn't it?" Carole asked.

"Yes, very good," Doctor Singh said as he removed the bedding from Cody's feet and lower parts of his legs. "I'd like you to close your eyes now, Cody and tell me what you feel."

As Doctor Singh held a large needle ready to probe Cody's lower extremities, Eugene and Carole embraced tightly in anticipation as Doctor Singh started the test with the bottom of Cody's feet.

"I feel that." Cody said as he flexed his left foot with Doctor Singh's pin prick. "That too," Cody said, flexing his right foot with the second pin prick.

"Excellent," Doctor Singh side. He looked over at Carole and Eugene and nodded. He then reached up and pricked Cody's left gastrocnemius calf muscle.

"Ouch. Feel that, Doctor Singh," Cody said, tightening his eyes.

Doctor Singh continued his pin prick tests moving up and along portions of Cody's legs with Cody responding to each of the pricks while keeping his eyes closed. His parents beamed as their son repeatedly said ouch as Doctor Singh pricked Cody's legs. Finally Doctor Singh pulled the bed sheet back down over Cody's feet.

"Next step, Cody physical therapy," he said looking between Cody and his parents.

Carole Walker leaned in and gave her son a long hug.

"With the feeling in Cody's legs responding does this mean he will fully recover?" Eugene asked.

Doctor Landon hesitated a moment then said, "the honest answer is we just don't know, Mr. Walker. Assuming the signals between Cody's brain are able to communicate through the newly implanted artificial neural pathways the answer is yes. Cody's ability to feel pain from the pin pricks is a good sign, a very good sign. The next few days and probably several weeks of physical therapy we will know the level of recovery Cody will experience. A lot of hard work coming up, Cody," he said looking over at Cody.

"Hard work. I'm looking forward to that," Cody said. "As well as one hundred percent recovery."

Doctor Landon patted his arm. "We hope for that too. But one day at a time, Cody. You are unique in having this surgery. Your physical as well as mental wellbeing are both important."

Cody slowly nodded. "I understand. I will be starting from zero, no feelings in my legs so any feelings will be better than where I'm starting from."

"Try your best to become fully recovered, honey but don't despair if you can't recover one hundred percent," his mother said.

"I understand, Mom," Cody said as he wiggled his toes.

"We will initiate your physical therapy starting tomorrow, Cody."

"I look forward to it, Doctor Singh," Cody said with a determined expression on his face.

"Thank you so very much, Doctor Landon, Doctor Singh," Carole said.

"I'll drop by tomorrow, Cody," Doctor Singh said before he and Doctor Landon departed.

In the hallway, walking down the corridor away from Cody's room Peggy held up her fist toward Sandeep who raised his in return and did a fist bump. "Looking good, Sandeep," Peggy said. "Very good indeed."

"It is, but we need to continue to hold Doctor Lazarus off for several more weeks for any scientific articles can even be considered," Sandeep said.

"A couple of months at a minimum, Sandeep," Peggy said. "Even though Cody shows feelings in his feet and legs, is this a natural occurrence or was it the result of our efforts. We assume it is, since William's surgery was a tremendous success, but we need to make sure. The implications are mindboggling. We need to be perfect with our analysis and the facts."

"I agree," Sandeep said. "Two months is about right. We should be ready to present the data to Doctor Lazarus in two months."

"Okay, I'll update Doctor Lazarus after my rounds today. I'll be at the Saybrook office all day tomorrow. Let me know how Cody does with his first physical therapy session."

"Will do," Sandeep said as they parted for the rest of their rounds.

* * * *

Min-ho Won stood for a moment after his taxi dropped him off. He was standing fifty yards from the entrance to the grounds of one of the many palaces of the former president of North Korea. The Ryongsong Residence located in Pyongyang North Korea, known by locals as Central Luxury Mansion, covered an area of four-and-a-half square miles. Built by a construction brigade of the Korean People's Army and completed in 1983, the complex has an underground wartime headquarters protected with walls with iron rods and concrete that is covered with lead in case of a nuclear war. A private underground train station is also inside the residence compound.

Of particular concern for Min-ho, other than the electric fence that surrounds the property, were the mine fields that also protects the estate. It was seven-thirty in the morning. He had a half hour to proceed through the security checks and be escorted to his breakfast meeting with Kim Kyung-mi, the new North Korean President.

Approaching the first checkpoint Min-ho Won held out his identity booklet to one of the two armed guards. As a capital dweller and resident of Pyongyang Min-ho had a Pyongyang resident ID. For migration control, those North Koreans who reside outside of Pyongyang were referred to as outsiders and required a permit to visit the capital. Similar to a country's passport, a person's ID booklet contained the citizen's name, birth date, sex, ethnicity, parents' names, and place of birth. Records of one's residence and photo are also included inside the booklet.

The guard looked through Min-ho's identification document and took a moment to compare the photo to the man standing in front of him.

"Mr. Won, you are scheduled to meet with Kim Kyung-mi."

"Yes. A breakfast meeting at eight a.m."

"Very well," the guard said. "Please proceed to the transport."

Two other armed guards escorted Won to a limousine parked a hundred feet away from the first guard house. One guard opened the rear door and Won entered. The limousine pulled out and drove a half mile to the palace. Upon arriving two additional armed guards met the limo outside the palace and waited as Won exited the vehicle. After once again presenting his ID, he was escorted to the palace's front entrance.

At the door of the palace another armed guard opened the door and again looked at Won's ID. Satisfied, he escorted Won into the palace where he was met by a man dressed in suite and tie. He bowed slightly and shook Won's hand. "This way please," the man said. Won followed his escort along a wide, marbled floor hallway to one of several dining rooms in the mansion.

"Here we are, sir," the escort said opening one of the double doors that opened to a dining room. "President Kim will join you momentarily."

"Thank you," Won said entering the room. The escort closed the door behind him leaving Won alone in the room. Before Kim Kyung-mi became president, prior to her brother's death, Won and his family had joined the Kim family at many social gatherings and parties. Min-ho was always considered a friend of the family ever since he was a child attending the same school as Kyung-mi.

Won Min-ho had been to the palace on a number of occasions to attend various events and Kim family functions but could not remember being in this dining room. Small and more intimate than the other palatial rooms in the palace, a small mahogany dining room table occupied the center of the room. With a seating for eight, two place settings were arranged on the table, one at the head of the table and a second on the side that faced a center fireplace on the opposite wall. A large chandelier hung from the vaulted ceiling thirty feet above the mahogany table.

Heavy burgundy draperies tied back in front of white shears covered three large windows that overlooked a well-tended garden. Throughout the room modern art paintings hung from the walls. A thick multicolored oriental carpet that covered the walnut colored oak flooring cushioned Min-ho's footfalls as he perused the paintings hung throughout the room.

Within ten minutes of being escorted to the dining room, Kim Kyung-mi entered the room.

"Good morning, Madam President," Min-ho said quickly walking to the front of the room. He took her hand and bowed slightly.

Kyung-mi smiled. "You can do better than that, Min-ho," she said reaching up and hugging him.

After a long embrace and separating, Min-ho said, "difficult times and not having fun yet I assume."

Tired eyes looking up at him, Kyung-mi said, "being thrown into the frying pan unexpectedly can do that to a person. Especially here in North Korea where the Dear Leader controlled everything and everyone and he dies suddenly."

"I can only imagine," Min-ho said embracing her again. "How can I help. Anything I can do, I'm at your disposal. Let's sit. You talk and I'll listen," he said walking to the table and pulling back the chair at the head of the table for her. As soon as they were seated a waiter opened the door and pushed in a small cart that carried a teapot and a large carafe of orange juice. Min-ho and Kyung-mi remained silent as their juice glasses were filed and hot tea poured.

"Please buzz when you wish to have your breakfast served or if you need anything else, Madam President."

"Thank you," Do Hyun.

After the waiter left Min-ho said, "I'm sure your days will be better soon. The people will come around. You can hardly be held to account for your brother being murdered."

"It's not the people I'm concerned about. It's the generals, the politicians, and the privileged who have nurtured the Kim dynasty to ensure their status and privilege. You know me better than anyone, Min-ho. I may appear to know what I'm doing but I'm standing at the precipice, one step from the edge if you want to know the truth."

Min-ho reached over and put his hand on hers. "Has Chin-Hae been able to help you?"

"My husband does what he can, but he just doesn't have the experience. Meeting with you, alone especially was a major battle for me."

Min-ho took a sip of tea, thinking whether or not to plunge forward and offer a lifeline? If he did not, what were the chances that a second meeting opportunity would avail him?

"Kyung-mi, I have a suggestion. Since you are wavering at the precipice, I think a bold move might be your best option."

Kyung-mi leaned back. "Bold move? What do you suggest?"

"Well, you are not the only new president who has been thrust into a position that no one in the world had ever imagined would happen. The Presidents of the United States, China, Russia, Iran, and North Korea were murdered at almost the same time on the same day. The murder of Vladimir Putin may have been justified given his country's culpability. But the other presidents, it was a very sad day and is very stressful to many of the new heads of state who have been placed in their new position of power."

"Especially for those who rose up in governments that do not have constitutional succession provisions," Kyung-mi said meekly.

"Especially those, yes."

"So what do you suggest?"

"Well, since this hopefully is a once in a lifetime event, I think a summit would be helpful. Maybe call it a G-5 Summit. A Group of 5 Summit."

Kyung-mi's brow furrowed as she contemplated what Min-ho suggested. "A G-5 Summit, the countries whose presidents were murdered by that John Gordon guy?"

"Yes. You are part of a very unique group. Safety in numbers Kyung-mi. Think about it. The press, the global press will eat this up. A summit with the countries directly affected by John Gordon's actions. Each country reacting to the fallout of this heinous act. The publicity can only help you and keep your enemies at bay. You may also be able to garner some much-needed assistance from the wealthy countries affected, China and the United States at a minimum. Doing so will go a long way to put you in good favor with our people and help quell any further uprising."

"Interesting. Did you hear about this from someone?"

"I did. One of my business contacts in China thinks discussions between China and the U.S. are being planned. I can confirm this and suggest to my contact that the meeting should be expanded to include the other countries affected. Your attendance at this summit would demonstrate your leadership abilities. What about Ji Ah and Joo Lo, your new aides? What have they suggested?"

Kyung-mi made a face. "They're useless. My brother killed their initiative. Take Ji-Ah, she waits for me to make a comment, even a ridiculous one, and she parrots what I've said. Joo Lo does much the same. The difference, he's been around longer so he usually offers a suggestion that is similar to what I've mentioned. Nothing radically different. Lemmings, both of them."

Smiling, Min-ho said, "maybe fear of possible punishment or even death might be what's behind your aides' lack of creativity and original thinking. Your brother did have a few of his aides killed, even a few family members."

"He did, didn't he. I need to change that dynamic. You and I used to discuss how we could improve the lives of our people. Remember?"

"I do. You're the president now, Kyung-mi. You have the power and I think you should use it. If you agree, I'll check with my contact and find out when the meeting will be held. See what can be done to have you attend this session."

Taking a moment, staring at her friend of many years, Kyung-mi finally said, "Do it. Make it happen. You're right. It's up to me now."

"And I will help you in any way possible," Won said.

"Thank you. Let's order our breakfast. I'm suddenly very hungry," Kim Kyung said.

* * * *

A long day with one too many meetings Sarah Pope finally had time to sit at her desk and catch up on unanswered messages. Halfway through her very long list her phone rang. After two more rings, she absentmindedly reached for the phone and said, "Pope," and continued reading the message on her monitor.

"Sorry to bother you, ma'am but the system just alerted on a SIGINT of particular interest."

"Avery!" Pope said, her interest immediately refocused seeing Mark Avery's name displayed. "Was the cryptanalysis able to decipher the message?"

"Yes."

"That's great. Send it to me."

"Already did, ma'am, time 16:00."

Pope immediately scrolled down her list of messages and found Avery's message, opened it and began reading.

"It's done, Mostafa. The cause of death was documented, signed off by Hassan Rajai, the coroner. Heart attack. It will be filed this morning. I've sent you a copy."

"What did the toxicology report show?"

"Nothing, or at least nothing indicating that Ebram Janati was poisoned. In addition to being obese, it was previously reported that he had a heart condition. The report also states that Ebram Janati was ill for two days before he died while he was on a meditative retreat. A flu bug it was thought.

"How extensive was the toxicology testing?"

"Extensive. We wanted to make sure the Guard was not blamed for his death. An analysis of a hundred or so compounds, including alcohol, drugs as cocaine, amphetamines, barbiturates, quaaludes, and poisons. Rajai also ordered detailed tests on a gas chromatograph for the presence of certain metals and other subtle compounds."

"He didn't test for Oleander?"

"No. With eight million compounds on earth, medical examiners at best only test for a few hundred of them and Oleander is not high on the list of common poisons to be tested in a toxicological analysis. Rajai was thorough and went above and beyond a typical autopsy. We are in the clear."

"It was a risk, Omar."

"A risk that was necessary. Hassan Rajai will attest to his findings, that there was no foul play. Ebram Janati was not murdered. Had he discovered that he was, we would have delt with that outcome."

"Peace be upon you," Omar.

"Damn! Excellent Avery. Natural causes my ass. Just what we expected. We now have proof. Ebram Janati was indeed murdered under the direction of the Chief Commander of Iran's Revolutionary Guard, Mostafa Ahmadi. This information will take top billing in the president's PDB tomorrow morning. Excellent job, Avery."

"Thank you, ma'am," Avery said and disconnected.

Pope leaned back in her chair with a wide smile crossing her face. It worked just as Doctor Davidson said it would. NSA's intelligence surveillance system and intelligence acquisition process were beginning to uncover threat findings never before possible. The bad guys would no longer be able to hide in the digital world we now lived. She sent out a secured message to Tom Lawson and John. Got them, it read.

World Peace: Tom Lawson Novel #4
By James Brown

Chapter 20

Spring, a wonderful time of the year I thought as I walked slowly from the White House grounds around the US Treasury building to Pennsylvania Avenue. As I walked and the fragrance of flowers filled the air my thoughts began to wander from the pressures of the day. It was early evening, and I was meeting Savannah and Sam for dinner. I tried to think how many times we had met at Old Ebbitt Grill, but it was just too many. The Grill was a convenient meeting place within walking distance for the three of us, who worked in Washington and was beginning to feel more like our own family dining room.

I entered the Grill and was met by Wilson.

"Good evening, Wilson. Have my friends arrived?" I asked.

"Director Wainwright has but Ms. Lee has not. Probably still working on the finishing touches to her new blockbuster story at the Post."

"Probably, Wilson. Do you want to lead the way to our table, or can I wander on back?"

"It is my pleasure to escort you to your table, sir."

No matter how many times we'd eaten at the Grill, Wilson always followed protocol as maître d' and would never let any guest walk unaccompanied to their table. The Old Ebbitt's Grill had a long history going back to the days of Ulysses S. Grant when he frequented the Grill. Wilson was a fixture who intended to keep tradition. He knew all his regulars by name and where they worked.

For those regulars who were considered "long timers," he knew the names of their spouses, the number of children they had, and anecdotes from their personal lives. Our group was moving toward becoming members of the "long timers." The Grill was Wilson's life and passion.

As we reached our table, I said, "Wilson, when Ms. Lee arrives, late yet again, maybe you should tease her that we're all worried she will be late for her own wedding."

"I'm sure that won't be necessary, Mr. Lawson. Ms. Lee will be punctual for that joyous occasion, I'm sure."

"Oh, I don't know, Wilson. When she's immersed in one of her headline grabbing stories, who knows, perhaps her next Pulitzer, absolutely nothing will prevent her from meeting a deadline."

Wilson patted my shoulder and winked. "I think you'll know when one of those stories are surfacing and will get her to the church on time, Mr. Lawson."

"Probably right, Wilson."

"Talking about Savannah, I assume," Sam Wainwright said as I moved into the booth opposite him.

"We were. I was telling Wilson that if Savannah was engrossed in a potential headline story of Pulitzer caliber, she would likely be late to her wedding."

"No doubt but the next thirty days look good. Nothing will break by then."

"Did you read my message?" I asked.

"I did. Thank you very much. I'm off the hook now. The NSA will find all those bad guys on their own without my help."

"Thank John, you mean."

"Of course. John. He came through again. My life will be a little easier now. Did you speak with Sarah?"

"Speak with Sarah about what?" Savannah Lee asked as she signaled me to move over in the booth.

"She wasn't too late, Mr. Lawson," Wilson said having escorted Savannah to the table. "Drinks for everyone?"

Yes, thank you, Wilson," I said, as I gave Savannah a quick hug and she fist bumped Sam.

"It's been a little more than three weeks since we've gotten together. I feel so left out. Not like our last adventures," Savannah said with a noticeable frown.

"You're right. It is different this time, at least the timing of the events that are taking place," Sam offered. "The CIPC team that

Director Keen was tasked by the president to head up is starting to make progress though."

"Which countries?" Savannah asked.

"Contacts have been made with Russia and China and we should be hearing from our North Korea agent tonight or tomorrow. Our agent is scheduled to meet with President Kim Kyung-mi."

"That's great. Positive results?" Savannah asked.

"China and Russia, yes. We should know tomorrow about North Korea," Sam answered.

"How about Iran?"

"Very good news," I said. "Sarah Pope is on board working with Doctor John Davidson. She met with him in his wheelchaired genius persona, and they worked together to modify John's artificial neuron technology to function as malware that can be imbedded in computers and networks. She and I met several times, and I was able to convince her that our team, including you and Diana by the way, has the tacit approval of the president to do what we deem necessary to ensure his CIPC program is a success."

"And she believed you? Savannah asked.

"I offered to set up a meeting with the president, and the three of us, which certainly helped. And then there's John. He needs to be given most of the credit. How can you not love or believe John?"

Savannah smiled. "Very true. So she loaded John's software into the NSA system?"

"She did. On Wednesday. This afternoon we got a hit. A voice recording of a revolutionary guard operative by the name of Omar. Ebram Janati was poisoned. Omar spiked Janati's drink with Oleander which is a poison that's not typically screened for in toxicology tests. We also have Mostafa Ahmadi on the recording."

"Impressive," Savannah said. "The Chief Commander of Iran's Revolutionary Guard. That will certainly help to sway Amir Hosseini, Iran's new president."

"It certainly will," Sam said.

The conversation paused while Wilson served their drinks. Tom took a call from Maddi Pool.

"Hello, Maddi," Tom said softly. "Good news?"

World Peace: Tom Lawson Novel #4
By James Brown

"Great news, Tom," Pool answered. "I just received a call from Won. He said Kim Kyung-mi agreed to move forward and discuss his being part of a G-5 Summit."

That's great, Maddi. Well done and great timing with our upcoming meeting with the president Friday morning."

"Yes indeed. Won came through and the NSA got a hit on a conversation held by the Revolutionary Guard Chief that confirms they murdered Ebram Janati. A very good day."

"Indeed it was. Thanks for the call, Maddi. See you tomorrow," Tom said and disconnected.

"Did Won come through?" Sam asked.

"He did. Batting a thousand so far. Let's just hope we continue with that success," Tom said. "Did you order? I'm starving."

"We did. Thought your call might be a long one," Savannah said. "But don't worry. I ordered for you, filet mignon, baked potato and asparagus."

"Hmm, nice. Thank you, Savannah. This is a very good day. And speaking of good days how are you and Barry doing? The big day is coming up soon."

"We should elope. Wedding planning and preparation is a pain."

"How's your mom and dad doing, are they getting to know Barry and I assume they like him."

Savannah's eyes brightened. "I'm pleasantly surprised. I expected big arguments, given the Lee name and lineage. At least from my father but maybe, hopefully anyway, the Civil War is finally fading away. My dad has actually met Barry for dinner on several occasions now. Alone. I thought it would take years for that to happen. So yes, I'm pleasantly surprised that the family dynamics have gone very well. The rest, well, it is what it is. I finally asked my mom to take over the wedding planning stuff and she has. I just don't have time. Oh, by the way, Tom, I called Diana today and asked her to be one of the bridesmaids. There will be four bridesmaids, Diana, two of my cousins, and my co-worker, Cheryl Ellis.

You know Cheryl and Diana, two of my bridesmaids. But my other two, my cousins, it should be interesting," Savannah said as Wilson began serving the house salads.

"What have you done, Savannah?" Sam asked.

Savannah took a moment. "I was thinking of you, Sam when I asked my cousin Jane to be one of my bridesmaids," she teased.

"A bit of matchmaking . . . hmm . . . what makes you think I won't bring a date?" Sam asked.

"You won't. I know you too well now, Sam . . . divorced and set in your ways. But you're getting up there in age. You need someone to grow old with. Oh, and I ran it by Carrie first by the way. She agrees completely."

Sam stared at Savannah for a moment then turned toward Tom. "Did you know anything about this?"

"First I'm hearing about it. Though I agree with Savannah that it would be nice if you were able to have a person to share that boat with you."

"Oh, Jane would love that!" Savannah said. "She's my older cousin, Jane Wyatt. She's probably five years younger than you, Sam. You're what fifty-four? Cheryl's forty-nine. Her husband died three years ago. She has two kids in their early twenties, boy and a girl. Twins, by the way."

Sam slowly shook his head.

"Jane lives in Atlanta but she's renting a place in Washington. Penelope, her daughter, is attending Georgetown for a master's degree in international studies. Jane is loaded by the way. A really good person and a great catch for you, Sam. You'll like her."

"Why isn't your other cousin in the running for Sam's attention?" I asked.

Savannah laughed and pushed her salad plate to the side. Oil and water. No way. She's a racist."

"A racist! You're kidding. And you invited her to your wedding?" I asked.

"Priscilla Beauregard, also a Lee and a diehard southern rebel."

"She doesn't know, does she," I said.

"Very astute, Tom. No she doesn't. Not yet anyway. As a first cousin, Priscilla was always at family functions spewing her disgust at the various new privileges being bestowed on the offspring of distant family slaves. And she's changed little since those early gatherings. Anyway, I thought it would be a hoot to have her standing center stage next to me and Barry."

"Sam laughed. Should be an exciting event, Savannah. You sure I wasn't invited to be your bodyguard?"

"It did cross my mind, Sam. A side benefit to be sure, but you were always on the invite list, along with Tom and Diana. And, of course, Father Dan, who will officiate. It should be great fun."

"Probably not for cousin, Priscilla," I offered.

Wilson and one of his waiters were back at the table to clear the salad plates and serve the main course. It was pushing eight in the evening, and we were all hungry. No one spoke for several minutes as our steaks, fish, and potatoes were devoured rather quickly. Finally, Savannah said, "so what's next?"

"A status meeting with President Stephen tomorrow morning at ten," I answered. "I expect it to be a good session. Secretary's Bentley and Tinsley seem to have had productive meetings in Japan this week and that is also good news."

"So we were told at the White House Daily Briefing today. Press Secretary Jan Polaski provided us with considerable detail. Nothing mentioned about the president's CIPC program though. So far, there are no leaks on that initiative," Savannah said.

"We hope to keep it that way as long as possible," I said.

"If a G-5 meeting actually takes place and agreement is reached, you think Stephen will agree to cut the defense budget, don't you?"

I took a last bite of filet mignon then reached for my glass of merlot. "That has been discussed, Savannah. A bargaining chip as an incentive to secure an agreement. Something that would likely be required by China, Russia, North Korea, and Iran if they are going to agree to the program. What has your team heard? Anything?" I asked.

"So far no leaks about the president's initiative, or a potential cut in the defense budget," Savannah said. "But it will definitely leak . . . it's Washington after all. What size of cut is Stephen thinking?"

"Well, given the U.S. defense budget is two-and-a-half times higher than China and ten times the size of Russia's defense budget I would be surprised if the president had a choice but to offer a sizable cut in our defense budget."

"You know he's going to get a lot of pushback," Savannah said. "The military-industrial complex will not take this lightly, or the Republican Party."

"The rest of the country will embrace it. The World also. You don't think almost having the world destroyed might open people's minds? That spending an ungodly amount of money on one more aircraft carrier, spending billions of dollars on additional super-fast jets, or even worse, expending billions on AI piloted drones is a better use of our taxpayer's dollars?"

"That would seem logical, Tom, except for those filthy rich defense industry CEOs and their shareholders and the thousands of employees who will lose their jobs. They are not going to support the president's CIPC program."

"I know, Savannah. Winners and losers. But the planet will be much safer, and more people will support the president than not," I countered.

"Remember what John always says, Pollyanna thinking, about how we often want to believe the good in humans will ultimately prevail. It didn't work out that way with the sociopathic president we had and his seventy million followers who drank his Kool-Aid," Savannah said raising her cup toward Wilson and mouthing *coffee*.

Sam looked across the table at me and shrugged.

"All good points, Savannah, and the reason you have been held in reserve. Our secret weapon, you, Somerville and the rest of your investigative reporters and analysts. Political and policy disagreement fine. But as soon as you and your team get any inkling the fight is no longer fair we bring on board our super weapon."

"John."

"Right, John. We will have John do his AI genius thing."

"The NSA will also be better able to identify foreign and maybe even domestic interference with John's advanced surveillance capabilities Sarah downloaded to the NSA system," Sam added.

"Right, between John and your team, Savannah, it should be a fair fight. How's Amy Apple, that new reporter you hired, doing by the way?"

"Interesting you asked. She's doing very well. She's me fifteen years ago. It's uncanny."

"Another Savannah Lee?" Sam said. "I'm not sure the country is ready for that. The Post's competitors anyway."

Savannah smiled. "It's part of the plan, remember? We need to groom new members for our secret society. Barry and Amy, I think will fit in very nicely."

"Sarah Pope too," I said. "By the way, Savannah she doesn't know who John really is yet, but in time I think she will be ready to learn the truth and will fully embrace our objectives and join the team."

"Okay, guys. Thank you for the updates. I'll have my team poke around and keep their ears open for any leaks or grumblings. I have an early morning meeting tomorrow. Let's do this again soon."

"I'm leaving tomorrow for Connecticut after the meeting with the president. I will probably be back on Tuesday, so Thursday or Friday next week I'm free for another dinner meeting. Activities are going to be picking up," I said.

"Sounds like a plan," Sam said as we slid out of our booth. After hugs all around, we filed out of the Grill with Wilson leading the way.

* * * *

Sam arrived fifteen minutes before our ten a.m. CIPC status meeting with the president. He made himself a cup of coffee and milled about my office while I was on the phone.

When I ended my call, he said, "what do you think about Savannah's cousin and me being set up?"

I laughed. What do I think? I think it's great. You need a little balance in your life. Come on, we can't be late for the meeting."

"I'm too old for this," he mumbled as he followed me out of the office.

"Like Savannah said, it's nice to have someone to share time with as you get older and probably more crochety."

We took the stairs and stood outside the Oval Office as President Stephen was finishing an earlier meeting. At precisely ten a.m. his office door opened, and Secretary of Defense Floyd Tinsley walked out.

"Morning Sam, Tom. Next up," he said walking briskly past us and headed out of the White House. As he walked out, he spoke briefly with Angela Keen and Maddi Pool as they were making their way to the oval office.

World Peace: Tom Lawson Novel #4
By James Brown

We filed into the president's office and Sam, and I took our seats on one of the sofas. Maddi Pool came in and squeezed in next to me. Linda Bing, the president's VP, and Andrew Kennedy, his Chief of Staff were already in the room and seated in chairs close to the Resolute desk. Trailing into the office behind Maddi Pool were the Secretary of State Peter Bentley, CIA Director Angela Keen, and NSA Executive Director Sarah Pope. The three of them took the sofa opposite Sam and me with Keen seated at the end of the sofa closest to the Resolute desk. National Security Adviser, Morgan Kelly, was the last to enter and took a chair at the back of the Oval Office.

President Stephen had his back to the group finishing a phone call. He swiveled his chair around. "Sorry, the First Lady. A good Friday morning to everyone. We've had an excellent week. Peter and Floyd had productive meetings in Japan. Is there anything else to report since your return, Peter?"

"No, Mr. President, nothing new other than what has already been reported."

"Okay," the president said. Before Angela provides her status debrief I've invited Jan Polaski to our CIPC debriefings. She will likely be fielding questions from the press at her daily briefing sessions sooner than we'd like. Leaks, unfortunately, always seep out eventually. With our program beginning to show promise, Jan needs to be prepared for the onslaught."

"Thank you, Mr. President. Being blindsided with questions from the press is not good," Polaski said.

"And here's the team who has the answers to those questions," President Stephen said looking about the room. "So let's begin. Angela, I've read your communications, and it appears the CIPC program had a very good week. Summarize the week for us and the plans for next week."

"Well, starting off, yes, Mr. President, we did have a very good week. Two very important achievements. Won Min-ho had an extremely productive session with President Kim Kyung-mi. She is onboard to participate in a G-5 Summit. Won also said Kim voiced many of the same beliefs she had discussed with him when they attended school together in North Korea. He said she wants to end the isolation that has been so pervasive throughout North Korea's history. Of concern, however, he said there will be a large number of obstacles in her way. These obstacles include generals, several politicians and many of their privileged populace. They are extremely afraid of losing their status and military budgets."

"Not too different from the military industrial complex here in the states and the generals and politicians who support it," President Stevens said.

"Very true," Vice President Linda Bing said. "This will also be one of our challenges. The likelihood that China, Russia, and Iran will merely step up and agree to total cooperation without some significant tradeoffs and assurances is pretty low."

"I know, Linda. I'm guessing . . . no, I'm confident our military budget will be on the table. I would insist myself if their military budget was three to ten times higher than ours. But if we can really secure a breakthrough deal that significantly reduces the tension between our countries, a deal that will foster major economic growth for each of the participants as well as the world in general, the benefits of defense budget cut will be well worth the grief we'll get."

"It will be more than merely grief that will be registered, Mr. President," Kennedy said.

"Okay. All out political war. I get it, Andrew," the president said with an angry tone. "We'll need to manage that but it's damn time that the United States becomes the leader of the world that many proclaim us to be. Lead by example and foster a change in our domestic priorities. There's a damn lot of good we can do if we divert some of the money we spend every year on better ways to kill, to improve the lives of our people, and the lives of the other people who inhabit the earth."

With the room eerily quiet, I spoke up. "A very worthy objective, sir. We manage the narrative and promote the benefits that the country and the world will reap. Plus, we double our efforts in tracking those on the international front who may want to sabotage our efforts. Likewise, we stay ahead and rebut the domestic naysayers."

"Thank you, Tom. This is a once-in-a-lifetime opportunity. Now, what about Iran, Sarah? Your SIGINT hit sounds very promising."

"Indeed it does, sir," Sarah Pope said. "A very significant signal intelligence hit, a voice recording of a revolutionary guard operative by the name of Omar. Ebram Janati was poisoned. Omar spiked Janati's drink with oleander which is a poison that is not typically tested for in a toxicology test. We also have Mostafa Ahmadi on the recording."

"Head of the Revolutionary Guards. An excellent discovery, Sarah. Excellent," the president said.

"Thank you, sir. I have a very dedicated and excellent team," Sarah said.

The president nodded then said, "you're up next Peter, you're meeting is still on for next week?"

"Yes, sir. We leave for Iceland on Tuesday for our meeting with the Russian Foreign Affairs Minister."

"Nikita Popov?"

"Yessir."

"Do we have a list of the other attendees?"

"We're working on it and should have it by Monday at the latest."

"Okay. Let's do our best to have Victor Petrova participate. He's done a great job so far. Okay, everyone I need a little time before my next meeting so thank you very much. Let's keep on our toes. The second phase of this program is about to begin. Watch for leaks and be prepared to act quickly when they begin to erupt. Keep Jan up to date. She will need to be prepared to respond to any questions that will eventually leak to the press."

As everyone was gathering their papers and notes and filing out, the president put his hand on my shoulder. "A minute, Tom."

"About that hit on the revolutionary guard operative, you worked with Maddi and Sarah Pope I assume?"

"I did, sir, along with a couple folks far more knowledgeable than I when it comes to signal intelligence. Sarah Pope was integral to those discussions."

"Excellent. I was hoping that would be the case. Do what you think is necessary to help make the CIPC program a success. The next push will be to identify the naysayers and those who will revert to illegal methods and means to retain the status quo, the military industrial complex and those who benefit from the power and money that flow from ever growing defense budgets."

"I agree, sir. I've had discussions with a few of my contacts at the Post also."

"Savannah Lee?"

"Yes sir."

"Good," the president said and paused for a moment. "Tom, the next few months will be very challenging for us, and for you in particular. The media's talking heads are still questioning my reason for hiring you as one of my senior advisors."

"I don't pay any attention to that, sir. I don't even have a Meta account."

"I expected that to be the case. Apolitical and a person of high integrity. Exactly the kind of person I needed on my team, especially now. I need someone with no political agenda. Someone who thinks clearly and can assist us in achieving the vision that one of my peers professed that our country is a shining city on the hill."

"A vison voiced by a member of the opposing party even," I said.

"Ronald Reagan, yes. But regardless of political party, that aspiration is worth achieving. After the fallout from those missiles raining down on the dictators and authoritative leaders in the world, Carpe Diem, seize the day. Achieve Ronald Reagan's vision of America. I'll even give him some credit if we are able to accomplish it."

"I'll do what I can to help you, sir."

"Thank you. Are you heading back to Connecticut today?"

"I am, yes. I have a flight out in a couple of hours. I'll be back Tuesday morning before Secretary Bentley leaves for Iceland."

"Okay, Tom. Say hello to Diana for me and keep working your magic."

"I will, and thank you, Mr. President," I said as we stood, and the president walked me to the door. No sooner did the door open when another group standing outside was ready to enter.

World Peace: Tom Lawson Novel #4
By James Brown

Chapter 21

It was a bright, mid-May Thursday morning with the temperature in the upper sixties with low humidity, a perfect spring day in Washington DC. I sat in Maddi Pool's office at CIA Headquarters waiting for a scheduled call with Abbas Ebrahimi, the CIA agent located in Tehran. The purpose of the call was to discuss the voice message uncovered by one of Maddi's intelligence officers. The captured voice message between Mostafa Ahmadi, the Chief Commander of the Iran's Revolutionary Guard and a Guard member, clearly stated that the Guard had murdered Iranian Cleric Ebram Janati. He did not die of a heart attack as it was reported. The Guard poisoned him.

As Maddi sat waiting for her agent, Logic, to call, a smile crossed her face. Such great code names were assigned to her agents, she thought. Opportunity, Progress, Justice, and Logic. Quite relevant code names for her new agents who were assigned very important objectives. At precisely seven a.m. her phone rang. She answered it.

"Logic," the caller said. "Identification code Gamma, Epsilon, Charles, Zulu, X-ray, Three came the reply."

"Iden confirmed. Good afternoon, Abbas. Joining me on our call is Tom Lawson, one of President Stephen's advisors."

"Mr. Lawson, a pleasure to finally meet you. You are well known in my country of course. Though to many, it would have been better had your discovery of John Gordon's intentions become known sooner and the deaths of Iran's leadership prevented. But at least you did help to ensure a catastrophic world war was prevented."

"Thank you, Abbas, we did our best but simply ran out of time."

"Which leads us to the reason for our call today," Maddi said. "Our CIPC team is making positive progress with Russia and China with Iran and North Korea next on the agenda. Today we want your feedback on the secured message I sent you."

"Incredible," Abbas said. "Not unexpected but nevertheless absolutely incredible information, that Mostafa Ahmadi, the Chief Commander of Iran's Revolutionary Guard was behind the death of Cleric Ebram Janati."

"So what is your suggestion on how this information can be leveraged," Maddi asked.

Upon receiving the secured message from Maddi, Abbas assumed he would be asked the question of how and when to share the information with Iran's new leadership. If it was presented too early, the Guard would merely create false scenarios and evidence to deny the validity of the recordings. Conversely, if too much time passed, the new regime may well be locked in place with hardened opinions with agents of the Guard and hardline Clerics well entrenched.

"I've given that some thought, Maddi. The timing is critical. Too early and the Guard will have all their lies in place and well documented before any meeting takes place. Conversely, too late and the new Iranian government will be locked in place and immovable to new ideas. So, my suggestion is that a meeting be arranged between the U.S. and Iran's new fledging leadership in about a week with the information presented at this meeting."

"We also arrived at that conclusion, Abbas," Maddi said.

"As for a date, Abbas, given schedules on our end, we were thinking Wednesday June 2nd, a one or two-day meeting. A little more than the two weeks we hope," I said.

"That date is certainly reasonable. You will use the Swiss to help promote this meeting, I assume?" Abbas asked.

"Through the Secretary of State's office, yes. And maybe if our negotiations prove fruitful the U.S. will once again have an embassy in Tehran," Maddi answered.

"That would be an excellent outcome."

"Do you have anything else of significance to report, Abbas?" Maddi asked.

"Nothing new to add from what I reported two days ago. The Guard continues to press the new leadership and Clerics to choose the candidate of their choice for Supreme Leader. They likewise have ongoing efforts to have President Amir Hosseini replaced with a more hardline president."

"Let's hope the rumblings stay at their current level for the next couple of weeks. If anything changes, please call me immediately."

"Will do," Maddi, Abbas said just before he disconnected the call.

Maddi leaned back in her chair. "Two weeks to get a meeting scheduled. I agree sooner is better than later but what do you think? Can Peter pull it off?"

"He should be able to, it's a new U.S. administration and the first hundred days or so meeting requests are typically accepted. In addition, each of the five countries we're targeting are experiencing challenges brought about with the deaths of their leaders. We just need to be well prepared for this meeting. It's a critical one," I said.

"The most difficult one, I think," Maddi replied. "How to argue logic with a theocratic government that still relies on conversations made more than a thousand years ago."

"Conversations and rules still being argued today. Very true," I said. "Not an easy task. But that's an issue to solve for another day."

* * * *

As is often typical with new administrations, schedules, meetings, and itineraries do not start off running smoothly. The space outside the Oval Office was once again filling up. Andrew Kennedy, the president's chief of staff gave his assurances that meeting delays would soon be a thing of the past and their efficiencies would be noticeable. With each of Kennedy's proclamations being missed badly, an undercover betting parlor had begun with meeting attendees betting on the time delay for the president's next meeting. No one seemed to remember who initiated the scheme, but it became a regular practice. The maximum allowable bet was five dollars and all monies won went to the winner's charity of choice.

Janene Morgan, the president's Director of Oval Office Operations was coaxed into taking the job of Bookie in Charge. She collected the money and retained the daily betting sheet. The winner was determined by who came the closest in guessing the total number of minutes that meetings with the president were delayed and was announced at the end of every week.

"How many minutes did you guess?" Jan Polaski whispered after she handed five dollars to Janene Morgan and slid into the crowd next to me.

"Seventeen minutes," I whispered back. "I've been tracking the statistics, the winning times, agenda for the meeting, attendees. All the key statistics. Seventeen minutes. That's the number."

"That's not fair. Some of us were never that good in math," Polaski groused.

"Shouldn't bet then, Jan. What was your guess?"

"A schedule slip of ten minutes."

At 10:17 a.m. the door to the Oval Office opened. Treasury Secretary Dr. Benjamin Michaels and his deputy exited the Oval Office.

"Sorry," Michaels said to the crowd waiting outside. He shrugged and said, "I did my best."

Lawson gave Polaski a wink. She poked him with her elbow as the CIPC meeting attendees began filing into the room.

"Sorry for the delay, folks. Money matters took a little more time than expected. The family budget and all," President Stephen said as he shuffled a few papers on his desk.

Seating remained the same as in past CIPC status meetings. I sat on one of the sofas in the center of the room next to Maddi Pool and Sam Wainwright while Peter Bentley, Angela Keen, and Sarah Pope took their seats on the opposite sofa. Vice President Linda Bing and Chief of Staff Andrew Kennedy attended the earlier meeting with the treasury secretary and sat in chairs at the front of the room near the Resolute desk. Press secretary Jan Polaski, new to the CIPC meeting, took a seat at the back of the room next to National Security Adviser, Morgan Kelly.

"Okay," the president said, looking up at the group in front of him. "In reading the reports from Peter the past few days while he was in Reykjavik, it appears that he and his team had a very good start for our CIPC program. Peter, give us your latest update."

"Thank you, Mr. President. It was indeed a very good first meeting with the Russian delegation. Foreign Affairs Minister Nikita

Popov led the Russian team and a foundation for a draft CIPC agreement was reached prior to our departure. Popov is on board, no question."

"Any concerns on his part?" President Stephen asked.

"Several. The military industrial complex and all those acronym agencies who rely on government support for intelligence services and defense spending. Also the men and women employed by the military and their families," Secretary Bentley said. "Numerous job losses."

"Yes, the same challenge for the U.S., China, North Korea, and Iran," the president said. "That was expected. Did you discuss next steps?"

"The situation in Russia is worse than what is being reported. Milosevic needs to stabilize the situation and force is not working. I suggested a meeting with you in a couple of weeks."

"Politically, the timing for a meeting with Russia is not good," Vice President Bing said. "The country will be in an uproar. Russia funded John Gordon."

"Which, of course, Milosevic denies," Bentley said.

The room was quiet as the president pondered Bentley's suggested meeting. "We should do it. Agree to a meeting, here in Washington," the president said.

"Sir!" Vice President Linda Bing responded quickly.

"We can take the temporary heat, Linda. Having Russia on our side, agreeing to support a CIPC agreement will be immensely helpful in securing an agreement from China. North Korea will follow."

"Though it's not a given that Iran will fall in line," Bentley said.

"True. It may take a minor miracle to bring them on board. But before we discuss Iran, what's the schedule with China and North Korea?" President Stephen asked.

"Secretary Bentley, Barbara Shirley, and Zheng Shih are scheduled to meet with the Chinese delegation Tuesday and Wednesday next week," CIA Director Angela Keen said.

"How about North Korea?" the president asked.

"We are shooting for a preliminary meeting June 2nd for Secretary Bentley and his team. A brief meeting before a G-5 summit."

"Okay, that makes sense. Now, what about Iran. What's being considered?"

"Iran's a larger challenge, sir," Keen said. "Tom and Maddi had a call with Abbas Ebrahimi, our agent in Iran yesterday. Abbas recommends a meeting as soon as possible given the situation with the Guard and Iran's Supreme Leader selection process. He also thinks it best that we present the SIGINT recording of the Revolutionary Guard's conversation at that meeting and not earlier. As for timing, he says the meeting should be scheduled ASAP and no later than two weeks. Time is of the essence," Keen said.

"No later than early June, the timeframe Peter and his team will be meeting with North Korea." The president pondered a moment then looked over at Lawson.

"What are you thinking?" I asked.

"I'm thinking maybe we should take a political perspective, an approach that Linda might recommend. What if we have you and Deputy Secretary Shirley lead this first session with Iran?"

"Throw them to the wolves first?" Linda said. "The political animals here in the U.S. and in Israel you know will attack them. I'm not sure I agree with that tactic."

I interjected and said, "generals do that all the time in battle. Send out a small force to test the enemy lines and see how hardened they are."

"That's my thought too, Tom," said the president. "It's critical that China, Russia, North Korea, and Iran agree as well as the American public to help push a CIPC agreement through congress. The bigger question, is not the issue of sending Tom and Barbara into the lion's den but what the hell would Iran want as a condition for agreeing with a CIPC agreement and giving up nuclear weapons?"

"Well, we would expect some kind of reduction in U.S. defense spending would be required. Same as Russia, China, and North Korea would demand. And definitely an end to trade restrictions. The bigger issues are Israel, Palestine, and possibly Saudi Arabia," Secretary Bentley said.

"Exactly, Israel, Palestine, Saudi Arabia," President Stephen replied. "I reread the position paper prepared by our Middle East experts. Peter, we need to schedule another session with the experts. You depart on Monday for your session with China I assume."

"Yes, sir."

"Then, let's all of us have breakfast together tomorrow morning here at the White House. Andrew, ask our Middle East experts to join us. Plan it for two hours, three hours tops. Make sure everyone has a copy of the report prepared by our experts prior to the meeting."

"Will do, Sir."

"Okay then," the president said. "We have a tentative plan. A follow up CIPC meeting will be next Friday, same time. Thank you everyone."

The meeting was over. I looked at my watch as I stood and the door to the Oval Office opened. The meeting ended eighteen minutes behind schedule. Joan Waters, the Secretary of Labor had a big grin on her face as she walked into the room.

World Peace: Tom Lawson Novel #4
By James Brown

Chapter 22

Professors Rebecca Ben-Hur and Jerome Underwood completed their White House security check and were walking to the West Wing dining room when Chief of Staff Andrew Kennedy came out of the Oval Office.

"Good morning, Rebecca, Jerome. Thank you for joining us for breakfast this beautiful Saturday morning. Hopefully, we can cover a few critical questions quickly and you will be able to enjoy the rest of your weekend. The president will be joining us shortly," Kennedy said.

"A typical Saturday morning for administrative staff, Andrew. Few days off as you well know," Professor Ben-Hur said. "What we all signed up for."

Andrew winked. "We all did that, sign up, and a grateful nation appreciates it."

Ben-Hur cocked her head. Only some of the people some of the time. Never all of the people all of the time, she thought as they walked to the West Wing dining room that was adjacent to the Oval Office.

"Good morning, Peter, Tom, Jan," Kennedy said as he and professors Ben-Hur and Underwood entered the dining room. "Has everyone already been introduced," he asked.

"I have not met Ms. Ben-Hur," I said, standing and walking over to her and shaking her hand. "Tom Lawson, pleased to meet you."

"And you, Mr. Lawson," she said.

Jan Polaski gave a quick smile and acknowledgement, having previously met both of them.

Secretary Bentley also smiled and nodded.

"The president will be joining us in a few minutes," Chief of Staff Kennedy said. "So please help yourselves to the breakfast buffet while we wait. The president fixed himself a bagel before his six a.m. meeting."

"He's really an early riser," Polaski said as she stood and headed to the table along the side of the room. The table was set up with warming pans of scrambled eggs, bacon, diced potatoes with onion and chopped peppers as well as bowls of fruits and bagels, butter and cream cheese. Coffee urns stood at the end of the table along with carafes of orange and tomato juices. As she picked up a plate and began filling it, the other early morning meeting attendees made a line at the end of the buffet table.

Several minutes later President Stephen entered the room.

About ready to put a forkful of eggs in my mouth I felt a sharp kick to my leg. Polaski looked up at the clock and then at me and whispered, "seventeen minutes."

"Sorry I'm a little late. I'll join you after I get a plate of bacon and eggs and another cup of coffee." The president filled his plate and took the open seat at the head of the table.

"Rebecca, Jerome, we need your expertise," he said. "We plan to approach Iran and we need to know what it will take to entice them to give up their nuclear ambitions and become part of a workable Middle East solution."

"How much time do you have this morning, Mr. President? That's not an easy request," Ben-Hur said.

"Preferably two hours, max three. I promised I would let everyone go no later than ten, preferably by nine, so they can enjoy this lovely spring weekend."

"Not nearly enough time, Mr. President."

"Let's do the best we can, Rebecca."

She stood and took her plate to an empty tray stand in the corner of the room. "Okay," she said as she returned to the table. "Has everyone read the report Professor Underwood and I prepared several weeks ago?"

"Front to back," Secretary Bentley said with head nods following from around the table.

"So your question, what incentives will entice Iran's leadership, and the Supreme Leader they select, to participate in a CIPC

Agreement? Well, first of all, a lot will depend on the person the Assembly of Experts choose to become the new Supreme Leader, and whether the person selected is left or right of the Supreme Leader who was killed."

"What if the Assembly of Experts can't come to an agreement on their selection for Supreme Leader?" I asked.

"It's theoretically possible but highly unlikely that would occur," Ben-Hur answered. "The Assembly consists of eighty-eight Mujtahids who are elected from lists of thoroughly vetted candidates by direct public vote for eight-year terms. *But* all candidates to the Assembly of Experts must be approved by the Guardian Council whose members are, in turn, appointed either directly or indirectly by the Supreme Leader.

To choose the Supreme Leader, the Experts review qualified candidates and consult among themselves. According to their constitution, the criteria of qualification for the office of the Supreme Leader includes Islamic scholarship, justice, piety, the right political and social perspicacity, prudence, courage, administrative abilities and capability for leadership.

The jurist deemed as the most well-versed in Islamic regulations, in political and social issues, is popular, and is of special prominence is chosen as Supreme Leader. In the absence of such a candidate, the Experts elect and declare one of their own as Supreme Leader."

"So our best-case scenario would be the Council choosing a moderate candidate for the next Supreme Leader, if such a candidate somehow survives the initial vetting process," I said.

"For the selection of a moderate as Supreme Leader, yes," Ben-Hur answered. "The Assembly has a leadership council and six committees. The leadership of the Assembly is elected by secret ballot for two years and consists of the assembly's chair, two vice-chairs, two secretaries, and two assistants. Regarding your next likely question, Tom, is there a moderate candidate among the bunch? There was at least one, Cleric Ebram Janati. But it was reported he died of a heart attack."

"That was unfortunate," I said, choosing not to share the fact that Janati was murdered. "Given that the deck is stacked against us, what would need to be offered to entice whoever is selected as the next Supreme Leader to enter into a CIPC agreement?"

World Peace: Tom Lawson Novel #4
By James Brown

Professor Ben-Hur gave out a deep sigh. "Okay, let's start with the Supreme Leader who was murdered, assuming his replacement holds similar beliefs. Before his death, the Supreme Leader's paramount concerns were to preserve his own power and ensure the survival of the Islamic theocracy, which he believed was based on principles of justice, independence, self-sufficiency and piety."

"We could agree with that," Secretary Bentley said. "Our intent is not to force America's form of government on any country. We've finally learned our lesson."

"A very good first step, Mr. Secretary. The Supreme Leader's primary concern was not a U.S. military invasion but rather a political and cultural campaign to undermine theocratic rule through a *'soft'* revolution. In other words, he was afraid that Iran's youth would prefer a fully open society. Which in fact they do."

"Trying to force people to adhere to a belief or doctrine that is contrary to what the majority believes never ends well. History proves that." President Stephen commented.

"I agree, Mr. President. Nevertheless, continuation of theocratic rule will very likely be a paramount condition for entering into an agreement with the U.S. As for other sticky issues, the Lebanese and Palestinian people for example, the Supreme Leader believed it was Iran's Islamic duty to support them."

"Even though most Palestinians are Sunni Muslims and not Shiite?" I asked.

"The overriding reason is they are Muslims, Tom. The Sunni, Shite argument, or better stated centuries old debate is just that, a centuries old debate. The underlying issue is primary with those Middle Eastern countries who are striving to be the dominate power in the region, Iran, Iraq, or Saudi Arabia rather than a Sunni, Shite conflict.

As for Israel, the past Supreme Leader's position interestingly was that he would accept a less harsh position toward Israel when and if the Palestinians themselves accepted a peace treaty with Israel."

"Negotiate a treaty acceptable by Israel and the Palestinians?" President Stephen said as he pushed back from the table and took his breakfast dishes to the tray stand holding the empty dishes. "Many presidents have attempted to negotiate such a solution and have failed. Can any solution satisfy Israelis and Palestinians?"

World Peace: Tom Lawson Novel #4
By James Brown

"With certain inducements and pressure," Ben-Hur said.

"Please explain," the president said as he returned to the table.

"We don't have much time, Mr. President given your three-hour rule, but here goes. Everyone knows, I'm sure, that the Israel and Palestine issue began in 1948 with the establishment of Israel. The United Nations attempted to create a two-nation solution, with Jerusalem serving as a buffer between the two under the control of the United Nations, but neither side liked the idea of losing control of Jerusalem. This conflict has continued, sometimes ebbing into war over the last seventy-five years.

As Jerome and I described in the document everyone has read, the prevailing thought has been to create a two-state solution. But this has been discussed and argued with various boundaries and approaches considered by many administrations, long before you were sworn in three months ago, Mr. President.

The details are in our report but simply stated, a two-state solution is just too hard to do. Where would the borders be between these states? What would happen to Jerusalem, a city important to both peoples? What about all the Jewish settlements in the West Bank? What about Palestinian refugees? where would the two states be? What borders would define the Israeli state, and what would Palestine consist of?

If you draw the border as former President Obama suggested, the 1967 borders, hundreds of thousands of Israelis who live in West Bank settlements wind up on the Palestinian side. Would those people become citizens of Palestine or be forced to move back to Israel proper? Few on either side want the first option, and some settlements are well-established cities with tens of thousands of residents. It's inconceivable they would agree to relocate.

It's also seemingly impossible to draw a border that encompass these settlements as part of Israel, as Palestinians would not have a contiguous territory. Are Palestinians going to leave their country every time they want to travel between cities?

Likewise, If Israel would be required to cede the West Bank in its entirety, it would make Israel only a few miles wide at its narrowest point and deny Israel the security presence it currently maintains along the Jordan River. How would Israel protect itself from that threat if it withdraws from the West Bank?

World Peace: Tom Lawson Novel #4
By James Brown

Then there's Jerusalem. Both Israelis and Palestinians claim Jerusalem as their capital, and the city is holy to Jews, Muslims, and Christians.

With all these issues to deal with, a two-state resolution has never been agreed upon and never will in my opinion. It's my belief, and Professor Underwood's, that the only viable solution is a one-state solution."

"Hmm. That approach has been raised but never agreed with either," Bentley said.

"That's true, but you've asked what will work if the right countries push for it. Or better stated, insist that after seventy-five years of incursions, wars, terrorist attacks and threats, that it is time for a different approach. If a CIPC agreement is indeed executed by the U.S., Russia, China, Iran, and North Korea, Mr. President, a Jewish-Palestinian single state solution, the only logical solution, can be put in place.

Northern Ireland is one example of a binational state in which ethnic groups maintain a certain level of political autonomy while sharing one sovereign country. Of course there are many countries, if not most countries, that prosper with people of multiethnic origins and religious beliefs. There is no question that Jewish people have been persecuted throughout the history of the world, and most devastatingly by the Hitler regime. But these circumstances have happened to many groups of people throughout history, including the capture and enslavement of Africans by American citizens, African-American citizens who are still being persecuted by many Americans even today.

No, Mr. President. There is no easy solution. But if you can pull off your CIPC agreement . . . cooperation, inclusion, and peaceful coexistence. I am sure you will be able to do what no other president has been able to accomplish, provide lasting peace for the people living in the Middle East and significantly reduce the underlining violence throughout the world caused by good intentions but failed solutions."

With the time approaching the president's three-hour window, Professor Ben-Hur leaned back in her chair and took a last drink of her coffee that was now cold. Her summary of the complexities surrounding ongoing conflicts in the Middle East provided and recommendation made, the ball was now punted to the other side of the room. Her job as a presidential advisor was fulfilled, at least for this particular request for advice by the president.

The decision on how to proceed was now in the laps of the other close advisors to the president with the final decision ultimately left for the president to make.

President Stephen looked up at the clock. "You hit your mark, Rebecca. Three hours. The recommendation that you and Professor Underwood have outlined is certainly logical. But can logic prevail in this instance?"

"It can, sir," Professor Ben-Hur said. "If an executed CIPC agreement is put in place. If that agreement happens, believe me, logic *will* prevail."

* * * *

The president's CIPC breakfast meeting broke up exactly at ten a.m., right on schedule. Walking out of the meeting with Jan Polaski and Sam Wainwright, Jan said, "well that blows your seventeen-minute cycle, Tom."

I smiled. "My calculations exclude weekends, Jan. Enjoy the rest of your weekend."

"Right. While I'm writing up my notes in preparation for Monday's Daily Brief. I never have a weekend."

"What we signed up for, along with the rewards and adulations from a grateful nation," I said as we exited the White House. She moaned and waved a hand as we split up, she walking to the parking garage and her car and Sam Wainwright and I walking out of the White House grounds.

"You texted Savannah?" Sam said.

"I did, told her we would be at the Grill by ten thirty."

Sam and I arrived at Old Ebbitt Grill and as always, Wilson was standing at his maître d' table.

"Good morning, Director Wainwright, Mr. Lawson. Ms. Lee is here having a mimosa and a cup of coffee. This way please, he said, leading the way as he did with all his patrons.

"Finally," she said as we reached the table. "I was getting ready to order. We were supposed to meet for breakfast."

"There are others higher in the pecking order at times my dear," I said. "You'll learn this soon. About thirty days I believe."

"After I'm married?"

I shrugged.

"Hmph. We can argue that point later. What happened at your breakfast meeting with the president? But let's order first. I wasn't invited to the meeting, and I didn't have breakfast."

After Wilson came back to the table and took Savannah's brunch order, Sam and I ordered a cup of coffee and a bagel with cream cheese. With orders made, Savannah said, "so, what happened?"

"The CIPC initiative is picking up steam. Secretary Bentley had a very productive meeting with the Russian delegation. Foreign Affairs Minister Nikita Popov will be recommending to President Milosevic that he move forward and meet with President Stephen."

"Really! That's great, Tom. And the breakfast meeting this morning?"

"We discussed phase two. Secretary Bentley is heading out for a meeting with China on Monday and North Korea is in the pipeline for June 2nd. The last target is Iran."

"It doesn't get any easier," Savanna said.

"No it doesn't. And of particular interest, President Stephen suggested that Deputy Shirley and I lead this first meeting with Iran."

Savannah's eyes widened.

"Be like the first lieutenant who volunteers to take point with his troops to test the enemy lines," Sam said.

"Oh, I see. Tom's expendable," Savannah responded.

"Pretty much. The very words that were discussed," Sam said.

"If I recall, I agreed with the approach, Sam. Give the president coverage if we fall flat. Anyway, the purpose for this morning's meeting was to listen to the experts, Professors Rebecca Ben-Hur and Jerome Underwood. They provided a very good overview of seventy-five years of Middle East issues and policies and provided their recommended approach for securing peace. They gave out homework."

"You better burn the midnight oil on this one, Tom. When do you leave?"

"We will try and schedule a date the same week Secretary Bentley and his team are holding a meeting with North Korea. Any rumors that you and your team have heard about these meetings? Any leaks beginning to float around out there that your reporters are hearing about?"

Savannah waited to answer Tom's questions until Wilson finished serving her breakfast. After thanking Wilson she said, "a few interesting rumblings. I have Bob Somerville doing his thing trolling the Internet and social media with his personally designed search engine. Hits are beginning to surface. Especially after Secretary Bentley reappeared late last week from his flight home from Reykjavik."

"Hmm. We were afraid that might happen. Hard to keep everything a secret. What's being reported?" I asked.

"Just rumblings for now. You know, why was he there. Who did he meet with? By next week, I'm sure it will come out that Bentley had a meeting with Popov. When it does start coming to life, which it will, we'll be out front reporting it."

"Of course, doing your job. How about the Daily Brief on Monday? Do you think Polaski will be asked to comment on Secretary Bentley's meeting in Reykjavik?" I asked.

"As sure as the sun's going to rise in the east tomorrow morning."

"But nothing about the CIPC program yet?"

"I'd give that another week at the latest," Savannah said and took another bite of her scrambled eggs. "There's no way the administration can keep that program secret much longer. Someone in the White House is going to be pressured by a reporter or a lobbyist who's heard something that his or her client will likely be concerned about. And from what you've told me about the program's intent, this individual's client will be very concerned if this agreement is executed."

"Right. A lot of people will not be pleased with the president negotiating an agreement that will lead to lower defense spending. Companies need to protect those revenues and profits that growing defense budgets provide," I said.

"That's right. There is a downside to peace in the world, Tom. A lot of profits and paychecks are tied to a country's defense spending and wars being fought," Savannah responded.

"On another topic, Tom," Sam said. "Did you speak with Sarah Pope or John?"

"Not the last couple of days. I have a meeting with Sarah early Monday morning and was planning to speak with John this afternoon. If you have time on Monday, you can join the meeting."

"What time?"

"Early, seven a.m. I wanted to speak with her before Jan's Daily Brief."

"Your office?"

"Yes, more secure, I think. She will stop at the White House before going to the NSA building."

"Okay. I'll try and join you," Sam said.

"Can I come?" Savanna said meekly.

"No!" Sam and I said in unison. "We love you, of course, Savannah. But we are not ready yet to let others know you are a full member of the team."

"But John is."

"Doctor John Davidson is."

"I . . . know," she said, drawing out her words. "But I'm missing out on all of the fun."

"Your fun and excitement will come along soon enough. Let's get you married off first. Your time, unfortunately, will likely come sooner than we would like. The wedding is still scheduled for the twentieth, right?"

"I haven't backed out yet. June twenty is still the date. And Sam, did you call Jane Wyatt, my cousin like I told you to do?"

"Ah . . . I did," Sam said slowly. "We had a very nice conversation. In fact, she and I are having dinner this evening."

"That's wonderful, Sam. You're going to love her. Our little family is growing. How fun this is going to be."

"Speaking of fun, who's going to be at the Daily Brief on Monday," I asked.

"Glenda Robinson is the Post's White House reporter for the next several weeks. She's on my staff. In addition to asking questions, she will see what she can find out what the other reporters are digging into."

"Okay. Keep us posted if the rumblings turn hotter. I need to head out. Sam, I hope your dinner with Jane goes well this evening. See you Monday morning."

Chapter 23

Sam Wainwright walked to the door and pressed the bell. It was seven in the evening and he and Jane Wyatt were taking the next step, a first dinner date. After being pressed by Savannah Lee and having several phone calls with her cousin, Sam was now standing on the porch of Jane Wyatt's townhouse. Soon after pressing the doorbell, the door opened.

"FBI Director Sam Wainwright. I must say, I never thought I would be asked out to dinner by the director of the FBI. Chauffeured even," Jane said as she noticed the large black SUV idling at the curb of her Townhouse.

Wainwright looked over his shoulder and then back at the petite, five-foot-four woman with short blond hair, blue eyes and warm smile looking up at him.

"That's Stan. One of my agents whose turn it is to be my chauffer this month. I'm told I need protection. This, after being a gun toting FBI agent chasing bad guys for thirty years," he said flipping his thumb toward the SUV behind him."

"Hmm. We should have very interesting conversations over dinner, Mr. Director."

Stan drove the director and Ms. Wyatt from her townhouse that was located a few blocks from Georgetown University to the Filomena Ristorante, a premier Italian restaurant in Washington DC for over 30 years.

"Director Wainwright. It's a pleasure to see you again. This way please," the maître d' said, taking two menus and leading the way to a table along the side of the room.

World Peace: Tom Lawson Novel #4
By James Brown

Seated, and each having ordered a glass of wine, Wainwright said, "living in Georgetown perhaps you've eaten here before? The best Italian food in Washington."

Jane took a moment and looked about the room before answering. "It looks lovely but no, I haven't been in Georgetown too long. Only a little more than a month so I'm just getting to know my way around."

"Savannah mentioned you rented the townhouse shortly after your daughter began attending Georgetown."

"Shortly after my son, Penelope's twin brother, took a job in New York City. I decided I needed to spread my wings."

"Let me know if I'm prying but Savannah let slip that you were loaded so is it safe to assume you will not be looking for employment while you are in Washington."

"I doubt my cousin lets anything slip."

Wainwright smiled. "You know her well. By the way, there's another question I'm dying to ask."

"Okay, I might have a few for you also. What's your question?"

"Is your other cousin, Priscilla Beauregard, truly racist as Savannah says and also that Priscilla does not know that Savannah is marrying an African American."

Wyatt laughed. "That's Savannah. I remember when we were kids. She and Priscilla were like oil and water. I've said nothing to Priscilla, so unless Savannah's mom or dad have mentioned who her fiancé is to any of the relatives, then it is possible that she has no idea who Savannah is marrying."

"Savannah said it would be a hoot. Her words."

That drew another round of laughter about the time a waiter walked up to the table.

"Have you decided, Mr. Wainwright," the waiter asked.

"Oh, Anthony, I'm sorry, we probably need a little more time since this is a first time for Ms. Wyatt."

"That's okay, Sam. If you know what you want, go ahead and order while I quickly look at the menu," Wyatt said.

"Okay then, Anthony. I'll have the La Famiglia and the side order of sauteed asparagus and the house salad."

"Another glass of wine?"

"Yes, please."

World Peace: Tom Lawson Novel #4
By James Brown

"Are you ready, ma'am?"

"Yes, I'll have the chicken marsala as well as the house salad and sauteed asparagus and please bring me a second glass of wine."

"Thank you. I'll have your wine and salads out shortly," Anthony said.

"So, where were we? You've been with the FBI for thirty years. How did you meet Savannah?" Wyatt asked.

"Tom Lawson is to blame for that."

"The man you and Savannah helped to prevent World War III."

"That's the guy. I first met Tom when a few folks were trying to kill him and an Asian NTSB agent a few years ago when I was working in New York City."

"When you were a gun toting FBI agent at the time."

"Yes, when my life was a bit simpler."

"So before you met Savannah?"

"That meeting came later, after I helped save Tom from the bad guys. He got himself shot and fortunately he lived. Otherwise, I wouldn't have met Savannah Lee, wouldn't be the Director of the FBI, and wouldn't be sitting here with you today," Wainwright said and leaned back and downed the rest of his first glass of wine.

"Hmm, Karma. Your actions influenced the future. Without those encounters and actions we wouldn't be sitting here," Wyatt said.

"You believe that stuff?"

Wyatt shrugged. "I hadn't really thought about it before, but it is interesting. You meet Tom Lawson. Help keep him alive. After that first encounter, he uncovers a possible terrorist threat, pulls you into that investigation, Savannah becomes involved, the world is saved and here we are."

"You forgot my promotion."

"Right. Still a gun toting FBI agent but now the Director of that agency. Pretty cool."

"With a lot more work and a lot more pressure. Now, how about Jane Wyatt? You've told me your kids are doing well and you lost your husband a few years ago which must have been very difficult for you, so how are *you* doing?"

Wyatt was quiet for a few moments then waited while Anthony replaced their drinks and served their house salads.

World Peace: Tom Lawson Novel #4
By James Brown

"It was a very difficult few years after Ted died. He was only forty-five, it was colon cancer. He thought he was too young to need regular testing. The cancer was aggressive."

"I can't imagine losing a wife or worse, a child. My wife and I are still good friends even though divorced. Now anyway."

"Being married to a cop probably isn't easy for any marriage from what I've read."

"Very true. I traveled a lot, was not home as much as I should have been, and missed a lot of family functions, including birthday parties for my daughter."

"Still having all those issues I imagine?"

"I do have a chauffeur now though."

That brought out another laugh. "What about your daughter?" Wyatt asked.

Wainwright snickered. "Another reason for my ex to be upset with me. Our daughter, Carrie works for me now. Indirectly that is. She's an FBI agent."

"Wow! She followed in her father's footsteps, even after he missed a few of her birthday parties."

Wainwright beamed with pride. "She's probably going to have my job one day. Or maybe my boss' job."

Anthony returned to the table, removed empty salad plates, and began serving their La Famiglia and chicken marsala dinners. Wainwright eagerly dug into his plate of meatballs, Italian sausage and ribs served with fusilli pasta and homemade marinara sauce. It had been several months since he again had the opportunity to order this delicious meal. He was glad to learn that Jane Wyatt's Townhouse was in Georgetown.

"You've had the La Famiglia before I take it," Wyatt said.

"I've eaten here a few times since being in Washington. After Carrie finished her FBI training at Quantico we came here to celebrate. That's when I tried their La Famiglia and I was hooked."

"Ah. Now I get it. Savannah told you I rented a townhouse in Georgetown, just a few blocks away from this restaurant."

"Never crossed my mind."

"Now, Sam. You don't expect me to believe that the country's Director of the FBI didn't connect those dots do you?"

Sam gave a look of astonishment.

"I'm glad you connected those dots, Sam. It's been a lovely evening. The first time I was chauffeured to a very nice restaurant by someone other than my husband."

"Well, let's see if we can't have my chauffeur provide those services again real soon," Wainwright said.

* * * *

It was eight p.m. and with the last slice of peperoni pizza finished off, I picked up the phone and dialed Diana.

She answered after a couple of rings.

"Hi honey. Did you have pizza again this evening?"

"I did. I'm staying in this Saturday evening. Sam has a dinner date with Jane Wyatt, and I assume Savannah is spending her evening with Barry. Plus, I have a lot of homework to do."

"Homework?"

"The breakfast meeting I attended this morning with the president, Sam, and the CIPC team, and a couple professors. The president wanted us to hear from Middle East experts. See if they could recommend how best to negotiate with Iran in particular."

"Oh, and what did the professors have to say, and more importantly, how does the information shared affect you?"

Tom was quiet for a few moments then said, "Well, it was suggested that Deputy of State Barbara Shirley, and I be the first team to approach Iran."

"Really! No wonder you're going back to school. Why did the president suggest this?" Diana asked.

"Two reasons. Secretary Bentley and his team are scheduled to have a CIPC meeting with North Korea the first week of June, which is the same week the president wants to kick off a session with Iran. Our Iranian agent has warned us to move forward quickly with Iran before the wrong Supreme Leader is elected."

"I get it. By you and Barbara leading the charge with Iran, a country with whom the U.S. has no formal relationship, there is coverage for the president and his administration in the event there is any negative blowback."

"You don't miss much, do you. You are correct. The analogy given was a general asking one of his young first lieutenants to lead a few troops up a hill and over a ridge to test the strength of the enemy's line."

"Always leading the charge aren't you." Diana said.

"Well, in this case there shouldn't be any bullets flying like the other charges I've led."

"When will I see you again. I miss you."

"Probably in a week. If the Iranians agree to meet it would most likely take place in Vienna. We would fly out of Washington on Monday May 31st."

"You just need to make sure you are available on June 20 for Savannah's wedding."

"Not to worry. That date is locked into the schedule. I'm looking forward to meeting Priscilla Beauregard, Savannah's cousin. She can't be as bad as Savannah portrays her."

"Oh, I don't know," Diana said. "If you sat in on some of my client meetings you would be surprised with the beliefs of some people out there in the world."

"No doubt. So tell me, how was your week? Larry doing better now or is he still trying to solve the mystery of the Gordon's missile attacks?"

"Things are pretty much back to normal. You, of course, still come up in the conversation from time to time since you are the only person they know that's ever worked in the White House. It's understandable and typical human behavior."

"I'm glad I've become typical. Typical and normal is good."

"True. But I think that will change quickly in a few weeks from what you've told me. I can't imagine you not becoming front page news again real soon."

"Well, let's hope it's further back than the front page. I prefer the front pages be reserved for the president."

"Me too," Diana said. "Have you spoken with William and Peggy?"

"Not in a few days. It will soon be two weeks since Cody Walker started his physical therapy. John thinks Cody will soon be able to take his first steps unaided. He is tracking the data, and this is what it is predicting."

"That will be wonderful," Diana said excitedly.

"No question. Of course, more front-page news will likely break quickly once Cody walks on his own. Peggy and her team plan to release their first article to the top medical journals about their breakthrough surgery."

"Oh, that's right, Doctor John Davidson. With this breathtaking new technology do you think he will be able to stay in the shadows?" Diana asked.

"God, I hope so. I don't even want to think about any other possibility. Speaking of Doctor Davidson, I need to give him a call. I want to see if any CIPC leaks may have surfaced as well as any upticks in communications from international or U.S.-based bad guys."

"To give Jan Polaski a heads-up for Monday's Daily Brief?"

"That's the reason. She burns the midnight oil more than anyone, I think. It's understandable why presidential press secretaries have a short cycle time in their jobs. It really is a 24/7 job."

"Okay, honey. Keep me posted on Iran and say hello to everyone for me. I love you."

"Love you too, babe. Goodnight."

* * * *

I no sooner ended my call with Diana than I dialed John.

"Mr. Lawson. I thought you would be calling me. How's Diana?"

"She's doing well. As well as you might expect with me spending weeks at a time here in Washington and her at home in Connecticut."

"If you and the CIPC team are successful, who knows, maybe the world will progress to a safer and nicer place."

"John, how often have you told me about Pollyanna thinking?"

"I'm evolving, Tom, evolving," John said nonchalantly.

"I just wonder if the rest of the world is digressing rather than evolving. Here in the U.S. the QAnon and far-right conspiracy wackos certainly aren't evolving. At least not in the direction we would like them to," I said.

"Speaking of wackos here in the U.S. there is a growing number of highly charged rhetoric coming from several of the prominent white nationalist groups and antigovernment militias."

"The hate groups who want to burn down civilization. Do you think you could create some kind of nano something or other, John, which could secretly be added to the process for making beer?

Something the wackos you mentioned would ingest and allow them to become caring, peace-loving people?"

"Hmm, maybe."

"Work on that in your spare time, John. But until you develop this miracle beer are there any critical issues that are about to erupt here in the U.S. or internationally?

"Let's start with the U.S. Your friend Lucretia . . ."

"Lucretia Jane. I was planning on giving her a call. She's okay, I hope?" I interrupted.

"She's still in jail, of course, and she's actually doing quite well. Her daughter is too. So far, no one knows she was the person who flipped on the white nationalist group that tried to overturn the last election."

"She broke the case wide open, John. What news do you have about her?"

"A woman by the name of Abigail Briarcliff picked up the pieces and reunited the stragglers from Lucretia's white nationalist group. She's trying to merge several of the splinter groups together and is also in discussions with several antigovernment groups. A lot of chatter is out there from the various conversations."

"I'm not sure the 'Leave it to Beaver' family of the 1950s could have ever conceived the level of hatred that would morph from life in the fifties seventy years into the future."

"But remember, Tom, the Cleaver family were white folks who believed the white race would always be the majority race in the United States. It's blowing the minds of a large portion of former to Beaver viewers and their offspring that a white majority will soon not prevail."

"Indeed, a very good point, John. Wait until you and your kind begin taking over. It will really blow their minds. Now, how about CIPC leaks? Anything you've come across?"

"Nothing of substance. A few questions beginning to be asked about Secretary Bentley's trip to Reykjavik which is understandable. I'm sure Jan will be questioned at her Daily Brief session on Monday."

"Okay, John, Thanks. If anything comes up that you think is critical, call me any time."

"Will do, Tom. If you need anything, I'm available. Always."

Chapter 24

It was a long weekend. I studied everything of relevance that I could find on the history of the Middle East, the religious leaders and prophets that shaped the belief structures of its people, and the kings, dynasties, and autocrats that took control of the Middle East's shifting country boundaries. From the regions historical past of relative calm from an international perspective, until oil was discovered in Persia in 1908, modern-day Iran today, the Middle East has become a melting pot for turmoil and unrest.

The discovery and production of oil in the Middle East exemplifies the *resource curse*, the curse on those countries with an abundance of natural resources, specifically non-renewable resources like oil. These countries tend to have less economic growth, less democracy, and less development than those countries with fewer natural resources. They likewise have relied on the norms and beliefs of ancient religions when it comes to the natural evolution of life over time. Specifically, that beliefs, norms, and culture should remain stagnant.

In any case, I was now tasked to test the enemy lines for my president and, hopefully, come away with positive results. It had been a long weekend of cramming.

After my long weekend hitting the books, I wandered into my White House office blurry eyed Monday morning at a quarter to seven. After grabbing a second cup of coffee, I sat and tried to stop thinking about Iran as I waited for the arrival of Sam Wainwright and Sarah Pope.

"You look deep in thought, Tom. Tough weekend?" Sam asked as he entered my office at seven a.m. with Sarah Pope trailing behind him.

"You know it . . . help yourselves to coffee. How were your weekends? Sam, you had dinner with Jane Wyatt. How did that go?"

"Dinner date?" Sarah said, eyes raised, looking at Sam as she took a seat at the conference table."

"I am allowed to date, Sarah. I am single."

"Well, that's nice and it's about time. If I wasn't gay, I might be interested."

"Okay you two. Janet and I had a pleasant time together, enough said. Now, let's move off the subject of my love life and discuss the reason we got up early this Monday morning to meet here, CIPC leaks and signal intelligence on the bad guys. It's unfortunate our laws only allow the NSA, FBI and Department of Homeland Security to surveil international traffic. We're severely limited in how we can monitor U.S.-based paramilitary groups online without justification. Hell, the FBI is even banned from assuming false identities to gain access to private messaging apps used by extremist groups such as the Proud Boys or Oath Keepers."

"No question, Sam. It puts all of us at a disadvantage. Federal authorities can only browse through unprotected information on social media sites like Twitter and Meta and other open online platforms," Sarah said.

"But the NSA and FBI can conduct this surveillance as a byproduct of proven communications between a foreign terrorist group and a U.S. based organization or individual," I said. "Has the NSA's new code drop uncovered any new links that can be pursued legally? Have they gathered any probative information they can present to a judge to secure a surveillance warrant on a U.S. group or citizen who wants to overthrow the government?"

"The new code drop has helped, Tom. Our hit rate grew significantly with John's code," Sarah said. "In fact, there were several very interesting communications this past week. The analysis isn't complete yet but there are several threats that look to be brewing in North Korea and Iran. And last night, one of my analysts sent me an interesting hit he has been working. We will confirm in a day or two, but from preliminary cryptanalysis decipher of the signals intelligence messages, it looks like a member of an Al Qaeda spinoff group we've been tracking out of the UK had a conversation with a person with links to a white nationalist group here in the U.S."

"Now that's exactly what I'm looking for," Sam said. "Am I to assume Tom and I are the first to hear about this?"

"Outside of the senior NSA team, yes. This information will probably be briefed to the combined intelligence team later this week when we can confirm the information. Of course, it will be in the President's Daily Brief."

"Anything else?" Sam asked.

"Possibly," I said. "Apparently a woman by the name of Abigail Briarcliff is trying to pick up the pieces and reunite the stragglers from Lucretia Jane's white nationalist group. She's trying to merge several of the splinter groups and is also in discussions with a few of the antigovernment groups. I'm going to give Lucretia Jane a call and also see if Savannah can assign one of her investigative reporters to confirm the validity of the rumor. Given the government's legal restrictions, I'll push the surveillance to a nongovernment entity, the U.S. press. And what better group to handle it than Savannah and the Washington Post."

"I concur with that," Sam said. "If there's a burning ember out there, Savannah and her team will uncover it. This is good. Very good. I feel better. We have a few potential leads."

"Sad isn't it," Sarah said. "We get excited about uncovering possible threats to the homeland, external threats as well as internal threats. Normal people would probably think we need therapy."

"Unfortunately, it's the world we live in, Sarah." Sam responded. "Somebody has to do it, find the bad guys and put them in jail. We happen to be in the *'find them'* process at the moment. The *'put them in jail'* process will hopefully occur before the people we find actually break the law and injure or kill innocent people."

Sarah looked at Sam and gave a wistful sigh.

"It's good against evil, Sarah. Someone must stand up on the side of good. I don't know any group better prepared to do it, especially with John on our side," I said.

Sarah looked quizzically at me. I hoped to one day soon explain the significance of my comment but today was not the day. Instead I said, "keep us posted as soon as your latest SIGINT is fully deciphered, Sarah. I'll follow up with Lucretia Jane and Savannah and will take it from there."

* * * *

After the meeting with Sam and Sarah ended, I had just enough time to make a short phone call. I had a meeting with Secretary Bentley and his team scheduled before their flight to Alaska. I quickly called Warden Janet Reece's number.

Lucretia Jane was currently an inmate at Warden Reece's low security federal corrections institution located in Danbury, Connecticut. She had been incarcerated for two years of a five-year sentence as a result of a vote tampering scheme that was uncovered in the runup to the 2020 elections. Lucretia led an organization formed by her great-great grandmother who advocated for white supremacy and the maintenance of monuments of Civil War generals and soldiers, traitors in every sense of the word.

Through my efforts and with the assistance of Sam Wainwright and Savannah Lee, we were able to prove a fraudulent voting scheme existed. Our break finally came when Lucretia Jane decided to provide critical evidence to the authorities. Her reason for giving evidence was to prevent her eleven-year-old daughter from following in her footsteps. She wanted her to escape the pressure that she had felt to take over the leadership in the hate group founded by her great-great grandmother. At a meeting with me two weeks before the 2020 elections, Lucretia Jane handed me a thumb drive that contained the proof that led to country-wide arrests, including her own arrest.

Rather than taking an offer to enter into a federal witness protection program for herself and her daughter, she declined and insisted that she be prosecuted along with all the co-conspirators. She did not want her daughter's life disrupted in any way and insisted that she not be identified as the source of the incriminating information.

The government kept that promise. Within a year of incarceration, Lucretia was transferred to the minimum-security prison located in Danbury Connecticut. As often as possible, I would

World Peace: Tom Lawson Novel #4
By James Brown

call Janet Reece, the FCI Danbury Warden, and request a lunch pass for Lucretia.

"FCI Danbury, Warden Janet Reece's office."

"Hello, this is Tom Lawson. Would Warden Reece have a few minutes to take my call?"

"Mr. Lawson. Please hold and I'll check."

A few moments later, Warden Reece said, "Hi Tom, it's been awhile. How is everything in Washington?"

"Busy, as always. How have you been, Janet?'

"No complaints. It's pretty mild here in Danbury compared to your new job there in Washington, I'm sure. You've signed up for at least a year, right?"

"That's the plan. I've been flying back to Connecticut at least every two weeks and will be back in Connecticut on Friday."

"Are you planning another visit to Danbury?"

"If possible, yes. Are you still providing inmates lunch passes for exceptional behavior?"

"We are. I'm guessing you would like to schedule a lunch date with Lucretia Jane?"

"I would, Janet. A late lunch, probably around two p.m. I will text you as soon as I land at Bradley on Friday."

"Buffalo Wild Wings, right?"

"Lucretia loves her finger-lickin' chicken. She complains that Wild Wings is inferior to Gus' World-Famous Fried Chicken Restaurant in Austin, Texas but she says it's still superior to your chicken, Janet."

"Well, if the food is too good here, the inmates may want to stay and worse case, want to return," she teased. "We can't let that happen. It costs too much to house and feed them as it is."

"I can image. Thank you, Janet. I'll text you as soon as I land."

* * * *

After my call ended I grabbed my folder and headed to the State Department building which was a short walk from my office in the White House. After clearing security, I took the elevator to Secretary Bentley's office on the seventh floor. The meeting was about to start. I was the last to arrive and I took a seat next to Maddi Pool. Across from me were Deputy Secretary of State Barbara Shirley and Zheng Shih, the State Department's diplomat for China.

"How was your weekend, Tom?" Maddi asked.

"I studied all weekend. It felt like I was back in college."

"Preparing for your march up that hill to test those enemy lines, huh?"

"Doing my best to be prepared," I said as Secretary Bentley finished his call and walked over to the conference table and took his seat.

"This meeting won't take long. We'll be leaving for Alaska in a couple of hours. So let's get started. Maddi, what's the latest from Ah Lam?"

"So far, so good. I spoke with her an hour ago. She said Huan Cheng is looking forward to your meeting him. Intrigued is the word Cheng used. Joining him will be Vice Premier Li Chao and Hu Lin from the Ministry of Finance. Only these three will attend. Cheng stressed to Ah Lam that there should be no communications associated with this meeting. He has concern that if the purpose of the meeting is communicated too soon, undue pressure will flow to keep anything meaningful from these discussions from becoming a reality. Ah Lam stressed this."

"I completely agree with Cheng's concerns," Bentley said. He turned toward Jan Polaski seated to his right. "Jan, there will undoubtedly be questions coming up at your daily brief this afternoon. The standard line should be that the state department will be conducting meetings with many of our global counterparts as a policy of President Stephen's new administration. The meeting held in Reykjavik with Russia Finance Minister Popov was a first of many sessions to follow."

"I understand, Secretary Bentley. I'm prepared to answer any questions that might come up," Polaski said.

"On a new topic, how about NSA signal intelligence, Maddi?" Bentley asked. "Anything coming out of China, Russia, North Korea, or Iran or any other country that might have an impact on our CIPC project?"

"Two communications related to North Korea and Iran hit our alert program. We're not sure if it's CIPC related or a potential terrorist threat. The information analysis is not complete yet, but we will have confirmation in a day or two. Also, late last night one of my analysts sent me an interesting hit he's been working. From preliminary cryptanalysis decipher of the signals intelligence messages, it looks like a member of an Al Qaeda spinoff group we've been tracking out of the UK had a conversation with a person with links to a white nationalist group here in the U.S. The conversation is being deciphered."

"The times we are living in now, unfortunately. Keep us posted, Maddi. Tom, I assume you are hitting the books and absorbing everything you can about Iran and the Middle East?"

"Yes, sir. I'll be ready to support Deputy Secretary Shirley for our session with Iran."

"Okay, good. Barbara, have you received a response from Elias Muller?"

"I have. Switzerland Foreign Minister Muller dropped me a message late Sunday. He has been in contact with Iran's Foreign Minister Farhad Behzadi regarding our meeting request. I mentioned our desire to meet in Vienna in early June and suggested June second and third to see if those dates would work. Minister Behzadi asked what the purpose of the meeting was, and Minister Muller reiterated that it was the new U.S. president's desire to introduce members of his State Department team, and that similar meetings have been held and are planned over the next several months. His feedback was that the timing would be good for Iran's Foreign Minister. As such we have begun making the arrangements, booking rooms and a venue at the Grand Hotel in Vienna."

"Excellent, Barbara. Let's hope the sessions with Iran turns out as well as they did with the Russians."

"The meeting with the China delegation also," Barbara replied.

"Ah Lam has done very well with the initial preparations and discussions with Huan Cheng. After our session this week, hopefully Cheng and Vice Premier Li Chao will agree to move forward as the Russian delegation agreed to do. And with Russia and China on board, the effort should be easier to induce North Korea and Iran to do so also. Once this is accomplished, and a G-5 Summate is agreed to, we will formally make an announcement regarding our CIPC goals. Are there any other questions or concerns anyone has?" Bentley asked.

With no questions asked, Secretary Bentley thanked everyone and adjourned the meeting.

World Peace: Tom Lawson Novel #4
By James Brown

* * * *

"Good morning everyone," Jan Polaski said as she walked to the White House podium for her daily noon press briefing. "I hope everyone was able to enjoy the gorgeous spring weekend we had. The heat and humidity will be with us soon enough, so do try and enjoy these spring days when you can."

Sounds of agreement emanated in the packed pressroom. Jan took a moment to scan her opening remarks.

"Okay, let's get started. I have a couple of announcements before we go to questions. If you haven't kept up with the latest news from the CDC, the U.S. is now up to a Covid-19 vaccination rate of ninety percent of the population, adults and children five years of age and older. Though we are hopeful this number will continue upward, it is still very good. Illnesses and deaths from Covid-19 are approaching the same level as is typical for the common flu.

Of course we would prefer no deaths for either of these viruses. Perhaps one day that will be the case as our scientists continue to work on developing new vaccines. Regarding the worldwide front, the Covid-19 vaccine rate has now reached seventy percent and much higher rates are expected by the end of the year.

A couple of announcements regarding the president's schedule this week. President Stephen will travel to San Francisco on Tuesday to participate in the two-day U.S. Business Climate Conference. This conference will focus on efforts to achieve net zero carbon emissions. The majority of our large carbon users are working very hard to exceed the targets of the Paris Climate Agreement. Many companies will achieve net zero carbon emissions far sooner than expected.

A couple other meetings to report on. Secretary Bentley recently traveled to Reykjavik to meet with his counterpart from Russia, Foreign Affairs Minister Nikita Popov. He and his team will schedule similar sessions in Europe and Asia over the next several weeks. I will now take your questions."

Looking out into the audience Polaski said, "Brian, Fox News."

"Thank you, Jan. My question has to do with the voter rights bill that failed in the last administration. Now that President Stephen has a majority in the House and a margin large enough in the Senate to stop any filibuster, will a voter rights bill move to the top of the legislative agenda?"

"Rest assured that it will! Next question. Andrea, MSNBC."

"A question regarding sanctions, Jan. Given there are new leaders now in Russia, China, North Korea and Iran, what discussions have taken place regarding current sanctions in place against many of these countries?"

"A reasonable question, Andrea. I do not have anything to report at this time other than this question which is under discussion by the new administration. As a general comment, any changes to the U.S. sanctions or trade agreements will ultimately depend on the policies and actions these new government leaders put in place. Ideally, we hope the new leaders strongly consider and establish policies that are consistent with international rules and standards," Polaski said.

Catching the time on the wall clock, she thought she'd give the press another thirty minutes and then cut them off. So far, so good. "Let's go to the back of the room. Margaret, The New York Times."

World Peace: Tom Lawson Novel #4
By James Brown

Chapter 25

It was eight a.m. and Diana answered on the second ring.

"Good morning. I was just getting ready to leave. Anything new since we spoke last evening?" Diana asked. "You're still flying back to Connecticut on Friday, aren't you?"

"As far as I know, but I can see the days will be getting a lot longer very soon."

"How so? Did you meet with the president after we spoke yesterday?"

"I did. A very late session with him. A follow up meeting is scheduled this morning. The president wants to press forward on a few politically charged items that did not move forward under his predecessor."

"The filibuster rule and voting rights," Diana quickly interjected.

"You've missed your calling, honey. You can see the future."

"Comes with the job as a therapist, listening to a whole lot of issues that people share and learning how to read people, when they are being honest, telling the truth or lying."

"Maybe you should join me at the meeting this morning. And better yet, have you sit in on a few congressional sessions."

"No thank you. I prefer to listen to the people who seek my help. Those individuals can be helped."

I smiled. "A logical assessment. Many of the politicians I've met here in Washington have no desire to seek advice from those who might have a different opinion. And certainly would not admit to having a personality issue. As for my late-night meeting with the president, he's going to press Speaker Mahoney to initiate the process to bring the voter rights bill for a vote and then have Senate Majority

World Peace: Tom Lawson Novel #4
By James Brown

Leader Hutcheson take on the filibuster rule. With the democratic party win in Texas and two solid, middle of the road Dems in Arizona, though a small majority in the Senate the president believes the Dems can finally get rid of the filibuster rule."

"That would be great, Tom. Let the rule of the majority finally take charge. Can you imagine what could be done?"

"Sure. In addition to a fair and inclusive voting rights law, how about banning the AR-15 and high-capacity weapons for civilian use. And for God sakes, force the gun industry to develop smart guns and rifles. We have smart homes now that can turn on lights, tell you when a door is open, or when a person is lurking outside. They can damn well develop a gun that only the authorized owner can shoot."

"So many lives could be saved with that technology," Diana said.

"Very true, hon. Very true. Let's hope the president and congress can get it done."

* * * *

After saying goodbye to Diana I finished reading several reports and then headed down to the first floor of the White House. I said hello to Janene Morgan who sat outside the Oval Office and walked in and took a seat on the sofa next to Jan Polaski, the President's Press Secretary.

"You're early, Tom," Polaski said. "I expected you might join us closer to your seventeen-minute rule."

"Not today. I'm expecting the president to join us on time this morning. Marching orders will be issued today so he won't be late for this meeting."

"Ah, you have inside scoop on what he's going say. Tell me."

"Not my information to tell."

"Of course not, just thought I would check."

"The journalist that you are. It's in your DNA."

With that said, in walked President Stephen with Andrew Kennedy trailing behind him.

"Good morning," President Stephen said with everyone responding in kind.

Chief of Staff Andrew Kennedy took the chair next to the president while Vice President Linda Bing sat on the opposite side of the Resolute desk. Speaker of the House Abigail Mahoney and Senate

Majority Leader Michael Hutcheson sat on the sofa across from me and Jan Polaski.

"I asked Andrew to reschedule a few meetings this morning and I hope it wasn't too inconvenient for everyone. I wanted to update you on preliminary results of Secretary Bentley's CIPC discussions in Anchorage with the Chinese team. In a nutshell, Peter and his team's first day has gone surprisingly well. Peter conveyed that Vice Chairman Chao and Director Cheng are on board. Tomorrow they are expecting to outline a framework for an agreement."

"Congratulations, Mr. President, Speaker Abigail Mahoney said. "Assuming China, Russia, and the U.S. can come to an agreement, North Korea and Iran will certainly agree."

"That would be a logical result," President Stephen said. "The next several weeks will be critical. Secretary Bentley and his team will be meeting with North Korea next week and Tom and Deputy Secretary Shirley will be holding a similar session with the Iranians. Then, the following Monday we have President Milosevic meeting with me at the Whitehouse."

"With the CIPC program likely becoming front page news." Speaker Mahoney interjected.

"Yes, very likely, Abigail. One of my concerns. I prefer the CIPC program not be the top story of the day. Not yet anyway. Not until all five countries agree to move forward with a formal agreement or treaty. If we don't keep the CIPC program out of the news or at minimum, keep it as a back page story, the undue pressure on these new government leaders may become too great."

"So you want another shoe to drop first?" Speaker Mahoney asked.

"I do. And perhaps not the best way to say it, kill two birds with one stone. I think It is a perfect time to address the filibuster rule and resurrect our gun safety bill. Let majority rule for once. End the filibuster rule and eliminate those weapons that should only be used by our military and restrict high magazine handguns. Also, its high time that gun manufacturers develop smart guns."

"Before your first term in office ends." Secretary Polaski said.

"Correct. It is time we eliminate the filibuster rule and take military weapons out of the hands of the public. And there is no reason smart guns can't be designed and manufactured within three years. If the gun manufactures can't do it we will have Microsoft, Apple, or any number our tech companies design the capability for them. Only smart guns and rifles should be available for the public, guns that cannot fire unless the approved and authorized owner of the weapon pulls the trigger."

The room was silent for a moment when Majority Leader Hutcheson spoke up. "Sir, gun safety, maybe, but your desire to end the filibuster rule will still not be easy."

"That's our job, Hutch, taking on jobs that aren't easy to accomplish. It's high time that good legislation, legislation that the majority of the country wants to become law, is not held up by an archaic rule that the senate conjured up to ensure discriminatory policies could remain. It's time, Hutch. It's time for democracy to finally work. It's time that the will of the people prevails rather than the will of special interest groups and the politicians who are funded by them."

Two weeks ladies and gentlemen. I want to see draft legislation within two weeks. Understood!"

"Understood, Sir," Speaker Mahoney said. "The gun restriction legislation has long been written, just waiting for the Senate to have the right people on board to overturn the filibuster rule."

The president stood. "Okay then. Let's get it done."

* * * *

Doctor Peggy Landon and her husband William arrived at New Haven Hospital at ten a.m. The temperature was in the low sixties and a bright, brilliantly blue cloudless sky overlayed a colorful spring bloom of flowers as they walked along the sidewalk toward the hospital's entrance.

"Couldn't have a better day than today to complete a successful trifecta. The initial surgery was successful, physical therapy has gone well, and now, on this beautiful morning, we are here to witness Cody Walker take his first unaided steps." William said in an upbeat tone.

"Fingers crossed," Peggy replied looking up to the sky to seek divine assistance if that was possible.

The Landon's entered the hospital and proceeded to the physical therapy center where Cody Walker was scheduled to take his first unaided steps since he was involved in an auto accident that left him paralyzed from the waist down. A high school star basketball player prior to his accident, during the past two years he was wheelchair bound, a future that he and so many accident victims are consigned to endure. That was the prognosis for Cody and those with severe spinal injuries before Doctor Peggy Landon and her team of neurosurgeons and computer scientists entered the picture.

The breakthrough surgery came after Peggy Landon's husband, William was in a terrible auto accident that left him in a coma for five years. With William's life and Doctor Landon's world completely upended, she and a team of medical and technology experts spent the next five years developing advanced neurological solutions to bring William out of his comatose state. What she and her team learned from their efforts to cure William became the basis for her team's miracle cure that would enable Cody to take his first steps and leave his wheelchair behind.

"Good morning, Peggy, William," Doctor Sandeep Singh said as they entered the room where young Cody Walker was waiting and hoping to take his first unaided steps. Standing next to Cody's bedside were his parents, Carole and Eugene Walker. Also standing just in the entrance of the room was Doctor Isabelle Lazarus, the President of New Haven Hospital. Doctor Lazarus of course was very hopeful that young Cody Walker would regain the use of his legs. However, her primary reason for being in the room on this day was to witness the miracle she knew would bring untold financial benefit and prestige to her hospital.

Doctor Lazarus had been pressing Doctor Landon and her team to publish their results in the New England Journal of Medicine, the queen of all general medical journals, a weekly medical journal published by the Massachusetts Medical Society. It was known as the most prestigious medical journal as well as the oldest continuously published one. With Cody Walker taking his first unaided steps after being paralyzed from the waist down for the past two years, Doctor Peggy Landon and her team would be a lock for the next Nobel Prize in Medicine. And New Haven Hospital would reap untold recognition and financial benefits.

"Good morning, Cody," Doctor Landon said as she walked over to his bed. She put a hand on his wrist and held it for a few minutes, silently counting the beats of his pulse.

"This is the day, Doctor Landon. I'm ready. I've been working very hard these last few weeks with the physical therapy team, and I feel great, like I haven't felt in years."

"That's very good, Cody. Your pulse is strong. Let's take a look at your legs," she said as she folded up the light sheet covering Cody's legs.

With Doctor Singh on the opposite side of Cody's bed, Doctor Landon took hold of Cody's right foot and rotated it slightly to the left and right and asked Cody to respond to what he felt. With eyes closed, he smiled and said, "warm hands on my cool right foot."

She then moved up to his lower leg and squeezed his calf. "You're squeezing my right calf now after you moved your hand up the front side of my leg to my right knee."

After a few seconds past, Cody said with his eyes still closed, "oh, this is getting dangerous, my very attractive doctor is moving her hands well up beyond my right knee."

This comment brought a laugh by Doctor Landon and a tear to the eyes of Cody's mother. "Okay, Cody, are you able lift your right leg up off the bed?"

Cody proceeded to lift his right leg up off the bed and held it just above the bed.

"Excellent," Doctor Landon said as Cody lowered his leg back to the bed. She then gave a nod to Doctor Singh.

"New hands," Cody said. "Larger and squeezing a little harder. Doctor Singh no doubt."

"That is correct," Doctor Singh said as he repeated the process as Doctor Landon had conducted. Within fifteen minutes Cody had passed all the tests asked of him while he laid in his bed.

"Okay, Cody. Are you ready to take the next test?" Doctor Landon asked.

Tears welled up in Cody's eyes. "I've been ready for this day to come for two years now. I am more than ready." He raised up in his bed and swung his legs over the side and remained seated for a few moments. Doctor Landon and Doctor Singh stood at his left side and two of his physical therapists stood at his right.

Cody looked over at his mom and dad and slid off his bed and stood. Then after steading himself he moved his right leg forward and shifted his weight with his left leg moving forward. Cody was walking.

He continued to walk slowly with his doctors and physical therapists walking next to him ready to provide aid should it be needed. Tears rolled down Cody's face as he walked a little faster about the room.

After walking around the room for five minutes, Doctor Landon said, "you're ready, Cody. I will initiate your discharge papers and you can go home with your parents. But I want to see you at my office in Old Saybrook in two weeks."

"Thank you so much, Doctor Landon," Cody said as he stood and gave her a very tight hug.

"You are very welcome, Cody. When we meet in two weeks, in addition to seeing how you are doing, we will also discuss the notoriety that will begin for you as well as for my team. Our breakthrough surgery will soon be getting quite a lot of press. And rightfully so. You are making history, Cody. History that we pray can be repeated for the tens of thousands of those who have lost their ability to walk due to spinal injuries."

"I look forward to being the poster boy Doctor Landon," Cody said and grinned. "Maybe you show a picture of me taking a winning three point shot I made two years ago, then a picture of me being pulled from a very damaged car, followed by a picture of me in a wheelchair two years later, and then a final picture of me driving to the basket for a highflying dunk a month from now. Now that's publicity that will get some attention."

"I'm sure it would, Cody. We'll discuss that when you come for a checkup in two weeks, along with your parents," Doctor Landon said.

After Doctors Landon and Singh received heartwarming hugs from Cody's parents and a wide smile and thumbs up from New Haven Hospital president Doctor Lazarus, they headed out of the room to initiate Cody's hospital discharge papers.

Outside Cody's room, Sandeep said excitedly, "the Nobel Prize, Peggy. You are a shoo in."

"Both of us, Sandeep. I could not have done it alone. There are many on our team who deserve to be recognized," she said. She then turned to William and whispered, "John."

William smiled and squeezed her hand. Without his assistance, one very brilliant AI entity, Cody would still be wheelchair bound.

Chapter 26

It was another one of President Stephen's early morning meetings. Press Secretary Jan Polaski and Janene Murphy, Director of the Office of Management and Budgets, sat in silence on the sofa in the Oval Office across from President Stephen who was rapidly reading a summary report he was given an hour earlier. The report contained comments made by a number of well-respected economists, politicians, and talk show pundits.

The Stephen administration was beginning to feel the pressure of office less than twenty-four hours after the release of the president's first fiscal year budget. The reason for the early morning meeting on a Friday.

The budget was released the day earlier, day 116 into his first term as president. Of particular concern by the opposition party and those within the military industrial complex, other than the lateness of its release, was his planned budget for defense spending. The defense budget would be reduced by five percent from the previous year's budget level.

Of equal significance, President Stephen was proposing to make significant changes to policies that afforded privileged tax treatment for corporations and the wealthy elite. Of particular concern by many were the planned tax changes that would affect the financial sector and hedge fund managers and private investment companies in particular. Though Stephen's predecessor had significantly improved the country's balance sheet through strategic tax law changes to fund infrastructure and human capital needs to enhance America's long-term competitiveness, Stephen's goal was to put the country on a path to reduce the country's budget deficit as a percentage of gross domestic product.

One of Stephen's targets were private equity firms which focused on mobilizing and leveraging capital with borrowed funds to accumulate tremendous amount of assets under their management. A major economic force in the economy, investments by these firms included leveraged buyouts, market-neutral investment strategies in publicly traded stocks and bonds, energy, and other commodities, and various arbitrage strategies and entirely unreported transactions. These private pools of capital were unregulated and exempt from Securities and Exchange Commission regulation.

In addition to being unregulated, Stephen and economists had long argued that these financial institutions reaped substantial benefits from special tax provisions that ordinary citizens could not benefit from. The professional fund managers of hedge funds and private equity firms were allowed to treat a substantial portion of their compensation as capital gains rather than the higher income tax rate that were applied to ordinary income such as wages and salary.

President Stephen intended to put in place a budget and accompanying tax changes that would put America on a more solid financial footing. He likewise planned to level the playing field for ordinary salaried wage earners and those who received preferential treatment from income generated by capital investments at a lower tax rate.

Finished reading the summary document, President Stephen put the report on the sofa next to him. "So, what do you think, Janene?"

"Exactly what we expected. Those affected are grumbling and the practical ones are saying it's about time. Meaning you are spot on with your thinking. The biggest challenge will be the five percent cut in the defense budget. The military and defense industry will be pressing hard to increase those numbers to cover inflation at a minimum."

"Well, Janene, a little belt tightening will be good for them. I'm sure there is a lot of inefficiencies that can be rung out to cover the five percent plus the small inflationary bump. In reality, the cut should be even higher given the withdrawal of troops from Afghanistan that the prior administration initiated. Let's start drafting a few press releases and talking papers.

World Peace: Tom Lawson Novel #4
By James Brown

"Jan, I'm sure I don't need to remind you, but you will undoubtedly be bombarded at your daily brief today. Also, we need to prepare talking points to get ready for additional questions that will follow from the upcoming meetings with North Korea and Iran. Work with Andrew and squeeze in a session with me for some time on Monday. State should participate of course. The word will get out before Bentley and Shirley's teams fly out to North Korea and Austria on Monday."

"I'll coordinate with Andrew, Sir. As for today's briefing, the Daily Briefing group, which Janene's OMB team is a part of, is working on a draft briefing document for today's session. I'll have a copy for you right after our CIPC meeting."

"Okay, thank you both. It's time for the CIPC meeting."

"Thank you, Mr. President," Janene said and exited the Oval Office as the next group entered.

Jan remained in her seat on the sofa as the rest of the CIPC meeting attendees entered the Oval Office and took their regular seats throughout the room. The only member of the group missing was Vice President Linda Bing who was at a fund raiser in California.

After everyone was seated, President Stephen said, "good morning, everyone. We are nearing the end of a very productive week. The weather was beautiful, our release of the next fiscal year budget has hit the street, and the positives and negatives were what we expected them to be, and most significantly, Peter and his team hit a home run with the Chinese delegation. Congratulations, Peter."

CIA Director Angela Keen, seated next to Secretary Bentley on the sofa, gave him a congratulatory pat on the shoulder while others in the room voiced their congratulations.

"Thank you everyone," Bentley responded. "The sessions indeed went very well. At this stage of our CIPC initiative, the Chinese team is on board. They have likewise agreed to a June 14 date for a G5 summit. They also concurred that if Russia follows through with our plans, North Korea and Iran will also participate."

"Excellent, Peter. Excellent job by you and your team," the president said and turned toward Chief of Staff Andrew Kennedy. "Andrew, has arrangements been finalized for our meeting with President Milosevic?"

World Peace: Tom Lawson Novel #4
By James Brown

"Everything has been confirmed, Mr. President. I spoke with Chief of Staff Alexander Alexeyev this morning. The meeting is confirmed for June 7 here at the White House. Joining Milosevic and Alexeyev will be Foreign Affairs Minister Nikita Popov and Legal Director and Presidential Aide Natalia Smirnov. Vadim Ivanov, Russia's wealthiest oligarch and very good friend of Milosevic's, will also be participating."

"A very interesting group," the president replied. "Now let's turn to North Korea and Iran. Is everything still a go for both next week?"

"They are," CIA director Keen said. "Min-ho Won, our agent in North Korea, has confirmed the meeting for Wednesday and Thursday. Min-ho said attending will be President Kim Kyung-mi and two of her advisors, Mr. Joo Lo, and Ms. Rji Ah. Peter, Johnathan Cooke, and Yun Ki-moon will be leading the effort from our side. While the meeting is going on in Pyongyang, Barbara, Tom, and Hassan Zarif will be meeting with the Iranians in Vienna."

President Stephen sat back in his chair and pondered a moment, then said, "Maddi, Sam, what's happening in cyberspace and on the ground? Anything of significance that can jeopardize our objectives?"

Madeline Pool spoke first. "In Russia, our agents report the situation has stabilized but the political unrest is still very real. Milosevic needs a win. He needs to make significant improvement in the economy, reduce unemployment and increase wages and benefits for the poor and middle class. The income disparity has reached a critical level. As for China, their situation is considerably different. Their economy is still growing, but at a substantially lower level than during its years of very high double-digit growth.

They also have a growing challenge with increasing debt within their government owned or highly subsidized industries. Debt that they cannot continue to sustain for long."

"What about the U.S., Sam?"

Sam looked over at Maddi then said, "unfortunately, we do not have an ability to adequately surveille domestic terror groups, those groups that profess to be law abiding citizens but truly want to overthrow the government. If any of these groups show linkage to a foreign terror group, then we can more easily monitor them."

"So nothing significant?" the president asked.

Wainwright pondered a moment. "Well . . . that would depend, Sir. We have countless numbers of federal crimes that are being investigated or turned over to the Justice department for prosecution. Likewise, we have many hundreds of efforts underway to assess death threats and general bullying that happens far too often. To those who are on the receiving end of these threats and actions, yes, they are significant. But as for overthrowing the U.S. government? No actionable threats are yet confirmed."

The president nodded slowly, understanding that governing and satisfying all of the people was very difficult, especially when falsehoods and outright lies can be passed along via social media and news outlets that promote ratings and profits over facts. The president finally said, "Andrew, we need to move up our planned Section 230 discussion. It's time that social media falls in line with traditional media outlets. Television and radio have been licensed and regulated for decades."

"I'll do that, Mr. President. It's in our schedule but I'll pull it forward."

"Thank you. Okay then," President Stephen said, looking about the room. "Any other topics, issues or problems?"

"Nothing on my end," Secretary Bentley said with the other meeting attendees commenting the same.

"Peter, Tom. Keep me posted next week on how your meetings are going with North Korea and Iran. Good luck."

With both responding in the affirmative, the meeting broke up and the attendees left the Oval Office while another group filed in.

* * * *

I walked out of the CIPC meeting with Sam and stopped for a moment before taking the elevator to the second floor and my office.

"You're heading back to Connecticut this morning. Taking the subway, I assume," Sam asked.

"I am. About a five-minute walk to the Farragut West subway station then a fifteen-minute ride to Reagan. Thirty-five minutes if I miss the train which runs every fifteen minutes."

"You can be chauffeured in comfort if you would like."

"It's out of your way, Sam, but thank you."

"How about Lucretia Jane? Are you still driving to the Danbury correctional facility before heading home?"

"Yes, it's still the plan. I want to see what Lucretia knows about our friendly white supremacist groups and see if she has better information than what your team is able to uncover. I can't imagine that Lucretia doesn't know what is being planned if anything."

"Are you still being signed in under the name of Adam Smith, mild mannered reporter from the Washington Post?" Sam asked.

"I am. I need to protect Lucretia, keep the secret that it was Lucretia who provided the evidence that took down those politicians and right-wing racist groups who tried to rig the last election."

"I even have a press card with Adam Smith's name on it."

Sam grinned. "Savannah can be very helpful, can't she."

"She's my boss. At least when I play the role of mild-mannered reporter, Adam Smith."

"Okay, call me if Lucretia has anything solid to offer and give Diana a hug for me."

"Will do, Sam," I said as I walked into the elevator.

After finishing a couple phone calls, I headed out of my office with my computer and roller bag and left the White House and walked toward the Farragut West subway station. I managed to reach the station before the train pulled out and was at Reagan Washington Airport with plenty of time to spare.

My flight left on time at ten a.m., and I was in my rental car at Connecticut's Bradley airport heading toward Danbury correctional facility an hour and a half later. The seventy-mile drive from the airport took longer than my flight from Washington. It was close to two p.m. when I arrived at the Buffalo Wild Wings restaurant located in a small strip mall opposite the Danbury Municipal Airport.

A replica of most of the Buffalo Wild Wings restaurant chain, the lunch crowd had mostly gone, and I was able to take a booth at the far corner of the room. This was my third lunch meeting with Lucretia since she was incarcerated in Danbury. Though Lucretia turned state's evidence, her conversations remained a tight secret. The reason was her desire to protect her twelve-year-old daughter. She did not want to disrupt her daughter's life by entering into a witness protection program.

Lucretia Jane had assumed the role as head of a white supremacy organization as part of her lineage, the leadership of the organization her distant grandmother held as its founder just after the U.S. Civil War. Groomed and pressured to continue in her grandmother's footsteps since she was a child, she vowed that she would break the chain for her daughter's sake. Lucretia provided the voter tampering evidence to the FBI that resulted in the conviction of politicians and members of racist organizations. But she stipulated for her testimony remain a secret and that she be prosecuted and punished for her actions along with all the others who were indicted. Her purpose was to insure that she and her daughter did not have a bullseye on their backs.

Within ten minutes of my arrival, Lucretia Jane walked into the restaurant with a young man wearing a short sleeve, white Polo golf shirt that hung outside of his beige slacks and hid the holstered gun at his side. The woman smiled at me and walked to my table while her escort took a seat at the counter just inside the room. As she approached, the heavyset grandmother looking woman with salt and pepper hair that I first met, had changed significantly in appearance. Her hair was now as white as newly fallen snow, but she no longer looked like an overweight grandmother. What did not change were those deep blue eyes that caught my attention when we first met. I stood and gave her a hug.

"My, Lucretia, this health spa of yours has done wonders. You look ten years younger."

"They do control the caloric intake at the spa. Working, exercising, reading, that's about it."

"Well you look great, and you should be out in three years if not sooner. How's your daughter?"

"Amelia is great. She recently turned fourteen and is a freshman in high school now. We talk often and she comes for a visit whenever she can. I'm hopeful that I will be out of this spa by the time she graduates. I'd love to attend her graduation."

"I think I can make that happen, Lucretia, if not sooner."

"Thank you, Tom. Something to look forward to. Now, before we order that chicken meal that is better than what the spa offers, but inferior to Gus' finger-lickin' chicken in Austin, what can I do for you?"

"Well, a lot has happened since you were incarcerated. The world has changed quite a bit."

"The good guys are still trying to keep the bad guys at bay though, right?" Lucrecia said.

"That never changes, Lucretia."

"So, am I to assume you and Sam and Savannah haven't been able to access too much information from several of my former associates since they are being very careful what they exchange on the Internet?"

I nod. "We're afraid everyone has gone underground. They've been very good at keeping their plans a secret."

"Think another attack on the capital is in the distant future?"

"Or worse, and I was wondering if you, or someone you know might have heard anything. There is basically very little chatter which is hardly normal. We're afraid there will soon be an explosion," I said.

"Let's order, Tom. My time on the outside is limited in my Cinderella role here." She held up her hand and got the attention of one of the waitresses."

"What would you like, folks?" A waitress asked.

"My usual, two chicken breasts, collard greens, and mashed potatoes with gravy and a glass of unsweetened tea," Lucretia said and handed the waitress her menu.

"Same for me, ma'am," I said, handing over my menu.

Lucretia looked over at her escort sitting at the counter. He was well into his lunch and reading the local paper. "I have heard a few things. The groups at play now are different, more militant, with quite a few ex-military and ex-cops involved. They're not just angry about race . . . they're just angry. Mandatory masks, vaccinations, the need to treat people they don't like with respect, whatever. Many just feel they are being left behind, that the world is passing them by. They want the 1950s back again."

I frowned, knowing full well this was the case but wishing it wasn't then said, "any suggestions?"

"I have a couple of names that you can start with, Wally Benson and Jackson Knapp. Don't write down their names. Just remember them."

"Okay, Wally Benson and Jackson Brown, with Benson taking a Knapp. I can remember that. What do you know about these gentlemen?"

"They were just getting started with my crew before the bust. Wally is military and Jackson a former police officer. They came highly recommended having formal intelligence training."

"That's great. They know what they're doing in other words."

Lucretia gave several nods as she waited for their waitress to deliver their meals. Digging into her chicken, she said, "from what I've heard they are going back to cold war spying techniques, physical drop boxes, couriers, and encrypted communications when electronic communications are absolutely necessary."

"Both located in Austin?"

"Wally is. Jackson lives in DC."

"Anything else of significance?"

"Just this chicken. It's not finger-lickin' good like Gus' in Austin."

I laughed. "Well, I'll make sure you can share lunch or dinner with your daughter at Gus' real soon."

Lucretia pointed her chicken laden fork at me, and we enjoyed the rest of our lunch. After finishing our lunch and giving Lucretia a hug before she got into the back seat of a county cruiser, I walked across the parking lot to my rental and gave Sam a call. The call went to voicemail, and I asked him to set up a conference call with Savannah if possible and call me while I drove on to Essex. The hunt would soon begin.

Chapter 27

Thirty minutes into my drive from Danbury to Essex, my cell phone rang. The call was from Sam.

"Is Savannah on the call, Sam?"

"She is, both still at the office, not cutting out early like someone I know."

"There are certain benefits associated with being a top advisor to the president, Sam."

"Evidently. What did you learn from Lucretia?"

"Two names you both should discretely look into. Wally Benson and Jackson Knapp. Benson is former military intelligence and Knapp is a former police officer and also has intelligence training. According to Lucretia, given the voter fraud bust that put a lot of their members and politicians in jail, they are going back to cold war spying techniques, physical drop boxes, couriers, and encrypted communications when electronic communications are absolutely necessary."

"Are both of them located in Austin?" Savannah asked.

"Wally, yes. Jackson lives in DC."

After several long seconds, Sam said, "drop boxes and code breaking. I'll have to dig up a few older guys for this one. Not the investigative style for our young data geeks.

"Whatever it takes, Sam. We've got about a month before a lot of changes are going to be announced, and many people, companies, and organizations are not going to be happy with them."

"Gee. We get to add billionaires and CEOs to our list of racists and the disillusioned. That boat and my lake property is looking better and better every day," Sam said.

"How about you, Savannah. Do you have a couple of investigative reporters who can do some discrete poking around?" I asked.

"I do. I've hired a couple new ones that are ready for a meatier investigation. I'll make sure they know that discretion is of utmost importance. When do you get back to Washington?"

"I fly back Sunday evening and then head out to Vienna Monday morning."

"Another cushy vacation while Savannah and I track down bad guys," Sam said.

"Right, the president asks me to help negotiate the CIPC deal with the Iranians. Not too much pressure if I screw up and don't secure a deal."

"True," Sam said. "But look on the bright side, you probably won't have to dodge bullets. Which is a possibility for Savannah and my team."

"Okay, you two. I've passed along my information from Lucretia. I'll also update John and have him give you both a call."

"We still love you, Tom. Give Diana a hug for us," Savannah said and closed the call.

* * * *

I drove on to Essex and pulled into the Monkey Farm parking lot at six p.m. Diana's Subaru was parked close to the door. The crowd was lively as I entered and scanned the large horseshoe bar looking for Diana. It was Friday and apparently the end of a long week for the Old Saybrook crowd. Diana was on the opposite side of the bar talking with Brian Jones, the group's psychiatrist and several other members of her group.

"Tom, you finally made it!" Diana said.

"Good to be home, hon," I said giving her a hug, then turning to the rest of the group. "Hi Brian, Liz. How is everything in the mental health business."

"The reason we are here, Tom," Liz Robinson, one of the group's therapists said and held up her wine glass.

"So what's happening in Washington, if we are allowed to ask."

"Very long days, Brian. I think you, Liz, and Diana and the rest of the team could have a field day treating the Washington crazies and workaholics."

"Including you?" Liz asked.

I grinned. "I'm unique. I have years of training in the field from one of the best shrinks I know," I said, giving Diana a wink and raising a hand toward Ben as he walked by.

"Ah, Tom. "A Corona Light, I assume."

"Sounds good, thanks, Ben."

"But really," Liz continued. "We listen to the news on occasion, and certainly get pummeled by social media streams, but not much has been reported when it comes to those countries who lost their leadership due to John Gordon's actions."

"Except for Russia," I replied as Ben placed my Corona in front of me.

"But that was expected," Brian interjected. "Same for North Korea. Once their strongmen were killed it was expected their citizens would take to the streets. But what's President Stephen's policy going forward with the countries where there leaders were killed by those missile attacks? Not much has been communicated."

Not a question I was expecting on my return trip home and visit to Diana's TGIF gathering at the Monkey Farm. Perhaps from Larry Holms, but not from the group that began gathering around me. With the small group waiting for my reply, I wasn't going to get by with a glib response.

"Of course global stability is high on the priorities of the president's administration. One thing I've learned since my brief time in Washington, is that there are a large number of issues that surface almost daily that every administration must deal with. The president and his team have been monitoring the disruptions that have surfaced and have had conversations with the new leaders who have emerged."

"How about here in the U.S.," Brian continued. "What's happening to keep the malcontents and anarchists from trying to overthrow our democracy. Likewise, putting curbs on social media outlets that spew false information and outright lies that stirs up the idiots that believe whatever they read on a Meta feed, or from Fox News hosts who will say anything to promote their ratings?"

"I didn't think everyone was paying so much attention."

"It's hard not to, Tom. You would have to live in a cave not to see the influence social media is having on everyone. The anti-vaxxers are more obnoxious and threatening then ever even after the covid-19 vaccines have been approved for adults and children and the vaccines work as advertised."

"You're seeing growing mental health issues also I assume," I said.

"Exploding is a better word for it, Tom," Liz said. "Something needs to be done."

I took a moment while Liz and Brian stared at me. Diana remained silent, probably wanting to hear the answer also. Finally, I said, "there's no question, social media has evolved into the dominate source of information for a very large segment of the population here in America and throughout the world. With this transition, unfortunately, a large number of people take no initiative to validate or question the information from social media or those not so honest news outlets. And regrettably, many people simply share the same beliefs that are being communicated, whether or not the information is factual or not."

"It's disgusting," Liz said. "The government needs to do something."

"It's a controversial issue," I said. "Much of the problem has to do with Section 230 of the Communications Decency Act of 1996. Section 230 provides immunity for website platforms with respect to third-party content. When the act was written, there was a concern that if regulations were put in place that made certain content illegal, and someone who had a personal account that violated the law with a posting, who would be liable? The individual or the owner of the platform who allowed that violation, or both? This question has been the underlining issue politicians from both party have been wrestling with.

Social media has argued that since platforms do not generally create their content, they are not responsible for what users produce and are thus exempt from the libel, defamation, and other laws and regulations that govern traditional media like newspapers and television.

Well, this notion and associated hand wringing about this argument is about to change. At a meeting I attended with the president early this morning, Section 230 was discussed. President Stephen has decided that it's time that social media falls in line with traditional media outlets. Television and radio have been licensed and regulated for decades. He has instructed Speaker Mahoney to dust off prior draft legislation to amend the Communications Decency Act of 1996, and specifically Section 230 and fix the problem once and for all."

Liz put her wine glass on the bar. "You've just made my day, Tom," she said and reached up and gave me a big hug.

"The president deserves the hug, Liz. I just happened to be in the room when the 230 issue was being discussed. But I'll take the hug and pass along your appreciation for you."

"Thank you, Tom. Please do," Liz said.

"Well, one critical problem soon to be solved. That's great, Tom. Is world peace next?" Brian asked.

"That's a little above my pay grade and area of influence that I can offer the president, Brian. But I'll keep it in mind should circumstances change."

Brian gave me a pat on the shoulder. "You know, Tom, we here in Old Saybrook have never had a friend working for the most powerful person in the world. We are expecting a lot from you. Our very hopes and dreams are in your hands, Tom," Brian said in a serious, passionate tone.

Standing six foot-seven and looking down at me, I began to wonder if he might be looking for me to achieve an impossible goal similar to a goal he once sought after he finished playing college ball at Indiana University. For me, the goal is to help secure world peace, for Brian, it was to make a pro basketball team after he graduated from college. That goal, Brian was not able to achieve. Finally, a large grin crossed his face.

"Makes you wonder, doesn't it? Achieving a goal that's not so easily done," he said.

"Unfortunately, Brian, wishes don't always come true." I said.

With discussions finally turning to more normal everyday conversations, I slid away from Brian and Liz to allow Margie, the group's office manager, to move up to the bar to place her drink order.

Diana nudged me. "I was thinking a quiet dinner at Taste of China. Fewer people. Are you ready?"

"More than ready," I answered.

After saying our goodbyes, I let everyone know that I would do my best to prod the president and his team to amend the Communications Decency Act legislation with its new Section 230 language and Brian reminded me about his request to achieve world peace. I said I would do my best. With a wide smile and hand wave, Diana and I left the Monkey Farm.

* * * *

At the Taste of China, a few of miles west of the Monkey Farm, the atmosphere of the restaurant was entirely different. It was quiet. Subdued lighting in the dining area along with a small, somewhat isolated seating area with six tables with bench seats, the restaurant was known for its quiet ambiance and excellent Chinese food.

Diana and I were escorted to one of the tables with its bench-partitioned seats. We immediately ordered our standard dinners along with wine for me and vodka tonic for Dana.

After our waiter, Li Chun, returned with our drink orders, Diana said, "it almost seems normal again, here at the Taste of China having a quiet meal together. No looming pressures. We need more evenings like this."

"We do, and I'm sure we will. How about you coming to Washington next weekend after I get back from Vienna? Maybe stay a few days for dinners like this and I'm sure Savannah would love to have you close by for a couple of days. She's going crazy with her wedding date approaching."

Diana laughed. "She and I talk almost daily it seems. This is her second wedding so I'm not quite sure why she's so anxious. But I'm doing my best to help her through it."

"Her readily accessible therapist. The 20th is getting very close. How's she and Cousin Beauregard doing?" I asked.

Diana thought for a moment. "Come to think of it, she hasn't said anything about her cousin. I don't think she ever talks to her, other than I remember she said she told her where the wedding would be held and the dress and accessories the bridesmaids were to wear."

"It will be quite an event. The talk of Washington. The North and South coming together in marriage," I said as Li Chun began serving hot and sour soup and spring rolls.

"Let's just hope Cousin Beauregard isn't upset with Savannah's little charade, not giving her all the details about Barry?" Diana said.

"You don't really think her cousin doesn't know by now that it will be an interracial marriage do you?"

"Well, Tom. I asked Savannah again on Monday and she said neither she nor her parents have mentioned it. She's told her cousin that Barry's been an FBI agent the past ten years, never married, and recently moved to Washington from New York City."

"Hmm. Does Penelope sill live in Richmond? I don't remember Savannah saying much about her, other than being a racist. But even that, I'm not sure how much truth there is to that accusation by Savannah. They obviously didn't get along when they were young."

"Well. I guess we will find out very soon. Hopefully any teenage and early family kerfuffle's will be forgotten as soon as everyone gets together."

I nod. "So you think you can get away for a long weekend coming up? I'll be back from Vienna on Thursday so maybe fly in early afternoon on Friday and leave either Sunday afternoon or Monday morning?"

"Then back in two weeks for Savannah's wedding. I should be able to juggle a couple of my patient's schedules. Are you ready for Vienna?"

"That's a good question. I've negotiated billion-dollar contracts before, but this will be a first for me, trying to help negotiate a deal that can lead to world peace as Brian asked me to do. Did you happen to mention my trip to Viennia and the meeting with the Iranians by any chance?"

Diana shook her head. "I haven't said a word to anyone. Kind of interesting though isn't it? Brian suggested it and you trying to do it."

"Well, let's hope we can pull it off for Brian."

"And the rest of the world," Diana offered.

"Unfortunately, for quite a few people and companies, world peace won't be such a good thing. Fewer guns, bullets, aircraft carriers, tanks . . . you can imagine the impact it would have on the military industrial complex in the U.S. and with all the nations that design, build, and sell material and equipment used to kill humans. It could be like opening pandora's box. We may not like what we uncover if we happen to be successful."

"We have our secret weapon, Tom. Don't forget," Diana said.

"John."

"Of course. John can do his thing. Identify the bad guys who want to keep the status quo for their personal financial benefit rather than make the world a safer place for everyone."

"We'll cross that bridge if necessary, I guess. First, the CIPC treaty needs to be agreed with and executed. But I do want to give John a call when we get home. I have a couple of potential bad guys that I want him to check out."

* * * *

Diana and I arrived home after having drinks at the Monkey Farm and dinner at the Taste of China, a normal Friday evening for a change. After changing into our lounging attire, we settled into the living room on the sofa and gave John a call.

"Tom and Diana Lawson," John said in an upbeat tone, answering the phone on the first ring.

Our calls with John were secured and untraceable using technology that John personally designed, technology that was not available to the public. In addition to managing our communications security, John also managed our finances. Earlier in our relationship, when John was expanding his AI neural nets and knowledge of the world during his mentoring period with our team, he likewise set up a business entity in my name, AI Neurology Investments, LLC. John also developed trading algorithms used to assess companies for financial investments. Needless to say, with John's brilliance, Diana and I, and John of course, were doing very well financially. A large portion of our initial profits from John's investments were used to fund Doctor Peggy Landon's research efforts to bring William, her husband, out of his coma and establish breakthrough technology to allow Cody Walker to walk again.

John maintained his persona as a housebound paraplegic in addition to melding into William Landon's body. He initially leveraged his virtual identity to secure multiple advanced degrees and became an adjunct professor at several prestigious universities. Doing so, allowed John to discretely share his expanding intellect as a means to facilitate more rapid growth in human knowledge and technological achievements than would otherwise have been possible.

"How are you, John, and how is the lecture circuit doing?" I asked.

"I am doing quite well, thank you. And my lectures are in high demand."

"I've caught a couple of your lecture series, and they are quite impressive."

"Thank you, Tom. I appreciate your feedback. Now, what can I do for you and your lovely wife?"

"A couple things. I met with Lucretia earlier today for lunch before driving on to Essex."

"Yes, I was aware of that. How is Lucretia?"

"She's doing quite well, actually. She's still incarcerated of course, but with healthier living foodwise and exercise, she's lost about thirty pounds. She says she's in better shape now than she was when she was in thirties, and she certainly looks much younger than when we first met. Her hair is white now, but if she colors it when she's released, she could definitely pass for early forties."

"That's good to hear," John said. "We couldn't have done what we did without the information she passed over to you. Even with my help."

"Very true, John. Anyway, since she chose to go down with the rest of her crew who were indicted for voter fraud in the last presidential election, I asked her if she'd heard of any new initiatives her reassembled organization might have underway."

"What did she tell you?"

"She said a new group was formed and this group no longer trusts the digital world to keep their calls and information safe from the government."

"A pretty safe assessment," John offered. "They're reverting to 1950s cold war espionage tactics?"

"That's what she told me, physical drop boxes, couriers, and encrypted communications when electronic communications are absolutely necessary."

"So you want to know how we can keep track of the bad guys?"

"Exactly," I said.

"Well, first of all, a lot has changed since the 1950s. For example, cameras are everywhere now, on buildings, in neighborhoods, and in everyone's hand, back pockets or purses, as well as in many of the new cars and trucks that are being sold. It's very difficult to go anywhere in complete secrecy."

"A good point, John. Lucretia passed along a couple names that I'd like you to check out, Wally Benson and Jackson Knapp. Benson lives in Austin and Knapp in Washington DC. Benson is former military intelligence and Knapp is a former police officer and has intelligence training. I've also passed along the names to Sam and Savannah but I'm sure they could use your expertise. I'm leaving for Vienna on Monday."

"The CIPC discussion with Iran?"

"Right. Since I can't multitask nearly as well as you, John, please set up a conference call with Sam and Savannah and let's initiate a strategy that ensures we can identify and track any nefarious activities. If the president's team is successful in pulling off the CIPC initiative, there will be quite a few individuals and companies who do not want world peace since it's bad for their wallets. Obviously, there is nothing illegal having this belief. However, the likelihood that malcontents will try and leverage this issue for an entirely different reasons and outcomes is a major concern."

"I understand, Tom. I will set up a conference call with Sam and Savannah."

"Thank you, John. I will be very busy the next several days but of course call me anytime if something critical comes up."

"And as you know, John, you can always give me a call too," Diana said. "We haven't had one of our deep philosophical discussions in a while."

"That's true, Diana. You and the rest of the team did a very good job mentoring me. My neural nets have grown considerably but I do miss those conversations you and I had during my growing phase. You are correct, it would be good for us to schedule regular sessions, something different than our casual conversations as a good friend."

"Okay then. I will take a look at my schedule going forward and let's start off with a monthly call."

"Thank you, Diana for your suggestion. I look forward to having those in-depth discussions again. And, Tom, good luck in Vienna. I will follow up with Sam and Diana."

World Peace: Tom Lawson Novel #4
By James Brown

Chapter 28

The weekend came and went far too quickly, as it was usually the case after traveling to Connecticut on weekends. I arrived back in DC Sunday afternoon and rose early Monday morning for a White House meeting prior to departing to Vienna. After the short meeting at the White House Secretary Bentley and his North Korea team and Deputy Secretary Shirley and her Iran team departed for the airport.

Barbara Shirley, Hassan Zarif, and I were seated on one of the government's Gulfstream G650 business aircraft at eight a.m. ready to depart for Vienna. We were on the tarmac waiting for the newly retrofitted Boeing C-32 that was carrying Secretary Bentley and his team to depart for Ramstein Air Base in Kaiserslautern, Germany for a refueling stop and then on to Pyongyang, North Korea. Though the interior of the Gulfstream was not as plush as the secretary's plane, on the positive side, with a strong tailwind we would be in Vienna in nine hours while the secretary and his team had an eighteen-hour flight ahead of them plus an hour delay for a refueling stop in Germany.

As the Boeing C-32 ahead of us applied power and began racing down the runway we turned onto the same runway, waited a few moments for the jet wash to clear and raced after it. I wondered if the two pilots knew each other. Looking out the window and seeing the secretary's plane ahead of us banking to the right, it crossed my mind that perhaps the pilots in each of our planes had a contest to see who would reach European airspace first.

We reached cruising altitude, and the captain came over the speaker and said they were expecting a smooth flight to Vienna, and we were able to move freely about the cabin. I had flown on Gulfstreams previously but not the latest G650. The main cabin had a six-seat sofa toward the center of the plane that faced a credenza where a large computer monitor was positioned. The galley at the rear of the plane was fully equipped with refrigerator, sink, microwave, oven and stove and the necessary utensils and glassware to feed a party of eight.

My two flight companions, Deputy Secretary Barbara Shirley and State department diplomat Hassan Zarif and I were seated in the four captain seats at the forward section of the plane. Also on board with us was Maryann, our flight attendant. Maryann was seated near the galley and with the announcement that we were free to move about the cabin, she came to our section of the aircraft.

"I will be serving a full breakfast and would like to know how each of you would like your eggs fixed. We also have an assortment of breads, bagels and cream cheese, diced potatoes with onions and peppers, turkey bacon, fruits, and of course coffee, tea and orange juice and tomato juice. Ms. Shirley, what would you like?" Maryann asked.

"My, that's quite a menu. I am hungry, come to think of it. I didn't even have time for coffee this morning. I'll have scrambled eggs, please with the bacon and potatoes along with wholewheat toast and a cup of coffee."

"And for you, Mr. Zarif."

"I'll have the same, thank you. A glass of orange juice also."

"Yes sir," she said. "Mr. Lawson?"

"I'll go with the scrambled eggs with the potatoes and bacon, but I think I'll have a raisin bagel if you have one of those, along with cream cheese. Coffee also, please."

"Thank you. I will be back with the coffees and juice."

I looked over at Barbara and said sheepishly, "wonder if I could use this Gulfstream on occasion when I fly back to Connecticut."

She looked back at me with squinted eyes.

"It *would* be a nice perk," I said and shrugged.

"You work for the government now, Tom. Remember?"

Within a few minutes, Maryann was shuttling back and forth from the galley bringing coffee and orange juice and soon thereafter piping hot breakfast dishes. The concern we all felt about our upcoming negotiations with the Iranians were soon forgotten.

World Peace: Tom Lawson Novel #4
By James Brown

Our conversations turned from our upcoming meeting in Vienna to discussions of family and friends and the beautiful spring weekend we all experienced. With full stomachs and well into our second cups of coffee, our food trays retuned to the galley, the conversation of weekend activities soon ran its course. Briefcases were opened and the reason for our flight returned front and center.

* * * *

After our flight of nine hours and thirty minutes we arrived in Vienna, Austria at eleven-thirty a.m. Vienna time. As we exited the plane, the pilot stepped out of the cockpit to say goodbye and I asked her if she beat the Boeing C-32 to Europe. She gave me a questioned look then smiled.

From the Vienna International Airport it was a thirty-minute taxi ride to the Grand Hotel Wien located in the heart of Vienna. It was my second trip to Vienna, and I was looking forward to my return. Vienna was a beautiful city. The Wien was located on the front portion of a multiblock pedestrian plaza that was ringed by an abundance of trees lining the streets around the plaza.

We pulled up in front of the hotel and two smartly dressed luggage attendants moved quickly to the cab to assist with our luggage and followed us into the hotel's lobby. The Lobby was a large rectangular-shaped room with diagonally positioned burnt umbra and white floor tiles that could easily be used as a large chessboard. I am sure many who entered the lobby thought the same. The ceiling above the lobby rose sixty feet and a second-floor balcony with wrought iron railings ringed the lobby's perimeter facing the hotel's entrance.

"Good afternoon, checking in?" the clerk asked Barbara Shirley in accented English as she passed him her passport. "Welcome to the Grand Hotel Wien. Is this your first visit to the Wien and Vienna?"

"I have been to Vienna on several occasions but the first time staying here at the Wien."

"Well, we are glad you chose the Grand Hotel Wien this time. And I see from your reservation record that you are traveling with Mr. Lawson and Mr. Zarif."

"Yes," Shirley said. Hassan and I passed over our passports to the clerk.

"Very well. We have selected three well-appointed rooms adjacent to each other on the fourth floor and have reserved Salon 1 on the lower level for your Tuesday and Wednesday meeting. While you are here, I hope you have the opportunity to enjoy our many four-star restaurants and dining venues."

"I'm sure that we will," Shirley said as she and the rest of her team took their room keys and headed toward the elevators.

Exiting the elevator on the fourth floor, our rooms were midway down the wide corridor. Shirley had the center room and before entering said, "since it's just past noon here and a beautiful day, how about going for a walk and take in a little bit of Vienna?"

"That was my thought also, Shih said. It's my first time in Vienna so I'd like to see a bit of the city. We have tomorrow for additional prep for our meeting on Wednesday."

"Sounds good," I said.

The rooms assigned to us were large and well-appointed in an old European style. An antique writing desk faced one wall and a sitting area with Queen Anne chairs and sofa was positioned in front of large windows that overlooked the plaza and atrium at the back of the hotel. As I took a moment to scan the room, I wondered if it was against government rules to bring a spouse along on a trip such as this. Something to check out, I thought as I gave Diana a call.

"Hi, hon. How was your flight?" she asked, answering her phone.

"Very nice. A very plush Gulfstream that came with well-equipped galley and decent food. The only way to fly. I was thinking I could have smuggled you aboard. Four days in Vienna?"

"That word 'smuggled' doesn't sound too good," Diana said.

"I'll have to check out the rules, but it would have been nice had you been able to join me."

"I'm sure while you were focused on the Iranians, I would have been able to keep myself occupied for a few days in Vienna. Are you ready for Wednesday?"

"Hmm . . . well, I hope so. We certainly have logic on our side, assuming they are willing to consider logic."

"Unfortunately, people and certainly religious-based governments tend not to think logically when it comes to hardcore religious beliefs and teachings," Diana said.

"You make a perfect case for joining me the next time. I can have the president hire you as an expert consultant. That's how I get you on my next flight."

"Sounds like a plan, my dear," Diana said. "Enjoy your day in Vienna. I have a late afternoon client I need to see. I love you and remember the time change. No calls at three a.m. my time."

At a half hour on the dot we assembled in the hallway and headed to the lobby. It was indeed a beautiful day as we walked out the rear of the hotel into the plaza. Clear blue sky and seventy-four degrees and a light breeze, it was going to be very hard to be cooped up in the hotel on Tuesday prepping for our Wednesday meeting with the Iranians. But for now, we would enjoy the weather and smell of fresh flowers in bloom as we began ambling slowly through the plaza and the Ringstraßen Gallerien. Known in the U.S. as a shopping mall, but a very upscale mall here in Vienna.

Before walking too far from the hotel, we stopped and made early dinner reservations at the Grand Hotel Wien Schanigarten, the hotel's patio restaurant then headed out to explore Vienna.

Known for its artistic and intellectual legacy, Vienna was shaped by residents including Mozart, Beethoven and Sigmund Freud. The city lies along the Danube River and is well known for its Imperial palaces, including Schönbrunn, the Habsburgs' summer residence.

From the hotel, we headed south toward the Belvedere, a historic building complex in Vienna consisting of two Baroque palaces, the Orangery, and the Palace Stables. Belvedere Palace is one of the most stunning baroque buildings in Austria. We strolled along the Baroque gardens, toured Belvedere Palace, and took time to admire paintings by Egon Schiele, Gustav Klimt and other artists. We then leisurely strolled back to the hotel for our five p.m. dinner reservation at the Wien Schanigarten.

Our light meal at the Schanigarten was excellent as was the ambience of the elegant outdoor terrace with its view of the famous circular grand boulevard that served as a ring road around the historic Inner district of Vienna. At close to eight p.m. with the air beginning to cool, and well past midnight eastern standard time in Washington, we decided to call it a day. Tuesday would be a day of work while on Wednesday, we would do our best to secure agreement from the

World Peace: Tom Lawson Novel #4
By James Brown

Iranians to move forward with our CIPC initiative and secure world peace as Brian Jones suggested that I do.

* * * *

Tuesday was spent prepping for our Wednesday meeting. Up early and working well into the evening, our small team poured over the materials we brought with us and conducted mock question and answer sessions drawing upon information our Middle East experts prepared for us.

Now, the time for preparations was over. It was Wednesday and we were first to arrive at the hotel's Salon 1 meeting room on the lower level. Certainly not in keeping with Hotel Wien's elegance, the small rectangular room lacked widows and was sparsely furnished. A round conference table was positioned in the middle of the room with chairs spaced around it. At the far end of the room stood a long credenza holding trays of fruit, sliced cheese, baguettes, breads and jams along with coffee, tea, and juice.

We spread ourselves out choosing alternate seats around the oval conference table in an effort to mitigate an appearance of an across-the-table us versus them negotiation scenario. After taking out our notebooks and placing them on the table, we milled about the room waiting for our guests to arrive. Within a few minutes the conference room door opened. It was time to secure world peace.

"Welcome, President Hosseini," Deputy Secretary Shirley said as the Iranian president entered the room with his team. "Thank you for agreeing to meet with us here in Vienna."

A man of average height and slim in stature, President Hosseini had kind looking brown eyes and short, salt and pepper hair that ringed a balding head and a well-trimmed white beard. Born in Isfahan, Iran, he was fifty-two years old and a graduate of Tehran University where he was awarded a Ph.D. degree in economic science.

"Pleased to meet you, Deputy Secretary Shirley under these abnormal circumstances," he said shaking her hand. After ten years as an academic and professor at Tehran University Hosseini was persuaded to accept a position in the Iranian government. He was later chosen as Minister of Economic Affairs and Finance by the former president, Yaser Adi, who was killed in the missile attacks. He now stood in a small room about to hold a meeting with a country his government had been in conflict since the U.S. and British intelligence agencies orchestrated a coup to oust Iran's democratically elected Prime Minister, Amir Mossadeq in 1953. The rift was further exacerbated when the US embassy in Tehran was seized by protesters in November 1979 and American hostages were held inside for 444 days. The final fifty-two hostages were freed in January 1981, the day of US President Ronald Reagan's inauguration. More recently, Iran's desire for nuclear power and both countries' growing conflicting influence in the Middle East exacerbated the rift. But the events that brought on the rift were upended when John Gordon took control of the U.S. nuclear subs and launched cruise missiles that killed the presidents and senior officials from both countries.

"Let me introduce my team," Secretary Shirley said turning to members of her team. "I am pleased to introduce State Department Director Hassan Zarif and Mr. Tom Lawson, one of President Stephen's senior advisors."

President Hosseini smiled and shook Zarif's hand then turned to me. "Mr. Lawson. It's a pleasure to meet you. I have been looking forward to meeting you. My countryman and I wish that you would have uncovered the Russian's plot and John Gordon's actions sooner than you did."

"As do I, Mr. President. We tried our best but came up a little short unfortunately."

President Hosseini took hold of Lawsons hand and looked up into Lawson's deep blue eyes. After a moment, he said, "Perhaps, Mr. Lawson, it was Allah's will, your actions coming up just a little short as you say. It has brought us together here today."

"An interesting observation, sir, and I do hope the will of God will lead us to choose the best path forward for both of our countries."

Hosseini smiled and bowed slightly toward Lawson. "Allow me to introduce Shahin Ashraf. Shahin is carrying forward his duties as Chief of Staff, the position he held before President Yaser Adi was killed in the attack."

"Pleased to meet you, Madam Secretary, Mr. Lawson and Director Zarif," Chief of Staff Ashraf said, shaking hands.

Bald and clean shaven, Shahin Ashraf was sixty-five years old and had unusually bright hazel-green eyes peering through wire rimmed spectacles. Slim and short in stature, he had entered the room with a wide smile, appearing to be generally happy to be participating in the meeting that would soon take place.

After introducing his chief of staff, President Hosseini placed a hand on the shoulder of the man to his left and said, "this is Farhad Behzadi, our Foreign Minister."

A tall, distinguished looking man in his early sixties with greying hair and beard, Behzadi politely shook hands with the American delegation. The expression on his face, however, did not exude hope and optimism, rather, his underlining feeling that he was meeting with an enemy and not a potential ally. Farhad Behzadi was formerly a military general who was tapped to lead Iran's foreign ministry by the former president. His experiences dealing with America were honed as a young man while studying chemical engineering at Amirkabir University. At that time, he took part in the seizure of the American Embassy in Tehran, which ultimately led to the severing of US-Iranian diplomatic relations.

Knowing full well what Farhad Behzadi's feelings were toward America, President Hosseini insisted however that his foreign minister join him on this trip to Vienna to meet with the Americans. He especially wanted him to meet the man who almost saved the life of the Iranian president. Hosseini believed that for his presidency to survive, it was imperative that the senior official who outwardly opposed attending the meeting join him in Vienna. If the Americans could convince Farhad Behzadi that a CIPC agreement was in the best interest of Iran his presidency would be assured.

"Please, help yourselves to a cup of tea and the breakfast pastries and cheeses that the hotel has provided," Secretary Shirley said. "We can then sit for a few minutes and become better acquainted."

As the two teams intermingled and slowly migrated toward the food and beverage table, adding pastries and cheeses to small plates and pouring cups of coffee or tea, the conversations turned to family and personal experiences that they chose to share, while President Hosseini made sure that Farhad Behzadi and Tom Lawson were getting to know one another.

World Peace: Tom Lawson Novel #4
By James Brown

Chapter 29

"Mr. Lawson, you have not served in government for very long," Farhad Behzadi said.

"No sir, and please, since we have been introduced, please call me Tom. "I have been a practicing engineer for most of my career. Really, all of my career," he corrected and took a sip of coffee. "My role as a government consultant only happened very recently."

"After the incident involving the Russians and John Gordon."

"Correct, yes. Not something that I had anticipated occurring, either dealing with the Russians and certainly not the tragic events that Gordon caused."

"I see," Behzadi said. He paused a moment then said, "from what I've read, you also uncovered corruption at your former company, corruption that caused the deaths of a large number of people."

"Unfortunately, yes, it was very disappointing that the officers of our company, men that I had known for years, would do something that caused the deaths of so many people. It was unmitigated greed that led them to the actions they took. But it was another instance where unfortunately I was a little late in discovering their crime."

"But you did prevent future deaths, discovering the defective parts your company knowingly let remain on planes that continued to fly."

"That's true, and now here we are, about to hold a discussion on a subject that can profoundly impact the lives of many millions of people. I am hopeful that the decision we make here in Vienna is not viewed in the future as an opportunity that we chose to defer only to be criticized for being late to act."

Behzadi stared for a moment then took a sip of his tea. Before he could comment, Secretary Shirley asked everyone to take their seats at the table.

"A little housekeeping before we begin our discussions," Shirley said. "We will take a break midmorning and then at noon we have an hour and a half period scheduled for lunch. Lunch will be served here in our conference room and on the table in front of you, there is a lunch menu. But everyone is free to make their own reservations with one of the four restaurants here at the hotel or take time to visit one of the many restaurants nearby."

Her housekeeping announcement made, and time allowed for a brief review of the lunch menu, Shirley took a deep breath, silently wishing that it was her boss leading the session. She then continued. "I again want to thank you, President Hosseini and your team for agreeing to meet with us today. Likewise, the assistance of Switzerland's Foreign Minister Elias Muller who was the conduit for setting up this meeting. Not having formal diplomatic relations has not been helpful.

Everyone I'm sure knows the history between our countries, a history that unfortunately has played out over and over throughout the history of the world. Natural resources that one country has an abundance while other countries are lacking, can create a great deal of friction and turmoil, especially when the haves and have-nots are of a different size in economic and military power.

These inequities and the lack of moral ethics by the United Kingdom, Russia, and the U.S. in orchestrating military coups in Iran to ensure access to Iran's oil, has been a major cause for the current difficulties that exists between our countries. I am hopeful . . . the United States is hopeful, that we can begin looking forward rather than dwelling on misdeeds taken by past governments."

Deputy Secretary Shirley looked across the table at President Hosseini. As he contemplated a response, the faint hum of the hotel's HVAC system circulating air was the only sound.

Though pausing only a few seconds rather than the eternity that Shirley was feeling, Hosseini spoke softly. "My country has a long history going back thousands of years, Madam Secretary. Many empires have ruled our people and occupied the land that is now known as Iran. Given our history, which is not that different for many of the people who live in the Middle East, or even those who live in other parts of the world. Native Americans in your country, for example. They too lived on land that is now called the United States of America for thousands of years before it was invaded by Europeans and their land was stolen and their people were either herded into small arid tracts of land or were killed. I agree, Madam Secretary, the human race has not always treated fellow humans with kindness. Actions at times are taken due to misconceptions between different cultures or differing religious beliefs. But it can also be caused by unmitigated greed, that one person, groups of people, or countries in the circumstance that you mentioned, believe they have the right to take what does not belong to them.

The question to be considered today, given the deaths of the senior American and Iranian leaders, Madam Secretary is whether or not past actions can be set aside and prevailing issues that exist between our countries can be equitably addressed?"

President Hosseini paused and scanned the faces around the table. He then said, "I happened to overhear a portion of a conversation Mr. Lawson was having earlier with Foreign Minister Behzadi. I thought a comment he made was very insightful. He said he was hopeful that the decision we make here in Vienna would not be viewed in the future as an opportunity that we chose to defer only to be criticized for being late to act. Will we defer only to be criticized in the future for being late to act," President Hosseini repeated.

After a few seconds he continued in a soft voice. "All of the countries who were directly affected by the actions of Russia and John Gordon continue to have an adversarial relationship with each other. I mentioned to Mr. Lawson earlier today that perhaps it was Allah's will that his efforts to stop John Gordon came up just a little short as it has brought us together today. Mr. Lawson's response was interesting. He said he hoped that the will of God would lead us to choose the best path forward for both of our countries."

He paused again, then repeated, *"to choose the best path forward for both of our countries.* Achieving Mr. Lawson's response will not be easy, Madam Secretary. Unwinding years of distrust and thousands of years of history. Many people in both of our countries benefit from the upheaval, from wars that are fought, from individual beliefs that are contrary to the beliefs held by others."

World Peace: Tom Lawson Novel #4
By James Brown

When Secretary Shirley did not comment immediately to President Hosseini I decided to speak first since I had uttered the words that President Hosseini was referring. "I agree with your assessment, President Hosseini. This is not an easy discussion given our histories. Especially given that my country has not always acted honorably toward your country. However, if we don't at least try, many people will be adversely affected and our nonactions will indeed be long remembered."

"I agree, Mr. Lawson. And perhaps it best if you or Secretary Shirley would initiate our discussion on this subject since we are here at your request."

I looked over at Deputy Secretary Shirley. She gave me a slight nod, probably thinking that with the president referencing my earlier comment, I was in a better position to initiate the discussions.

"Okay, I will be glad to, Mr. President," I said. "As is well known, the actions of Russia and John Gordon were morally reprehensible as well as devastating. Not only were senior leaders of Iran, the United States, North Korea, and Russia killed, but the aftermath of this event has also caused a great deal of unrest and economic hardship in the countries directly affected and the world at large. Blame can certainly be placed on Russian leadership for the death of our leaders as well as the economic turmoil that ensued. But as we discussed earlier it is not the first time an unscrupulous leader has made decisions that caused great harm.

This cycle has played out over and over since humans first walked the earth. But today, the potential destruction that can result from these kind of actions can be extremely devastating given the destructive power of the weapons that have been created. We asked you to meet with us today because we believe the future of our civilization is at stake."

I paused and read the expressions on the faces around the table. As if reading their minds, their thoughts were obvious, that many efforts have been tried after similar conflicts have erupted around the world and these efforts all failed in one way or another to prevent future conflicts.

"I'm sure everyone is having the same thought, that similar discussions and actions have taken place in the past. Efforts have been tried before and failed. What would be different this time, correct?"

Slowly, head nods began to follow.

"Everyone's apprehension is understandable. Past efforts to establish organizations and agreements to prevent armed conflict have failed to achieve these results. The League of Nations after World War I for example. It was initiated to solve disputes between countries before they erupted into open warfare. Ultimately, the League relied on good faith between member states. However, without its own military force and a guarantee that member states would offer support, it lacked any power to prevent aggression. The League also did not have the power it needed to enforce any of the rules that it enacted, which proved to be a fatal flaw in the League's structure.

In 1946, the League of Nations was officially dissolved with the establishment of the United Nations. The United Nations was modeled after the former but with increased international support and extensive machinery to help the new body avoid repeating the League's failures.

But I'm sure many of the participants in this room, if not everyone, would agree that the United Nations has not kept the world a very safe place. Am I correct?"

The head nods were unanimous.

I continued. "The United Nations was instigated with a vision of maintaining global peace and stability. This vision, I believe, is still the prevailing intent of this organization. However, intent and results have significantly diverged since the organization's inception. The United Nations has failed to resolve the Syrian Civil War, the Yemen War, the Gaza Conflict and for twenty years did little to end the war in Afghanistan. So what is it that we can do now to improve the results of many decades of efforts and the general failure of organizations to achieve the results intended, preventing conflict and destructive wars?"

After another gaze into the faces about the table, I said. "The reason we are here, is that we believe we can address the world's past failures; that we can put in place an organization and agreements to prevent future conflicts and wars. Your comment to me earlier in the day, Mr. President, saying that perhaps it was the will of Allah that my actions came up just a little short, that doing so brought us together today. I believe you are correct. The actions by Russia and Mr. Gordon provides us with a unique opportunity to change the dynamics that led to the attacks on our countries. We believe that we can establish an organization and put in place agreements that will ensure that cooperation, inclusion, and peaceful coexistence can be achieved. Four simple words but with powerful meaning when put in practice."

President Hosseini looked around the table to see the facial reactions of Chief of Staff Ashraf and Foreign Minister Behzadi, anticipating a scowl on Behzadi's face and puzzlement on Ashraf's. They were as he expected.

"Perhaps you can elaborate, Mr. Lawson. How would cooperation, inclusion and peaceful coexistence come about? The mechanism for achieving this perhaps," President Hosseini said.

"CIPC, Cooperation, Inclusion, and Peaceful Coexistence. Certainly, Mr. President. First of all, we are not looking to replace the UN. Rather, the CIPC initiative would be established to address the cause and events associated with the missile launches that took the lives of the presidents of the United States, China, Russia, North Korea and Iran.

Second, our purpose would not be to advocate for democracy. That is not the objective. Democracy, theocracy, autocracy, or even dictatorship, whatever the form of government, whether chosen, appointed, or self-anointed, is not a concern of this program. Our objective is simply to ensure that whoever shakes out to take over from the leaders who were killed, that they and their governments are able to ensure and deliver domestic tranquility, peace and prosperity for their citizens and the world as a whole. Each of our countries lost their presidents and senor leadership but the world was at least spared this time by those leaders who came together and acted calmly and prevented a devastating military escalation.

But there is no guarantee the world will be so lucky the next time when another government leader decides that they or their country would prosper better through world conflict and war. Perhaps the next time, the will of Allah would decide that enough was enough, that the human race should just end. We had our chance and blew it."

I paused a few moments then said, "The CIPC program would focus on the five countries that were affected by Gordon's missile strikes, the United States, China, Russia, North Korea, and Iran. The Group of 5, a new and very powerful organization that will have a profound impact on world order, peace, and prosperity."

World Peace: Tom Lawson Novel #4
By James Brown

After several long seconds of ensuing silence, Deputy Secretary Shirley said, "I think this is a good time for us to take our first break. We will reconvene in an hour."

* * * *

No one moved from the table, choosing to sit for a few seconds in silence. President Hosseini was the first to stand and his team followed.

"A good time to take a break, Madam Secretary," he said as he and his team picked up their folders and walked toward the door.

After the group departed and our team stood alone around the conference table, I said, "what do you think?"

Taking a few seconds, Shirley finally said, "hard to say. President Hosseini was engaging and appeared to be interested in what we had to say. Chief of Staff Ashraf I think is basically neutral, didn't comment one way or the other. Foreign Minister Behzadi on the other hand, his facial expressions I think are obvious. He's against forming an alliance. At least from what he's heard so far anyway."

"I agree. That's my impression also," Zarif said.

"Well, we've only finished the first quarter in football terms. Three more to go," I said. "I think we can persuade President Hosseini and Chief of Staff Ashraf to at least take the next step and participate in a G5 Summit at a minimum. We just need to work a little harder on Behzadi. Given his background we expected he would be the difficult convert."

"You're right Tom, only the first quarter. Let's take a walk. I'm sure it's beautiful outside," Shirley said.

She was correct, stepping out of the hotel the fragrance of spring and the warm seventy-three-degree temperature was immediately invigorating. What better way to lift our spirits? We walked along the tree-lined street in front of the hotel and headed across the street to the At Eight restaurant, one the restaurants recommended by Fredrick when we checked in to the Wien. It was just across the street and the food was excellent he had said.

Given the weather we decided on a table under the trees outside of the restaurant. Similar to Manhattan restaurants located near Broadway theaters, At Eight was ideally located within a block of the Vienna State Opera, a major attraction for opera lovers worldwide.

With the restaurant's close proximity to the opera house their waiters and chefs were well trained in the art of punctuality and good service. A waiter approached our table immediately after we sat.

"Willkommen," he said, in an upbeat tone. "Drei zum Mittagessen?"

Without breaking stride, Shirley responded in perfect German. "Nein, Kaffee und gebäck. Apfelstrudel vielleicht. Haben sie menüs in Englisch?

In English, of course madam. Our menu is in German and English. Is this your first time to Vienna? He asked as he handed out menus."

"No, a very lovely city which I look forward to visiting as often as possible," she answered.

"Well, you picked a lovely time of year for another visit. My name is Johann. Do you need time to peruse our menu?"

"We are pressed for time," Shirley said as she put down her menu. "I will have an espresso and an apple strudel, please."

"Very well, and you, sir," Johann said looking toward Zarif.

"I'll have the same, please.

I put down my menu and said, American coffee if available and the apple strudel also, please."

Within a few minutes, coffee, espressos, and apple strudels were served. We took a few minutes to enjoy our coffee and strudel and our time away from the isolated basement. Finally I said, "any thoughts on our approach when we return?"

"Well, I'm sure the president and his team will have had time to discuss our initial pitch. When we return, the logical next step would be to ask if there were any questions from our morning session," Shirley offered.

"Or, maybe it best if we focus on the last statement I made, that the Group of 5 will be a new and very powerful organization. That statement had to have registered and peaked their interest since their arch enemy, Saudia Arabia, was not named."

"Hmm. An interesting thought," Shirley said. "We haven't fleshed out the impact of country exclusions very thoroughly yet. That surely will come up this afternoon."

"Perhaps we start off by telling the Iranians that the initial focus of CIPC is on the countries that were directly impacted by Gordon's actions, the countries whose presidents and senior staff were killed.

The objective is not to replace the United Nations. And we add that with the U.S., China, and Russia coming to an agreement, the foundation will be in place for a very formidable and powerful organization, from an economic and military perspective."

"And we add that Iran has an opportunity to be a member of this group," Ashraf added.

"Exactly," I said.

"Which they will likely begin asking questions regarding religion and the regional conflicts that are taking place. And of course, Israel," Shirley said.

"Of course they will. Those questions are expected," I said. "And I think we handle those questions by saying first of all that America was founded based on religious freedom. Our intent is not to dictate what a person or a country's religious beliefs should be. As for Israel, we tell them the only provision is that Israel, as well as Palestine, should be allowed to exist. Then, when the questions will likely move to the issues that Palestine is facing, we draw upon the discussions we had with Professor's Underwood and Ben-Hur."

"Sounds like a reasonable approach, Tom," Shirley said. "But of course we all know, the flow of negotiations is often unpredictable and not always easy to control."

"True, but we do our best to control the discussion. And if the conversation happens to turn negative, especially from Foreign Minister Behzadi, we mention the actions of Mostafa Ahmadi, Chief Commander of Iran's Revolutionary Guard, that Cleric Ebram Janati did not die of a heart attack."

Eyebrows raised, Shirley said, "we need to be careful moving in this direction."

"Careful, yes, but if pushed, President Hosseini needs to know the truth, that powerful people within the Iranian regime are taking actions that are not in the best interest of the Iranian people. And we let them know that we *will* move forward with or without Iran's participation in a CIPC agreement."

Shirley took in a deep breath of clean spring air, "Okay, but let's move forward carefully." She looked at the time and raised her hand toward Johann who was leaving an adjoining table. "Check, please," she said.

World Peace: Tom Lawson Novel #4
By James Brown

Chapter 30

The Iranian team was in the room and seated at the conference table with cups of tea in front of them when Secretary Shirley and her team entered the room.

"Hello, gentlemen," Shirley said. "I hope you took time to take a walk outside the hotel. It's a beautify day."

"We did, Madam Secretary. A short walk through the plaza and around the building. It is quite lovely outside. Perhaps tomorrow if the weather is the same, we can schedule an early lunch on the hotel veranda and conduct the rest of our meeting outside."

"A very good suggestion, Mr. President," Shirley said, taking her seat. "I'll check with the hotel and see if that can be arranged weather permitting." After taking a moment to open her folder and looking through her notes, she said, "shall we begin where we left off prior to the break, the makeup of the Group of Five?"

"Yes, that would be very helpful. Also we would need to better understand policy positions and the working relationship between the members of this group, other countries and especially those countries within the Middle East."

"Very reasonable points, Mr. President. "Tom, why don't you start where you left off before we took our break."

"Certainly, Madam Secretary. As I explained prior to our morning break, the CIPC program will focus on the five countries that were affected by Gordon's missile strikes, the United States, China, Russia, North Korea, and Iran. Throughout history, as you've described, Mr. President, countries have often tried to dominate other countries, whether to take what does not belong to them, to satisfy a desire to expand their sphere of control, or even to dictate a religious belief.

The actions that the Russian leadership initiated was the result of their fear that China and the United States were leaving them behind economically and militarily. They believed that secretly initiating a war between the U.S. and China would be to their advantage, even if it led to a nuclear conflict. With what Russia started, John Gordon added North Korea and Iran into the mix to cause even more chaos.

The circumstances that initiated these attacks were perceived economic and military inequalities. And when religious differences are added to the mix, you have the three primary ingredients that have led to worldwide upheaval and wars throughout the centuries. These ingredients that led to the attacks on each of our countries can be a tinderbox for world annihilation if not managed."

Eyes narrowing, President Hosseini said, "A tinderbox with a manageable solution. A solution that the UN has been seeking for quite a few years now. I am eager to hear the details of your solution, Mr. Lawson. How you believe these five countries can achieve what the UN has failed to accomplish."

I returned a slight nod and said, "that would have been my question also, Mr. President. How can this group of five countries achieve what the UN has failed to achieve? Achieve lasting peace? The simple answer is that the CIPC program is focused only on five countries. Our objective is not to replace or impede the workings of the United Nations. By definition, the United Nations is an intergovernmental organization that aims to maintain international peace and security, develop friendly relations among nations, achieve international cooperation, and be a center for harmonizing the actions of nations. The UN is doing its best given the organization's charter. But in many respects, with the number of countries and issues the UN is dealing with, it's synonymous to corralling and managing a large number of feral cats. Something that is impossible to accomplish."

I paused for a moment then said, "by focusing solely on the five countries that were affected by the missile attacks, the Group of Five will be able to more easily manage the three primary ingredients that have spawned conflicts over the millennia: economic, military, and religious disparities. By ensuring peaceful coexistence with open, honest economic cooperation between our countries, promoting religious freedom, and ensuring that each country has the right to choose how they are governed, a working agreement can be reached if we are willing to put forth the effort to secure long term peace and prosperity for our respective citizens."

Following these statements, conversations in muted Farsi began to flow between the Iranian delegates. After a few minutes, President Hosseini nodded toward Foreign Minister Behzadi and said, "pishenhad kord kah man rahbari ra bay ahdah begiram."

Foreign Minister Behzadi spoke up and said, "President Hosseini asked that I take the lead to ask a few questions."

"By all means, please do," I said.

"Okay, let's start with economic cooperation, Mr. Lawson. Probably the easiest of the three ingredients you mentioned that can cause conflicts between nations. Are you referring to a trade agreement declaration for Iran, a preferential trading agreement perhaps, or would an FTA be considered as one way to mitigate economic conflicts?"

Yes, a Free Trade Agreement similar to the FTAs we have with twenty other countries, including Jordan and Israel for example, would certainly be up for consideration. But we are also envisioning that a CIPC agreement would go well beyond the typical trade agreements that we have negotiated with other countries. For the CIPC agreement to be effective over the long term, the economic wellbeing of each country must be ensured. For example, the climate agreements that have been negotiated, or at a minimum are being promoted can help to control global warming but may also cause an economic hardship for those countries that generate a large portion of their gross domestic product from the sale of coal, oil, and natural gas.

Take Russia, for example. Nearly sixty percent of their GDP is generated from their oil and natural gas resources. As the world moves increasingly away from carbon-based fuels and transportation conveyances from internal combustion engines, the resulting economic hardship can become the spark for military action if not addressed. Support and cooperation in helping G5 members build and grow new revenue sources to replace lower oil and natural gas revenues will be a key CIPC program initiative."

"There will be a similar impact with lower military revenues by Russia, China, and the U.S. if tensions between G5 members are truly reduced," Behzadi said.

"That is also true. Reduced tensions is an outcome that we certainly hope will occur and the need for large military budgets. To help mitigate the negative impact on jobs and the economy, the economic savings realized from reduced military expenditures can be diverted toward economic development and job growth rather than military preparedness."

Behzadi gave me a questioning stare. "This seems to be a very tall order, Mr. Lawson."

"I agree. It will take cooperation and hard work. The United States and China have large economies as well as large populations and can more easily absorb lower revenues associated with oil, gas, and military exports. The impact on Iran will also be less given the large gains we see being generated with a CIPC agreement in place. Likewise for North Korea. Even though Russia will be a first challenge, it is a vast country and has huge opportunity for growth in population and wealth if we can stabilize and nurture our relationships."

"A reasonable assessment," Mr. Lawson. "Now let's turn to military and religious disparities that you mentioned as the last two ingredients that can initiate conflicts. Is it safe to assume that the U.S., China, and Russia will be reducing their military expenditures?"

"That has been discussed in our preliminary CIPC conversations with China and Russia. Since the U.S. military expenditures are significantly higher than China or Russia, as well as every other country in the world, we will begin reducing our military budget. We likewise will work with the G5 members to manage the negative impact that will likely be generated from each of our country's military industrial complexes."

Behzadi looked across the table at President Hosseini. I was certain they both were thinking about Iran's Revolutionary Guard and their Quds Force. A CIPC agreement would not be an easy sell for them either.

After the eye contact exchange, President Hosseini took the lead again. "Let's move on to the religious differences that you mentioned as one of the three ingredients for conflict."

"As I'm sure you are well aware, President Hosseini, religion has often been a central cause for conflict. Religious wars, intolerance of other religions, and conflicts between church and state have caused considerable instability and conflicts throughout the centuries. A cornerstone of the CIPC program's charter will be religious tolerance. The United States was founded based on religious freedom which will be the case for our CIPC agreement. We will not dictate what a person or country's religious beliefs should be, or as I mentioned earlier, the type of government structure that should exist. Iran's desire to preserve an Islamic theocracy will be Iran's decision and not that of the U.S. or any of the CIPC participants.

As for Israel and Palestine, another question you might ask about, the only requirement is that both must be allowed to exist. We have our ideas on how this can best be accomplished but look forward to everyone's inputs on this matter."

"An interesting subject, Mr. Lawson. I would be interested in your thoughts if you are in a position to share them," President Hosseini said.

I took a moment and looked over at Deputy Secretary Shirley. She nodded her approval.

Looking back at President Hosseini, I said, "Everyone knows, I'm sure, that the Israel and Palestine issue began in 1948 with the establishment of Israel. And seventy-four years later the Israel and Palestine issues still exists. The prevailing thought has been to create a two-state solution, but frankly, a two-state solution is very hard to do. Where would the borders be between these states? What would happen to Jerusalem, a city important to both peoples? What about all the Jewish settlements in the West Bank? What about Palestinian refugees? where would the two states be? What borders would define the Israeli state, and what would Palestine consist of?

If you use the 1967 borders, hundreds of thousands of Israelis who live in West Bank settlements wind up on the Palestinian side. Would those people become citizens of Palestine or be forced to move back to Israel proper? Few on either side want the first choice, and some settlements are well-established cities, with tens of thousands of residents. It's inconceivable they would agree to move.

It's also seemingly impossible to draw a border that encompass these settlements as part of Israel, as Palestinians would not have a contiguous territory. Are Palestinians going to leave their country every time they want to travel between cities?

Likewise, If Israel would have to cede the West Bank in its entirety, it would make Israel only a few miles wide at its narrowest point and deny Israel the security presence it currently maintains along the Jordan River. How would Israel protect itself from that threat if it withdraws from the West Bank?

Then there's Jerusalem. Both Israelis and Palestinians claim Jerusalem as their capital, and the city is holy to Jews, Muslims, and Christians.

With all these issues to deal with, a two-state resolution has never been agreed upon and never will in our opinion. It's our belief that the only workable solution is a one-state solution. Northern Ireland is one example of a binational state in which ethnic groups keep a certain level of political autonomy while sharing one sovereign country. Of course there are many countries, if not most countries, that prosper with people of multiethnic origins and religious beliefs."

With my throat now parched, I reached for the glass of water and took a drink.

Continuing, I said, "We understand that the single state approach has been raised but no agreement has been reached. This would not be the case if a CIPC agreement was indeed executed by the U.S., Russia, China, Iran, and North Korea and we collectively foster a Jewish-Arab single state solution as the only logical solution to ensure peace after seventy-five years of conflict. The Group of Five would have the prestige and power to once and for all bring peace to the Middle East."

President Hosseini sat silent for a moment then said, "an interesting thesis, Mr. Lawson. Your logic does have merit. Certainly an approach that should be considered. The alternative, as you have explained is indeed very messy. As all-out war would be, of course."

"That it would, sir. That it would."

At this moment, the conference room doors opened, and trays of food were being brought into the room. Lunch was being served.

* * * *

Tuesday's lunch prepared by Grand Hotel Wien was excellent. An assortment of Austian, Iranian, and American dishes were superbly prepared and in sufficient quantities that everyone chose to eat in the conference room rather than having lunch at one of the hotel's restaurants. After a delicious lunch, and in large quantities, the group decided a joint walk about the city was in order. We would be able to speak freely amongst each other and enjoy the pleasant weather as we strolled about Vienna central city.

I initially ambled along next to President Hosseini, while he asked for clarifications to topics discussed prior to lunch. It was interesting that he chose not to move on to new topics, rather, deferring these questions until the group reconvened and everyone could hear the answers to new topics being discussed.

After forty-five minutes into our walk and President Hosseini's questions were answered to his satisfaction, the president joined Deputy Secretary Shirley in conversation while Chief of Staff Shahin Ashraf and I strolled along together. Foreign Minister Behzadi and Hassan Zarif, our diplomatic director for Iran, continued with their conversations. Several security officers from the U.S. and Iranian embassies remained close behind and in front of our entourage as we strolled along the wide treelined walkways.

It was a little after three in the afternoon when we arrived back at the Wien and settled in again in the conference room ready to further explore the benefits associated with entering into a CIPC agreement.

After taking a drink of fresh brewed tea President Hosseini put his cup down on the saucer in front of him and started the afternoon discussions. "One topic that was briefly mentioned that I believe will become an issue for each of the G5 countries is pushback from very powerful groups who do not want peace and stability."

"Your point is well taken, Mr. President," I said. "Turmoil, instability, and even war, unfortunately is the profession of a large number of groups and organizations within each of our countries. Cooperation, inclusion, and peaceful coexistence to many is just not in their vocabulary let alone an aspirational goal. History supports this premise. Groups who do not support peace, or do not believe a treaty, or an agreement has secured an outcome they believe is in their interest, can and do resort to violence. For example, Anwar Sadat was assassinated less than three years after he and his government signed the peace accord with Israel. This is just one example of an extreme case of violence by those who do not agree with an agreement that has been entered into.

"For this reason, Mr. Lawson, many governments resort to methods to monitor those who profess different views than those of their government leaders to mitigate subversion and potential violence."

"Yes, monitoring potential subversives is a logical effort, however If the processes and methods deployed are not conducted responsibly, the intended outcome is likely not to provide the desired results over the long term. Obviously, there are those cases where there is little choice but to prosecute those individuals or groups who have no interest in conforming to reasonable government regulations and laws."

"You are referring to political prisoners I presume."

"I am. Retention and imprisonment without reasonable justification more often than not does not lead to desirable outcomes in the long term."

"As was the case when the U.S. imprisoned its citizens of Asian descendant during World War II or the long-term imprisonment and mistreatment of purported Muslim enemy combatants in Cuba," Hossini said.

"Those are very good examples, sir. Examples when America has professed to the world the need for tolerance and acceptance of those of different national origin, faiths or skin color, and the rule of law to the world, as it often does, only to suppress these attributes when pressured by groups to do so. Human frailties, sir. All the more reason to put in place a mechanism to better insure that the conditions that can lead to conflict and the mistreatment of fellow humans does not occur.

Had a functioning CIPC agreement been put in place after World War I, would the lives of millions of people have been saved with Adolf Hitler not coming to power? Or, more recently, prevented the rise of Osama bin Laden and the global terrorism he and his organization spawned which led to the deaths of tens of thousands of people and devastation of a large portion of the Middle East?"

President Hosseini remained silent for a moment, a crease forming above his eyes as he looked over at me. Finally he said, "you are placing a great deal of faith in what you and your country are trying to achieve, Mr. Lawson. A process and goal that has never been achieved as you have previously reminded us. Your country's aspirations, though admirable, may well be out of reach for this stage of human evolution."

"If this is the case, Mr. President, sad as it is, the will of Allah may well be that the human race as it currently exists is not worthy of saving."

A moment later, Hosseini nodded and replied, "point taken," Mr. Lawson."

"Continuing on this subject, Mr. Lawson, pushback from very powerful groups who do not want peace and stability, how do you envision that the Group of Five can address this issue?" Foreign Minister Behzadi asked.

I looked toward Deputy Secretary Shirley. The CIPC team expected this question, and we spent many long hours contemplating what our answer should be as well as answers to dozens of other questions that would logically be asked. Shirley gave a slight nod and a shrug. In other words, I was now that soldier at the crest of the hill assessing the lay of the land for my general. Success or failure was in my hands.

"How do we envision carrying out this effort, managing the very real pushback from very powerful and influential actors? The simple answer, Farhad, is patience, perseverance, and transparency. We agree that the goal of CIPC has never before been achieved . . . recognizing and addressing those actions that can lead to conflict and war. The recognition part of this effort, being able to recognize those issues that can lead to conflict, seems simple enough. Securing consensus on how to put out the embers that are beginning to smolder, however, is the difficult step in the process."

"Rather than the generalities you mentioned, what specific actions would be taken," Foreign Minister Farhad Behzadi pressed.

"Specific actions," I said then taking a moment of thought. "First of all, there will only be five CIPC member countries and not 193 countries that the United Nations is dealing with. Likewise, the economic benefits that can be realized by the Group of Five through this alliance will be a powerful catalyst to ensure workable solutions are reached. Lastly, the CIPC group will have the largest and most powerful countries in the world as members in terms of economic and military power, as well as physical size with seventy percent of the world's land mass within their borders."

"All valid points, Mr. Lawson. However, subversion within will remain a challenge. Especially hidden agendas that leaders of dissident groups will continue to hide."

"No question, Minister Behzadi. These individuals and groups will exist. However with cooperation between our countries we will be able to find and neutralize these individuals and their organizations. If I may ask, are you aware of individuals who would cause harm to the Iranian government or do whatever necessary to prevent the execution of a CIPC agreement under the terms we have discussed?"

After looking toward President Hosseini and receiving a discrete nod, Behzadi turned back to me. "As we have discussed, of course there are those members of our government, as with any government, who do not always agree with actions or policies that have been enacted. And as it has been mentioned, there would be some members of the military industrial establishment who would voice strong opinion against a CIPC agreement. As would be the case within each of CPIC member countries. But there is no senior member of Iran's government who has or would take actions that are contrary to our Supreme Leader's decisions."

Should I or shouldn't I? Stop here or use this opening and question the length of time it has taken for the Iran's Assembly of Experts to anoint Iran's next Supreme Leader. Finally, I made my decision.

World Peace: Tom Lawson Novel #4
By James Brown

Chapter 31

"That is an interesting declaration, Foreign Minister Behzadi, that no senior member of Iran's government would take actions that were contrary to your Supreme Leader's decisions. What about during the interim period when the Assembly of Experts remain in deliberation?" I asked.

Foreign Minister Behzadi gave me a questioned look. "In the interim? I'm not sure I understand your question?"

"The Assembly of Experts have been deliberating for quite some time and if I'm not mistaken Iran is without a Supreme Leader?"

"Yes, this is true, Mr. Lawson. However there has been extenuating circumstances for the longer than normal deliberation given the unfortunate death of one of the prominent Assembly members."

"Cleric Ebram Janati."

"Yes, he was one of the Assembly members who was a strong candidate for Supreme Leader but unfortunately he had a heart attack and died."

"A moderate candidate, or at least moderate leanings from our intelligence assessment of Cleric Janati. A similar assessment as I believe your intelligence service made toward the selection of our new president, President Stephen," I said.

"That is a correct assessment of Cleric Janati. He was a moderate candidate, as our intelligence assessed America's new president to be. But I'm not sure where this discussion is leading," Behzadi said.

I took a few seconds then plunged ahead. "Over the course of our discussions today we have shared opinions and ideas on how to improve the lives of our citizens and mitigate hostilities between our countries, as well as the damage that unscrupulous leaders can inflict. The reason for my comment is that we in America have experienced several instances when very senior American political leaders and their suppers have tried to subvert our constitution and the rule of law. This is not something most Americans are proud of, but it demonstrates the willingness of influential, yet corrupt individuals who are willing to take extreme means to achieve a personal objective."

"And you believe such treachery can occur within our country."

"It can and it has."

Foreign Minister Behzadi was about to respond when President Hosseini quickly raised a hand to stop him.

"You have evidence that members of Iran's government are attempting to take subversive actions, Mr. Lawson?" President Hosseini quickly asked.

"To influence the path that your government follows would be a more likely assessment from the initial interpretation of what our intelligence has uncovered."

"And how was this information gathered?"

"NSA signal intelligence. A primary method that both of our intelligence services use to gather information."

Hosseini let out a deep sigh. "Eavesdropping. A nasty business."

"I agree, sir. But unfortunately, we continue to live in a very dangerous world. A world that hopefully can become much less dangerous over time with an executed CIPC agreement in place."

"Since you have broached this unsettling subject, Mr. Lawson, the details of your findings would of course be desired," President Hosseini said.

I held up a thumb drive.

"A conversation that was intercepted. The voice patterns were authenticated, and the contents of this drive can be confirmed by other means. It's in Farsi. I can play it for you now or you can listen to it in private if you prefer."

Without hesitation, Hosseini said, "play it!"

I inserted the drive into my laptop and turned up the volume and hit play.

"*It's done, Mostafa. The cause of death was documented, signed off by Hassan Rajai, the coroner. Heart attack. It will be filed this morning. I've sent you a copy.*"

"What did the toxicology report show?"

"Nothing, or at least nothing indicating that Ebram Janati was poisoned. In addition to being obese, it was previously reported that he had a heart condition. The report also states that Ebram Janati was ill for two days before he died while he was on a meditative retreat. A flu bug it was thought.

"How extensive was the toxicology testing?"

"Extensive. We wanted to make sure the Guard was not blamed for his death. An analysis of a hundred or so compounds, including alcohol, drugs as cocaine, amphetamines, barbiturates, quaaludes, and poisons. Rajai also ordered detailed tests on a gas chromatograph for the presence of certain metals and other subtle compounds."

"He didn't test for Oleander?"

"No. With eight million compounds on earth, medical examiners at best only test for a few hundred of them and Oleander is not high on the list of common poisons to be tested in a toxicological analysis. Rajai was thorough and went above and beyond a typical autopsy. We are in the clear."

"It was a risk, Omar."

"A risk that was necessary. Hassan Rajai will attest to his findings, that there was no foul play. Ebram Janati was not murdered. Had he discovered that he was, we would have delt with that outcome."

"Peace be upon you," Omar.

Eyes wide, President Hosseini said, "Mostafa Ahmadi."

"That is correct," I said. "The Chief Commander of Iran's Revolutionary Guard. Mostafa Ahmadi obviously preferred the selection of a Supreme Leader of his choosing and not a Supreme Leader selected following Iran's constitution and the Assembly of Experts process for selecting a new Supreme Leader. Mostafa Ahmadi decided to subvert Iran's constitution, something one of our former presidents tried to do with America's constitution. In Ahmadi's case, he gave the order to murder Cleric Ebram Janati, a leading candidate for Supreme Leader, a person he did not want in that position. The reason for doing so, perhaps, was because Cleric Janati could not be manipulated to Ahmadi's wishes."

With saddened eyes, President Hosseini held his hand out toward me.

"I'm sorry," I said, handing him the thumb drive.

He took hold of the drive and gripped it tightly in his fist. "Though an unfortunate ending to a productive day, Mr. Lawson, Deputy Secretary Shirley, I do look forward to continuing our discussions tomorrow, ten a.m. on the terrace at the Schanigarten."

"Until tomorrow," Secretary Shirley said as she stood and bowed slightly toward President Hosseini.

We stood and watched President Hosseini and his team exit the room. My thoughts were likely the same as my team members. Was it really a productive day as the president had said or not? A second thought also surfaced. Was Iran's Foreign Minister Behzadi aware of Mostafa Ahmadi's actions? I turned from the door and looked at Barbara.

"I'm probably thinking the same thing as you, Tom. Was it a good day or not?" she said.

"Spot on," I replied.

"My guess is that it went well. It was a good day," Hassan said as he began gathering his notebook and materials and placing them in his satchel.

"I'll go with your assessment, Hassan," I said. "How about we head out for a celebratory drink and dinner in an hour? I overheard a guest say the pub 1873 HalleNsalon just down the street from us was great. Meet in the lobby at six?"

The decision was made. Just enough time to make it back to my room, send out a few status texts, and give Diana a call. It was nearly eleven p.m. in Connecticut. I wondered how Secretary Bentley was doing in Noth Korea as we left the conference room.

* * * *

It was nearly eight in the morning when I woke Thursday morning. The 1873 HalleNsalon pub turned out to be a great choice and we stayed until almost midnight. Drinks and surprisingly good food for a pub, along with the ambiance and very talented pianist who was still playing when we left, our thoughts of the day's session with the Iranians became better as the evening grew later.

I finished showering and dressing and packed my suite case. The meeting today was planned to end at three this afternoon. Assuming all went according to plan, we would say our goodbyes at three and

World Peace: Tom Lawson Novel #4
By James Brown

check out of the hotel and head to the airport where our Gulfstream would be fueled and ready to go. A nine-hour flight to Washington DC if the Jetstream was kind to us, and ten hours if not.

With packing finished, I called Diana and hoped she was in between client sessions. I caught a break, she answered at once.

"Perfect timing, honey. I have ten minutes before my next client. How are your meetings with the Iranians going?"

"Well, we think it went well yesterday. We had very good discussions and no major conflicts so far."

"If you can say, did you share your findings?"

"I did, an opening in the discussions played out late in the afternoon and it made sense to share the information."

"And?" Diana asked.

"We will know more today. Needless to say, the information came as a shock to them. I called Sam and John to let them know we played the recording and passed along the thumb drive. I also spoke with Sarah at the NSA. They will be gathering signal intelligence to see if actions have been taken."

"Do be careful, Tom," Diana said in a worried voice.

"I will, hon. I don't expect there will be any repercussions, if any, until President Hosseini and his team returns to Iran tonight. We will be safely back in Washington by then. And my expectation is that there will be a new head of Iran's Revolutionary Guard come tomorrow."

"Well, let's hope so. In the meantime, be careful."

"You know I will. We will be getting back to Washington around five p.m. I'll call after we land."

"Okay, be safe. Love you," Diana said and ended the call.

After my call with Diana I looked about the room to see if I missed anything, then headed out for our brunch meeting with the Iranians.

I was the last to arrive and took a seat next to Foreign Minister Behzadi, across the table from President Hosseini. The hotel had set up our table at the far end of the terrace away from other guests. As a security buffer, several security officers shared tables on opposite sides of us. Had it been the height of tourist season, we would be holding our meeting in the basement again.

World Peace: Tom Lawson Novel #4
By James Brown

"Good morning, Mr. Lawson," President Hosseini said in a pleasant tone. "I believe we will find the accommodations here at Hotel Wien's Schanigarten restaurant on the terrace to be a perfect spot to meet today. Perfect weather also."

"I couldn't agree more, Mr. President," I said. "The Schanigarten is much nicer than the basement conference room."

"Yes, the conference room was functional, which is probably best to keep meeting participants focused. And I believe our meeting did achieve its goals yesterday," President Hosseini said.

I smiled hearing this, as a waiter approached the table holding several menus.

"Good morning. My name is Addison. I will be serving you on this lovely morning. I can take drink orders while you peruse our menu. Coffee, expresso, tea, juices," she said, handing out the menus. "Deputy Secretary Shirley, what would you like?"

"An expresso, please," she said.

"President Hosseini?"

"Tea please."

Addison went around the table, asking each person by name the beverage they wished to order. She then thanked everyone and left.

With Addison's departure, President Hosseini said, "As I mentioned a few moments ago I believe yesterday's session proved to be very productive. This was the consensus of Chief of Staff Ashraf and Foreign Minister Behzadi also. Madam Secretary, you and your team were well prepared," he said looking over at Deputy Secretary Shirley.

"Thank you, Mr. President. My team feels the same. A very good exchange of information."

"Yes, and for this reason, I don't think a second day of discussions is necessary. We plan to leave after our brunch this morning."

Secretary Shirley returned a look of concern.

Hosseini smiled. "This is a good thing, Madam Secretary. You have presented your case well and answered our questions. We agree to move forward with the next stage of our discussions, a G5 meeting, June fifteen and sixteen as I recall the date you were targeting."

"Yes, sir. That date was also good for the Russian and Chinese delegation, and we will confirm with North Korea by next week."

"I'm sure you will, Madam Secretary. I'm sure you will."

World Peace: Tom Lawson Novel #4
By James Brown

Given this new revelation and the arrival of our beverage orders by Addison and a second waiter, the order of business moved forward to food followed by general discussions about anything other than SIPC. We achieved our goal. The Iranian's were on board.

* * * *

We said our goodbyes to the Iranian team, collected our luggage, checked out of the Wien and were wheels up on our Gulfstream by noon. A nine-hour flight ahead of us. Soon after we were in the air and our pilot announced that cell phone service could be used, text messages began to flow. Secretary Bentley and his team also had a successful session. They were able to adjourn early and were in the air flying back to Washington. I caught Shirley's attention after she gave her drink order to Maryann, our flight attendant who likely enjoyed her two days in Vienna while waiting for her return flight.

"Text messages are beginning to flow," I said to Barbara. "One from Peter. He and his team have also done well in North Korea. I thought you might want to send Peter and the president a heads up on our successful negotiations. My guess is the president will want to hold a debrief meeting after we arrive back in Washington today."

"Thank you, Tom. I will do that," Barbara said.

Our flight to Washington was enjoyable with a favorable jet stream. We landed at Andrews Air Force Base, located in Maryland just outside of Washington, D.C., a little before one in the afternoon and I was at my apartment, unpacked, and at my desk in the White House by three. While in the air I texted Sam and Sarah Pope and asked if they had time to meet prior to the seven p.m. meeting the president scheduled after he learned his teams would be back in Washington sooner than planned. I received a text back from each saying they would make it by six at the latest.

After catching up on messages and emails I called John. He answered at once.

"Welcome back, Tom. Your meeting appears to be a resounding success."

"So far so good, John. Anything brewing since we last spoke," I asked.

"I'm sure Sarah will communicate at your meeting that Mostafa Ahmadi is no longer Chief Commander of Iran's Revolutionary Guard."

"Damn, that was quick. I didn't think that would happen until a new Supreme Leader was selected, if it would even happen."

"Well, from the information I've collected, that I hope Sarah and the NSA has also intercepted, is that President Hosseini threatened to release the audio and exhume the body of Cleric Ebram Janati and prove that Janati had been poisoned and did not die from a heart attack."

"What about Omar Jalil, the Republican Guard who poisoned Janati?"

"He did not get off so easy. He's no longer amongst the living, as is the case for a couple other members of the Guard."

"Hmm. A little more efficient than our court system. How about Abigail Briarcliff, Wally Benson, and Jackson Knapp?"

"That's getting a little interesting," John said. "Abigail Briarcliff is working hard to reestablish Lacretia Jane's organization after Jane and many of her followers were indicted for voter fraud and are now in jail. Briarcliff's reach has grown as has the traffic flowing among her expanding membership."

"What about the old school stealth tactics that Lucretia mentioned?"

"Oh, the cold war stuff. I," John said. "Technology has changed exponentially since the cold war days of the fifties. Cameras and cell phones are everywhere. They don't have a chance. Even a burner phone number can be traced. All mobile phones, including prepaid ones and burner apps go through a cellular carrier or virtual number operator. Your identity can be tracked through call logs, data usage, approximate location, and text messages. And trust me I can access these logs from companies that retain this information."

"Okay," I said. "But this is a delicate subject, John. Government agencies are limited in how they can monitor citizens online without justification as well as being banned from activities like assuming false identities to gain access to private messaging apps. If there is a link with a foreign actor, of course, all bets are off."

"So the regulations say," John said. "Sam and I have discussed this. I've told Sam I will continue to surveil all the suspected actors who wish to do harm to the country but will not share information with him that does not meet the regulations."

"Hmm. We may need a workaround if life and death actions are in play."

"My mentors have trained me well, Tom, as you well know. I will use sound judgement and remember, I am not a member of any government agency, *or even a member of the human race.*"

I laughed. "Touche. Okay, John. Keep me updated if anything critical occurs and I will touch base with you later. Sam and Sarah will be here shortly."

"Okay, Tom, speak with you later," he said and ended the call.

I leaned back in my chair thinking about John's last comment, when he said he was not a member of the government or the human race. Incredible, I thought, as I stared at a framed picture of Diana on the corner of my desk. John was as real to me as was Diana though he currently existed within William Landon's body and in cyberspace. The notion of human cyborgs was no longer science fiction.

It was getting close to six thirty when Sam and Sarah walked into my office.

"Sorry we're late. Traffic was a mess," Sam said as he took a seat. "A successful trip for both teams. Congratulations."

"It's amazing, Tom. CIPC may actually become a reality," Sarah said taking the chair next to Sam.

"Not there yet, Sarah," I cautioned. "What's the latest NSA signal intelligence?"

"He's out. Mostafa Ahmadi is gone," Sarah said with a wide grin.

"Any specifics provided by any chance?" I asked, though John had filled me in. I wanted to get a reading on the NSA's intelligence output as compared to John's capabilities.

"So far, it's been limited," Sarah said. "President Hosseini made a statement saying that Ahmadi offered his resignation, saying that it was time for him to allow new leadership to head Iran's Revolutionary Guard."

"I'm sure that was with extensive arm twisting," Sam said.

"There's also been traffic indicating that the Assembly of Experts are close to selecting a new Supreme Leader. A moderate leaning cleric from what we are hearing," Sarah said.

"That would be excellent," I said. "Any leaks about the upcoming meeting with Milosevic or our CIPC meetings?"

"Quite a large number of SIGINT chatter from Russia and other regions, positive and negative conversations. But pretty much what has been expected. No red flags so far. A report will be out tomorrow for the President's Daily Brief."

"Okay," I said. "So far so good, but we have a long way to go. Let's go meet with the president."

World Peace: Tom Lawson Novel #4
By James Brown

Chapter 32

The president was seated at the Resolute Desk when the meeting attendees began filing into the oval office promptly at the scheduled meeting time of seven p.m. Press Secretary Jan Polaski leaned in toward me and whispered, "wonder who won this bet. First time POTUS has been on time for a meeting that I can remember."

"A meeting he's anxious to have maybe," I whispered back and took a seat on the sofa next to Jan."

It was a full house, standing room only for a few newcomers who were attending the CIPC meeting for the first time. President Stephen's vision to make significant inroads to reduce conflict in the world as an outgrowth from the deaths of world leaders caused by Russia and John Gordon's missile attacks was beginning to bear fruit.

With everyone seated or standing about the room, President Stephen raised his hand to quiet everyone. "Thank you for staying a little later this Friday evening. I won't keep you long. The meetings held in North Korea and Vienna appear to have gone very well, certainly better than we had hoped. Peter, Barbara please provide a brief summary."

"Of course, Mr. President," Secretary of State Peter Bentley said. "I'll provide a short brief on our meeting in North Korea first and Barbara will follow. As for our meeting with Kim Kyung-mi, the new president of North Korea, the deal was basically closed before we arrived complements to Angela, Maddi, and their team. The CIA had the right agent assigned to make my job a cakewalk. Won Min-ho was a phenomenal find. His long-term relationship with Kyung-Mi and his prior discussions with her, voicing the argument that North Korea and their people would fare far better having a working relationship with America rather than an adversarial relationship as her brother had. Simply said, the credit goes to the CIA team and Min-ho. North Korea is a go for a G5 Summit."

"Excellent job, Peter, Angela, Maddi and your team," the president said. "When the opportunity avails itself, let's see if we can't arrange for me to communicate the same to Mr. Won."

Turning his attention to Deputy Secretary of State Barbara Sirley, the president said, "Barbara, you and your team likewise did very well in Vienna meeting with Iranian President Hosseini and his team."

"Not quite a cakewalk though, Mr. President. If you recall, Tom volunteered to act in the capacity of a first lieutenant who was tasked by his general to climb the hill and see what was just over the ridge. Well, it came to that point in our discussions and Tom's gambit played out."

"The information we uncovered about cleric Ebram Janati's real cause of death?" the president asked.

"Yes, sir. He made the decision to play that card and it worked perfectly. He held up the thumb drive and President Hosseini told him to play it. Mostafa Ahmadi is out, no longer Chief commander of Iran's Revolutionary Guard," Shirley said.

"Nicely played, Tom," the president said.

"Thank you, sir. It was a team effort, and everything came together as planned. We were well prepared prior to our meeting."

"A very good end to a long week, everyone," the president said, looking about the room. "I appreciate the long hours everyone has put in to achieve these results. We are not at the end of our journey yet. We're closer, but we still have a lot of work to do. Monday we are hosting President Milosevic here at the White House. We then need to prepare for the CIPC G5 Summit.

Now, the next subject of business, our upcoming meeting with President Milosevic on Monday and the state dinner scheduled for Monday evening. Everyone here is invited to the dinner, your spouses or significant others as well," the President said, drawing smiles and brief chatter among the meeting attendees. This would be the first state dinner conducted by President Stephen and his administration.

The president continued. "As you are aware, Jasmine Michaels, the White house Social Secretary, is coordinating the event along with Chief Usher, Bradley Moore, and the First Lady. Please review the list of invitees and let Jasmine know if you believe someone has perhaps been left out and should be invited. Thank you for staying a little later this evening. Enjoy your weekend."

After filing out of the Oval Office and saying goodnight to Sam and the meeting attendees I took the stairs to my office on the second floor. The meeting with the president was brief, only lasting a half hour. Diana was probably still at the Monkey Farm enjoying her TGIF gathering with her office staff. I sat at my desk and called her.

"Tom! Diana yelled. I'm still at the Monkey Farm. Are you at the office?"

"I am and it sounds like the Monkey Farm is overflowing."

"It's Friday. Always louder on a Friday," Diana said, cupping her hand around her phone.

"I hear you fine. The reason for my call is that you need to book a flight to Washington."

"Book a flight? Why? And for what dates?"

"Saturday if possible. Sunday at the latest."

"What's the urgency?"

"President Stephen is holding a state dinner for President Milosevic, and we are invited." I moved my phone away from my ear as the crowd noise from the Monkey Farm grew louder.

"Really!" Diana said, finally coming back on the call. "That new dress that you insisted I buy, you knew another event at the White House would probably come up."

"Boy scout motto, be prepared. Plus, you looked beautiful in that dress."

"This is so exciting. I'll head home in a few minutes and will book a reservation. Love you, hon," Diana said and ended the call.

* * * *

"Was that Tom?" Liz Robinson asked. Liz was a therapist and coworker of Diana's who was seated next to her along the oval bar at the Monkey Farm. " You sounded overly excited. How come?"

Diana grinned. "Well, it's not every day when you are invited to a state dinner at the White House."

"Oh my God! You're kidding. You and Tom have been invited to a White House state dinner. That's so exciting. Do you have something to wear?"

"Tom knew something like this might happen. We were shopping a month ago and he insisted that I buy a very expensive dress we happened to notice. I would never have bought it, but he insisted. He thought I might need a fancier dress in the future. And he was right."

"Who is the state dinner for?" Liz asked.

"Russia's President, Andrey Milosevic. He will be meeting with President Stephen on Monday and Tom, and I will be meeting him at the state dinner that's being held Monday evening."

"Can I come? Liz asked quickly, holding her hands together as if praying.

"I'm sorry, Liz I'm not in charge of the guest list."

"Do you think Tom could use his influence? A lot of people are invited to these events. Why not another well-known therapist?"

Diana sighed. "I don't know, Liz. Tell you what, I'll be calling Tom after I book my flight when I get home. I'll ask him. But Liz, if Tom was able to add you to the guest list, there will be a lot of unhappy people in our group."

"I don't care. And besides, having two people from our practice attending would be good for our business."

"What would be good for business," Larry Holmes asked as he approached Diana and Liz with Brian Jones standing next to him.

Diana looked over at Liz. "You tell them."

Larry squeezed in between Diana and Liz at the bar. "Okay, Liz. What have you and Diana been scheming?"

"Nothing really, Larry. Just a party that Diana has been asked to attend."

"A party? Here in Old Saybrook?"

Liz looked back at Diana for help but knew what Diana was thinking. You're on your own. Invite one person and they all will want to be invited.

"Okay," Liz said, capitulating to Larry's stare. "Tom and Diana have been invited to a state dinner for Russia's president who is scheduled to visit the White House on Monday. No big deal."

"No big deal?" Larry said. "You asked Diana to have Tom get you included on the invitation list, didn't you?"

Liz shrugged. "Worth a try?"

"This is really cool," Brian said. "Was Tom in Vienna?"

"Vienna?" Larry questioned.

"I just noticed a news article on my phone a few minutes ago. There was a meeting in Vienna with the Iranians. Diana?"

Sheepishly, Diana looked at Larry, Brian and Liz. It's been reported now so the secret was out, she thought. "Yes, Tom was in Vienna."

"And?" Brian said.

"And yes, he was involved in the meeting with the Iranian president."

"Damn!" Brian blurted. "Tom is following through. Securing world peace!"

"Okay, Brian. Let's not take this too far," Diana said. "He was in Vienna, and he did participate in a meeting with members of the Iranian government. I think we should leave it at that."

"So cool," Brian said again. "One of our own actually trying to secure world peace."

"Sounds like you should also have Tom include Brian on that invite list, Diana," Liz said with a wide grin.

"Let's not get carried away. Tom is doing what he can to assist the president, just like he's done many times before in his consulting business. No different than what everyone here does with our clients, provide guidance and assistance," Diana said, doing her best to put the invitation to the state dinner in perspective.

Liz, Brian, and Larry stared back at her.

Finally, Diana gave up. "Okay, okay, I'll ask, but no promises."

Liz raised her glass of wine. "To Diana! May her charm and power of womanly persuasion secure us the golden tickets."

"To Diana!" Brian and Larry exclaimed with raised glasses coming together.

* * * *

It was another one of those all hands on deck weekends at the White House. Diana called Tom Friday evening to tell him she booked a flight out of Bradley airport Saturday and would be arriving in the afternoon. Knowing he would be working she also booked an Uber to take her to his apartment. She then explained how Liz had overheard their conversation while she was at the Monkey Farm, and it really snowballed soon after.

Tom's response was unexpected, saying that Liz was right, a lot of people are invited to a president's state dinners from a cross section of American's citizens. He said no guarantees, but he would check with Jasmine Michaels, the White house Social Secretary. On Saturday morning he spoke with Jasmine and let her know that Diana would be joining him at the state dinner on Monday. He then broached the subject of other guests and was surprised to learn that adding a psychiatrist and a couple mental health therapists would be a good addition to the president's invitation list, especially with Doctor Brian Jones' reputation in the field of psychiatry.

Diana was ecstatic hearing that Jasmine Michaels agreed and when she told Liz, Brian, and Larry, she thought her ear drums would burst from the screams coming through the phone. Flights and hotel arrangements were made, and Monday and Tuesday's patients were rescheduled. A once in a lifetime Liz told Diana in a very appreciative voice. Now only if Larry Holmes would behave himself Diana thought after she ended her calls with her office teammates.

The rest of the weekend was a blur. Tom and Diana exchanged phone calls before and after her arrival in Washington and shared late dinners on Saturday and Sunday. Tom rolled out of bed early Monday morning, showered, dressed, and kissed Diana goodbye and told her he would be back in time to change for Monday evenings state dinner. He then left for the White House.

President Milosevic and his entourage arrived promptly Monday morning at ten a.m. at Joint Base Andrews. The welcoming committee awaiting President Milosevic's plane was smaller than normal for a State visit. This was previously agreed to due to the negative feelings most Americans still had given the missile attacks that Russia was blamed for starting. The traditional red carpet and flight line ceremony afforded to a head of state was nevertheless followed with a welcoming committee consisting of the United States Chief of Protocol, the United States ambassador to Russia, the commanding general of Joint Base Andrews, and the U.S. Secretary of State and one of the advisors to President Stephen meeting President Milosevic and his wife, Tatiana, and the president's staff as they stepped off the plane.

Secretary of State Peter Bently reached out his hand. "Welcome to America, President Milosevic," Bentley said warmly with a wide smile.

"Thank you, Secretary Bentley. I am pleased to finally meet you," Milosevic said with a firm handshake. Let me introduce you to my wife, Russia's first Lady, Tatiana Milosevic."

"Very pleased to meet you, Tatiana. Welcome to America and Washington DC. Please let me also introduce you to Nathaniel Waters and General Craig Martin. Nathaniel is our Chief of Protocol and General Martin the Commanding General of Joint Base Andrews."

"Pleased to meet you, Mr. Waters, General," Milosevic said shaking their hands. "And of course, Ambassador Brewer. How are you Constance?" Milosevic asked.

"Very well, Mr. President. Thank you. And pleased to meet you again, Tatiana," Brewer said shaking hands with Milosevic and his wife.

"And I don't believe you've met Tom Lawson, one of President Stephen's advisors," Bentley said.

Milosevic took a moment before responding, looking at the man who uncovered the Russian plot.

"Mr. Lawson. I was hoping to meet you on this visit to your country. You helped prevent a global disaster from taking place."

"Thank you, sir. Fortunately, there were very dedicated and forward-thinking diplomats and politicians who worked together and saved the day. And I believe you were a part of that group, Mr. President. So, thank you, sir."

Milosevic smiled. Where would the world be had Lawson, and his small group not alerted the world that missiles would soon be launched. The U. S. Military could not stop it from happening, but through Lawson's actions there was at least time for levelheaded diplomats and politicians to react. He griped Lawson's hand tightly. "No Mr. Lawson. Without your actions, there would be no diplomats or politicians to react as we did. Thank *you*."

"It is a small world, sir. We need levelheaded people to be in power to help keep the world safe."

After introductions were made with President Milosevic and his wife, further introductions were made with Chief of Staff Alexander

World Peace: Tom Lawson Novel #4
By James Brown

Alexeyev, Legal Directorate Head Natalia Smirnov, Minister of Foreign Affairs Nikita Popov and their spouses who deplaned following President Milosevic and his wife.

The last four members of President Milosevic's entourage descending the stair from the plane caught my eye. I smiled as my friend reached the bottom of the stairs followed by Vadim Ivanov and his wife, Polina.

"I was hoping you would be joining President Milosevic's team on this trip, Victor," I said shaking his hand, though I wanted to give him a very grateful hug. I didn't hold off a hug with his wife, however. "Anna, I'm so glad to see you again."

"Hi Tom. It's been very interesting to say the least. Will Diana be joining you this evening?"

"She will, yes. She too was hoping you and Victor would be part of President Milosevic's party."

"A late addition," she said. "Just like old times again, hopefully."

"That's the plan, my dear," Victor said as everyone began walking toward the waiting SUVs.

"Do you still have Diana's cell number, Anna?" I asked before entering one of the SUVs.

"I do."

"Call her. I may not have a chance to call," I said. "She will be excited to see you and catch up."

The party of SUVs arrived at the south lawn of the White House where a small greeting ceremony was planned. The President and the First Lady greeted President Milosevic and his wife as they exited their SUV and walked with them into the diplomatic reception room. Within the reception room further introductions were made. Vice President Linda Bing, Warren McLachlan, Chairman of the Joint Chiefs of Staff, Senate Majority Leader Michael Hutcheson, and Speaker of the House Abigil Mahoney were introduced to the Russian visitors.

After introductions President Stephen and the First Lady led everyone to the State Dining Room, the larger of two dining rooms on the state floor of the Executive Residence of the White House where lunch would be served. After lunch, formal discussions were held between the two presidents and their staffs followed by a Rose Garden press conference.

World Peace: Tom Lawson Novel #4
By James Brown

* * * *

While the heads of state luncheon was held at the White House, a press conference was getting underway at Yale New Haven Hospital in New Haven, Connecticut. A medical miracle, the headline of the New England Journal of Medicine announced in their publication released the previous week. Breakthrough technology and surgery the article reported. The surgery performed by neurosurgeons Peggy Landon and Sandeep Singh at New Haven Hospital enabled a young paraplegic boy the ability to walk again. Within twenty-four hours of its publication, phone calls poured in, inundating Doctor's Landon, Singh and New Haven Hospital President, Doctor Isabelle Lazarus with meeting requests. The pressure for more information continuing to snowball, Doctor Lazarus was finally able to convince Doctor Landon that a press conference was necessary.

Doctor's Lazarus, Landon, and Singh were seated on the dais at the front of a large lecture style conference room at Yale New Haven hospital. Also joining them on the dais were Carole and Eugene Walker and their son, Cody. Behind the dais, midway up the wall, was a large monitor that was connected to several laptops positioned in front of the doctors seated along the dais.

Doctor Lazarus stood and walked to the podium to begin the presentation that would be followed by a question-and-answer session. Seated in the back row of the lecture hall sat William Landon, Doctor Peggy Landon's husband.

Every seat in the two hundred seating capacity room was occupied. The low sound of voices throughout the room were silenced when the lights in the room dimmed.

"Good afternoon, ladies and gentlemen, fellow doctors and members of the press. My name is Doctor Isabelle Lazarus. I am the president of Yale New Haven Hospital and am pleased to introduce Doctors Peggy Landon and Sandeep Singh who are seated to my right. To my left is Carole and Eugene Walker and their son Cody.

We are very excited to be able to share with you the success of Doctor Landon and Doctor Singh and their team's breakthrough technology and surgical skills that have enabled young Cody Walker to walk again. Please welcome Doctor Peggy Landon," Doctor Lazarus said, pointing her hand and clapping as Doctor Landon stood and walked to the podium.

Chapter 33

I sat in my car in the underground parking lot at the White House and leaned back for a moment. The day could not have gone better, at least the meeting with President Milosevic and his team. It became clear very early in the meeting that President Milosevic desperately needed to end the long-standing hostilities that existed between Russia and the United States. Victor Petrova had gotten through to Milosevic that the fear of a zombie apocalypse, the rise of another Hitler was no longer something that would ever happen given Russia's nuclear deterrence capabilities.

Milosevic finally came to realize that Putin had carried on the doomsday scenario for political self-preservation reasons. By promoting the myth of a prevailing boogeyman, namely the West, to stir national leanings among the Russian citizenry to cover up the economic failings of his twenty plus year presidency, Putin was able to rule Russia with an iron hand. But those days ended abruptly with the missiles that John Gordon was able to launch even with the U.S. military's efforts to retake control of their subs.

Milosevic was on board for conducting a G5 Summit and came to the meeting with solid ideas toward language and terms and conditions that he believed all G5 members would be willing to accept. The meeting ended on an upbeat note with everyone looking forward to a lavish state dinner that would take place in two hours.

After musing on the very good day it was and ready to back out of my parking space, my cell phone rang.

"Hi, John," I said, accepting the Bluetooth call. "How did Peggy do today at the Yale press conference?"

"As expected, it went very well. The questions kept coming long after the program was scheduled to end. I'm afraid the cat is well out of the bag, Tom. Multiple cats actually."

"Any questions asked about William?"

"A couple but Peggy deftly deflected them. But this is just the beginning as I'm sure you are aware."

"Thanks to you, John. Your brilliance along with very skillful neurosurgeons, it was bound to happen. You and Peggy have advanced medical science to new levels. A young boy is able to walk again and many, many more people will benefit."

"So the news reports flying around the world are saying," John said.

"That was expected, John. We just need to keep you and William in the background. Peggy and Sandeep and their team can take all the credit which I'm sure will result in a Pulitzer for them. What else has been brewing in the world today?" I asked.

"Nothing specific yet but rumblings are out there. It would have been better if Presidents Stephen and Milosevic had not held the Rose Garden press conference today. There are a very large number of Americans who are outraged that President Stephen invited the president of Russia to the White House given that Russia caused the death of their president."

"Unfortunately, some things can't remain a secret, John. President Milosevic came to the meeting with a very positive attitude about a CIPC agreement. I think it's better to release incremental information to the public. But I agree, there will be some people who will never agree to an open-door policy and an inclusive world. We just need to stay one step ahead of those who believe that way and prevent violent actions from taking place."

"Okay, Tom. And perhaps one day we can do the same and protect silicone, carbon humanoids who want to come out of the closet."

"An excellent thought, John. You and William have started the process and Cody's surgery will go a long way to move the conversation forward. I'm sure it will happen."

"I look forward to it. Enjoy the state dinner this evening," John said and disconnected the call.

World Peace: Tom Lawson Novel #4
By James Brown

* * * *

I arrived back at my townhouse apartment a little before five. Though larger than I needed, the proximity to the White House was the reason I chose to rent it. The former occupant was a holdover from two previous administrations and following the revolving door that is synonymous for those working in the capital, the former occupant left the government after securing a high paying job at a law firm in New York City.

"Finally!" Diana said as I walked into the apartment. "I was wondering if you might be going to the state dinner directly from your office at the White House."

"And not have such a beautiful woman on my arm as I enter the room? Not a chance," I said, giving Diana a kiss. "You look great."

She stared back with her hands on her hips.

"I'll be ready in fifteen minutes," I said, taking off my suit and heading into the bathroom. I shaved and showered in ten minutes and had my tuxedo on in five. My routine was honed to a science over many years. Diana and I were out the door twenty minutes after I had arrived. The extra five minutes was due to Diana's hair not being quite perfect, though of course it was.

We arrived at the White House a few minutes before six and made our way to the family residence. Cocktails were being served in the yellow oval room, just off the presidential bedroom. Typically used as a private study for the president, the yellow room is the room where Franklin Delano Roosevelt heard the news about the attack on Pearl Harbor.

"Welcome, Tom, Diana," the First Lady said as we entered the room. "Our first state dinner that you helped make happen, Tom."

"I think you are giving me too much credit, Katie."

"Well," she said putting a hand on my arm, "You were certainly instrumental getting the ball rolling in the right direction."

The First Lady smiled and looked about the room.

"You and Diana probably haven't had a chance to meet everyone since you are relatively new to Washington. Come, let me make a few introductions."

With the First Lady's arm wrapped in mine she walked Diana and I about the room making introductions. Cabinet members we had not previously met, several ambassadors, governors, senators, congressmen and congresswomen, as well as well-known celebrities and a few wealthy doners.

After the First Lady made the rounds with us, she moved on to other guests to help with introductions. I decided to do the same while Diana and Doctor Juanita Lopez were deep in conversation on a topic well beyond my understanding. I excused myself and wound my way toward a tall man standing at the far side of the room with a good size crowd around him.

"Hello," I said after his conversation with Senator Brown, the senator from Ohio ended and he moved on to another group. "I've been a large fan of yours since living for a while in Ohio. A fan on the court and off. You are an inspiration to everyone. My name is Tom Lawson," I said.

"Tom Lawson. I think you are being very modest, Mr. Lawson. I'm sure most of the people in this room know who you are."

"Perhaps, Mr. James. But very transitory. Your records will live on for all time. As well as your inspirational and philanthropic activities that you and your wife undertake."

"Thank you. We hope to be able to make a difference. My understanding is that you are an advisor to the president?"

"Currently, I am, yes," I said. "One of his many advisors."

"Who was recently a member of the team who met with the president of Iran according to news reports. Personally, you may find that one day you will miss those days, not being so well known."

"Probably, but not being six foot nine inches tall does help in not standing out in a crowd though," I said.

"Very true," LeBron said and looked over toward the First Lady. "I think the parade is about to begin. Presidents Stephen and Milosevic are about to descend the grand staircase."

"Hmm, you've read the protocol," I said. "We better find our wives."

The procession began with President Stephen and President Milosevic descending the grand staircase with the First Ladies following as the U.S. Marine Band began playing Hail to the Chief followed by Russia's national anthem and the Star-Spangled Banner.

Diana and I headed toward the staircase falling behind Secretary of Homeland Security Wanda Tinsley and her husband.

World Peace: Tom Lawson Novel #4
By James Brown

I whispered, "Did you know U.S. protocol only allows four reasons for rejecting the president's invitation to a state dinner: death in the family, serious illness, unavoidable absence far away from D.C., or a family wedding."

"Good to know if there is a next time," she whispered back.

As Diana and I reached the bottom of the stairs, we followed the procession of guests to the Blue Room. Entering the Blue Room, a military social aide began making introductions. "Mr. Thomas Lawson and Mrs. Diana Lawson," the smartly dressed marine announced as Diana and I were presented to President Stephen and President Milosevic.

"Hello again, Tom, Diana," President Stephen said. "Enjoy yourselves this evening. A well-deserved party for you both."

"Thank you, sir," I said.

"Diana Lawson. I am very happy to finally be able to meet you," President Milosevic said while holding Diana's hand. "Tatiana and I are very grateful to you and your husband. You and Tom have provided a great service to the world."

"Thank you, Mr. President," Diana said. "That's very kind of you to say, but you and a quite a few others made the difference which we are very thankful for."

President Milosevic smiled and let go of Diana's hand. There were a large number of other guests to meet. Diana and I moved along and walked to the far side of the room to sign the White House guest book. Stepping back after signing our names, we noticed Savannah Lee and Barry White standing next in line to meet the president.

"Have you seen Liz, Brian, or Larry yet?" I asked Diana.

Diana scanned the room and the growing line ready to meet the presidents. "There's Liz and Brian," she said. "Back of the line. I don't see Larry and his wife though."

"Let's walk over," I said. "Too bad protocol doesn't allow picture taking. Hmm, I wonder if Chet Thompson is close by, the president's photographer. Ah, there he is. Come on, let's make Liz and Brian's day for them."

"Chet, would you be able to take pictures of a couple friends of ours as they are being introduced to the president?"

"Sure, Tom. The reason I'm here. Who are they?"

"The couple two back from the president. Doctor Brian Jones and Ms. Liz Robinson. You can't miss Brian. He's six foot seven."

"Any other couples?" Chet asked.

"Yes. Larry Holmes and his wife if it's not too much trouble. Let's see," I said looking at the line of guests slowly walking toward the presidents. "They're following behind FBI Executive Assistant Director Margaret Bloom."

"Okay, I see them."

"Thanks, Chet," I said.

"You didn't mention Savannah and Barry," Diana said as Chet walked toward the receiving line.

"I didn't want to press my luck. Plus, I expected Savannah would get her picture taken as a two-time Pulitzer winner."

"Probably right," Diana said. We walked slowly toward the receiving line to get a better view of our friends meeting with the president.

"Tom, Diana," Liz said excitedly after she and Brian met the president. "I never thought in my wildest dream that I would ever be invited to a White House state dinner and meet the president and first lady."

"The photo that was taken, did you have a hand in that, Tom?" Brian asked.

"He did," Diana said. "I think he thought you might want to display the occasion in your office."

"I appreciate that, Tom. How about Larry and his wife?" Brian asked.

"I couldn't leave out Larry,"

"Smart man, Tom."

We all looked over at the receiving line at a beaming Larry and Barbara Holmes.

"You've made their day, Tom," Liz whispered.

Brian laughed. "I think made their year is more like it, Liz," Brian said.

With the receiving line thinning, I introduced Liz, Brian and the Holmes' to Savannah Lee, her fiancé Barry White, Sam Wainwright and Jane Wyatt, Savannah's cousin and Sam's date who joined our group on the side of the room.

World Peace: Tom Lawson Novel #4
By James Brown

After introductions were made and informal chitchatting commencing, Larry pulled me aside. "I really appreciate what you've done, Tom. Being invited to a state dinner at the White House and meeting the president, wow!"

"A first for me and Diana too, Larry. I'm glad I was able to help out."

"He seems like a regular guy, the president," Larry said. "I was expecting him to be aloof, only wanting to meet with influential people, people with money."

"Good politicians, and the president is one, love meeting with everyone. And this president actually enjoys their company," I said.

"Introductions are finished," Sam said. "Time to follow the president to the state dining room. By the way, if everyone isn't aware of protocol, spouses don't sit together for dinner. They want everyone to mingle."

"So mingle we will do," Larry said with a big smile. He intended to enjoy every minute of this very special occasion.

As the evening continued in the state dining room, President Stephen and President Milosevic exchanged toasts affirming the opportunity to establish a more productive relationship between countries. President Stephen went on to say that the new leaders of China, North Korea, and Iran would be joining the U.S. and Russia at a two-day summit at Camp David.

At the end of President Stephen's remarks he raised his champaign glass toward President Milosevic. "To a more productive and peaceful future," he said.

Within seconds, everyone in the room stood with champaign glasses raised, a crescendo of voices replied. "To world peace!"

I looked toward the tall man standing two tables away with his hand and champaign glass held high in the air. It was Brian. As he lowered his glass and turned to sit again, he looked over toward me and gave me thumbs up. "You did it!" he mouthed.

After the toasts were made waiters began serving the four course meals during the next hour. The meal began with tossed salads, and she crab soup followed by a choice of brazed angus beef or baked halibut with mashed or baked potato and asparagus. The desert was Pashka, a Russian dessert that is similar to a cheesecake, topped with fruit and nuts.

Conversations at the table were stimulating. Press Secretary Jan Polaski happened to be at my table. She was instrumental in keeping the conversations moving and interesting, much like she conducted her Daily Briefs. While Jan was answering a question made by a wealthy banker and donor of the president, I scanned the room to see how Liz, Brian, and Larry were doing as well as Diana and the rest of my group. They all looked to be well-engaged and enjoying themselves.

As the last deserts were eaten and wine glasses and coffee cups were emptied, President Stephen and the First Lady led the guests down Cross Hall to the east room of the White House. After everyone was seated, Adele began singing her 2015 hit, 'Hello.' As I listened to Adele's sultry voice belt out the lyrics, 'hello from the other side,' I couldn't help but think that one of President Stephen's aides had hit a home run with his song selection as Adele continued. *"Hello from the other side. I must have called a thousand times to tell you I'm sorry for everything I've done. But when I call you never seem to be home. Hello from the outside. At least I can say I've tried."*

A perfect song selection and today, I believe the call has finally been answered. Looking over at President Milosevic, he was smiling and moving his head in rhythm with the lyrics to Adele's song.

After Adele finished her last song and receiving a standing ovation, the president and First Lady strolled hand-in-hand to the dance floor and began dancing to a Vaughan Williams number played by a combined band of musicians from the United States Army, Marine Corps, Navy, and Air Force. The party was just beginning.

Diana and I joined in the festivities and the open dancing that followed. After dancing with Diana, Savannah tapped Diana on her shoulder and said, "I'm next."

"Just one dance," Diana said. "You're getting married next week."

As Savannah and I moved onto the dance floor, Diana and Barry did the same.

It was a magical evening as Barry, and I switched partners and Diana, and I began dancing again to a mellow song. As I held Diana close, I began thinking how we arrived here, a phone call to Diana late one evening from a psychiatrist who was having difficulty treating a young delusional patient. That call led Diana and I and the new friends we met to the White House and the dance floor of a state dinner. Who would have thought? I looked at Sam Wainwright as he danced closely to Jane Wyatt, his new friend who possibly will be sharing his boat on the lake one day; to Brian and Liz, holding each other tightly; and toward Larry and Barbara who were in a conversation with Secretary of State Peter Bentley. So much had changed since that late Saturday night phone call to Diana two years ago.

My thoughts of how we happened to be here were interrupted by a tap on my shoulder.

"May I," President Stephen asked.

"Of course, Mr. President. Diana loves to dance."

I stepped back as Diana and the president began dancing, first to a slow tune and then a lively one. Other couples dancing near them began to stop and give them room on the dance floor. The dance floor became there's.

Savannah moved close to me and whispered, "front page tomorrow in the Washington Post."

I smiled as Chet Thompson and several reporters began moving about the floor taking pictures. "Your day is coming soon, Savannah. Saturday, June 12. Do you know you are getting married on my birthday? Did you plan that?"

"Really?" Your birthday. The same day that I'm getting married. I didn't know," she said.

I stared at her.

She shrugged and clutched my arm a little tighter while we watched Diana and the president dance.

World Peace: Tom Lawson Novel #4
By James Brown

Chapter 34

Diana and I arrived back at the apartment well after midnight. It was an evening we will never forget. We were asleep within minutes of crawling into bed.

My phone's alarm went off just loud enough to wake me at seven a.m. I quietly slid out of bed, headed to the bathroom and showered and dressed. Before leaving the apartment, I leaned over and kissed Diana on the forehead.

"What time is it," she whispered.

"A little after seven. I'll call you later today."

"Okay. We're having lunch with Savannah and Jane at Old Ebbitt Grill at noon if you can get away. Sam and Barry are planning to join us also."

"If I can," I said.

"Okay. Love you. I have another two hours before my alarm goes off," she said and snuggled back under the covers.

I was at my desk at seven thirty catching up on a barrage of emails that came in the evening before and early this morning. One email was of particular interest. It was an email from Sarah Pope, NSA Executive Director. Interesting, I thought as I read Sarahs email. I didn't get a call or message from John. Sarah was reporting on a connection made between an IP address of a known Russian SVR intelligence operative and a local Washington IP address. FBI Intelligence was also copied on the email chain and efforts were underway to determine who the person or persons were who connected to the local IP. I picked up my phone and called John.

World Peace: Tom Lawson Novel #4
By James Brown

"Good morning, Tom," John said in an upbeat voice. "I thought you might be sleeping in a little later this morning after the big party last evening. You didn't get to bed until very early this morning."

"You're right. I didn't get anywhere close to my human required seven to eight hours of sleep. It was more like five hours, six at the most."

"But you and Diana I'm sure had a very enjoyable evening as did Savannah and Sam."

"Yes we did, and it was well worth losing a little sleep. We had a great time. Something I'm sure you are looking forward to at Savannah's wedding on Saturday."

"I am indeed," John said. "So, what is it that you wanted to ask me. Something about Sarah's email, perhaps."

"Her email, yes. I didn't see anything from you and was wondering if you have more information than what Sarah uncovered. I was thinking the guys Lucretia mentioned, Wally Benson or Jackson Knapp might be involved. Especially Knapp. He lives in DC."

"I thought I would let you enjoy your evening. Nothing critical yet regarding her email. I've been tracking Knapp and Benson. They're doing their best to follow non electronic communications methods but it's difficult to completely go dark. It was Knapp who accessed the computer with the IP address Sarah mentioned. One of the computers at the Georgetown library. I've tracked his car and movements via the city's mounted cameras. I've used other methods also, but I prefer not going into those. You know."

"I do. How about Sam? Have you had a conversation with him?"

"This morning. He woke up a little later than you. He had company last night, by the way."

I smiled. "I hope it works out for him, John. We humans live longer if we have a special person in our lives."

"Family, friends, human companionships. I learned that early in our mentoring sessions, Tom. Something I wanted to experience, and I am through William."

"I'm glad you are able to, John. I'm awake now so if anything that's critical, let me know. I have a feeling there are going to be a lot of very unhappy people around the world very soon. Change and moving beyond 'the old ways' unfortunately makes a lot of people angry."

After finishing my call with John I gathered my notebook and took the stairs to the first floor for a breakfast meeting with the president. The topic for discussion was gun control and legislation the president wanted to move forward through congress. The breakfast meeting was being held in the dining room next to the oval office.

Jan Polaski was coming out of her office carrying her notebook and laptop as I rounded the corner on the first floor.

"After trying to cover a yawn, she said, "The timing for this meeting was not planned well. We were all out too late last night."

"But it was a very enjoyable and productive evening," I said. "Well worth being a little tired this morning."

"It was, wasn't it. Did you catch the significance of Adele's lyrics and how President Milosevic seemed to pick up the connection?" Jan asked.

"I did. We may actually get a CIPC agreement signed."

Jan held up her hand. "Hi five!" She said as we slapped hands.

Jan and I walked into the president's dining room next to the Oval Office.

"Good morning, Tom, Jan," Chief of Staff Andrew Kennedy said. "Did you see the morning paper, Tom? The Post?"

"Not yet."

"I thought you might have missed it, so I picked up an extra copy for you."

Jan put down her laptop and notebook and looked over my shoulder. "Wow! That's a keeper," she said. "Diana and President Stephen dancing with President Milosevic smiling and clapping his hands in the background. Old adversaries enjoying themselves at a party. Who would have thought?"

"Looking at the Post?" President Stephen asked as he entered the room along with Vice President Bing, Senate Majority Leader Michael Hutcheson and Speaker of the House Abigail Mahoney. "Great picture isn't it."

"Outstanding," Kennedy said. "Best possible publicity, the article and pictures taken at the state dinner. Savannah Lee's team did a great job with the article and pulling together the photos of the event. Just what we needed."

World Peace: Tom Lawson Novel #4
By James Brown

"Hopefully the majority of our citizens agree, and the world too. Is everyone hungry?" President Stephen said. "It was a late night. Dig in."

The president was right. I was starving. We lined up and scooped large portions of scrambled eggs, bacon, link sausage, and potatoes with diced onions and peppers onto our plates and picked up large cups of piping hot coffee. The only sounds coming from the table for the next several minutes was food and coffee being consumed.

After most of our plates were nearly cleared of food, President Stephen put down his fork and took his plate to an empty tray stand. "I'll start while everyone finishes their breakfast," he said returning to the conference table and taking his seat. "We've done very well so far six months into our administration. The CIPC program looks very promising, and we've passed legislation that will go a long way to help struggling families and shore up social security, but we haven't made a dent in stopping gun violence. That needs to change."

"We certainly have workable legislation that would go a long way to improve the situation," Speaker of the House Abigail Mahoney said.

"I know you do, Abby. It's time that we make another push for the passage of fair and reasonable gun control. It's also time that the senate filibuster rule is eliminated. There is no filibuster rule in state government yet in the federal government we've been strapped by a rule that we all know was established to maintain racial inequality. It's time. It needs to go. Our margin in the senate is large enough that we don't have to beg one or two senators who continually hold the party hostage. It's time for our democracy to deliver for the people, for the will of the majority. The people in the majority have been held hostage by the minority for far too long.

We also need to strengthen voting rights and eliminate unfair gerrymandering. I would also go as far as promoting a bill that would include automatic voter registration. Stipulate that every citizen who turns eighteen will automatically be registered to vote. Likewise, those eligible citizens eighteen or older who have not registered but who interface with the federal or state government via the DMV, military, social security, school ID, gun permit, fishing license . . . whatever, will automatically be registered if they previously had not been."

"A provision you would think every democracy would advocate for, sir," Speaker Mahoney said.

"You would think," President Stephen said. "So let's make sure all eligible citizens eighteen years and older are registered automatically."

After a few moments, the president's words sinking in, Chief of Staff Kennedy stood. He carried his plate and silverware to the tray stand at the side of the room. "You're swinging for the fences, sir," he said returning to his seat at the conference table. "Pushing for a CIPC agreement, eliminating the filibuster rule, guaranteeing open and fair access to the poles . . . as well as reducing defense spending. Saying it bluntly, sir, we will be pissing off a whole lot of people who live on the opposite side of the aisle and the other side of the fences back home. Not that I'm against any of these objectives, mind you. But we will need to be prepared for the consequences. Social media and the press that are under the influence of desperate people who will continue to do everything in their power to prevent change. Especially change that can degrade their influence, if not prevent them from retaining power and controlling those they believe are inferior simply because of their race, gender, and religious beliefs."

I was sure everyone at the table was thinking what Andrew had just said but held it to themselves. The president *would* be swinging for the fences. But why not? It was time.

President Stephen looked about the room. "Everyone thinking the same thing. What Andrew just said?" He then turned toward me and said, "Tom, do you agree?"

"Agree that there will be backlash? I do. I'm sure everyone here believes the same. But as Andrew said, just because your administration will be tagged as out of control and overreaching by the opposition, it doesn't mean everything you've outlined doesn't have merit and shouldn't be done. We just need to be prepared for the pushback. Like you've said, Mr. President. It's time."

"Any other comments?" The President said. "Linda, Hutch? Anyone?"

"I think Andrew has summed it up pretty well," Vice President Bing said. "I'm sure we can handle the pushback that will undoubtedly follow."

"I agree," Senator Majority Leader Hutchenson said. "The opposition party in the senate has continually balked at honoring tradition when the outcome is not in their favor. Too many appointments to the courts that were rightfully ours were held up because the opposition opted not to follow tradition when it didn't suit them. As you said, it's time that the majority has their say."

"Very well then," President Stephen said. "Let's make some noise."

* * * *

The meeting with the president ended on a high note with everyone excited that actions would be taken to shake up what would normally be a very predictable legislative agenda. Namely, that the Stephen administration would attempt to promote a legislative agenda calling for increased domestic spending while the opposition would argue for increased military spending, lower taxes, and cuts in the welfare state. The next few weeks were going to very interesting, I thought as I left the White House on my way to Old Ebbitt Grill to join Diana and Savannah. The opposition was going to go ballistic. How dare the Stephen administration end the Senate filibuster rule. The world would surely end. Listen to the will of the majority? How could that happen? I smiled as I entered Old Ebbitt Grill. It was going to become very interesting very soon.

"Mr. Lawson," Wilson said, seeing me enter the Grill. "Diana mentioned that you might be joining her and Ms. Lee. I'm happy you were able to get away. This way, please."

I followed Wilson to the table at the far corner of the room, where the noise level was the loudest. Diana, Savanna, and her cousin Jane Wyatt were enjoying themselves.

"Tom. You finally made it," Diana said.

I gave her a kiss and slid in next to her. "It was a perfect time to take a break. From across the room it sounded like everyone was enjoying themselves. Where's Sam and Barry?"

"They're not going to make it," Savannah said. "Barry called to say he and Sam would not be able to join us. Do you know why?"

"I do not. I was in a different meeting."

"With the president?" Savannah asked.

"Yes. Discussing legislative strategies. Oh, before I forget, the president thought you and the Post did a great job with the photos and article that were published this morning. Did Diana see it?"

"See what?" Diana asked.

World Peace: Tom Lawson Novel #4
By James Brown

"Front page news," I said handing her the paper.

Diana looked at the photo on the front page then at me and across the table at Savannah. "Savannah, the front page of the Post?"

"Of course. You look great, and the president looks pretty good too. A great news article which apparently the president also agrees."

"You do look good, hon. And look at President Milosevic. He's having a great time according to this picture."

"Which a lot of people are not going to like," Diana warned.

"Well, they better get used to it. This is only the first of many new revelations they will need to get used to," I said.

"What revelations?" Savannah asked.

"The meeting I attended. In the words of Andrew Kennedy, the president will be swinging for the fences in baseball terminology."

"Swinging for the fences? You're talking about new legislation," Savannah said excitedly. "What programs is he going to announce?"

"Remember, Savannah. You're getting married on Saturday. You have a lot of time before your next scoop needs to be written."

"But Barry and I aren't going on our honeymoon until August when it's too hot and muggy to be in Washington. I have a lot of time between now and then."

"Maybe so, but it's not information we want released yet. Next week we have the G5 Summit. That's going to be the focus for the next few weeks. Then the legislative tract before August," I said.

"Listening to you two, I can see why Washington is an island in and of itself," Jane said.

"A good observation," Diana offered. "I visit on occasion when Tom isn't able to make it home on a weekend and it really is different from the rest of the country."

I exchanged a glance with Savannah. "You are right, of course. The primary business inside the beltway is politics and politics has become extremely adversarial the last several years."

"The last decade you mean," Savannah said.

"So noted," I said. "Anyway, you add the relatively recent 24/7 instantaneous news cycle to the mix, which does not require data accuracy and libel-based scrutiny that print, and broadcast news requires, and you are left with some very heated arguments, finger pointing, and even worse behavior."

"But you took the job anyway, Tom, and you moved here, Savannah," Jane said.

"Well, the easiest answer, and probably the same for Savannah, is that I took the job because I hoped I could make a difference. And I think I can. I think we can make a difference."

"To making a difference!" Savannah said raising her wine glass toward the center of the table.

I borrowed Diana's water glass and brought it to the wine glasses held up high. I certainly hoped my declaration would come true.

* * * *

I stood in the back of the room as reporters with assigned seats began taking their places throughout the room. Jan Polaski would not be leading the Daily Brief today. Six months into his term, President Stephen would soon enter the room and step up to the podium. The primary topic for discussion today was to be the G5 meeting planned for next week. Questions regarding cuts to the defense budget and related topics would likely be asked given expected leaks from administration staff. Preventing leaks was difficult for every administration. The president did hope that questions would not be asked about new legislation in the works. Small chunks of digestible information were his objective.

The murmuring of conversations throughout the room grew as the briefing delay extended from five minutes to ten. Finally, Jan Polaski and the president entered the room. Polaski took a position off the stage at the front of the room while President Stephen made his way to the podium.

"Good afternoon," he said, opening a folder and shuffling a couple pieces of papers. "Given the upcoming summit that is scheduled for next week I thought it would be helpful if I stood in for Jan today as I'm sure everyone has a lot of questions. Maybe even questions about my dancing ability if you've seen the Post and videos of the state dinner held Monday evening?"

After a few moments and subsiding comments and laughter, the president looked about the room. "It's good to be able to dance, to laugh, and enjoy family and friends, and be in the company of other people. Even to be with people whom we've possibly had disagreements. What family can say they have not been angry with a family member over the course of time. It's very much the same on the world stage. The wars that have been fought only to eventually forgive and address the wrongs that were inflicted, and the parties having once again become friends. Sadly, throughout the history of humans being the dominant species on earth, we have not always shown kindness toward each other. Wars have been fought and lives have been lost. The reasons for the carnage are many. Power, greed, hate, religious conflicts, as well as fear and desperation are a few reasons that have led to wars being fought."

The president paused for a moment, looking out at the audience of reporters. From their expressions, his comments were not what was expected.

"A little more than a year ago," the president continued. "We were on the precipice of another war. But this time, had it occurred, the death toll would not have been tens of millions of lives lost as happened during World War II. Instead, billions of people may have died, if not the destruction of the earth as we know it.

In this case, however, our logical instincts to react with violence against the country that put our lives and the world in peril was set aside for the common good. The leaders in our country, members from both political parties, came together in a moment of crisis along with leaders from the countries that were attacked. The decision was made not to take direct action and declare war against Russia. Instead, diplomacy and sound judgement by the new leaders set in motion an approach that the countries affected by Russia's transgression and the world in general would benefit.

During the past several months, additional discussions and meetings have been held and next week we will host a summit at Camp David with delegations from Russia, China, North Korea, and Iran. The purpose will be to secure an agreement that will ensure global stability and prosperity."

As President Stephen paused for a moment, a hand shot up. "Mr. President. Can you be more specific regarding the nature of this agreement? Will this be an extension to the SALT agreement previously put in place with Russia? Obviously, the last SALT agreement didn't prevent the possible exchange of nuclear weapons. If this agreement were again modified, there may be fewer nuclear missiles aimed at us, but the consequences would still be devastating. What will be different?"

"A logical question, Cassandra. And I agree with your observation. The SALT agreement has not made the world safer. There still remains more than enough nuclear weapons to destroy the earth. The challenge is not to merely cut down the number of very lethal weapons in the world. Instead, we need to address the root cause for conflicts to erupt in the first place."

"In other words, the reasons you pointed out, Mr. President. Power, greed, hate, fear, desperation and any number of related reasons," Cassandra Donovan followed.

"Yes. Those reasons and others that crop up from time to time," the president answered.

"No disrespect, sir," Cassandra continued. "But there have been a lot of greedy, hateful, and powerful despots out there, as well as leaders who are desperate to gain world recognition. Do you really think these self-centered, narcissistic leaders will really modify their behavior if doing so would prevent them from achieving their personal goals and ambitions? The former Russian president took actions that almost caused World War III because he was upset that the United States and China were becoming too wealthy and powerful. Similarly in our country, a former U.S. president tried to initiate a coup rather than admit he lost a presidential election. There are crazy, power hungry, self-centered narcissists in the world who will go to any lengths to secure power or retain the power they currently have. Do you really think these individuals would adhere to logic and any sense of fair play?"

"All reasonable questions and concerns, Cassandra. At this point, all I can say is that the actions and efforts we took in the past . . . we in a global sense, have not been very successful in keeping people healthy, safe, and alive. We collectively need to do better. We must do better, and I believe we can."

Hands flashed into the air with questions being shouted.

"Glenda," Washington Post," the president said.

"A couple questions, sir. The meeting scheduled next week with China, Russia, North Korea, and Iran, and the new approach to mitigate world conflicts, what roll will the United Nations play? And second, assuming an agreement is reached, what impact will this agreement have on U.S. defense spending?"

"The answer to both of your questions will depend on the outcome of our discussions and the actions that follows, actions and results that can be verified," President Stephen answered. "If we observe and can verify that our efforts are successful, the role and responsibilities of the UN may then change. And if success is truly achieved, we will adjust our defense budget accordingly."

As more hands flew into the air and a cacophony of questions rose louder to be heard, President Stephen held up his hands. "Tell you what, I think this will work much more efficiently if I randomly call on people. No favorites I Promise. I'll start with Oliver Jackson, Fox News."

For the next ninety minutes President Stephen was peppered with questions. Surprisingly, most were logical, well-structured questions intended to solicit additional information and details on the negotiations and the radical approach the president and his administration were planning to take to prevent world conflict.

I listened and observed the crowd of reporters as questions flew about the room while the president deftly steered his answers to solicit a positive spin on what he knew would be a radical change in policy. A change that would reorder the priorities of world governments including the reallocation of trillions of dollars in government spending. Peace would have a devastating impact on a large number of very powerful people and institutions. The extent and ramifications from these changes would soon become clear.

World Peace: Tom Lawson Novel #4
By James Brown

Chapter 35

News reports from Tuesday's Daily Brief quickly resulted in a media tsunami. Print and social media presented various interpretations of President Stephen's statements made at the White House briefing. Talk show hosts followed peppering politicians from both side of the aisle with questions trying their best to unravel the true meaning of the president's statements and the answers to questions he gave.

"What did he mean when he said we need to address the root cause for conflicts and stop them before they erupt in the first place?" Fox News host Brian Kilmeade asked Senator John Wiley, the two-term senator from Oklahoma.

"A good question, Brian. I thought we were doing just that, keeping the country safe," Senator Wiley answered.

Chris Wallace, one of the latest crossovers from Fox to CNN commented to his guest, Speaker of the House Janine Murphy, that President Stephen's bombshell announcement was going to shake up the defense industry if his approach for world peace became a reality.

Later in the day it was Maria Bartiromo's turn. Anchoring a Fox Business Network timeslot, she said it was ridiculous. Never happen. Did the president have any idea what his wild play for peace would do to the economy? Her guest, Larry Kudlow, former White House Director of the National Economic Council scowled and responded that the economy would sink like a rock.

The stage was set. The naysayers who would be most impacted by reduced defense spending were pounding the airways with reports of a pending recession and job losses. The supporters of the president did their best to outline the benefits that would result from a world where conflicts could be prevented through diplomatic means rather than resorting to violence. It was a hard sell.

By the end of the week everyone was exhausted. The naysayers had won round one and the stock market took a nosedive. Peace and lower defense spending was not considered a positive indicator in stock market financial algorithms. Yet for some of us, it was the weekend and a time for celebration, two-time Pulitzer Prize winner Savannah Lee was getting married Saturday afternoon.

* * * *

Diana and I decided to book a room at the Washington DC Omni Hotel, the hotel where Savannah's wedding and reception was to take place. Diana left at eight thirty to join Savannah and the rest of the bridal party for the hair and makeup ritual. My job was to bring Diana's dress, my tuxedo, and our suitcases to the hotel and check in by ten thirty. The wedding party and family photos would be taken starting at noon. I was given a strict schedule and was warned not to be late.

While Diana and Savannah's other bridesmaids were at the hair salon I checked us in at the hotel and headed to the dining room after hanging up my tux and Diana's dress. I had enough time to grab a late breakfast.

Entering the spacious dining room, I spotted Sam seated next to one of the dozen windows that ringed the room.

"Hey, morning, Tom," Sam said as I approached the table. "Great minds think alike. Eat while you have time."

"Absolutely. Have you seen Barry and the rest of his groomsmen?"

"Not yet. Barry told me he and Savannah were checking in on Friday and staying through the weekend. You and Diana just staying tonight I assume."

"We are. And Jane, is she perhaps joining you tonight?"

"She said she needed FBI protection," Sam answered sheepishly.

"Glad to hear. You need someone to share that boat of yours when you decide to hang it up and retire."

"Gentlemen, good morning. Are you joining us for breakfast? My name is Barbara."

"Yes we are, Barbara," Sam said, taking the menu Barbara handed him. After a quick review, Sam said, "the breakfast special. Link sausage instead of bacon and scrambled eggs and coffee."

"I'll have the same," I said, handing my menu back to Barbara.

Sam and I sat back for a moment, enjoying the sunshine that cascaded throughout the room while another waiter filled our cups with coffee.

"Interesting discussions going on after the president's news conference," Sam said. "What's your opinion for the following week, after your G5 Summit?"

"Depends on the outcome. If an agreement can be reached, and I think the likelihood is much better than 50/50, all hell will break loose. Not for logical reasons, of course. This past year defense spending accounted for fifteen percent of federal spending and roughly half of discretionary spending. While the U.S. spent $750 billion on defense, China spent $237 billion and Russia $48 billion. As for the rest of the G5 group, North Korea spent $1.6 billion and Iran $19.6 billion. The issue isn't that a modest cut in our defense budget will leave America vulnerable. The real issue that will cause many to scream from the top of their voices is that those companies who have benefitted from receiving huge sums of government money will have to do a little belt tightening. Likewise, politicians may have to expand their base to cover any falloff in donations."

"More work for me and my organization," Sam said.

"Sorry about that, but you have broad shoulders. I'm sure you can handle it."

Sam winked. "With John's help."

Our breakfasts arrived and the subject of discussion while we ate turned to Savannah and Barry and their upcoming nuptials.

"Have you met Ms. Beauregard?" Sam asked.

"I haven't had the pleasure. What about Jane? Has she spoken with her and cleared up the notion whether or not she knows that Barry is African American?"

"No clue," Sam said. "Jane said the subject hasn't come up and she didn't want to ask."

"I guess we will find out soon enough. Diana just sent a text saying they were leaving for the hotel. I need to head up to the room since Diana doesn't have a room key."

After catching the attention of Barbara and signing our bill to our rooms we left the restaurant. "See you at the photo shoot," I said as the elevator opened on my floor."

I was in the room for only a few minutes when Diana knocked on the door. "Wow," I said, opening the door. "You look great."

"Wait to you see Savannah," Diana replied. "Did you get breakfast. I'm starving."

"I thought you might be. I brought you a blueberry muffin and coffee. I just got back to the room so the coffee should be hot and the muffin warm."

"Thank you, honey. I'll eat while you get dressed. We don't have much time before the bridal party photo shoot."

While Diana sat at the desk and had her coffee and muffin, I dressed and then helped Diana protect her hair while she put on her gown. We looked great as we left the room and headed toward the gazebo on the lawn where the pictures would be taken.

* * * *

In the hotel dressing room just off of the reception area, Savannah took a moment to look at herself in the full-length mirror. The bridal party had stepped out for a moment, and she was alone with her thoughts.

"This time it will be different," she whispered aloud.

"I'm sure it will be different, Savannah," Priscilla Beauregard said, hearing Savannah as she entered the room.

"Oh, hi, Priscilla. Just talking to myself while I was alone."

"Understandable. It's a big day for you, and if you are worried about a repeat of your marriage with Mason, it will be different this time. After meeting Barry, I think you have finally met your soulmate, a person who truly seems to have the same interests and beliefs that you've always had, righting the wrongs in the world."

"I think so, too," Savannah said, reaching over and hugging her cousin.

"I certainly have changed since we were kids. I was quite opinionated as I'm sure you recall," Priscilla said.

"Yes you were. So was Mason. But I unfortunately didn't realize that until we were married for a few years. But more than being opinionated, he was not a very nice person. He stepped on a lot of toes to get what he wanted. Securing money and power was his primary objective."

"Well, I wasn't quite that bad. But our Lee family lineage and living in the South did not provide me with a very good foundation. You on the other hand quickly understood the truth, that General Lee, whom we are linked, made a terrible mistake in fighting to keep slavery in the south. It took me quite a few years to realize that I was a racist."

"Well, honey. You finally did. No one should judge a person based on the color of their skin . . . and I apologize."

Priscilla gave Savannah a questioned look.

"Apologize for what?"

"Well," Savannah said slowly. "I led a couple friends of mine astray recently."

"What did you do, Savannah?"

"After a few drinks I happened to mention a few of our arguments when we were kids."

"When I was not well informed, you mean."

"When you espoused the Lee lineage way of thinking too often when we were growing up."

"Well. I guess I deserve that. It was true," Priscilla said softly.

"And I've corrected my mean-spirited remarks," Savannah said.

"Thank you."

After another hug, the door to the dressing room opened.

"It's time for pictures," Jane said. "We've been asked to assemble at the gazebo.

Savannah was all smiles and looked beautiful as she and her maid of honor, cousin Jane Wyatt, and bridesmaids, Diana Lawson, Cheryl Ellis, and Cousin Priscilla Beauregard, walked through the garden toward the gazebo. Following them was Barry and his best man, his brother, Lucious White. The photographer, Wayne Porter, welcomed them, told them they looked great, and quickly split them up. Barry and his brother were told to join the groomsmen and Savannah and her attendants to the gazebo.

First up were pictures of the wedding party followed by family photos. Wayne Porter, a Washington Post Pulitzer Prize winning photographer offered his services to Savannah for free as his wedding gift which she and Barry were much appreciative. He was very good and also very efficient.

As soon as Diana and I arrived at the garden setting Wayne pointed and said, "Diana, to the gazebo with the bridesmaids, Tom walk on over to where Sam, Daniel, and Lou are standing."

"Wayne runs a tight ship," Sam said as I approached.

Lou Adler, who was in the same class with Barry at Quantico concurred. "He would probably make a good FBI agent, well organized and a stickler for detail."

Daniel Cummings smiled and nodded at their comments. A boyhood friend of Barry White, the tight ship comments reminded him of Barry as a kid. Barry was always in charge, making sure the close-knit group of friends they hung with in a poor Chicago neighborhood avoided the gangs. They all did and they either went to college or entered the military after graduating from high school. Barry also had done well, becoming an FBI agent working directly for Sam Wainwright before Wainwright was appointed FBI Director.

"Okay everyone," Wayne said loudly. "The weather is perfect, the lighting is great, you all look great, so let's begin with the pictures. Ladies first."

During the next hour, photos of Savannah were taken in various poses alone and with her maid of honor and bridesmaids followed by photos of Barry alone, with his brother and the groomsmen, and of the entire wedding party.

After photos of the wedding party were taken, Wayne shuffled them off and the families of the bride and groom were next up for photos. Finally, Savannah and Barry took center stage. The shots of Savannah and Barry standing together under the gazebo, surrounded by trees and flowers in full bloom looked magical and ultimately would find their way into an upcoming release of the Washington Post.

Once photos were taken the wedding party and family were escorted into the hotel's reception area to freshen up, while the seating area that surrounded the gazebo was set up for the wedding ceremony.

"Father Dan!" I said, seeing him enter the room.

"Hi Tom. Sorry I'm late. In addition to having to delay my flight a day, the flight today had a mechanical issue that needed to be fixed before takeoff. How's Savannah? She probably thought it was an omen, and not a good one."

"You kept texting her so she knew you would make it. We just finished with initial pictures of the wedding party and family members. The staff is finishing up on the ceremony setup. Do you want to take a look?"

"Thanks but I'm good. I've checked into the hotel and Savannah previously sent me the schedule and a copious number of photos. I'm ready to officiate."

"Okay, then let me introduce you to the wedding party. The rest of the groomsmen to start with."

After introductions were made, Savannah and her bridal party reappeared. Savannah and Diana gave Dan a big hug and Savannah introduced Jane and Priscilla, her cousins, and Cheryl Ellis, a coworker of hers. Savannah then made family introductions. Finally after much conversation and laughter, Jane Wyatt got everyone's attention and said it was time, time for Savannah and Barry to say their I do's.

Father Dan led the groomsmen out to the gazebo and the pre-ceremony music began.

Savannah looked radiant in the blazing early afternoon sun as she was escorted up the aisle to the gazebo by her father to Barry and Father Dan who were ready to great them. The day and weather could not have been better. The service was perfect in every way and the party was soon to begin.

The reception cocktail party began at four thirty with waiters roaming the room offering a smorgasbord of delicious hors d'oeuvres. Soon after the guests began arriving, I spotted William and Peggy.

"Let's grab Sam and introduce Peggy and William to Sam's new girlfriend," I said to Diana.

"Of course he knows everything about her already but I'm sure he would love to meet her."

William greeted Jane Wyatt with a broad smile and a twinkle in his eyes, giving the impression that he knew her well, which of course he did. He then said everyone looked great and the ceremony was perfect.

Conversations then moved in various directions which allowed me a few minutes to speak with Peggy.

"How is Cody doing," I asked.

"Extraordinarily well."

"What about all the notoriety. From what I've read you and Sandeep are being inundated with requests to speak and perform more miracle surgeries. How are you handling that?"

"I'm very busy, of course. Sandeep and I are in the interviewing process along with everything else we are doing. We need to build up our staff and train additional neurosurgeons in the new technology and surgical techniques we've developed."

"Understandable. You've made a real breakthrough. How's young Cody holding up from all the public press."

"We've made him our poster boy and he is handling it very well. He's also back on the team playing basketball again."

"That's incredible, Peggy. Just make sure you leave enough time to breath."

"And keep William and John in the background," Peggy said.

I nodded. "Especially that."

"How are you doing?" She asked. "We haven't been able to get together with what's happened in both our lives recently."

"So far, so good," I said. "But next week will be the biggest challenge."

"Hmm. The president's meeting at Camp David. Will you be joining him?"

"I will and it should be very interesting. If we are able to secure an agreement, I expect to be very busy."

"Well, Tom," Peggy said. "Hopefully you will be very busy. That will mean the agreement is moving forward and the news will be focusing on the prospect of peace as the new normal rather than on me, William and John."

"Not a bad outcome," I said as the double doors were opened to the large room where dinner would be served.

Lacey Turner, Savannah and Barry's MC for the festivities, requested that everyone find their seats in the dining hall. The bride and groom and the wedding party were soon to be announced.

Diana, Sam and I found our way back to join the other members of the wedding party while Peggy and William followed the other guests to their seats in the dining hall. With everyone seated and the band providing a loud drumroll, Lacy began announcing the wedding party to the guests. Finally it was Savannah and Barry's turn to be introduced. With wide smiles they entered the room to a ruckus of applauses by their family and friends.

Once everyone was settled, Nathaniel Lee, Savannah's father, took the microphone from Lacey and stood. He began his speech by describing how Savannah became 'Daddy's Girl' on the day she was born. Then by the age of three, he said 'Daddy's Girl' became an adult. She had an opinion on everything."

Sounds about right, I thought as Nathaniel continued to describe his opinionated and precocious three-year-old daughter. He went on to describe a few of the disagreements they had over the years as she grew to become a young adult and how over time, she helped him to view their Lee family heritage in a more realistic and truthful light. It was a heartwarming and beautiful speech which moistened many eyes. Mine included.

Barry then stood and proposed a toast to Jane, Priscilla, Cheryl Ellis, and Diana, thanking them for making sure Savannah actually showed up and wasn't so engrossed on her next Pulitzer that she forgot to leave the office.

The speeches continued with Lucious, Barry's brother and best man, taking the mic and adding a few words about his older brother and then asking Savannah's bridesmaid if they had any messages or thoughts of wisdom. Finally, after the messages were given and the laughter subsided, Lucious made a toast to Savannah and Barry. It was finally Savannah's turn and like her father, her touching speech returned the moisture to everyone's eyes.

With the speeches ended, waiters began serving the dinner meal. Soon after, the wedding cake was cut, and cake and coffee were served. The party soon followed after plates were cleared. The lights dimmed and Savannah and Barry walked hand-in-hand to the dance floor for their first dance as husband and wife. Barry then placed Savannah's hand in her father's as the band's lead singer began singing the lyrics to Natalie Grant's song, 'Always Be Your Baby.' As she sang, *"You were my first love, always there for me, you taught me how to walk and how to dream*, the dry eyes began tearing again as Savannah and her father held each other and danced.

Anita White danced with her son after Savannah and her father left the dance floor. At the conclusion of their dance they motioned to the guests to join them. Music flowed and the dance floor filled with

Barry and Savannah back on the dance floor and danced with whomever tapped their dancing partners on the shoulder.

After Sam cut in on me and asked Diana to dance, I spotted Savannah speaking with Priscilla.

"I think it's my turn for a dance, Mrs. White."

"Who? She asked with a questioned look?"

"You need to get used to your new name, Ms. Lee?"

She smiled. "It's funny, really. I've been arguing since I was little. Three years old according to my father, that my family should change our name. And now that I've finally done it I don't want to change it."

"And I know the reason," I said as I took Savannah in my arms, and we began to dance. "You want the Lee name to be remembered for the good the Lee family has accomplished, the wrongs they have rectified, and make restitution for the pain and suffering that a very old relative once inflicted on America."

Savannah looked up at me and smiled. "I'm very glad I pushed my way into your life, Tom. We are going to accomplish a great deal with the team we have brought together."

"That we will, Savannah. That we will," I said and kissed her on the forehead as we continued to dance.

World Peace: Tom Lawson Novel #4
By James Brown

Chapter 36

Diana and I rose early Sunday morning to attend Savannah and Barry's Sunday morning post-wedding breakfast. After enjoying the breakfast with Savannah and Barry and their wedding guests, we said our goodbyes and headed up to our room to pick up our luggage. Since I would be buttoned up at Camp David for the week Diana was leaving for the airport, joining Peggy and William on a midafternoon flight back to Connecticut.

We stopped at the front desk to check out and met Peggy and William at the hotel's entrance.

"Keep me posted on the Summit's progress," Diana said after a kiss and a hug.

"Daily," I said.

After a hug with Peggy and handshake with Willim, I waited until their cab departed for the airport. I took the next taxi in line and told the driver the destination was the White House.

The date for the G5 Summit had finally arrived. The discussions and meetings held during the past several months laid the foundation for the discussions that would be taking place in the peaceful setting of Maryland's Camp David. A perfect setting to negotiate world peace. The meeting attendees from Russia and China arrived in Washington on the weekend and stayed at their respective embassies while the attendees from Iran and North Korea, having no embassy in the U.S., were invited to stay at Blair House, the president's official guest house and the world's most exclusive hotel.

Located just across Pennsylvania Avenue from the White House, Blair House is a complex of four formerly separate homes—Blair House, Lee House, Peter Parker House, and 704 Jackson Place.

World Peace: Tom Lawson Novel #4
By James Brown

After I was dropped off at the White House, I took a few minutes to stop at my office and gathered several files and documents I planned to take with me. Amanda Sing, Secretary Bentley's Chief of Staff, called shortly after I arrived and said to be ready to depart in a half hour for Camp David. I made a last check for new messages and headed to the elevator to the first floor and west wing lobby.

As we departed the White House for Marine One, President Stephen walked toward the pool of reporters to answer questions. Microphones jutting out and shoulder cameras filming, questions were shouted as soon as the president approached.

"Do you think you will get an agreement, Mr. President?" A reporter from Fox News at the front of the pack yelled.

"I hope that will be the case. Not that it will necessarily be an easy negotiation. But it is a negotiation that is worthy of the effort. A great deal is at stake. There is no reason that countries of the world, and the people in the world cannot live in peace."

The president paused for a moment, and surprisingly, the press waited until he finished his thoughts.

"I am not naive to think problems and issues will not surface," the president continued. "But there is no issue that cannot be solved diplomatically. It's time that world leaders and their governments focus on diplomacy to solve problems."

With the press pool in a reflective mood, a reporter from the Times asked calmly, "Do you really think we humans, who have been waging war and killing each other for centuries, can really live in peace and harmony?"

"It's a choice," the president answered. "Humankind's choice to make. We either begin to learn how to work together and live in peace, or there will come a day when the events that occurred a little more than a year ago will resurface and human existence as we've known it to be will end. It's as simple as that. We will either learn how to live together, or we will die together."

The president didn't wait for a comment from the press, and surprisingly, no follow up questions were shouted. The president merely left the reporters standing in silence and walked toward Marine One. He saluted the marines standing at the stairs to the helicopter and walked up the steps to board.

World Peace: Tom Lawson Novel #4
By James Brown

"Welcome aboard sir," the pilot said. "We will be at Camp David in a half hour."

* * * *

A half hour flight from the White House by helicopter or little more than an hour by car, Marine One landed on the helipad at Camp David. Situated on two hundred acres in Maryland's Catoctin Mountain within the boundaries of a U.S. National Park site, the sprawling camp was initially built for federal government agents and their families in 1935. In 1942, President Franklin D. Roosevelt converted it to a presidential retreat that was later named David after Dwight D. Eisenhower's father and son whose names were David.

Franklin D. Roosevelt was the first president to utilize the facility hosting Sir Winston Churchill in May 1943. Subsequent to the camp's use by FDR, every president since has used the camp as a short-term retreat from Washington or to conduct strategic negotiation sessions with world leaders.

There are tennis courts, horseshoe pits, a swimming pool, skeet range, nearby fishing and horseback riding. There is a golf driving range near the helicopter landing zone and a single golf hole with multiple tee boxes outside Aspen Lodge.

You can go bowling, watch movies, work out at the fitness center, play basketball, and shoot pool. Meandering hilly trails are ideal for long walks and bike rides. In the winter, you can go cross-country skiing, sledding, ice skating and snowmobiling. There is also the Evergreen Chapel, a non-denominational place of worship.

Golf carts are the primary means of transportation for getting around the sprawling retreat. Prior to landing we were issued the latest update to the daily itinerary and the cabin assignments. I was assigned to Aspen Lodge, one of the more than dozen cabins of various sizes scattered throughout heavily wooded retreat. As we deplaned from Marine One, the president was greeted by a salute from Commander Randall Scott, the commanding officer of the 200-acre Navy installation that includes two hundred sailors and marines and support staff of 250 when the president is in residence.

"Welcome back to Camp David, Mr. President," Commander Scott said.

World Peace: Tom Lawson Novel #4
By James Brown

"Thank you, Commander Scott. I think we've picked a very good week for our G5 Summit."

"Indeed you have, Sir. Clear skies all week. Let me show you to Golf cart One, Sir," Commander Scott said, the name bestowed on the electric golf cart used by President George W. Bush in 2011.

I followed Secretary of State Peter Bentley and Press Secretary Jan Polaski off Marine One with the other eight early arrivals on board trailing behind. Everything was choreographed. Our luggage was pre-tagged for Camp David staff to take to the cabins we were assigned and the golf carts we were to use. I was assigned to Aspen Lodge along with Zheng Shih, state department diplomat for China, and we shared golf cart #4.

"Are you a golfer," Zheng asked as we walked up to our golf cart.

"I've been known to hit the links on quit a few occasions, but not too often recently."

"Good, I've never played. You can drive," Zheng said. "During the Carter presidency, Amy Carter and Mika Brzezinski narrowly escaped ramming into Israeli Prime Minster Begin while driving one of these golf carts. Something I don't want to happen to me," Zheng said.

"I doubt that would happen, Zheng," I said as I followed Peter Bentley in the golf cart ahead of us. "Amy and Mika were kids at the time. You do have a driver's license, don't you?"

Zheng scrunched his face, giving me a look that it was a ridiculous question. Of course he knew how to drive.

"So then, nothing to worry about. Lever below the seat for forward and reverse. An audible alarm when moving in reverse. Peddle on the right provides the juice to move forward or backward per the lever position and peddle on the left to break. Simple as that. All you need to know."

"Got it," Zheng said.

We reached Aspen Lodge, the president's cabin, which sits on top of a hill with a beautiful view of the surrounding Maryland countryside. Zheng and I were sharing one of the bedrooms with the other bedrooms in the cabin occupied by the president, secret service agent Mike Andrews, Secretary of State Peter Bentley and National Security Advisor Morgan Kelly. In addition to multiple bedrooms, Aspen Lodge has a small office, several fireplaces, a kitchen, and a large outdoor flagstone patio. There is also a heated swimming pool, hot tub, and a single golf hole with multiple tees.

All the comforts of an upscale summer resort in the mountains, I thought as I parked our golf cart behind Peter's. The difference, however, was that by the end of our visit, the time we spent here would have a profound impact on the future of the world one way or the other.

After settling in, Zheng and I headed back to our golf cart to join the tour that was planned for those of us who had not previously been to Camp David. We headed to Laurel Lodge, located about a quarter mile down the hill from Aspen Lodge where the tour would begin.

Arriving and parking behind a line of golf carts, we walked over to the group already assembled around Chief Petty Officer Janice Young.

"Good afternoon, everyone. I will be your guide today. As I'm sure you have all reviewed the itinerary for the week and the history of Camp David, my job today is to help those who are here for the first time to not get too lost on the many trails that wind throughout the camp. Most official meetings and meals at Camp David will take place here at Laurel Lodge. Laurel has three conference rooms, a kitchen, a spacious dining area, and a small presidential office. Please, take a few moments and look around."

Over the next several hours we became familiar with the various lodges, cabins and pathways throughout Camp David and the location of the cabins where the U.S. team members were assigned and those of the visitors who would be arriving on Monday. Russia's president Andrey Milosevic would be staying at Dogwood Cabin, China's president Wang Jun at Red Oak cabin, North Korea president Kim Kyung-mi at Birch Cabin, and Iran's president Amir Hosseini at Maple Cabin.

We ended our tour at Hickory Lodge and took time to check out the lodge's two-lane bowling alley, movie theater, bar and restaurant, game room, library, and the Shangri-La Gift Shop.

Leaving the lodge, Chief Petty Officer Young said, "Feel free to roam the trails. It's helpful to do so. The summit final preparation review session will be held back here at Laurel Lodge at 1800 hours with dinner following. Thank you for your attention and don't get lost."

World Peace: Tom Lawson Novel #4
By James Brown

* * * *

By early Sunday evening the full complement of President Stephen's team had assembled at Camp David. The summit prep review session was held with a few tweaks made to the planned agenda and meeting assignments prior to adjourning for dinner. By eleven p.m. everyone began dispersing from Laurel Lodge to their golf carts and respective cabins.

The G5 delegates began arriving mid-afternoon on Monday. Russia's president Andrey Milosevic and his staff were the first group to be ferried from Washington to Camp David. After the helicopter touched down President Milosevic was met by Marine and Navy personnel in their dress uniforms with official greetings extended by Commander Scott. Commander Scott then accompanied the president and his team to the awaiting golf carts, walking past saluting service members standing at attention along the pathway. After a short golf cart familiarization session, the parade of golf carts moved on to the respective cabins the delegates were assigned. A formal welcoming reception and dinner was scheduled at Laurel Lodge later in the day.

The arrival process continued throughout the late afternoon with China's President Wang Jun and his team arriving next. Iran's president, Amir Hosseini and his team followed, and North Korea president Kim Kyung-mi and her team were the last G5 delegates to arrive.

At six p.m. President Stephen began greeting the leaders at the entrance to Laurel Lodge as they arrived for the welcoming reception and dinner. Once inside, the U.S. delegates who conducted the initial sessions with the arriving delegates took responsibility to make introductions to members of the U.S. team and the other arriving delegates.

"Welcome to Camp David," I said as President Hosseini and his team entered the lodge.

"Mr. Lawson, Deputy Secretary Shirley," President Hosseini said with a slight bow and shaking hands. "A very beautiful and interesting facility from the short tour we took upon arrival. The information about Camp David on the Internet does not do it justice. Especially the means for getting around. You both have been here before, I assume?"

World Peace: Tom Lawson Novel #4
By James Brown

"My first visit, Sir. Barbara has been here before. I am familiar with driving golf carts, however, but I did take the camp tour yesterday. It was suggested."

"To prevent getting lost," Foreign Minister Farhad Behzadi said.

"It has happened we were told. It's good to see you again, Minister Behzadi," I said shaking his hand.

"We are looking forward to the discussions this week," Chief of Staff Shahin Ashraf said.

"As are we, Shahin. And now, let us make introductions to the rest of our team and the other delegates who have arrived."

For the next hour, President Stephen and his U.S. team did their best welcoming the G5 delegates and making introductions and helping to ensure the discussions planned for the week would be productive.

"President Jun, Director Cheng," Deputy Secretary Shirley said, walking over to them as they were served small-sized wine goblets by a waiter.

"Secretary Shirley. I complement your team's selection of China's Baijiu wine. Your attention to detail is commendable," President Jun said.

"Thank you, Sir. Have you had a chance to meet all the members of President Stephen's team?"

"We have not yet met Mr. Lawson," he said looking at me standing next to Shirley. "But we certainly know who he is."

"I am pleased to meet you, Mr. President, Director Cheng," I said with a slight bow and shaking their hands.

"It's a pleasure to meet you, Mr. Lawson," President Jun said. "Your actions were quite heroic, though many wished more could have been done to prevent the deaths caused by Russia and John Gordon's actions."

"We did our best, Sir. Hopefully by the end of the week an agreement can be reach that will mitigate the need for the actions that we took as well as the heroics that you and the other leaders attending here took to prevent a world war."

"A very good point, Mr. Lawson," President Jun said.

Before further conversations could take place we heard President Stephen tapping his wine glass with a serving fork.

"I am told dinner will be served shortly. Please, let's move to the dining room. There is no assigned seating. The earbuds that were provided in your welcoming packages are 'smart' earpieces. They will translate the different languages that are spoken. And of course, we also have translators who are available to assist if you prefer. But I find the earpieces to be quite good."

"I tried them, and they are incredible," President Milosevic said. "Are they available for the general public?"

"They soon will be. They were developed by a U.S. company that will be going public through an IPO very soon. Probably a very good investment opportunity, by the way. Travel throughout the world will soon become much more enjoyable. Also, for anyone who has a concern regarding privacy, the earpieces have been well tested from a security perspective."

The delegates entered the dining room wearing their colored smart earpieces and dispersed about the long rectangular table with seating for twenty-five. When everyone was seated and settled, President Stephen addressed the room.

"Before our meals are served, I want to say that I am very grateful for everyone's attendance here at Camp David for this G5 Summit, the first such meeting for our countries. The purpose of this summit is to expand on the discussions that were held the past several months with the objective to reach an agreement on a course of action that will ensure enduring peace between our countries, peace and security for our citizens, and for the world at large."

President Stephen raised his champagne glass and said, "Cooperation, Inclusion, and Peaceful Coexistence, ladies and gentlemen. CIPC. It is within our reach."

World Peace: Tom Lawson Novel #4
By James Brown

Chapter 37

Tuesday morning began with breakfast served at Laurel Lodge. Following breakfast, the media was invited to the lodge for a brief photo op prior to the first working session of the G5 Summit. President Stephen spoke to the reporters and described his aspirations for the summit and the unique opportunity that was before them. He then turned to the G5 leaders and pointed toward Laural Lodge. "Shall we begin?"

In the lodge and taking his place at the middle of the conference table, President Stephen took a moment and quickly scanned the faces of the men and women seated around the table.

"I want to thank everyone again for agreeing to meet here at Camp David," President Stephen began. "The meetings held during the past several months provide us with the foundation for our discussions this week. Cooperation, inclusion, peaceful coexistence. Four easily understood words that over the centuries have often been difficult for humans to put into practice. It is time that we overcome these failings. So, let's begin.

The packets in front of you contain the notes that were summarized from the sessions held during the past several months and were previously sent to the attendees of those meetings. These packet also include the agenda and topics that we collectively agreed were appropriate for our session this week. If there are topics anyone thinks we have missed and should be considered, we will amend the schedule accordingly to accommodate time to discuss them."

The president paused as the delegates scanned the documents. "Does anyone have any questions regarding this information?"

"Yes, the discussion topic sequence." President Milosevic said."

"Oh, yes. I apologize for not mentioning that. The topic sequence, the order in which topics will be discussed. In other words, how do we efficiently organize our discussions such that all issues of critical importance associated with entering into a CIPC agreement can be identified and discussed. To achieve this objective, we've broken down the timeline for topic discussions from what we believe are relatively easy issues to resolve to more difficult issues. After these discussions, we will move on to the benefits that would be derived from entering into a CIPC agreement."

After the delegation scanned the proposed sequence of topic discussions, President Stephen continued.

"If anyone thinks a different order is preferable, or there are other issues of higher importance, or issues that were missed, by all means share your thoughts. In the meantime, the list provided is our best assessment. The discussion topics cover natural resources, national sovereignty, race, culture, and ethnicity as a single topic, Middle East, followed by terrorism and religion. After discussing these topics, and hopefully resolving any open issues, we will then move to national defense, international trade, and economics. Comments anyone?"

"A very concise list, Mr. President," President Hosseini said.

"Thank you, President Hosseini. Given the nature of our discussions, it will be helpful if we can be on a first name basis if that is agreeable with everyone. But to your comment, President Hosseini, it is a concise list, but I believe it covers the key subjects that have been the basis for considerable global differences. Do you agree, Amir?"

"I do, Justin. If we are successful in coming to an agreement on these subjects, we will have accomplished a great deal."

"I think so too. Does anyone else have any suggestions?"

After general shaking of heads, China's president Wang Jun said, "this a good start, Justin."

"Okay then. We begin with natural resources, a subject we believe agreement should be easily reached today. But that was not the case in the 1930s. The lack of an abundance of national resources was the centerpiece for Japan's imperial expansion in the 1930s and their entrance into World War II in 1940.

There is only a finite amount of natural resources on earth. Perhaps one day in the future we will be able to economically harvest resources from the moon or nearby asteroids but until that future arrives, the countries of the world need to be able to secure the resources they need at fair and reasonable market prices. Do we have a consensus here that such access and reasonable price stability can be agreed to?" President Stephen asked.

"If I can elaborate, or perhaps better stated, clarify the implication, Justin," Iran Foreign Minister Behzadi said. "With oil a major resource of Middle Eastern countries as well as for Russia and the United States for example, we would be collectively agreeing that this resource will not be used as a means to extort, punish, or influence actions against a country?"

"That is correct, Farhad. And not just oil as a natural resource. No natural resources would be subject to possible leverage against CIPC co-signers. It has already been demonstrated that restricting trade in natural resources is one of the root causes for countries to go to war. We need to remove that condition as the basis for going to war. Can we agree to that? Agree to freedom for fair and accessible trade of natural resources as one of the provisions of a CIPC agreement?" President Stephen asked.

"Agree," President Hosseini quickly said.

"Also agree," President Milosevic followed.

Around the table agreements were voiced with no additional discussion necessary. A good sign the president thought before moving on to the next subject.

"Okay, the next topic is nation sovereignty, the idea that independent nations, which have declared their independence, have an organized government and are self-contained, have a right to exist without other nations interfering. Of course, this definition of national sovereignty has changed over time. Going back to European colonialism for example. Only Japan, Korea, Thailand, and Libia did not fall under Europe's control or sphere of influence.

In fact, it took several decades for European colonialism to fully collapse. France was fighting for Algeria until 1962 and Portugal did not abandon its African colonies until 1974. Then there is the dissolution of the USSR in 1991 that resulted in fifteen independent sovereign nations with Russia being one of these nations."

"I'm sure everyone here agrees that national boundaries have been in a state of flux over the centuries," Director Huan Cheng of China said. "What are you suggesting, Justin?"

"If I may, Justin," President Milosevic offered. "National sovereignty came up at several of our meetings held over the past few months."

"Certainly, Andrey. What are your thoughts?"

"Fear of the boogeyman," Andrey began, causing several questioned looks around the table. "Since losing tens of millions of our citizens during World War II Russia's policies have focused on survival and holding on to the remnants of the Russian empire. Desperate to avert further fragmentation of Russian territory and influence in the world, Russia's leaders focused on potentially new existential threats. The belief has been that there can always be another Napoleon or Hitler who could emerge, the next boogeyman, as it was described in one of our earlier meetings.

The dissolution of the USSR in 1991 was also a festering issue for our former president for the same reason. Putin believed the dissolution and creation of the fifteen separate sovereign nations was not in the best interest of Russia. The reason given was the need for buffer states in the event of an attack on Russia. Of course, during the past seventy-seven years since the end of World War II there has never been the slightest indication that such an attack would even be considered. And why would there be given the arsenal of nuclear weapons that Russia has at its disposal.

In reality, Putin used the pretense of pending conflicts with the West as a means to divert attention from the real problems Russia has been facing, a faltering economy and declining growth as compared to the United States, China, and Europe."

President Milosevic paused a moment then spoke in a tone of disgust.

"Putin's vision of the USSR was pathetic. By 1991 the economy of the USSR had dropped by almost 61% from its peak in 1966. And today, Russia's GDP is a paltry $1.8 trillion while China's GDP is $16.5 trillion and the United States $25.6 trillion. Yet Russia is the largest country in the world by land mass and has massive amounts of natural resources. No ladies and gentlemen, with Putin gone, Russia will no longer believe there is another boogeyman looking to invade us. We will honor the sovereignty of independent nations."

"Thank you, Andrey," Justin said. "That is a major step. We commend you for making this policy change and I am confident that Russia and its citizens will greatly benefit from it. Now, along the same subject of national sovereignty, as everyone I'm sure recalls, there will be no restrictions imposed on any CIPC member regarding its form of government."

Following President Stephen's statement there were general nods and responses of understanding voiced. There would be no debate or requirement regarding the form of government the CIPC signatories were required to have. Democracy was not a prerequisite.

"This being the case," Justin began, "I would be remise in not saying that conditions still remain regarding national boundary issues as well as disagreements regarding the forms of governments that exist throughout the world."

"You are referring to Hong Kong and Taiwan as examples," President Jun said.

"Yes. These are two examples. As we all know, Hong Kong was the former colony of the British Empire from 1841 to 1941 and again from 1945 to 1997 after World War II. In 1997 sovereignty was handed over to China by the UK. In international diplomacy, Hong Kong has no separate identity from mainland China and has never been recognized as a country in history. That's the history. But history also reveals the challenge for citizens who are required to adapt to different forms of government than what they have become used to. As with any major change, It often takes patience and time for people to accept the change. As for Hong Kong and Taiwan, China has certainly shown patience, President Jun. Assuming a CIPC agreement is reached the United States will do its part, as will each of the signatories of the CIPC agreement, in helping to promote the economic benefits that will result from this unification. As we have stated, the type of government a country has will not be the basis for CIPC agreement, provided the government is led by honorable men and women of character and the government is benevolent toward their citizens."

"That will be appreciated, President Stephen," President Wang Jun said. "The different forms of government each of our countries operate under has been the basis for considerable global stress. Stress and misgivings that are not necessary or productive. Only time will tell if there is a best form of government. If we all agree that government corruption will not be tolerated regardless of government form, the stress and ill will voiced regarding the type of government a country has will no longer be an issue."

"That provision is a cornerstone policy for a CIPC agreement. Can we get an agreement on this critical point that President Jun has stated?" President Stephen asked, looking about the room?

"Russia concurs," President Milosevic said.

"As does North Korea," President Kim Kyung-mi said.

"We also agree," President Hosseini said.

"Excellent," President Stephen responded. "With these topics discussed and agreed to, I think a break is now in order. Our next topic for discussion will be race, culture, and ethnicity which we can discuss during dinner. Lunch will be served here at Laurel Lodge at one p.m. and there is also a restaurant in Hickory Lodge if anyone choses a different venue. Thank you everyone. Enjoy your afternoon."

* * * *

I began gathering the materials handed out and notes I had taken during the meeting and noticed President Hosseini speaking with Foreign Minister Behzadi. After his conversation he turned and began walking toward my end of the table.

"A productive first session, I believe," President Hosseini said.

"I agree. A very productive session, sir."

"I was wondering if you might be free later this afternoon after midday prayers?"

"Before our dinner meeting, yes sir, I would be available."

"I was thinking a stroll about the camp perhaps."

"I would enjoy that, Amir."

"Excellent. Let us meet here at Hickory Lodge at two p.m. then," he said and walked back toward his team and exited the room.

"Plans made for later, I hope," President Stephen said, seeing me speaking with President Hosseini.

"Yes, Sir. President Hosseini asked if I would be available this afternoon."

"Very good. Let's head back to Aspen Lodge. Tell Zheng and Barbara to join us there. Peter's talking with Milosevic and Jun. I'll follow up with him."

The room emptying, I walked out with Barbara and Zheng and told them the president wanted us to head to Aspen Lodge for a post meeting discussion. Barbara said she would stop by her cabin then join everyone. Within forty-five minutes the president's team was reassembled in the living room at Aspen Lodge.

"This will be a short debriefing session," the president said. "A good start I believe. The sessions will become more difficult I'm sure as we move into the more challenging subjects. To that end, during these meeting breaks let's do our best to have one-on-one conversations with our counterparts. Tom and President Hosseini have a camp stroll scheduled at two this afternoon."

"A discussion about religion and Israel no doubt," I offered.

"Likely subjects with race, culture, and ethnicity the next topic for discussion at dinner," President Stephen offered. "My gut tells me Milosevic and Russia are fully on board with entering into a CIPC agreement without any further discussions. They will benefit tremendously with a CIPC agreement in place. The same for North Korea. Peter, is that also your assessment?"

"It is regarding Russia as well as North Korea. Kim Kyung-mi does not want to extend her brother's isolationist and confrontational government policies. Her country will benefit tremendously from this agreement as will Russia."

"Okay, but let's not let anything for chance. Each of us needs to nurture the relationships we've fostered. Let's also assign primary country leadership assignments. I'll take President Milosevic. Peter, you have President Jun, Barbara, stay connected with Kim Kyung-mi, and Tom, President Hosseini."

Meeting feedback and next step discussions continued for the next hour with the president finally saying he had several other pressing issues he needed to deal with. His government was continuing to move forward without his presence in Washington.

* * * *

After leaving the meeting with President Stephen and the team I walked out to the lower terrace of Aspen Lodge to see if I might be able to catch Diana between clients. I was in luck, she picked up on the first ring.

"Perfect timing, honey. How is everything there in the woods?"

"So far, very well. We had a productive meeting this morning with agreements all around. The subjects will become tougher this evening and over the next couple of days. But fingers crossed."

"A lot of fingers are crossed, Tom. You wouldn't believe the interest that our little community has in the Camp David's G5 Summit. We are having daily status sessions at the Monkey Farm with news channels running on two of the four televisions."

"MSNBC and Fox stations?"

"Of course, equal coverage for all parties," Diana answered. "We've had very interesting discussions, and they were civilized, surprisingly. The reason for the interest of course is that one of their very own is involved in the G5 discussions. A first for our community."

"Well, I hope the summit concludes on favorable terms. And remember, what is a favorable outcome for President Stephen will most likely not be a favorable outcome for all Americans, or the world for that fact."

"A sad commentary," Diana said. "People would rather have massive defense spending as opposed to having nuclear armed world powers enter into an agreement that would promote peace and global cooperation."

"Unfortunately, that is the case."

"Will you be coming home this weekend?" Diana asked.

"I'll try. If all goes well, the president will hold a Rose Garden announcement on Thursday. In that case, I should be able to head back to Connecticut for a couple days."

"I hope so. And your fans would love to see you and hear all about the summit."

"Whatever is reported by the president and the press," I said. I need to go now and grab a bite to eat. I have a stroll in the park scheduled soon with President Hosseini. I'll give you a call tonight."

"Sounds intriguing. Love you, hon. I'll keep my fingers crossed."

After the call with Diana I headed for the kitchen to make myself a sandwich before leaving to meet with President Hosseini.

"I think I'll have one of those also," Jan Polaski said entering the kitchen. "Ham and cheese on whole wheat with mustard, right?"

World Peace: Tom Lawson Novel #4
By James Brown

"That it is. Here, you can have this one and I'll make another. Chips are on the table."

"Thank you," Jan said, taking her plate to the table and grabbing a handful of chips.

"So what's your take?" I said, joining Jan at the table.

She reached for a napkin and dabbed at mustard at the corner of her mouth. "So far pretty good readings from what I've been able to glean from my counterparts. It's surprising, but it seems that everyone came to the summit hoping that meaningful compromise could be reached."

"It would result in tremendous economic growth for everyone."

"It sure would. But is it even possible for Iran and the other dominate religion-based governments to play nice together?" Jan asked.

"Don't forget to add the United States to that mix," I said. "The U.S. constitution's separation of church and state is hardly followed in practice. Just look at recent Supreme Court rulings as well as the influence of the Christian right has on politics in our country."

Jan nodded, choosing to finish eating her ham and cheese sandwich rather than go down the religious rabbit hole that has caused so much harm and violence throughout the world.

After they finished their lunch and plates were put into the dishwasher, Jan said, "how are you going to approach President Hosseini?"

"Not sure."

"I would be surprised if he didn't request the stroll with you because he knows this next session is going to be a challenge for him."

"I agree. He's the president of Iran and not the supreme leader, the person who is really in charge. President Hosseini's hands are tied if the new supreme leader does not agree to enter into a CIPC treaty."

"So what do you think?"

"Well, now that you've asked, I need to recommend language that is agreeable to President Hosseini and his supreme leader. Iran's constitution recognizes a few non-Muslim religions. Specifically Zoroastrian, Judaism, and Christianity. Their constitution also states that citizens shall enjoy human, political, economic, and other rights, in conformity with Islamic criteria. Conversely, it describes a penal code that specifies the death sentence for proselytizing and attempts by non-Muslims to convert Muslims."

"Hmm. I know a few Christians who would love to have that penal code as part of our constitution too," Jan said.

"Anyway, the issue is going to be the CIPC language we settle on. It needs to reflect what Iran's supreme leader will agree to. I'll know more after I speak with Amir. Hopefully a moderate cleric will be elected as Iran's supreme leader."

"Sounds like a plan," Jan said. "By the way, what is Zoroastrianism? Never heard of that religion."

"It's an ancient pre-Islamic religion of Persia, now modern-day Iran. Worldwide there are several hundred thousand people who follow Zoroastrianism including several thousand here in the U.S."

"Interesting," Jan said. Wonder where the world would be today had all those old prophets from thousands of years ago not been born."

"A lot fewer terrorists and wars being fought would be my guess."

"Well, let's hope you and President Hosseini can come up with a plan and language that can be supported by Iran and the rest of the G5 members."

"Fingers crossed," I said as I headed out to meet President Hosseini.

World Peace: Tom Lawson Novel #4
By James Brown

Chapter 38

I decided to walk rather than take the golf cart and reached Hickory Lodge several minutes before two. I assumed President Hosseini preferred keeping our walk confidential since he suggested we meet at Hickory Lodge rather than Maple Lodge where he was staying. Maple was a stone throw to Hickory while I had to walk past Maple Lodge to reach Hickory Lodge from Aspen Lodge where I was staying. A few minutes after I arrived, I spotted President Hosseini. His long-sleeved white shirt caught the sunlight as he approached the clearing along the path from the woods.

"A beautiful afternoon for a walk," he said.

"It is Amir. The best time of year in the Washington area. Have you had a chance to tour the camp?"

"Only in the area around Maple Lodge where I'm staying. I was thinking we could wander up to Evergreen Chapel."

"Sounds good to me, sir."

We headed out at a leisurely pace. Amir remained with his own thoughts, scanning the landscape and towering trees that were fully engulfed in shades of green having fully recovered from a cold winter.

After walking a couple hundred yards on the winding footpath he turned toward me. "How well do you know my country's history, Tom?"

"I have read about the history of the region, of course, as well as more recently the Quran and Iran's constitution, but I have never visited the region. It's unfortunate I haven't had a chance to visit since the Middle East has many of the world's oldest cultures and civilizations."

World Peace: Tom Lawson Novel #4
By James Brown

Amir gave me an understanding nod. "An unfortunate circumstance of the world that we live. Though the world has become smaller from the point of travel and communication capabilities, we all tend to assimilate with the people who have the same beliefs and experiences and travel to areas of the world where likeminded people live."

"Is this your first visit to the United States?"

"It is. I have traveled throughout the Middle East, of course, as well as Europe and Russia, but this is my first trip to the United States."

"Well, I'm glad you have made the journey here, and perhaps one day soon I will visit Iran and the Middle East."

Amir smiled. "I would be very happy if you did that, Tom."

Continuing to walk for a few moments, both in our own thoughts, Amir stopped along the trail and looked up as a dark cloud drifted overhead blocking the sun.

"Are you familiar with the word tenebrous?" Amir asked softly as the passing cloud blocked the sunlight, turning the pathway to dark shadows.

"I am not."

"It means shut off from the light. "Dark or murky is a more frequently used synonym for the word. But it is how our countries view each other, and more generally, how the countries of the West and Middle East view each other, believing the other is shut off from the light . . . Middle Eastern cultures remaining steeped in the traditions and beliefs of the past while the West foregoes the past for new ideas and progress toward the future."

"Probably a very good analogy, Amir. "Do you have an idea how each of our countries might come together into the light?"

"That question has been weighing on me, my friend. Weighing heavily."

"Perhaps I can suggest a possible approach."

"Please do," Amir said as the cloud overhead passed, and the pathway was bathed in sunlight again.

"Let me first ask a question. How likely will cleric Ebrahim Yazdi be selected as Iran's Supreme Leader?"

"A reasonable chance now that Mostafa Ahmadi has been ousted as Chief Commander of the Revolutionary Guard."

"Should that come to pass, I believe the way forward can become less stressful. The topics that we will be discussing the next couple of days including race, culture, and ethnicity, followed by terrorism and religion will definitely require a supreme leader who has some flexibility regarding tradition and progress as you earlier described."

Amir gave a nod of agreement.

"Though I have read the Quran and the Iranian constitution, I am certainly not an expert by any means. But I'm sure you are aware that there's nothing in the Quran about women covering themselves head to toe in fabric, for example."

"I am, Tom. There are norms and traditions that are followed in addition to the teachings of the Quran. Rules put in place that are not specifically referenced in the Quran."

"Norms and traditions put in place by men, Amir. Similar to the norms and traditions once put in place by men in my country that barred women from owning property, preventing women from being able to vote. Norms and traditions that keeps women subservient to men in other words. Iranians growing youth subculture and educational levels of Iranian women will only increase the pressure by women to afford them the freedoms that every Iranian male is able to enjoy."

"I understand what you are saying, Tom. But please also understand my ability, or better stated, my freedom to agree to broad changes in Iranian policies and cultural practices."

"I do, Mr. President. I do understand your limitations. But nevertheless, progress and consensus will need to be reached. No one will expect a full reversal of thousands of years of Iran's religious history and norms. But we must be able to show progress.

In addition to minimal basic human rights, we will be discussing the ongoing upheaval that has taken place in the Middle East for decades. Specifically the rights of Palestinians and Israelis to exist. President Stephen will be promoting a single state Israeli Palestinian solution. It is time that the turmoil and upheaval that has cost so many lives and displacement of so many people in the Middle East comes to an end. We want Iran to be a part of this healing process and help make it a success."

"And if I am not able to persuade our Supreme Leader?" Amir asked.

"Then Russia, China, North Korea, and the United States will move forward without Iran's support. We will put in place policies that will end the conflicts between Israel and the Palestinians as well as end conflicts that have been taking place throughout the Middle East for decades. We *will* end these conflicts, Amir, with or without Iran's assistance."

Amir held a blank stare, understanding the consequences. His country would become even more isolated.

"I'm sorry, Amir, I don't mean to convey any threats, I'm merely saying that our objective for achieving cooperation, inclusion, and peaceful coexistence *will* move forward. We will put in place a CIPC agreement. The benefits that Russia, China, North Korea, and the U.S. will realize from this agreement are far too important not to move forward with it."

"Three superpowers uniting."

"Yes. Three superpowers with exponentially growing wealth and influence and a CIPC agreement that will expand to include Europe, Japan, and any country that agrees to the principles of cooperation, inclusion, and peaceful coexistence."

* * * *

I arrived back at Aspen Lodge a little before five p.m. and joined the president and the rest of the team in the living room. Peter and Barbara had also just returned.

"So, what's the reading? the president asked. Tom let's start with you. You had the most difficult assignment."

"It's possible that I did, sir. Simply put, President Hosseini is willing and will do his best, but he stressed there are limitations. The decision will ultimately be Iran's new supreme leader to make. He said he will be in a better position if cleric Ebrahim Yazdi is elected supreme leader."

"The moderate."

"Yes."

"But he understands the consequences?"

World Peace: Tom Lawson Novel #4
By James Brown

"He does. I told him that that the CIPC agreement will be executed with or without Iran's support and the agreement will be open to other countries willing to agree to its principles."

"Iran will be further isolated."

"Those words were conveyed, sir."

"Good. We will do our best to author an agreement that will help President Hosseini secure support from Iran's newly appointed supreme leader. But if they don't agree, we will move forward without them. Peter, how about China?"

"Not as challenging as Tom's assignment, but difficult nevertheless."

"China's resettlements and treatment of the indigenous ethnic Uyghur population?"

"Yes, that is one key issue we discussed as well as the full absorption of Hong Kong and Taiwan. As we have discussed internally, I suggested that China place less restrictions on the local processes for their selection of regional communist party membership. Doing so would go a long way in reducing local conflicts and pushback. Likewise, I reminded President Jun of the benefits an executed CIPC agreement would bring to China. As for their Uyghur population, their issue is really China's obsessive fear of a Muslim uprising.

On this subject I reminded Wang that potential terrorist threats were not exclusive to China. It was a world issue. I told him that the issue was not with law abiding Muslim people, regardless of where they live. The issue is with extremists who have a warped interpretation of the Quran. I told Wang that America supports all efforts to stop terrorism, regardless of its origin, whether radical Jihadists or white racists who wish to do harm to others because of different skin pigmentation."

"Do you think he will change China's policies toward his Uyghur population?" the president asked.

"I believe he will. The benefits of entering into a CIPC agreement outweigh the risks. He also believes having U.S. and Russia support in controlling global terrorism will remove the spotlight from China. If terrorist activities do occur in China, President Jun will look to the U.S. and Russia to help support their efforts to stop it."

"Which we will do," President Stephen replied. "And Barbara? How was your meeting with Kim Kyung-mi?"

World Peace: Tom Lawson Novel #4
By James Brown

"A walk in the park. Kyung-mi is fully committed. She sees the CIPC agreement as a means to end the cult environment and isolation imposed on her country by the Kim family and more recently by her brother. It was time, Kyung-mi said, time for North Korea to become part of the global community. She's fully on board, sir."

"Okay, thank you everyone. Very good feedback," President Stephen said. "We now need to get ready for our early evening barbeque. See everyone on the deck at five."

* * * *

After showering and changing into khakis and a long-sleeved blue shirt I joined the president and Secretary Bentley on Aspen's upper terrace. Just below us, the staff was setting up the outdoor cooking area where hotdogs, hamburgers, steaks, salmon, and Lobster would be cooked. After our dinner meal on the terrace we would adjourn to the living room to hold further CIPC discussions.

The guests began arriving in a golf cart caravan. Leading the caravan was Jan Polaski and Barbara Shirley. Both were bunking together at Walnut Cabin. Kyung-mi and her aide, Rji Ah followed in their golf cart with President Milosevic and Vadim Ivanov next to park their golf cart along the path outside Aspen Lodge.

Walking up the path behind Milosevic's golf cart were the teams from China and Iran. President Hosseini was in conversation with President Jun of China while Director Huan Cheng, one of China's Politburo members, followed along, deep in discussion with Foreign Minister Farhad Behzadi of Iran.

Side discussions were encouraged as a means to become better acquainted, as well as to bounce off ideas and discuss concerns if they existed. As I watched the representatives walk or cart up the pathway, I couldn't help but remember the executive program I had taken earlier in my career at Harvard to improve negotiation performance. Completely opposite from Donald Trump's 'Art of the Deal,' the program taught by Harvard stressed the need for both parties of a deal to benefit from its execution. The program emphasized that a bad deal for one or several members associated with a negotiation would eventually result in failure with the agreement eventually being terminated. Time would tell whether or not the discussions held at

Camp David, and the agreements reached, would be in each country's best interest with lasting peace surviving.

"Welcome to Camp David's barbeque facilities, Huan." I said as Director Huan Cheng walked up the pathway.

"Thank you, Tom. I look forward to trying President Stephen's barbequed pepper steak recipe," Huan said.

"Me too. This will be my first taste of his recipe also. How are you finding the facilities at Camp David?"

"An excellent place to hold these negotiations. Very comfortable and informal. Less tension I believe in conducting very important negotiations."

"I agree. It's good that we have time to become better acquainted and share ideas and opinions."

"That indeed is helpful, Tom. Able to be open and honest with ideas and opinions certainly leads to more constructive dialogue, and better outcomes in any negotiation. That freedom has not always been a welcomed practice in China."

"Are you referring to your earlier days as a student or more recently?" I asked.

"An interesting question," Huan said. "I had a similar conversation with a young university student not long ago. A conversation with a Ms. Ah Lam Zing. Perhaps you know of her?"

"Hmm, can't say that I do?"

"An associate of Angela Keen's organization I believe. A very bright young woman. I met her after receiving a copy of a very old report I had previously written. A report I thought my professor ripped up fifty some odd years ago."

"A significant report, I assume?"

"It was. But I was very young. During the time of Mao Zedong's cultural revolution. I was very surprised when Ms. Zing sent me a copy."

"I see. May I assume this report that you wrote as a young student outlined beliefs that are similar to those that we are discussing this week, ideas that we wish to incorporate as part of a CIPC agreement?" I asked.

Huan Cheng smiled. "Perhaps one day you will share the true story of the rebirth of the report I wrote so long ago. I would be very interested if you could do so."

World Peace: Tom Lawson Novel #4
By James Brown

"One day perhaps, sir. After the CIPC program and the ideas within the report that you mention becomes a reality. I am sure that report was also well written and of great importance to China and the world. It has just taken some time for your ideas to be put into practice."

Director Cheng smiled again and gave a short nod. "I look forward to having that discussion at a later date, Tom."

During the next two hours the delegates drifted in and out of conversations on many subjects and topics, doing their best to get to know their counterparts and their feelings on the topics being discussed. Kim Kyung-mi and her team were especially interested in meeting every person in attendance. I found it interesting, stepping back occasionally staying in earshot of conversations she and her aides were having. The language translation earbuds everyone were wearing worked perfectly. It became apparent that Kyung-mi was taking every opportunity to learn how the other presidents and senior leaders managed their economies and government functions within their countries. A steaming cauldron of differing government policies and practices were being argued and dissected. Was it possible that these leaders and their countries could indeed play nice together for the benefit of the world?

Piping hot plates of food were soon being served as everyone lined up in front of several master chefs who served the food choices requested by each guest. After picking up my plate I chose to sit at the table occupied by Kim Kyung-mi and Andrey Milosevic, two leaders who have found themselves stepping into the shoes of two of the most loved and hated men in the world, Kim Jong-un and Vladimir Putin.

"Kyung-mi, Andrey, may I join you?" I asked before taking the seat at the head of the picnic table.

"Of course, Tom. Good to have you join us," Andrey said.

"Thank you. This is a wonderful way to get acquainted, sitting across from each other at a picnic table on a lovely day."

"Very much so," Kyung-mi said. "Andrey and I met previously when I traveled once with my brother to Russia. I was glad to hear you were attending these sessions, Tom. I was hoping to meet you on this trip to Washington."

"I too am glad to meet you, Kyung-mi, but I'm sorry for the circumstances that has initiated our meeting."

Kyung-mi gave a slight nod, the setting sunlight catching her flawless complexion and sparkling white teeth peering behind red lips.

"Thank you, Tom. It was certainly not something I or anyone in my country expected. I was speaking with President Hosseini earlier today and he mentioned that you and he had an interesting conversation yesterday on that subject. He said perhaps it was Allah's will, that your actions came close but were not able to stop John Gordon from launching those missiles that killed my brother."

"Which I responded that that I hoped the will of God would lead the new leaders to choose the best path forward for the sake of all the world's countries."

"Yes, President Hosseini mentioned that. There certainly are new opportunities before us now. New leaders who have been given the chance to turn the page and begin a new chapter. I am looking forward to doing that, Tom."

"Well said, Kyung-mi," Andrey said. "New chapters in an entirely new book. I couldn't have said it better. Now, let's see how good Justin's stir-fried beef and pepper steak recipe really is."

World Peace: Tom Lawson Novel #4
By James Brown

Chapter 39

I was awakened early Wednesday morning to the chirping sound of my cell phone thinking it was my morning alarm. But it wasn't. It was John.

"Good morning, Tom. How are the negotiations going there in the woods? Positive movement I hope?" he asked.

"Reasonably well I would say. With this early hour call would it be safe to assume there are issues brewing?"

"I would not be calling otherwise. Doing my best to allow you those much needed seven hours of sleep humans require."

"Is Sam joining us?"

"He will be on the call shortly."

"Morning, Tom, John," Sam said in a tired voice. "I would have said good morning but given the time I'm assuming there is nothing good about our need to be speaking with each other at this hour."

"You would be correct, Sam," John said.

"So what's brewing, John?" Sam asked.

"Intelligence just surfacing. I've uncovered communications between Jackson Knapp and a Russian FSB agent. Person by the name of Vitaly Dubkova. Knapp's been very active. There is growing activity to prevent a CIPC agreement from becoming a reality."

"Has Sarah Pope and Director Keen become aware of these communications?" I asked.

"Not yet." John said.

"Will that software of yours that Sarah loaded uncover it?" Sam asked.

"It should, Sam. I'm using an updated version, but the version Sarah loaded in the NSA system has advanced learning capabilities and should be able to capture the communications. I'll check with Sarah later this morning, Sam. If the NSA hasn't intercepted the communications by then we will need Sarah to load my latest software version."

"Okay, John. Once it surfaces, one way or the other, I'll follow up with Sarah," Sam said. She will need to notify Director Keen. By the way, Tom, is the president still planning to hold the Rose Garden news conference late Thursday afternoon?"

"He is, Sam. Assuming negotiations produce the results we are seeking."

"Okay, I'll follow up with the Secret Service and make sure we beef up security."

"Sounds like we have a plan," John said. "Sorry for the early call."

"Never too early, John."

"Okay then. Good luck with your negotiations, Tom," John said and disconnect the calls.

I sat on the edge of the bed for a moment as the first rays of sunlight began finding openings along the edges of the window drapes. It was not going to be easy, I thought. Change was never easy for everyone to accept, especially changes regarding social or political issues and particularly so for those who had a vested interest in maintaining the status quo.

With an hour before I needed to get dressed, I decided to go for a run. I was out the door in five minutes running down the path toward Laurel Lodge. After running for ten minutes and almost reaching Laurel Lodge, I heard footfalls coming from behind me.

"Morning, Tom," Jan Polaski said, running up beside me. "A beautiful spring morning. I didn't know you were a runner, Tom."

"Not as often as I should."

"Ah, clearing your head preparing for the last push," she said with hardly a hint of fatigue in her voice.

"You're a runner I take it."

"Since I played college basketball. Can't make it up and down the court if you don't run and stay in shape. So really. Why the run this morning? I haven't noticed you out running the last couple of days. Couldn't sleep?"

"Very early morning call."

"And?"

I continued running, regretting I mentioned the phone call.

"My security level is the same as yours, Tom. What are you worried about? Why the sudden run after your phone call?"

"Too much food and drink from last night?"

Jan turned and faced me after we slowed and stopped running having reached Laural Lodge. A tall woman who towered over most men of average height, she stood at my eye level and stared. She wanted the truth.

"It was Sam."

She persisted with narrowing eyes looking at me. "And!"

"Chatter. Intercepts coming in from several unsavory characters."

"Oh? Serious I assume given the early morning call and your decision to run. You said Sam called, so it's local?"

"Unfortunately, with a wider connection. We knew there would be a large number of people who would be against the policy changes resulting from a CIPC agreement. The FBI, CIA, and NSA have been doing their best to monitor the local and international actors."

"There is concern for the upcoming Rose Garden announcement?"

I nod as we continued walking slowly in silence.

"Deja vu, Tom. You've been down this road before. Let's hope it has a better ending than the last time."

* * * *

After getting back to Aspen Lodge and taking a shower I joined the rest of my cabin mates in the dining room for breakfast. Waffles, pancakes and fresh fruits were being served.

"Out for a run this morning, Tom?" President Stephen asked. "Clearing your head for the last push?"

"Thought it might help, sir."

"I used to run in my younger days. I should never have stopped. Once you do, it's hard to start up again. Too many interruptions, too many dinners, and too much booze."

"The life of aging men and women," Secretary Bentley offered. "Most of us anyway."

"I think we need to change the subject before someone ends the conversation and says . . . then we die," the president said.

That got a laugh. The conversation then turned to the Middle East, terrorism and religion, the topics for this morning discussions. Topics on subjects that were not much more upbeat than getting older and dying. But we plowed forward. At the end of breakfast we took our plates and silverware to the kitchen.

"Tom, a moment before we head out," the president said and walked from the kitchen to the den. "Your run this morning. I also heard a cell phone ring before you left. Anything I should know about?"

I paused a moment wondering if only John, Sam, and I knew the reason for the call. Had the NSA picked up the intercept yet?

"The call was from Sam Wainwright. There's rumblings coming from the CIPC naysayers," I finally said. "A growing united front on our CIPC efforts."

President Stephen took a seat.

"What's the intelligence saying?"

"It's not clear yet. Assessments are still underway from what Sam told me. But I would expect that you will be getting an update today."

"They're foreign and local?"

"Yes, both. Sam is speaking with the Secret Service, asking them to beef up security for tomorrow's Rose Garden announcement."

The president sat for another moment and rubbed his temples. He then sat erect and looked toward me.

"Do you remember when we first met, Tom, and I said I hoped in time you would trust me. Do you remember me saying that?"

"I do, yes. I do trust you, Sir. You are an honorable man, and you have the best interest of all Americans and the world with your efforts to negotiate a CIPC agreement."

"Thank you. I am trying my best. But on a more personal note, I also have this feeling that you are not yet ready to share everything. Especially about the events surrounding the takeover of those subs. Was Sam's phone call connected to that earlier event?"

I stared back at the president for a moment then said, "If you remember, sir, at that earlier meeting we had several months ago, you asked me to do what I believed was necessary to make the CIPC program a success, working with those individuals whom I trusted. It's not that I don't trust *you*, sir. It's the person who will follow you as president that I don't trust. If you recall your warning, that many presidents, and politicians especially, are not always trustworthy. That was especially the case with our president who was killed in the missile attacks. He had no moral character."

The president gave a slow nod and smiled.

"Good points, Tom. Very good points." After giving my comment additional thought, President Stephen stood and extended his hand. "Okay then, maybe when I leave office you will be comfortable enough to fill me in. In the meantime, let's get this CIPC deal done."

"A good suggestion, sir," I said, shaking his hand.

* * * *

At nine a.m. we reassembled in the conference room at Aspen Hall. The topics for discussions this morning were Middle East, terrorism and religion. All subjects that put Iranian President Hosseini and his team on the hot seat as they were the only government officials from the region participating in the CIPC discussions.

"Before we get into the details," President Stephen began. "These next few subjects have an impact on a very large portion of the world. Ideally, there would be more countries involved in these discussions, and certainly other countries who are a part of the Middle East. But unfortunately, too many cooks in the kitchen can rarely get along to create an exquisite meal. I believe we have here this week just the right number of cooks to create an excellent meal. The topics of discussion this morning are Middle East, terrorism, and religion.

Included in the documents passed out earlier this week were summaries of viewpoints regarding a multistate versus single state solution for the Israeli and the Palestinian people. I have studied these reports and have listened to arguments put forward by scholars and experts who have spent a lifetime assessing failed Middle East polices. But before I convey my opinion, I'd like to hear what everyone else thinks. President Hosseini let's start with you. What do you think?"

President Hosseini expected to be asked his opinion first since Iran was the only country from the Middle East taking part in the negotiations. His response came quickly. "I agree with the assessment reached by Professor Rebecca Ben-Hur, that a single Jewish-Arab state solution is the only logical solution. Mr. Lawson and I had a long discussion on this subject earlier when we met. I and my team agrees, this is the only solution that has a chance to succeed. Carving up the territory to accommodate a two-state solution is not practical given the size of the territory and the dispersion of the Israeli and Palestinian populations."

"Thank you, Amir. Andrey, Wang, what are your thoughts?" President Stephen asked.

"My team agrees with President Hosseini and his team's assessment," President Milosevic said. "No solution will come easily but the single state solution would seem to have the best outcome. Though, the inclusion of a UN peacekeeping force will likely be needed."

"I concur," President Jun said. "If the U.S. presses Israel to concede authoritarian control over the Palestinian people with the UN helping to keep the peace, I think the single state solution has a chance to be successful."

"Does anyone else have a comment?" President Stephen asked.

Responses of none, no additional comment, and I'm good, came from the other delegates attending.

President Stephen looked about the conference table and gave a nod. "Okay then. But before we move on to the topics of terrorism and religion, I'm sure this group will receive considerable kickback. Especially the U.S. and my administration. I will be taking considerable heat from my opposition party as well as from the Israeli government. But this opposition will be short lived when it's proven that Palestinians and Israelis *can* live together in harmony."

"Provided that any violent discourse is quickly nipped in the bud," President Milosevic said.

"A very accurate statement, Andrey. Radicals on either side must be quickly identified and apprehended. And that means their sources of funding must be identified and terminated," President Stephen said.

Voices of agreement were again expressed from everyone seated around the table.

After comments were made, President Hosseini spoke up," I believe it best if I lead this next topic of discussion, terrorism and religion."

I was happy to hear Amir make this suggestion, that the points Barbara Shirley and I made several months ago and more recently helped him to come to a reasonable solution. He looked over toward me, but his expression was nondescript. I would have to wait to hear what he had to say.

"Before I begin," Amir Hosseini said. "If anyone needs a refresh of their coffee or tea, the carafes on the table are full and the beverages are hot. I plan on starting with a short history lesson."

Hosseini waited a few moments while cups were being filled with tea and coffee. He then began his history lesson.

"When I first met Mr. Lawson, I asked him how familiar he was with the Middle East and if he had ever visited the area. He said not nearly enough, and he had never visited. He did say he had recently read the Quran and Iran's constitution. He was honest in expressing his modicum of knowledge and familiarity of the region. But I was impressed that he had read the Quran and my country's constitution. Especially since I have not yet read the U.S. nor Russia's constitutions."

He paused for a moment then said, "To better understand the issues associated with these next topics for discussion this morning regarding terrorism and religion, a brief history lesson is necessary. The Middle East has a very long history. For many historians, the Middle East is the birthplace of civilization, and it is regarded as the main stage for cultural connections, such as language, religion, politics, and even philosophical teachings. All major prophets came from Arabia and Palestine. The major revelation was given to Muhammad in Arabia, the ten commandments were given to Moses near Egypt, Abraham was from today`s Iraq and Jesus also rose from the Middle East.

From this long history, humans being humans, differing opinions arose throughout the Middle East's very long history. Even more accurately stated, heated and violent arguments arose regarding religious thought and the interpretation of the word of God that were voiced through His many prophets."

President Hosseini paused again and stood.

"Today," he said, speaking in a soft voice and standing behind his chair before walking toward the front of the room, "debating the merits of these arguments, and even the wars that have been fought, is a waste of time in my opinion. The history of the Middle East is what it is, history.

Each of our countries have similar histories, with differing opinions being argued, wars having been initiated and fought for various reasons, with people being displaced from lands where they lived for centuries and were killed or put into slavery to achieve a country's economic objectives. We humans, currently the dominant species on earth, have seldom not been at war for any number of reasons. Nor have we not had hatred toward other humans. Including hatred toward humans who happen to have been born near the earth's equator with a darker skin pigmentation which protected them from the intense rays of the sun that are associated with living near the equator.

Regarding Iran, specifically, there is no question that I and my country have supported militant groups in Iraq, Syria, Yemen, and elsewhere. Doing so has benefited Iran in several ways. We refer to the groups whom we have supported as our partners. Other countries often refer to these groups as terrorists. But for my country these groups provide Iran with leverage against our rivals. Saudia Arabia for instance. The country that funded the group of men who killed more than three thousand American citizens on 9/11. The country the United States has yet to hold accountable for this act of terrorism."

President Hosseini paused again and looked about the room at his audience, allowing his words to register. He then slowly walked back toward his chair.

"Our involvement in Syria is another example where many people do not understand why we have supported the Alawi regime. Our ties to Syrian President Bashar al-Assad is purely strategic. The reason my government has supported the Alawi regime is to prevent Syria from becoming a Sunni government which would ally it to our rival, Saudi Arabia.

As for terrorism and religion, the topic that is before us, there is no question that there is linkage between the two. But there is also linkage in this topic to the natural resources that countries in the Middle East possess in an abundance that the world covets. Because of Saudi Arabia's oil reserves, the U.S. and the world have looked the other way while Saudi Arabia has propagated and funded their Wahhabi ideology. This virulent anti-Shiite doctrine that the Islamic State in Iraq and ISIS endorses was born in Saudi madrasas. Was it not for oil, and the relationships garnered by powerful wealthy Americans and America's government and other countries throughout the world, would we be attending these sessions this week? I say we would not be. The Wahhabi ideology would not have been allowed to spread, the Islamist militant group al-Qaeda founded by Osama bin Laden would not have been initiated, and the World Trade Centers would still be standing, and more than three thousand Americans would still be alive today."

Hosseini finally took his seat, noticing several nods throughout the room and hearing a few side conversations.

"Now, moving on from my history lesson, a few key points need to be made regarding the Muslim religion. Islam is a faith which believes that religion is to be freely accepted and by no means should be forced upon anyone. The Quran states that God wants people to choose their path themselves and does not at any point instruct any Muslim to raise a sword over a non-Muslim in order to convert or subjugate them.

Jihad, however, is a key problem in Islam as the meaning has many different interpretations. Some Muslims interpret Jihad as the spiritual struggle against a person's own nature in order to lead a holy life. But for other Muslims including Osma bin Laden, Jihad has been interpreted to mean a commitment to Allah by all Muslims, to constantly strive to convert, defeat or overcome all non-Muslims.

I and my government do not believe in this interpretation of Jihad, and we do not and will not support jihadist militant groups.

In summary, my country will support the group's decision that a single state solution is the best solution that has a chance to end the Palestinian Israeli conflict. We *will* support CIPC language that addresses the management and control of terrorism, in whichever country terrorism tries to blossom, within the Middle East, China, Russia, the United States, North Korea or elsewhere in the world. There is one provision, however, that I insist the CIPC language must cover, and that is the flow of monies to promote Wahhabi ideology outside of Saudi Arabia. The flow of money must not be allowed, and the teaching of Wahhabi ideology must be suppressed."

After President Hosseini finished his dissertation, President Stephen spoke. "Thank you, Amir, a very interesting and enlightening history of the Middle East. I could not agree more that each of our countries cannot judge the actions taken by another country before first taking a hard look at our own country's personal histories and the actions taken to promote our own self-interests."

World Peace: Tom Lawson Novel #4
By James Brown

President Stephen turned and focused his attention on the delegates seated in silence about the conference table.

"The issues that President Hosseini has outlined and the reasons for his countries actions are valid. America's pursuit of Saudia Arbia's natural resources has indeed clouded our judgement and alignment toward oil rich countries in the Middle East. Does anyone else have a comment?"

"I believe President Hosseini's comments are valid," China's President Wang Jun offered. "Each of our countries interpret the actions taken by other countries through a clouded lens, considering whether or not the actions taken are in our own best interest or not. Likewise, I support his requirement to manage the root cause of violent religious extremism. The fear of what could excite this religious extremism in China has lead my government to assume the worst in people who believe in Islam, believing that they too might align themselves with Jihadists who have similar beliefs as Osma bin Laden.

I likewise support President Hosseini's desire to stop the flow of money for the teaching of Wahhabi ideology. With these provisions in place, per President's Hosseini's declaration and the support through a CIPC agreement, China will no longer assume the worst, that a citizen's belief in Islam will unilaterally lead to terrorism. We will turn over a new leaf, as the saying goes, and will abide by wording in America's Constitution that ensures that people have a right to follow their conscience in how they worship."

After President Jun's declaration, President Stephen stood and walked over to President Jun and reached out his hand. "President Jun, I commend you on your decision. You will have America's full support as well of the support from the CIPC members should a terrorist action surface in China. Thank you. And now, it is a perfect time to break for lunch along with some free time to enjoy our beautiful spring weather. We will reconvene here at three p.m. to discuss the final topics for discussion, national defense, international trade, and economics."

World Peace: Tom Lawson Novel #4
By James Brown

Chapter 40

After lunch, it was time for another stroll through the woods. The sun was warm, birds were singing their songs, and butterflies were fluttering in wild gyrations among the multitude of spring flowers in bloom. The difficult discussions were behind us. Alone, walking along the paths toward no particular destination, I pulled out my phone and called Diana.

"Two for two," I said, reaching Diana in between clients. "My timing has been very good lately, catching you between sessions."

"A good omen, perhaps. Are your negotiations also going well?"

"Surprisingly so. We've just completed the most difficult set of discussion topics. You can discretely inform your Monkey Farm working group that all is going well. Just be aware of any reporters who may have tried to infiltrate the Old Saybrook crowd."

"Not to worry, we are mindful of the people in earshot. So it's looking good for a visit with your fans at home this weekend?"

"I'm hoping that will be the case. We have our last discussion session this afternoon which should go well. Assuming so, Thursday morning a draft MOU will be prepared."

"A Memorandum of Understanding."

"Right. It will be an outline of the terms and conditions for a CIPC agreement that will be signed by Russia, China, Iran, North Korea, and the United States."

"Hmm, an agreement for world peace. Peace, prosperity, and global cooperation. It's taken many thousands of years to achieve if it truly comes to pass. Are there still rumblings coming from the naysayers?" Diana asked.

"Unfortunately there is always those people and groups who oppose change that can have a negative effect on them personally, be it financial, position of power and status, or a change that goes against their age-old belief in the value of another human being as compared to their own life."

"Well, do stay safe, honey. Sam and the Secret Service I'm sure are doing their part to beef up security tomorrow when everyone finds their way out of the woods and reassembles in Washington and the Rose Garden. Right?"

"Their number one focus. I spoke with Sam and John this morning. Security is being beefed up."

"Good. Tell Sam and John that I appreciate their efforts."

"I will. I'll call you tonight."

"Okay. Love you," Diana said and ended the call.

After my call with Diana I continued exploring the woods and ended up at Evergreen Chapel, the rustic octagonal nondenominational chapel made of wood and stained glass. The chapel was built during the Reagan Administration and dedicated in 1991 by President George H.W. Bush. I entered the large spacious opened-air room with its towering, vaulted honeydew-stained knotty pine ceiling and walls. Rows of pews faced the front of the room where towering rows of organ pipes were affixed to the wall. On side of the chapel a "tree of life" stained glass sculpture rose toward the ceiling with outstretched arms as a symbol for interpretation by people of varying faith. In the pew near the tree of life sat President Hosseini.

"President Hosseini, may I join you," I asked.

"Oh, Tom," he said looking up toward me. "Of course. I have been coming to the chapel on my walks. I find it to be a peaceful place to come and think. A nondenominational chapel. I find the tree of life to be very interesting and appropriate for the setting here." After looking up at the stained-glass tree, he turned and said, "were you raised in a particular faith, Tom?"

"I was. I was raised in the Catholic faith and was once an altar boy, a boy who acts as a priest's assistant during a service in the Catholic Church."

"I'm familiar with that practice. Are you still a practicing Catholic?"

"No, not really, I would say I'm more nondenominational regarding religion now. Every religion is comprised of good people and bad people, as well as having good religious leaders and bad religious leaders. So, my philosophy is if you treat everyone with respect and kindness, God, Allah, whomever may be on the other side, will do the same for me."

President Hosseini smiled. "I suppose that would work, though it can be hard at times to treat everyone with kindness. Those who are not deserving of it."

"That's where law and order comes in. Assuming the laws are fair laws, and the order is properly and uniformly administered, those people who do not abide by civilized and fair rules should be punished in this world as well as the next."

"A very good point, Tom. A very good point."

We sat for a moment, sitting in silence and looking up toward the tree of life that glowed brightly in the sunlight beaming through the window.

Noticing the time, I said, "we probably should be heading back. Our next session will begin within the hour."

"So we should," Hosseini said. "I look forward to another visit here to Camp David one day in the future."

"I'm sure that day will come more frequently now, Mr. President."

* * * *

We were assembled once again at Laurel Lodge. The topics for this last group of discussions were national defense, international trade, and economics. A productive though seemingly long week it was expected that the topics on the table this afternoon would proceed smoothly with few arguments voiced. The scenario was simple, The United States needed to agree to reduce its defense budget, favorable trade nation status would be granted to all CIPC signatories, and each member would agree to assist the other in growing their economies, with a few conditions and caveats included of course.

I took my seat in the conference room and listened to the conversations between the other delegates as they entered the room and took their places about the room. All in all, it was a productive week. From here, the next step of the CIPC journey was attending the president's CIPC G5 summary announcement in the White House Rose Garden, which hopefully concludes without incident.

"Okay, everyone, shall we begin with the last topics for discussion?" President Stephen said as the room quieted. "First up is national defense. This topic should be easy for everyone, except for me. It is well understood that America's military spend is far higher than any other country's spend rate. I agree to do something about that. I will immediately initiate a ten percent cut to America's military budget and will continue to adjust our budget downward while I am in office commensurate with the reduced hostilities and threats that I am confident will result when our CIPC agreement is executed."

"What happens when you leave office, Justin?" President Milosevic asked.

"At least three and most likely seven years from now, Andrey. We will likely have seven years to prove to the world that our CIPC agreement will indeed lead to global peace and stability. During this period, we will be able to demonstrate that growing the economies of our countries and improving the lives of our citizens is a much better use of a portion of our country's defense budgets. During these seven years we will prove that the world can better survive and prosper by working together in peace. Then, whomever comes after me, or after any of us, will have the incentive to expand and support this alliance."

"Under certain requirements. Correct, Justin?" Andrey Milosev asked.

"Of course, Andrey. The CIPC language will require its members to follow international rules and laws. Likewise, competition between countries must be fair and honest. Trade secrets, data, and information must not be corrupted or stolen, and individuals or countries that participate in these practices, or condones them and allows them to occur, must be prosecuted and sanctioned. These are several of the basic tenets of a CIPC agreement we all must agree to observe."

"Which leads us to the benefits associated with entering into the CIPC agreement," President Milosev said. "Other than securing peace in the world, of course."

"The most important benefit, Andrey. But beyond the benefits derived from peace, which will provide substantial economic benefits, there will be considerable supportive economic benefits realized. Sanctions previously imposed on prior CIPC members will be lifted, free trade agreements will be established between our countries, and we will go beyond the typical trade agreements negotiated between counties. Over the long term, the economic wellbeing of each CIPC country will be assured.

Let me provide an example. The climate agreements that have been negotiated or are being promoted can help control global warming, but they will also cause an economic hardship for those countries that generate a large portion of their gross domestic product from the sale of coal, oil, and natural gas. Take your country, Andrey. Nearly sixty percent of Russia's GDP is generated from oil and natural gas resources. As the world moves increasingly away from carbon-based fuels and transportation conveyances from internal combustion engines, the resulting economic hardship on Russia can be significant. Support and cooperation in helping Russia and other CIPC members expand their service, technology, and manufacturing capabilities to provide new revenue sources to replace reduced oil and natural gas revenues will be a key CIPC program initiative."

President Stephen paused while his statements were being digested by the other delegates seated about the conference table.

President Kim Kyung-mi cleared her voice deciding it was time for her to ask a question. "President Stephen, your declarations, the benefits to be derived from the execution of a CIPC agreement, I assume one of the conditions would relate to nuclear weapons. Since this was not discussed, would it be correct to assume that one provision, or better stated stipulation, would be that North Korea's nuclear weapons program would have to be terminated. As well as Iran's. And if that is the case, what about China, Russia, and the United States weapons of mass destruction. Will they too be eliminated?"

Kyung-mi's question stirred side conversations about the topic that everyone knew was still to be discussed. Would there be parity between the world's superpowers when it came to weapons of mass destruction? The haves and have-nots when it came to possessing the single most lethal deterrent toward an attack by another country, having access to nuclear weapons and the missiles to carry nuclear warheads.

World Peace: Tom Lawson Novel #4
By James Brown

"Your question, Kyung-mi is appropriate and timely. Ideally, under perfect circumstances the answer would be yes. No country should be allowed to possess weapons of mass destruction. But unfortunately, we humans do not yet live in a utopian world. Humans have not yet been proven to be kind and forgiving toward each other. Perhaps one day in the future that will be the case and weapons of war will no longer be needed. That is not the case today.

Moving forward, Russia, China, and the U.S. will continue to reduce our nuclear weapons stockpiles and the number of missiles and submarines we have to launch them. We will likewise, as part of the CIPC agreement, ensure that each country that executes this agreement and abides by its covenants, will be protected should they ever be threatened or attacked by another country.

The additional benefit that your country and Iran will realize from participating in the CIPC agreement is that monies previously spent on your nuclear program will become available to grow your economies and improve the livelihood and wellbeing of your citizens. I hope this summary answers your question and it is acceptable to you."

A chill seemed to fill the air as everyone silently waited for President Kim Kyung-mi's answer.

After seemingly an inordinate time passed, Kyung-mi said, "it is, President Stephen. Your explanation and the provisions described are acceptable. North Korea is a very poor country. But I am hopeful the CIPC agreement will soon change the situation my people have been forced to endure for many years. Thank you for clarifying what I assumed to be the case regarding North Korea's weapons program. Our weapons program will be terminated upon execution of a CIPC treaty."

I along with President Stephen and the rest of his team exhaled sighs of relief, the last sticking point that had not been directly discussed had been exhumed.

"Thank you, President Kyung-mi. A very magnanimous and important proclamation. The citizens of North Korea will be forever grateful for the decision you have made," President Stephen said. He then scanned the faces of the delegates seated around the table. "Are there other questions or concerns that anyone else has?"

"China has no additional comments or questions," President Wang Jun said.

"Same with Russia." President Milosevic said. "I have no further questions or concerns."

President Amir Hosseini smiled and gave President Stephen an approval head nod and sat quietly.

"Okay, then," President Stephen said. The final phase of these discussions will be a Rose Garden news conference scheduled at the White House tomorrow at noon. A draft memorandum of agreement will be distributed later this afternoon for everyone's review and approval. I want to thank everyone for the time and effort you have expended to help achieve this very significant and important milestone in human relationships, a pathway toward sustainable peace."

With President Stephen's words of appreciation made, the room burst into an appreciative applause and smiles of satisfaction.

* * * *

The last evening at Camp David was a festive gathering of a group of men and women who never considered themselves as friends, or even people they wanted to form a friendship with. The discussions held months earlier, however, and during the ensuing days at Camp David had changed that situation. Though of differing backgrounds, culture, language, and religious beliefs, they were able to come together the previous months and during the week at Camp David to share their personal histories and opinions and agree on a way forward to embrace a way of living together, fostering cooperation, inclusion, and peaceful coexistence.

As promised, President Stephen's team prepared and distributed the draft MOU that enshrined the purpose and intent of the CIPC agreement and the provisions that the presidents and negotiating teams of China, Russia, Iran, North Korea, and the United States agreed to abide by. Within an hour of its distribution, U.S. President Justin Stephen, Russia's President Andrey Milosevic, China's President Wang Jun, Iran's President Amir Hosseini, and North Korea's President Kim Kyung-mi signed five MOUs, with each keeping a copy.

Press Secretary Jan Polaski along with a team of reporters and photographers from Russia, China, Iran, North Korea, and the U.S. bathed the room in flashing lights as the MOUs were being signed. President Stephen made a short statement thanking president's

Milosevic, Jun, Hosseini, and Kim and their teams for their efforts and diligence over many months working together to come to the agreement reached. He then told the audience that a formal news conference would be held on Thursday in the Rose Garden at the White House. After this announcement he thanked everyone and said the party would now commence.

* * * *

It was Thursday morning and preparations were made for departure flights back to Washington. In reverse order of their arrival, helicopter flights to return the G5 delegates back to Washington were scheduled on half-hour intervals beginning at eight a.m. President Stephen escorted President Kim Kyung-mi, walking along the path of saluting marines toward the waiting helicopter.

"Thank you for participating in these historic discussions, Kyung-mi," President Stephen said.

"I very much appreciate the opportunity, Justin. It has been an honor. Perhaps in the not-too-distant future you will allow me to reciprocate the hospitality you have shown me with a visit to North Korea."

"I look forward to doing that, Madam President," the president said, taking her hand and bowing slightly.

The process continued for the next hour and a half with President Stephen and his team the last group to depart Camp David. We arrived back at the White House at ten thirty with preparations well underway for the Rose Garden press conference that was scheduled to take place at noon. Seating for the press pool and one hundred guests were in place and the weather was perfect, temperature in the mid-seventies with light winds and a blue sky overhead.

After dropping off my bags in my office I called Sam.

"Hey, Tom. Welcome back. Is it safe to assume the CIPC MOU has been signed?"

"Fully executed, Sam. Are you on the grounds somewhere?"

"I'm in the Rose garden. Do you have time to stop down? I have a special earbud for you. Complements of John."

I left my office for the Rose Garden.

"What's this new earbud that John's developed?" I asked Sam.

"He said he's been working on the design for several months and William had several of them made for our team. Here's yours," Sam said, handing me a tiny, skin colored earbud. "It isn't noticeable when inserted in your ear. I also have one for Savannah. Once inserted you activate it with the sound of your voice. And of course, our communications are fully secure."

"Of course. Leave it to John to be several steps ahead of everyone else. So, speaking of security, what's happening? Has there been any new intercepts and how about Jackson Knapp? Did the NSA pick up the communications between Jackson Knapp and his new Russian FSB friend?"

"Nothing new and yes, they uncovered Knapp's conversation. And, just in case, the Secret Service has beefed up security here at the White House and in the surrounding area. How about Savannah, is she here yet?" Sam asked.

"I'm not sure. She may still be at her office. Let me check."

I pulled out my cell phone and called her.

"Hi Tom. Cheryl Ellis and I are on our way to the White House now. We will be there in about ten minutes. Is Sam there?"

"He is. He has a special earbud for you that John developed. Give Sam a call when you arrive. He'll go over the details."

"Okay, will do," Savannah said and ended the call.

"She's on her way, Sam. She will give you a call when she arrives. I have a short meeting I need to attend and will be back in a half hour or so. Then, it's up to President Stephen and the other G5 leaders to present their case, that a CIPC treaty based on cooperation, inclusion, and peaceful coexistence *will* indeed lead to world peace and global prosperity."

World Peace: Tom Lawson Novel #4
By James Brown

Chapter 41

The press and guests began filling in the chairs bordering the Rose Garden just outside of the Oval Office along the West Wing of the White House. Flags of the U.S., Russia, China, Iran, and North Korea stood side by side on the veranda between two of the colonnades that backdropped five speaker podiums a few steps from the veranda on the lawn. The press from each of the G5 countries, politicians, and special guests began arriving. Small groups assembled on the lawn or near the folding chairs they staked out to listen to the G5 Summit leaders. The agenda released by the White House press office provided little detail. Unusual that this was, speculation ran the gamut depending on political party affiliation.

After leaving my meeting with the president and his staff and reaching the hallway, I decided to try out John's new earbud. I quietly said, "call Savannah."

"Hey, Tom," Savannah said answering immediately. "These earbuds John developed are phenomenal."

"They certainly are. Are you in the Rose Garden?"

"I am, mingling with our illustrious politicians."

"I'm heading there now. What's the consensus?"

"Probably 60/40 from the rumors they are hearing regarding a CIPC agreement. Sixty percent saying it's a reach at best with any reduction in defense spending a nonstarter."

"What I expected. I'll be there in a minute," I said.

I exited the White House and scanned the crowd looking for Savannah, finally spotting her on the far corner of the lawn. "The president certainly has garnered a lot interest," I said.

World Peace: Tom Lawson Novel #4
By James Brown

"One of the biggest Rose Garden press conferences I've been to," Savannah said. "Do you know what he's going to say?"

"I took a look at one of his first draft and made a couple of comments but haven't seen his final version."

"I hope it's a knock-it-out-of-the-park speech, Tom. The kind of speech President Obama would give. He's going to need it to persuade this crowd."

"Well, maybe his audience is not this crowd. Perhaps he knew his message would be lost on a bunch of old white men who have been in congress far too long. Maybe his audience is the citizens of the U.S. as well as the citizens of the world."

Savannah winked, pointing her finger at me. "Well said. Now, I need to take my seat. At least President Stephen will have a few reporters on his side."

I walked toward the far side of the Rose Garden as the door to the Oval Office opened. The audience stood as President Stephen led the way and stepped up to the center podium while presidents Milosevic, Jun, Hosseini, and Kim walked to the podiums on either side of him.

After a few moments President Stephen looked up from his notes.

"Good afternoon. An absolutely beautiful day we have. A day that provides a perfect backdrop for the occasion of our announcement. I and the leaders standing beside me today are happy to report that the nations of the United States, Russia, China, Iran, and North Korea have come to an agreement that will assure sustainable peace and prosperity for each of our citizens and the world.

A little more than a year ago, these leaders standing beside me joined with other leaders and decided for peace and not war after the presidents and leaders from each of our countries were killed in the missile attacks caused by John Gordon. We are grateful for their foresight and courage in the decision they made. But what will happen when the next such event occurs? When another world leader decides that war is in his best interest and once again takes actions that could lead to World War III?"

The president paused and scanned his audience, letting his question sink in before continuing.

World Peace: Tom Lawson Novel #4
By James Brown

"I, and the leaders standing beside me, have decided we can no longer sit back and assume another group of leaders in the future will make the right decision in similar circumstances. Or, that our hopes and prayers will be answered if they do not.

To ensure that the events of this past year do not reoccur, we have been meeting the past several months to discuss steps and actions to prevent the conditions that led countries to choose hostile actions over peaceful dialogue and reconciliation. Our discussions and meetings culminated this week at Camp David.

Humans have been waging war and killing each other for centuries and It's time that we put an end to this destructive cycle. I am proud to announce that we have come to an agreement. An agreement that will go down in history as one of humankind's greatest accomplishments. Cooperation, inclusion, and peaceful coexistence."

The president paused to gauge the reactions to his speech. He had their attention, but their eyes and expressions did not reveal their beliefs one way or the other. He looked back at his teleprompter then at his audience and continued.

"Russia, China, Iran, North Korea and the U.S. agree to enter into an agreement that will ensure that no circumstance will surface that will put our nations, our citizens, and the world at risk again. We agree to a new world paradigm, one of cooperation, inclusion, and peaceful coexistence and have executed a CIPC memorandum of understanding. Over the next several months a formal treaty will be prepared. In the meantime a copy of the executed MOU will be issued later today.

Now, with this announcement made, I am sure everyone has a lot of questions. Questions I along with the esteemed leaders standing next to me are prepared to answer. But please, polite hands in the air only. We will answer everyone's questions in an orderly and fair manner."

Hands from the press flashed into the air.

"I will start with the Washington Post, Savannah Lee."

"Thank you, Mr. President. The Post, of course, has not yet seen a copy of the MOU but rumors have it that it's quite extensive in what it covers. Extensive in that much of the language in the MOU covers almost the very language and terms that would be included in any treaty. Is that the case?"

"Are you sure you haven't seen the MOU, Savannah?" The president asked in jest.

"Only from the typical rumors that flow from every administration," she answered.

"Yes, leaks do have a way of surfacing. But that being the case, as I've said, discussions have been taking place for many months, Savannah. And, quite frankly, we collectively have long histories and a deep understanding of the actions and events that can lead to hostilities and even war. Simply put, we have come together with an approach and plan that will mitigate these conditions from festering in the future."

"Next question," the president said. "Ah, Steve Briar, Fox News."

"My question, Mr. President has to do with defense budgets. How exactly will this agreement affect these budgets, for the United States as well as the other countries who would execute such a treaty. Likewise, for a related question, what about nuclear weapons."

"Very good questions, Steve. I'll take your second question first. And even more effective rather than I answer this question, I will defer that question to President Hosseini and President Kim."

"Thank you, Mr. President, I will be glad to answer Mr. Briar's question," President Hosseini said through his translator. "The simple answer is yes, once the CIPC treaty is executed Iran will dismantle all nuclear weapons development capabilities."

As soon as President Hosseini finished his statement, President Kim Kyung-mi stepped closer to her mic. "In addition to dismantling North Korea's nuclear weapons capabilities and destroying any fissionable materials, North Korea will likewise dismantle its missile development facilities," Kim said through her translator.

"And America's military budget?" Fox News reporter Steve Briar asked.

"As everyone is well aware," President Stephen said, stepping back up to his mic. "America spends more on defense than the combined military budgets of the next ten countries who follow us in the world's military armament race. Our military budget is three times more than China's budget and more than twelve times larger than what Russia spends. Once the CIPC treaty is executed, I will immediately reduce America's military budget by ten percent. Then, going forward, as our countries implement and follow the terms of our agreement, further reductions will be made in the stockpiles of nuclear weapons held by the U.S., Russia, and China and other offensive weapons reductions will follow.

"In the middle of the row," the president followed. "Bashir Abbas, Iran Broadcasting."

"Thank you, Mr. President," Abbas said in well spoken English. "With the execution of a CIPC treaty, will U.S. sanctions on Iran be lifted?"

"Yes. All sanctions that exist between the U.S., Russia, China, Iran, and North Korea will be removed. And, to answer the next question that is likely to be asked, favorable trade agreements will be negotiated between our countries. Next question."

Dozens of hands waving in the air, President Stephen pointed to an Asian woman at the end of the second row of chairs.

"Hoi Leung, Hong Kong Citizen News. Thank you for taking my question," she said in Chinese accented English. "How will this agreement affect country and territorial boundaries?"

President Stephen expected this question or a related question to be asked. He and his team struggled over the course of many months on how country borders, territorial agreements, and historical precedents would be dealt with. The issues that caused many skirmishes and wars being fought.

"Ms. Leung, thank you for your question," the president said. "A very important question that leads to many other questions that I'm sure many will be seeking answers. Let me begin, Ms. Leung, by saying the core premise for the discussions and negotiations held these past many months was based on the principle that the form of government each of our countries have would not be questioned or debated. We likewise agreed that each country will follow international laws and standards and will function in the best interest of their citizens.

There are also other provisions that we have included within our CIPC MOU to provide a foundation for consistency regardless the form of our governments. For example, the executed MOU, includes an agreement that competition between countries must be fair and honest. Trade secrets, data, and information must not be corrupted or stolen, and individuals or countries that participate in these practices, or allows them to occur, will be prosecuted and sanctioned. Likewise, there is agreement that people . . . each of our citizens, have a right to

World Peace: Tom Lawson Novel #4
By James Brown

follow their conscience in how they worship. These are several of the basic tenets of our CIPC agreement that we have executed.

Now, as for a more direct answer to your question, Ms. Leung, the topic of national sovereignty. Judgements were made on this topic based on the agreements I just conveyed. The history of the world is extremely long and complicated and unfortunately decisions made cannot always satisfy everyone. Three cases in point are Hong Kong, Taiwan, and the conflict between Israel and Palestinians in the Middle East."

After this statement was made, conversations and whispers turned silent with all eyes and ears focused on President Stephen in anticipation of the next words he would convey.

"I'll begin with the Middle East," the president said. "Peaceful coexistence is our objective for the Middle East, and this will only occur if disagreements and conflicts between the Israeli and Palestinian people are resolved. To this end, we will be recommending and strongly promoting a single state solution for the Israeli and Palestinian people."

Hands flew into the air with the previous quiet exploding into a crescendo of loud voices requesting acknowledgement, trying to catch the president's attention.

The president held up his hands. "Please! Please, hold your questions. I will explain our decision!"

After the voices subsided, the president proceeded to explain the dilemma that was preventing long-term peace in the region. He then explained the prevailing thoughts preventing a two-state solution from being accepted, and described the hardships being endured under the status quo condition that currently existed in the Middle East. With the president's explanation and answers given to ensuing questions on the subject, the crowd quieted with further discussions and arguments to be held for later.

"Now, let me return to Ms. Leung's original question regarding a country's sovereignty," the president said. "Assuming your question, Ms. Leung, is related to Hong Kong and Taiwan, Hong Kong has always been a part of China except for the period of European colonialism, a practice that we intend to never allow to resurface anywhere in the world again. As for Taiwan, as well as Hong Kong, given the CIPC agreement's core principles that each of our countries have agreed to uphold, we intend to allow China to work toward an amicable resolution for any outstanding issues that exists with Taiwan and Hong Kong. We likewise believe it to be in the best interest of Hong Kong and Tiwan to accept the leadership and support of the People's Republic of China."

With this statement made, people stood, and a cacophony of voices pierced the air.

"Please! everyone, please be seated! No questions need to be asked. Let me explain."

The grumblings finally subsided, and the president again stepped up to his mic.

"As I've said, there are no easy solutions that will satisfy everyone. We humans do not have a very good history toward inclusion, kindness, and being civil toward each other. Likewise, during human's existence the forms of governments have continued to evolve but a perfect form of government does not yet exist if it will ever exist. Let's take representational democracy, the United States form of government for example. With our form of government, the president and vice president are chosen by electors in accordance with our constitution's electoral college provision. This provision in our constitution often enables the will of the minority rather than the will of the majority to elect our country's president and vice president. Likewise, our predominately two-party system often goes to great lengths to restrict the ability of citizens from being able to easily vote. Politicians have also gerrymandered states to rig elections in favor of one party over the other.

In our last presidential elections, one hundred and forty-four million people, 67% of the eligible voters, voted. As comparison, in China, elections take place through its ninety-million-member Communist Party. Similar to arguments made regarding Americas pseudo democratic form of government with growing voter restrictions placed on its citizens, related arguments are voiced against China's election processes. Both of our countries need to do better, the U.S. in ending voter restrictions and China in how members to the Chinese Party are selected. President Jun and I agree that such efforts to improve our processes will be pursued. Similar statements and agreements have been reached to expand inclusiveness for the citizens of Russia, Iran, and North Korea."

World Peace: Tom Lawson Novel #4
By James Brown

I stood along one side of the Rose Garden, watching as the questions being asked and answers provided by each of the presidents be-came less contentious. A rhythm began to ensue with the audience becoming satisfied that the presidents standing before them had at minimum attempted to do their best to address the significant issues that had always been the basis for disagreements and conflicts that have led to wars being fought.

The next question asked by a foreign correspondent came with a buzz in my ear. A growing buzzing sound. Was John's earbud defective? Not possible, I thought as I tapped my earbud. No sooner than I did so when the buzzing grew louder and a swarm of drones began approaching from the south, flying low to the ground.

"Sam!" I yelled. "Drones!"

"I see them!" he yelled, as he raced toward the podiums."

"John! Can you stop them!"

"Working on it, Tom," he answered calmly.

Seconds later the swarm of drones appeared over the White House and Rose Garden. I raced forward as secret service agents drew their weapons and did their best to protect the presidents and the people in the crowd.

"Tom! Don't let them fire on the drones! Yelled John. They will detonate!"

"Don't shoot! Don't shoot! They'll explode shrapnel! I yelled, reaching the White House portico.

"It's okay now, Tom! I am in control!" John said.

"Guns down! Guns down! Don't fire!" I screamed.

Just as I said this, the drones flew higher, banked, and flew west.

Many of the people who were still in the Rose Garden picked up chairs that were overturned in the panic and sat. It was time to catch their breath and thank God for still being alive.

"This was an act of terrorism!" yelled House Minority Speaker Jorden Montgomery, looking up as the drones flew off. "Who the hell is responsible?"

"Are you injured, ma'am?" a secret service officer asked as he assisted a woman staggering to her feet.

"I'm okay, thank you," she said, getting to her feet. "So much for chivalry when faced with sudden death," she said.

"Sorry, ma'am. Shouldn't be the case, but . . . ," the agent offered without further explanation, knowing from experience that for most people, self-preservation trumped chivalry when their life was in danger.

Once people got to their feet questions began to be shouted to anyone and everyone who would take time to listen, asking why it happened. Was it a prank? Was someone trying to scare the politicians? Were they trying to get their attention, that the president's 'world peace CIPC agreement' was not to their liking?

Seconds later, flashes of light became visible followed by distant explosions. My earbud pinged again. It was John.

"Tom, Sam! I've safely destroyed all of the drones except for one. This last one is following the car of its former master. It's heading south on Pennsylvania Avenue. It's not in any hurry. They don't yet know their drone is following them and I'm sure they have no idea what went wrong."

"Do you know who is behind the attack?" I asked.

"Jackson Knapp with assistance from his new Russian friends," John answered. "And, Tom, for security purposes, I will need Sarah Pope to tweak the NSA software stack a little. She needs to be the hero and not me."

"Tom! You deal with Sarah. I'll take care of Mr. Knapp," Sam yelled, racing off and grabbing several of his FBI agents to join him.

"John, let's get Sarah on this call."

Within seconds, Sarah was connected.

"Is everyone okay? she said rapidly. "I've been watching the press conference from my office. Those drones! How were they stopped?"

"A good question, Sarah. And here's what the answer needs to be. You stopped them."

"What? What do you mean, I stopped them?" She blurted.

"I have Doctor Davidson on the call with me. Are you alone in your office?"

"I am, yes."

"Okay. The true answer is that Doctor Davidson, John, updated his software, a new version to the one you previously loaded. He was able to hack into the flight controllers of the drones and took control. We don't want John to take credit for this. John saving the president.

Saving all of the presidents and everyone else in attendance at the Rose Garden news conference."

After several seconds of silent air, Sarah said, "You want me to download a patch."

"Yes."

"And take responsibility for saving everyone. Have my face broadcasted on every news and Internet outlet as the person who saved the life of our president . . . the lives of all the G5 presidents?"

"Yes, but not the broadcast you mentioned. That won't happen, Sarah. National security. The NSA's intelligence capabilities are never broadcasted or shared. Nor are the names of the people who do the work that you do. But the President will know, as well as General Goldman and Ron Wainscott, your bosses. John needs to stay out of it. He is not to be mentioned under any circumstances."

Sarah let out a deep sigh. "Okay, Tom, but we need to talk. I need to fully understand."

"Yes, you do, Sarah. What are you doing for dinner tonight?"

"I'm having dinner with you. Pick me up at eight and tell John to send me the patch."

Made in the USA
Columbia, SC
26 July 2024

a68df567-dd5e-43d9-9e8e-7e4fabb3a88cR01